BY ZOE SAADIA

Obsidian Puma
Field of Fire
Heart of the Battle
Warrior Beast
Morning Star
Valley of Shadows

The Highlander
Crossing Worlds
The Emperor's Second Wife
Currents of War
The Fall of the Empire
The Sword
The Triple Alliance

Two Rivers
Across the Great Sparkling Water
The Great Law of Peace
The Peacekeeper

Beyond the Great River
The Foreigner
Troubled Waters
The Warpath
Echoes of the Past

Shadow on the Sun
Royal Blood
Dark Before Dawn
Raven of the North

WARRIOR BEAST

The Aztec Chronicles, Book 4

ZOE SAADIA

Copyright © 2017 by Zoe Saadia

All rights reserved. This book or any portion thereof may not be reproduced, transmitted or distributed in any form or by any means whatsoever, without prior written permission from the copyright owner, unless by reviewers who wish to quote brief passages.

Cover art attribution: Mural by Diego Rivera showing the life in Aztec times, by Wolfgang Sauber under the GNU Free Documentation License.

For more information about this book, the author and her work, visit www.zoesaadia.com

ISBN-13: 978-1522031079

AUTHOR'S NOTE

To the south of Lake Texcoco spread fertile areas of easily cultivated valleys bordered by highlands of various elevations. Plenty of cities and towns dotted those, some subdued by Tenochtitlan prior to the second part of the 15th century and Axayacatl's rule, some "unattended" as yet.

The part of the region Miztli came from, indeed, joined the growing empire when those areas were annexed by joined forces of Tenochtitlan and Texcoco under their famous rulers and the founders of the Triple Alliance – Itzcoatl, the fourth emperor of Tenochtitlan and Nezahualcoyotl the emperor of Texcoco. Back then, in the early 15th century, this same fertile south was reported to be divided in two areas of tribute collection: Oaxtepec in the south, near which Miztli's village was located, and Cuauhnahuac in the southwest, a large, very important city that rebelled several times and was finally re-conquered by Tenochtitlan fifth emperor, Moctezuma Ilhuicamina, or Moctezuma I.

By the time of Axayacatl's rule and the later parts of the 15th century, the people of these regions talked Nahuatl, absorbed into the growing empire quite thoroughly, but their native tongues – Matlatzinca, Mazahua, and several Chichimes dialects – were still dominant and well known. The southwest beyond Cuauhnahuac was barely touched by Tenochtitlan at this time.

However, after the fall of Tlatelolco, the young Aztec emperor had to set his sight on the unexplored west and the fertile Toluca Valley with its dominant cities and their political rivalry, especially between the strong and influential Toluca or Tollocan and less important but no less ambitious Tenantzinco, who promptly came to Tenochtitlan asking for help against their troublesome neighbors.

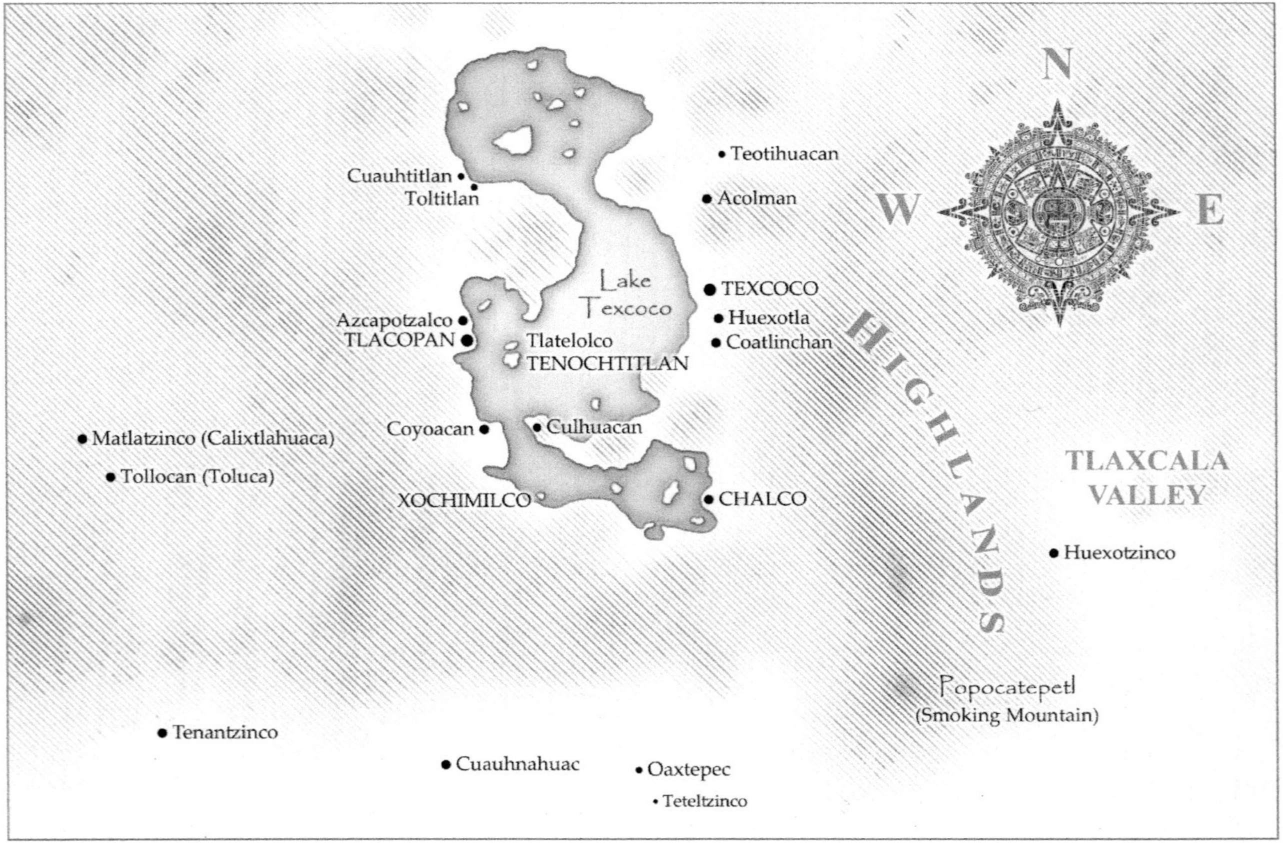
N
W
E
Teotihuacan
Cuauhtitlan
Toltitlan
Acolman
Lake
Texcoco
TEXCOCO
Huexotla
Coatlinchan
Azcapotzalco
TLACOPAN
Tlatelolco
TENOCHTITLAN
HIGHLANDS
Coyoacan
Culhuacan
Matlatzinco (Calixtlahuaca)
Tollocan (Toluca)
XOCHIMILCO
CHALCO
TLAXCALA
VALLEY
Huexotzinco
Popocatepetl
(Smoking Mountain)
Tenantzinco
Cuauhnahuac
Oaxtepec
Teteltzinco

CHAPTER 1

Teteltzinco village,
1474 AD

It always got eerily quiet when the earth was about to shake. Even though when in its depths, its real depths, one had less means to actually hear the upcoming disaster. Chirping birds and insects didn't bother to leave the safety of the world lit by sun or washed by rains. Certain animals did it for safety reasons. And people. People did it for greed.

Freezing in his tracks, Elotl listened, daring not to breathe, let alone to call out. As did the men he had left behind. The sounds of massive hammers striking the hard surface did not echo against the rocky walls, not anymore.

Clenching the heavy basket he held with both hands, he fought the urge to throw it down and just rush out, pell-mell. Never caught in a crumbling tunnel or a mine until now, he knew Father's instructions for such cases by heart, crisp and clear, and many, his directives repetitive, insistent, his stories vivid and frightening. Things happened. A badly constructed mine could crumble if it was dug without proper care, or sometimes *Tonantzin* Mother Earth would decide to move with no reason, as though shaking off sleepiness. Then it was up to a miner to survive, not to panic and thus die terribly, a bad death. There were ways to dig oneself out, means to crawl and make one's way back. As long as the man didn't panic, kept his thinking lucid, assessed the situation, and did what needed to be done.

Clutching his basket with all his strength, feeling the coarse handles cutting into his skin, he listened to the ominous creaking of the mountain's insides in which they all had been prowling, small insignificant forms, belonging less than the animals daring to make their homes between those same broken rocks. Was Mother Earth angry with those who did it to her? Somehow, he knew that she was.

The gravel began to rain on the uneven surface, crumbling into bigger stones before his mesmerized eyes.

"Elotl!"

Father's voice overcame the screeching, his footsteps hurried, light upon the shifting earth. His hand was rock-hard as it locked around Elotl's upper arm, the other tearing the basket in what seemed like the continued movement of his desperate leap. The powerful pull made Elotl struggle to stay on his feet, yet it broke the stupor, making his legs join the running.

There were footsteps of other miners, intermingling with the groaning earth, the stones bouncing off the craggy walls, eager to falter their step. A few torches flickered, then died. The speed of the running did this, he knew, a corner of his mind noting the details, curiously detached. Father had too many things in his hands: his favorite hammer – no surprise that! – two unlit torches, ceramic ladle, and a basket of smaller tools that held bone scrapers, precious obsidian blades, and wooden wedges. All this, in addition to his, Elotl's, basket laden with pieces of greenish copper to the brim, created a heavy cargo. Still somehow, Father ran as fast as the rest, faster than some, pushing him, Elotl, along, making sure his son ran before him. The realization shamed him and he made an effort, sensing the breeze upon his sweaty face, faint but there. The safety!

The makeshift stairwell was still there, wide slabs piled one above another, to make the climb out more comfortable. They were wavering precariously now, sliding away. Just like the rocky walls around them did. He darted away from a rolling boulder, swaying as a smaller stone crushed against his side, bouncing off his shoulder.

Clutching an uneven edge for support, he felt it swinging away and this time actually went crashing down, unable to fight the force that was pulling him back, terrified by its ferocious determination. Someone's basket bounced off the falling rubble, but before he could understand the meaning of it, Father's palm was again locked around his arm, its yank painful and strong, as though attempting to tear his limb off. Then he was hurled up and toward the freshness of the breeze, landing painfully, sprawling upon the gravel that for a change didn't dance like maize husks in boiling water but lay there as the solid earth should.

Blinking, he tried to understand, feeling rather than hearing another body landing beside him. The shuffling of the running feet resonated against his head. Father? The thought hit him and he leapt up, swaying but holding on.

The opening in the rocky hill was still there, gaping. A hateful presence. Only now he realized that he always feared it, always mistrusted it. His brothers didn't seem to have any such misgivings. The oldest, Tletl, worked those mines with not a word of compliant, as efficiently as Father did, especially since taking that girl of the neighboring village and thus becoming the head of his own tiny segment of a family. Yet Tletl was in the fields now, a relief. As for the youngest, Miztli, Father's favorite; oh, that one Father took along into mines since the boy could walk straight, but he was away now too, in that giant *altepetl*, the capital of the mighty Mexica-Aztecs, the cause of everyone's worry. Only he, Elotl, was stuck here, crawling in the belly of the earth, angering the powerful deity. What happened now was proof, wasn't it?

More people clawed their way through the narrowed opening, now nothing but a crack in the rocky side. It wasn't moving anymore, but people's voices and cries for help were pouring out. Of Father, there was no sight. But of course! An elder everyone looked up to, Father must be in there, helping to extricate everything and everyone, reflected Elotl, shamed. To rush back toward the yet-again unstable ground came as an effort. He had to force his legs to do that.

"Take the things. Carry them away, where the fires are!" Father's face peeked out of the opening, hurling a basket full of tools, making it land behind the nearest rocks, its contents scattering. But for being so close, he wouldn't even recognize the man, his features hiding under the thick layer of dust and worse. Blood was trickling from the cut upon his forehead, making him blink.

"Father, you are bleeding!"

"Not now!" The man's gaze willed him away. "Do what I said, then come back. Help the wounded."

Only when the sun was about to disappear behind the ridges of the hill that tried to bury them, all miners were accounted for, the wounded taken care of, broken limbs put back in place, secured by improvised splints – a hideous procedure that left Elotl's back covered with cold sweat, unpleasantly sticky. Five men were hurt to this or that degree. The others sported bruises and plenty of grazed skin. Nothing worthy of an additional look. Father refused to attend even his own bleeding forehead and smashed, badly swollen finger. The miners were looking up to him; it was imperative that their leader would present as unhurt a façade as he could.

The old admiration was back, laced with an equal bitterness. Father was too strong, too efficient, too perfect, impossible to measure up to. He, Elotl, was old enough to admit that by now, if only deep inside. At the count of seventeen summers, a person could face himself. And yet, Father or not, he was not a nonentity either. If only Father decided to send him to that legendary Tenochtitlan, choosing his second over his favorite youngest son only this once.

"We need at least one carrier. Take care of that." Father's hand landed upon his back, sweaty and ragged, yet encouraging, letting him know that he did well. It didn't help. He knew that he didn't. "You two, go with him."

Even though he was the youngest in this group, being the son of his father and an efficient enough person in itself helped, as did his recently quite open involvement with Oaxtepec and its rebellious elements. He tucked another worry away. Tomorrow, there was another meeting to be held, well away from the better parts of the town, where the villas of Tenochtitlan aristocracy sprinkled the lavish hills. Not anywhere near the fields, of course.

The smell of the cultivated land and the swarms of insects it brought was too much for the delicate noses of the Great Capital. However, it made it easier for those who wanted to conduct unobtrusive meetings and gatherings, the same despised peasants who weren't that thrilled with the honor of serving spoiled urban aristocracy apparently. Elotl ground his teeth at the very thought, then forced his mind back to the problems at hand.

"We'd better search in the piles of firewood first, before spending time collecting branches out there. There must be long enough sticks to help us make at least half a carrier." Glancing at his companions, two ruffled bruised men in their mid-twenties, older than him but not by much, he shifted his eyes back toward the sun. "It will become dark not long from now."

They nodded dourly, not caring enough to claim the lead that their count of summers alone warranted. Exhausted by the long day and shaken by the possibility of being smashed in the crumbled mines, all they evidently wanted was to go back to their homes, wash and rest, and offer on their private altars, thanking various deities for keeping them safe. Both didn't care about the happenings in Oaxtepec, even though he, Elotl, did approach one of them. Oaxtepec's dissident elements didn't mind his little count of summers either while asking him to recruit possible sympathizers from his fellow younger villagers.

"You search through the piles and work with what branches are fitting," he said absently, eyeing the high stalks of firewood that were always piling down the slopes of the rocky hill, for the miners to work on some of the minerals, separate the rubble from the precious metal elements, something only fire could do well with ease and unerring efficiency. The trouble was that more than half a day of work was beyond them, which served to reduce the piles considerably. A bother!

"I'll go down there, bring more sprouts and such. The green ones that they didn't pick for the fires will serve us as well."

"Want me to come with you?" asked one of the youths, frowning with discomfort.

"If you want to. But it's better that the two of us get to work on the carrier right away."

His volunteered help nodded numbly, dragging his feet toward the rustling pile with little enthusiasm. The other one was already at work, more vigorous than his peer. Again, he wondered why this man didn't agree to participate in the Oaxtepec meetings. Then the task at hand took the entirety of his attention. It was imperative to construct those carriers, better two than one, before they finished salvaging people and tools. He had let Father down enough through the course of this day and organizing people was easy with no rocky walls closing from every direction, repressing every feeling and thought. If only he could do that out there in Oaxtepec or, better yet, large towns like Cuauhnahuac that he only heard about but never even dreamed of visiting instead of being stuck in his village's fields and the ominous tunnels, the terrible pits out to trap people and make them die terribly.

It was well after dark when Father managed to free himself from various visitors and worried family members and address the matter of the visiting trader. Exhausted by the demands of the terrible day, even if washed, fed, and with his wounds taken care of at long last, Father did not succumb to the temptation of the well-deserved rest. Instead, he had set out for the place the visitor had indicated his possible whereabouts, the flat grounds next to the widening track, and a favorite place for the rare passersby to camp when on a journey.

The man was one of the long-distance *potcheca* traders who were always on the road, traveling far and wide, bringing goods or distributing them, and he had come to their house in the early evening, when they were still in the mine apparently, recovering the last of the tools and taking care of the wounded. Luckily, no one was hurt seriously, caught in the rubble, or buried under the earth for good. The mountain trembled, but only slightly. Enough to damage a well-built adit, but not enough to ruin it for good.

When done with the first most immediate troubles of broken

limbs and most alarming bleeding, some people went back, carrying the wounded on the two makeshift platforms Elotl and his improvised crew managed to put together in a remarkably short time, which pleased Father and made Elotl feel better. Still, until everyone was accounted for, succored or calmed, and sent home, Father wouldn't leave. Only when there was barely any light left to obstruct going into the gaping opening with no stairs and no comfortable access, the rest of the salvaging efforts were put off until the first light of tomorrow.

At home, Mother was frantic with worry, having already received the worst of the news. Not a fussy type, she had everything at hand and ready: warm food, ointments, bowls of water, and strips of tanned leather. Tletl's young wife was the one to make most of the noise. It grated on Elotl's nerves worse than anything, the silly fox's stupid crying and sobbing. Her husband hadn't even been in the ruined mine, busy in the fields on this particular afternoon, coming no closer to danger than a woman overturning a boiling pot while cooking. Still the stupid baggage carried on, gasping and beginning to sob every time the thought of her husband's going down this same mine on occasion crossed her empty, feather-light head.

Tletl himself had rushed to the site of the disaster the moment he heard the news. Exceptionally strong and efficient, he of course had been a great help. Only Miztli, their youngest of siblings, was missing in this urgent family gathering, reflected Elotl, grimly amused. Another wonder of strength and helpfulness. Out of all three, he was the only one to inherit Mother's slimness, if not her even temper and presence of mind. Neither Tletl nor Miztli sported hot tempers. None in the family did, except for him. As always when he thought about it, he felt like cursing under his breath. All the wrong traits were his to enjoy, the middle son, not the first and the strongest, nor the last and the favorite.

A shrug came out on its own this time. Father was good to him; patient, supportive, going to certain lengths in trying to understand his restless middle son better, to help him direct his fire into useful channels. Or so Father would say, smiling. A fire was a good thing in a young man. In right amounts and while controlled tightly, it could make a person go far, become a leader, even. Not everyone possessed such a trait, and combined with a keen mind like his, his temper could be a treasure, not a curse.

It sounded nice while coming from Father's mouth, in the quiet evening time, when only the dying fire was left to lighten the world and allow a peek into one's converser's face. Neither of his brothers possessed leadership qualities, was Elotl's conclusion; or rather, a secret hope. At least that. Tletl was too placid and indifferent, too unpretentious, happy with his lot as a miner and a field worker; while Miztli was too quiet and too humble, unsure of himself. Being the last and so obviously the favorite, possessing it all: good looks and a Father-like keen, analyzing mind, combined with exceptional strength and surprising agility at times, their youngest of siblings could raise his ambition to the skies, chancing to become the most unbearable thing in the world, a true thorn in his elder brothers' paws. But he didn't. He was too reticent, too thoughtful, thinking too much before doing something, not seizing on opportunities, examining those until they passed before his very eyes. Oh yes, Miztli could use some of his problematic brother's fire, was Elotl's semi-amused conclusion. It was clear that they should have been sharing their gifts; maybe mixed together, then divided again, like the bones from the Underworld when Quetzalcoatl, the Beautiful Serpent, mixed it all before creating the people of this world of the Fifth Sun.

Shaking his head, Elotl went on watching Father pacing the earthen floor of their house, before reaching for the treasured bag that accumulated precious material every miner stored against bad days. When prowling the belly of the earth, extracting copper or sometimes other minerals for melting, one chanced stumbling over prettily shiny objects, glittering marble or even beautiful green stones. Traders paid nicely for those things, and it was easy to store such pieces, to keep them against the time of need.

Like now, he thought, watching Father examine his treasures, not attempting to hide his activities from the fascinated glances of his family members, even that silly thing that was Tletl's wife. He had paid this same trader two glittering jade pieces close to two moons ago, when first asking the man to detour through certain areas while visiting Tenochtitlan, the Capital of the World.

No one argued with Father back then as well. They all wanted to know what was happening with Miztli; they all worried to various degrees. But not like Father, for some reason. Even Mother was not that frantic over her youngest son's fate. She believed in the boy and his talents and abilities to do well, she would say. But still Father worried. That was why he had approached the only long-distance trader he knew, a man of distant Cuauhnahuac, not a local merchant of Oaxtepec. To detour through the metalworker's shop while doing his business in Tenochtitlan should not be a problem, to ask questions, talk to the boy himself preferably, give him news of his family and an encouraging word in case he needed it. Two fairly large pieces of green stone and another larger one promised when the news was delivered constituted an ample compensation in exchange for such a service, more than they could afford to spend. And yet, no one argued against it.

Elotl shrugged again, missing his younger sibling, like all of them. When Miztli was born, he was ready to hate this new addition to the family, the baby and, later on, the boy Father clearly preferred to spend his time with. Mother took long to recover from the difficulty of this last birth, but when she did, she also was fussy about the new son, spoiling him whenever she could, giving him special treatment, the wonder of a boy with a spectacular name and a talisman that out of all Father's sons only he had – an obsidian puma, of all things, a wonder one could only crave to touch. No one was allowed to do that, but on his tenth birthday, Miztli received the whole thing, an annoying piece of rotten meat that he was.

Oh yes, he, Elotl, did wish to hate his younger brother with all his heart, all his alleged fire, and underlying passion. However, even this was not possible. Miztli was too nice of a person, never even noticing the special treatment he received, let alone making use out of it. Everyone would have benefited from such a state of affairs, everyone but that good-natured, unpresumptuous Miztli. This one didn't even notice.

It would be good to learn that the annoying thing did well, thought Elotl, following Father out and onto the patio, not sure why he was doing this. Did Miztli enjoy his new life in the legendary great *altepetl* that ruled the world? It was too much to expect of the shy piece of meat to go out and explore the life of the big city for real, but maybe a little, at least some of it. He tried to imagine what Tenochtitlan might be like. Like Oaxtepec but bigger? With a marketplace alley, maybe, and pretty girls frequenting it, carrying their baskets while swaying their hips. In Oaxtepec, there was a special alley for sellers to come and offer their goods every now and then, mainly things no one needed but the holidaying nobility from the surrounding estates, so huge and well guarded no one even tried to sneak into and wander about, let alone attempt to imagine what they looked like. Was Tenochtitlan like that but bigger? Or was it something else, something different, sporting a bigger alley for market, or even a square with something impressive built upon it?

Trust Miztli not to look out for something like that, though. That one would be working day and night, making shiny jewelry like Father wanted him to do. A silly skunk! Was that why Father preferred to send his favorite out instead of him, Elotl, as available and much more eager than Miztli, less useful in the fields and the mines? Miztli was happy to perform whatever job there was on a given day, doing everything well and beyond required. The annoying piece of work, and yet the most likable thing, bashful but not insignificant like some other shy boys were. It was a pleasure to mess with this one sometimes, to piss him off until his namesake, the puma, came out. That quiet, self-conscious Miztli did have his share of fire, even though Father wasn't aware of that.

"They will begin their journey soon. I must hurry." Spoken atypically loudly, Father's words made him nearly jump out of his skin, too deep in his musings to notice that the man was looking at him now, not pacing the patio anymore, his forehead a mess of ointments and dried blood, both prominent cheekbones scratched raw, rubbed with balms too. Trust Mother to be thorough and uncompromising about the necessity of the treatment. From inside the house, the voice of Tletl was coming quietly, monotonously, overcoming his wife's hysterical shouting, making it fade.

"Who, Father? The trader?"

The man nodded, then motioned him to follow, charging toward the edge of the narrow plot that separated their private growths from the road out there, peering into the darkness. If one could make people appear out of the thin air by the sheer power of their will, the trader would be here now, hovering, reflected Elotl, his heart going out to Father. He was worried so. Why?

"I didn't know you knew any long-distance traders," he offered, thrilled with the opportunity to accompany Father, to have this man all for himself. Rare were the chances of such private conversations, not without a good reason to have one. But for him being anxious to meet the trader, Father would be meeting with other respectable elders of the village now, discussing the ways to minimize the damage of what happened today, or how to redirect their settlement's working forces.

An indefinite motion of the head was his answer. Father's silhouette was broad, as solid as the rocks around the mines. And as rigid now.

"How do you know him?" pressed Elotl, craving this private talk all of a sudden. Maybe he could find the courage to bring up his inadequate behavior down there in the mine, to talk to Father about it, his hatred of tunnels and pits, this emptiness in his stomach and the lack of proper air to breathe. "I mean, he doesn't buy things from us, does he? Only people of Oaxtepec do that, no? The local traders. They don't have long-distance traders, do they?"

Father's head swayed in a way one shakes his limbs to get rid of mosquitoes. Yet, when the man glanced at his son, his eyes were attentive and kind. The moon broke from between the sweeping across clouds in time to let him know that.

"This man is not an Oaxtepec trader, even though he does spend some time there. Not among the locals but among the highborn visitors. Supplies them with things they need, plenty of those. Items you wouldn't even dream to imagine, the strangest of foods and drinks." Father's pursed lips were twisting in a reluctant grin. "But do they eat strangely, those people from big *altepetl*s. Foamy stuff of spice and bitterness, he says. Raising dogs for cooking; imagine that. Would you go after a wolf in the woods for the taste of its meat? Would you even crave such thing if you were forced to kill it?"

"Wolf? No!" He heard his own words bursting out in a loud exclamation. "Who would try to eat a wolf, or bother to go after it?"

Father laughed, clearly pleased with the effect. "The dwellers of those *altepetl*s. They raise hairless dogs and they keep them in their houses sometimes. When they don't eat them, I suppose."

"In the houses? Like inside?" He thought about the faintly flickering opening of their dwelling, the fire inside probably made larger by now. By Mother's efforts, of course. Not the useless fox his brother bedded. Screams of their new baby would be coming out as well now. Elotl made a face, then pushed his resentment at this additional thing in the crowdedness of their hut out of his mind. The pleasure of conversing with Father and about most bizarre things was too good to mar it with familiar frustrations. But for him being sent to Tenochtitlan as well!

"Do you think Miztli eats wolves now?"

But Father's face closed again, and as the broad shoulders lifted heavily, Elotl cursed himself, watching the man turn his head away and toward the road. "I hope he gets to eat well, yes. Whatever they consume in that island-capital. I hope he is not treated badly or harmed."

"Why do you worry about him so? What could happen?"

The dark silhouette of Father's head did not move for a long while, besides the motion his long paces created. "I don't know, Son. It's just..." The sagging shoulders lifted again. "I have a bad feeling. That man, the trader, he promised to find that workshop, talk to Miztli, pass him a word of encouragement, ask about his life." The night rustled softly, moving with the heaviness of Father's sigh. "He is just a boy, after all, so very young and naïve. Maybe I should not have sent him away. He has great potential, so many outstanding qualities that are waiting to be awoken. But his thinking was always too simple, too trustful. He doesn't command your understanding of people. He does not see their nature as quickly as you do, does not act accordingly. In that, you might have done better out there in the strangeness of the great *altepetl*."

Then why didn't you send me instead? he thought, but didn't dare to utter the question, knowing the part of the answer, if not all of it. In order to learn new skill or trade, one needed a good measure of diligence, of patience and ability to deal with mundane, boring work, to accomplish tedious tasks without shortcuts or spells of hot temper. That great *altepetl*'s craftsman might have thrown him out of the workshop before the moon ran its course.

"The Tenochtitlan metalworker is said to be a respectable, decent man," went on Father, clearly needing to talk, speaking into the darkness as though eager to convince the surrounding hills. "Miztli should do well there, should learn enough, practice his newly acquired knowledge."

"Do you want him to stay out there for good?" The question nagged at him for a long time; since his younger sibling's leaving, truth be told. Was Miztli destined to come back, share in the knowledge, help Father open a workshop of his own, maybe? Would they manage to produce shining jewelry the visiting aristocrats of Oaxtepec were reported to wear all over their bodies? That would put their village over quite a few of the neighboring settlements, would make even Oaxtepec's dwellers stop looking down on them.

"I don't know." Father's sigh startled him again, such a loud sound. "And I probably worry for nothing. There is no reason why Miztli would not thrive out there in Tenochtitlan."

The lights were flickering in the distance, proving Father right on one count. Oh yes, the traders were still camping, preparing to resume their journey in all probability, following the old time custom of traveling through the night.

"Who are you?" A man armed with a club stopped them when they already reached the outskirts of the hill, narrowing his eyes against the darkness. "What do you want?"

"I came to meet Honorable Ixollin." Father's voice rang authoritatively and it made Elotl straighten his shoulders, his pride welling. No, they wouldn't be told off like simple villagers, not even by exclusive long-distance traders. "He sought my company not long ago."

The man hesitated, then motioned them to proceed, following closely, clearly on guard. Elotl edged nearer to Father, just in case.

"Wait here."

By the glimmering embers of a fire that had already been put out, two silhouettes were moving packages, preparing to tie those to their foreheads in a practiced manner. He remembered the market square of Oaxtepec, the last time he had sneaked there with two of his friends, two youths that he had managed to talk into attending one of the Oaxtepec's meetings. There were minor traders there, a pair of young men with large bundles hanging behind their backs but tied to their foreheads in an intricate manner. Others were there too, some from surrounding villages, some from Oaxtepec itself, talking about places he hadn't heard of before, Toluca or Tollocan out there in the north, and then somewhat closer Tenantzinco. And Tenochtitlan, of course. Everyone feared the masters of the Great Lake, their continued presence here in the fertile south. It was not enough that larger towns like distant Cuauhnahuac had to pay the mighty island a tribute, collecting it from the entire area, of course, every town and village, no matter how small and insignificant. Even Oaxtepec, even their tiny village Teteltzinco. And yet now Tenochtitlan warriors might be showing up in their valleys and hills again, called here by the ruler of this same mysterious Toluca against Tenantzinco, both more than two days of walking from here. Or maybe it was the other way around. The man who tried to talk them into an organized resistance had not been clear about such details, only about the need to do something, to beat Tenochtitlan off and show those snotty islanders what the people of the south were made of.

"It's good to see you, Matlaltepetl." A voice jerked Elotl from his memories, its owner approaching them, not an impressive type, short and stocky, with a clear hint of an extra padding on his limbs and what one could glimpse of the stout body. His eyes were difficult to see in the glimmering darkness, but the features surrounding those were relaxed, expressing mild interest. "I was looking forward to seeing you before we left." The inquiring gaze narrowed with sudden intensity. "Has there been trouble with one of your mines?"

"No," said Father quickly, too quickly. "Just a minor inconvenience."

Some inconvenience, thought Elotl, but was wiser than to comment on any of that; even had he been allowed to sound his mind in such respectable company, which he wasn't.

"I wish I could escort you back to my house for a decent meal and a conversation," went on Father, politeness itself. As though they didn't stand in the middle of the road, surrounded by darkness and the shrieking of the wind, among obvious preparations for the nighttime journey being almost completed. "It would be my honor to do that."

"It would be a pleasure to accept your generous invitation, elder of Teteltzinco, but for the pressure of our impending journey. My next visit to this area will not see me leaving without paying you my respects."

Surprised with such deference a clearly important town man was paying his father and in such an open manner, Elotl braced himself for a long wait, trying to pay no attention to the chill of the night. Such respectable talk heralded more flowery words before either of the speakers would get to the point of the conversation, reluctant to profess impatience and thus lose face.

However, the journey must have been pressing indeed, as after a few more flowery exchanges, the trader nodded solemnly, then pursed his lips. "I'm afraid I'm not a bearer of good news, Matlaltepetl."

Not a muscle moved in Father's face, but the night became somehow colder, less friendly than before. "You bring word from Tenochtitlan?"

The stocky trader nodded again, then glanced at his fellow travelers, all ready and waiting by the roadside, hovering at a respectable distance, politeness itself.

"The workshop you asked me to visit wasn't difficult to find. The craftsman who manages it is a prominent enough man, enjoying commissions of even the Royal Enclosure temples, let alone other important institutions of the Great Capital. You could not have placed your boy in a better establishment."

Father's nod was as stiff as that of a rocky mountain after the slightest of the earth's quakes. An imperceptible motion. "It is good to hear that." Even his voice had stony quality to it, not of brittle obsidian but of a hard marble piece.

"However, it seems that your boy did not appreciate the respectability of this establishment, nor everything that has been done for him in this place." A dramatic pause had Elotl holding his breath, afraid to miss a word.

"What did he do?" Father's voice didn't change, the same impassive stone, polished to perfection.

Their tormenter sighed. "He has left, never to return. After living there for about two, maybe three moons, treated like a family member, taught the intricate craft and being encouraged to learn, the boy has repaid all the kindness by leaving in an ungraceful way, causing damage, behaving appallingly, or so the respectable craftsman claimed. He could have applied to the local courts, the metalworker said, for the damage the boy had caused was substantial. However, knowing your situation, he decided to let this matter go. Which is a good thing, Matlaltepetl. The Great Capital has means to collect debts, even from such faraway places."

Still Father didn't move, but the air hissed, drawn forcefully through his widening nostrils. Elotl didn't dare to stir, aware of the tickling in his limbs, his skin crawling, covering in goose bumps. Could it be true? And if so, what did it mean? For him and his private plans as well, Oaxtepec and the meetings.

"Where is the boy now?" Father's voice tore the night, low and gritty, no polished marble, not anymore.

The trader shook his head. "They don't know. Otherwise, he would be in the courts, wouldn't he?" he added gently, with what seemed like genuine sympathy. "But the metalworker's sons said that they had seen him around the city, engaging in dubious activities, up to no good." Another pause. "They didn't elaborate what exactly. No positive feeling is harbored toward your son in these quarters. These people are hurt and angered. It was easy to observe that."

The men with bundles were shifting uneasily.

Father drew in another rasping breath. "I thank you for bringing the news to me, Honorable Ixollin. My gratitude knows no bounds." A quick fiddling produced the cherished small bag. "Please take this as a token of my gratitude, and if you hear something further concerning this matter, please do not hesitate to let me know. A father in you understands my position as much as a respectable person of honor and responsibility."

But did Father know how to talk well! Elotl bit his lips, moved by the reserved words, ashamed of thinking about himself before. His younger brother was in trouble, maybe even in danger of some mysterious courts and whatnot. Spotted in a bad company, engaged in dubious activities? Miztli? No, it couldn't be. Anyone but him! And what were those activities? What did Tenochtitlan's dubious people do? Robbed passersby like some criminals out there on the roads, witness those same traders traveling armed and on the lookout? Would Miztli join something like that? The mere thought made him wish to chuckle, even if nervously.

Father was nodding, answering platitudes offered by their dubious bearer of bad news. Then the surrounding silhouettes began melting in the darkness, leaving them blissfully alone, with only the angered wind for company.

"What do you make of what this man said, Father?" he asked after the silence lasted for too long, beginning to grate on his nerves. The way Father just stood there, a lifeless form made out of cold marble, made him feel dreadfully alone, surrounded by mounting danger. He shot a nervous glance behind his shoulder, then looked at Father again. "What he said can't be true, can it? He must have gone to the wrong workshop."

"The wrong workshop with a wrong boy from Teteltzinco?" Father came back to life at once, his features a brief study of anger, a disturbing sight. "Some other boy from our village who came to learn the trade but got tired of it, unlike our diligent ItzMiztli. I'm sure this is the best explanation!"

Elotl pressed his lips, unused to Father flaring at him in such a demeaning, belittling manner, unsettled by it. Indeed, what were the chances? And yet, it was inconceivable to think of the sensible, trustworthy, diligent Miztli doing something violent, irresponsible, something so wild it warranted a complaint lodged in one of these courts, a place one could only hear about out there in important cities like Cuauhnahuac, where people would be judged by strangers and not local elders familiar with both the accuser and the accused, knowing the undercurrents. What a terrible thought!

"It doesn't make sense, yes," Father was saying, his voice low now, hardly disturbing the night. His paces as he began walking were slow and measured, like that of a person progressing at someone else's will. "But he is just a boy, so very young. Impressionable. Maybe he did pick bad company. Maybe he fell under the wrong influence."

"Not Miztli surely!" He said it without thinking, resolving to keep quiet, not to sound as childish as before while suggesting a mistaken conclusion. Still, to think of his younger brother falling under a bad influence was strange. Miztli was not that sort of a person. He always thought before he did something. Too much and for too long sometimes, missing opportunities or avoiding something worth joining. There were plenty of dubious activities to engage through the midst of the rainy season, when not forced to spend days and nights in the fields or the mines. He, Elotl, himself never missed out on any of this, getting in trouble sometimes, lying his way through or wriggling out of trouble in another manner when possible. He was the gambler between the two of them, not the responsible deep-thinker Miztli. If anything, his brother was just the opposite.

"He must have been lonely, maybe confused." Again, Father stopped, addressing his words to the wind, clearly thinking aloud. "Yet this man said he was treated like a family, given a warm home." His massive hands came up, clutched the strands of his receding hair, tied in a loose knot but ruffled by the wind already. "I don't understand. It's not like him, not like him at all! To be so... so selfish and unkind, to do bad by the people who did him nothing but good."

Elotl put his face into the wind as well. It felt good to let its force cleanse him. "How do you know that they are telling the truth?" he asked quietly, afraid to do so but needing to utter the words aloud. "If not the trader, then maybe that Tenochtitlan workshop man; maybe he lied about Miztli. Maybe other things happened and he didn't want to tell the truth. With Miztli not being there, what was to stop him from telling what he wanted? What was—"

Father's snort cut his words short. "Stop talking like a child, Elotl!" That came out harshly, again with atypical anger and disdain. "The metalworker has no more motive to lie than the trader has. Your childish thinking is unacceptable!" The burning eyes bore at him, piercing the darkness. "You have seen closer to twenty summers than half twenty. Start thinking like a man, not like a mischievous boy. The trips to Oaxtepec will stop unless I send you to this town. Otherwise, you will work like the rest of the family does, with no more dubious sneaking away. Not anymore!" Another deep breath was drawn through widening nostrils, the effort of controlling his temper obvious, impossible to miss. "Speaking of bad influences, you came dangerously close to one yourself! Therefore, pull yourself together, boy, and start working like the rest of us. It will do you nothing but good."

The darkness shattered as the man turned around, resuming his walk, his paces now long and determined, challenging the night. No more uncertain pacing and no thinking aloud. Elotl stared at the drawing away back.

CHAPTER 2

The sun was glaring through the partly closed shutters, outlining straight paths upon the flagstones of the floor. Tlemilli followed the merrily blazing patterns, then let her eyes wander across the room. Nothing would change there since she did the same thing some hundred or less heartbeats before; still, it was better than to stare at the folded papers containing too many dots and flags alternating with the occasional glyph symbolizing a higher number of those. Boring!

The surprisingly young priestess, a woman in her mid-twenties with a pleasantly round face and astonishingly even temper, was repeating the same thing again and again, rephrasing herself painstakingly, trying to explain in different words. Still, the stupid fowls that crouched around the book in question asked silly questions, as though no explanations were given before, not a word in regard to the ways of dealing with amounts larger than twenty. Stupid turkeys!

Tlemilli suppressed a snore, letting her eyes rest on her neighbor to her left, the commoner girl. This one was the only person to keep quiet, to venture no comments, but the way she leaned backwards and away, side-glancing the unfolded pages warily, as though ready to spring to her feet and flee in case those came to attack her, suggested a glaring lack of understanding, if not worse. Poor thing. Tlemilli rolled her eyes at the twinge of pity that knotted her stomach, even if for the briefest of moments. This girl was the nicest, not mean and not spiteful, smiling quite readily, meaning it too. Not the thin smiles some of the beauties clad in the finest of gowns would give you, that cold, careful twist of lips, letting you know that you couldn't be further from its owner's real interest, the insignificant insect that you were. Matlatl was an expert on those, but now Matlatl was nowhere near, thanks all the great and small deities for that. The contents of the Tlatelolco Palace had been emptied speedily and briskly on the day following the conquest, given away, or rather, sold to various provincial rulers brimming with a surplus of goods and ambition. The general price for royalty and various aristocratic offspring must have fallen dreadfully in the market intervals following her city's fall. Or so claimed one of the boys, another friend of Miztli's friend Necalli, a funny troublemaker named Axolin. For some reason, Miztli did not warm to this other boy, keeping a reserved, non-committal façade of amiable enough politeness. Only with the other one, Necalli, would he smile this wonderfully open, sweetly shy smile of his, would joke and mess around, and laugh openly. But only when outside the school's fence. Inside their *calmecac*, he would turn into a stony statue; sober, tight-faced, on guard, speaking little, watching his step.

Never with her, of course, and yet, when she began attending their school and on rare occasions when they managed to meet, he would remain tense and alert, looking ready to defend them both against some danger that was waiting to spring from everywhere, behind every corner or every glancing pair of eyes. It made her remember his grazed cheek and the hideously split lip of the night before her Tlatelolco fell. It made her feel cornered too, in a way. Although this school was actually nicer than the one she was forced to attend back at home. The priestess teaching the girls was all sweetness and good looks, and the girls were distant but not outright nasty like some of her half-sisters and other annoying Palace's brood.

The commoner girl Chantli was the nicest, always smiling and ready to strike conversations when forced to work in the temples together, treated well by her fellow other girls despite her glaringly humble origins. Like Citlalli, the commoner was too nice not to enjoy her company, but not too nice to let others take advantage of her. Even though a few of the spiciest girls in the class did bother to make this one remember that she wasn't one of them, even if allowed to tread the same elegant flagstones of the exclusive establishment for the noblest youth of the land. They did so with typical misleading sweetness, as though unaware of the nature of their remarks, but every arrow went in, of that Tlemilli was sure, herself not the most perceptive person, not until her previous life had fallen apart. Back then, she also thought that the commoners were all an uncouth, ignorant, unworthy lot, good for carrying heavy loads or cleaning, existing for the sole purpose of serving, growing or making food, and doing other useful things, incapable of anything more intricate or clever anyway. Even though some maids were the nicest, of course. Tlaco, for one, and some of the others; still beneath Palace's dwellers, but nice nevertheless.

Well, all mighty deities bear witness, it was still hard to believe that Miztli was one of them. Or maybe even worse, not being even one of the city's commoners, a spicy uneducated lot, yet dwellers of the big *altepetl*. A peasant from a gods-forsaken village, growing food out there or seeking rocks in the depths of the mountains? But did he like to talk about it, about his father and the precious things only he knew how to spot, to dig in the earth and extract carefully. It was still hard to believe that this was his life before Tenochtitlan and that he thought it was something good, worthwhile, talking about it with longing and only when no one was there to listen but her. It made her wish to go out and seek all those places too, the way he talked about it – the forests and the hills, and the underground tunnels and mines, or so he had called those – mines or adits. And why wouldn't she? With him by her side. And yet, when alone and in the privacy of the nicest suite of rooms Citlalli had been given, small but so very cozy, bearing Citlalli's touch, she had always found it hard to digest the fact that he was not noble, not even a little, with all his courage and spirit, his looks, and his inner and outer strength. The greatest of heroes from Tlaco's stories, and yet just a peasant from stinking fields of a stinking province, or so the nasty fowls kept claiming on that day when she had a huge fight with them all.

It was a few market intervals after the fall of her city and she had been in school for some time by then, over the shock of the relocation and coping with it better than expected – even better than Citlalli did! – because he was there every time she managed to sneak away or send him word. The other boy, his spunky friend with wild ways, the boy at whose father's house she had been hidden on the night of the fighting, had managed to establish communication between her and Miztli through a net of other *pillis*, like the Emperor's youngest brother, a rascal of barely half twenty summers and the most likeable thing she ever met named Ahuitzotl. They had gotten along well from the very first moment and, if no subject of politics came up, especially her Tlatelolco, now reorganized and still on everyone's lips, they had even managed to keep it so. Otherwise, she and the royal *pilli* would yell at each other fiercely and with much spirit, exchanging the most colorful curses one could fish in one's arsenal of such things. Still, even in the heat of an argument and mutual name-calling, she knew that she preferred the royal rascal's company to any of her former female adversaries from the Tlatelolco Palace any day.

Also the young Emperor's brother kept smuggling her out of the Palace and toward their school for Miztli to meet and make everything right again. *His* arms were so strong and his chest so broad, with his eyes the most beautiful and his lips still as enticing as she remembered from that night in the Tlatelolco Palace. Even though to find enough privacy to kiss like back then was a challenge, either near school or under various temples' stairs. He was the reason why she agreed to start attending local *calmecac*, surprising them all with her alleged adaptability. It made the opportunities to meet him multiply like dots and flags on *amate*-paper.

Speaking of dividing and multiplying, she forced her ears to listen to yet another silly question she knew the answer to, then let her mind roam again. The girl who had difficulty calculating how many flag glyphs of twenty dots could fit in the feather-like glyph of four hundred was not the part of the group she had gotten into a fight with on her second market interval in this school, less than a moon ago.

Grinding her teeth, she remembered that day, sunny but cold, typical to this part of the seasons, with not a rainy cloud in sight despite the relevant temples doing plenty of rites to honor Tlaloc, the earth and rain deity. It had taken the aristocratic fowls in her class less than a day to come to grips with her presence before the regular rolling eyes and poisonous needling took place. However, a veteran of such altercations, she returned them their treatment with enough viciousness to silence them for some time, making them slink back into the dark holes they had come from. Evidently, Tenochtitlan *calmecac*'s female population was soft, unused to an out-front war. Which made her wonder about Tenochtitlan school males as well. If they were as easily intimidated, then maybe her Tlatelolco should think of a rematch.

However, the following two market intervals proved her conclusion to be a hasty one. Or maybe it was that she had given them too much ammunition by sneaking around the Plaza with Miztli whenever they managed to meet outside the school's fence. Such juicy gossip was difficult to ignore. Even she knew that.

When the needling and goading resumed, it was on that sunny day, when they all had been out there, watching the ceremony, coming to a peak when she lost her temper and attacked one of the girls who kept commenting not only on the pitiful state of Tlatelolco, but on her sister's lustful ways that at least included imperial coupling and not the disgraceful thrashing about with commoners still smelling of fields.

In the beginning, she had had enough presence of mind to return measure for measure, scaring the nice commoner girl Chantli, who kept staring with her eyes round and huge and her cheeks burning in all sorts of coloring. This one tried to stick to her, Tlemilli, to put in a good, encouraging word like she did through the past market intervals; hesitantly, but she did. However, the other girls kept ignoring this one, a dubious element in herself when the commoners' virtues or the lack of those were discussed, and by then, Tlemilli grew too angry, furious with their jabs against Citlalli and Miztli altogether, seeing nothing but red. Just who did they think they were to talk about her most precious people like that? Villager or not, they would be lucky if he deigned to side-glance one of the fat fowls favorably, let alone condescended to show an interest in them. As for Citlalli, the most refined, perfect, accomplished person...

"Your lustful sister at least cast her immoral ways on the ruler of a petty island, not marring her noble body with someone beneath her," went on one of her tormenters, her eyes narrowed into slits, with no more pretended sweetness of the initial verbal assault. "While you are lusting after a commoner still smelling of feces that they put in the fields, all smeared in it." The girl's lips were twisting in ugliest of manners, dripping poison. "Does it amuse you to—"

But by this time, the words stopped reaching her and there was nothing remaining but the hated face and the wickedly glimmering eyes, as she threw herself at it, letting her fists decide what to do, where to strike, how hard; the way he did back in the war-torn marketplace, with wonderful abandon. And it didn't matter that they both toppled over, not as long as her offender ended up underneath her, squealing in this stupidly high-pitched tone, making her wish to shut her ears.

There was plenty of additional noise all around, as annoyingly shrill cries and other authoritative voices. She had fought against hands that pulled her away from her victim, her fingers claws, tearing something – strands of hair? The stupid poisonous empty-headed fowl! But she would not let this one talk about him in this way. Neither her, nor the others. And certainly not while badmouthing her sister along the way.

"Now unfold your papers and take brushes and red and black coloring."

The priestess's voice jerked her back from her reverie in time, before she grew angry about the incident yet again. She didn't feel bad for losing her temper to such an extreme, even though it never happened to her before. Various clashes and altercations with her half-sisters never came to physical violence, and the rest of the girls in the Tlatelolco *calmecac* were a somehow quieter lot. They might have made faces and rolled their eyes aplenty when she would argue with the priestess against this or that admonition or slide into another public altercation with her foul-mouthed siblings, but they would not add to it, just smirk. While the Tenochtitlan snakes turned out to be quite vicious. No wonder, really. Even though later on, before the matter was hushed by the Palace's authorities despite the other girl being hurt to a relatively serious degree – this torn hair and bleeding face, a pure pleasure! – Citlalli had explained to her why back in Tlatelolco no one dared to pick on her but their immediate siblings. Apparently, their former *altepetl*'s aristocratic progeny was afraid of Father, them and their families. Which, of course, was not the case here in Tenochtitlan. Puffy-eyed and alluringly pale, thin and gaunt, but somehow more beautiful than ever, Citlalli had held her close, huddling in the small cozy alcove their set of rooms contained, trembling visibly, unsettled for real.

"We must watch every step of ours now, little one," she repeated again and again. "You cannot let your temper loose, certainly not in such terrible ways. We must not give the slightest excuse." The hands enfolding her tightened. "You will stop going to school. I want you to stay here with me and not to go out anymore, not for a while."

From there, of course, it spilled into a heated argument, as Tlemilli was not about to give up on her newfound freedom, the joy of seeing him often and with no special effort made to achieve that, no intricate net of messages and wearing waiting in between. And then, Citlalli was again talking bad about him, pointing out his common origins and his tendency to land her in trouble again and again, dismissing the fact that he was the one to save them both from a terrible fate as something small, insignificant, and angering her, Tlemilli, on that count greatly.

The quarrel was threatening to turn noisy but for the royal messenger that came to summon her into the royal presence, and to do so with no delays. An unsettling summons. Especially when following an assault on a member of local nobility. Citlalli again grew unbecomingly frightened and tried to delay, pleading Tlemilli's unbecoming state of wear, not appropriate enough for the royal side of the Palace. But the servant was apologetic, yet adamant. The young girl had to accompany him, no matter the state of her clothing. The revered person who wished to see her could not be kept waiting. So she had followed with her heart fluttering but her head held high. What could they do to her after all? Throw her out of the Palace? Who cared? He would arrange something better for her if that happened, he and his friends, Necalli and Ahuitzotl. Who wanted to live in the Palace anyway?

Hiding her smile now, a whole moon later and ensconced in the sleepy mood of the classroom in the high afternoon, with the sun flowing in gently, lulling, she remembered her surprise and then this slight splash of fright, or at least a twinge of immediate alarm upon seeing the identity of her summoner. This familiar strikingly beautiful face, as groomed and perfectly arrayed as she remembered, not a tendril escaping the intricate coiffure, not a piece of intricately embroidered cotton out of place. The Tenochtitlan snake! As unbearably haughty, as annoyingly sure of herself. She remembered gathering the remnants of her courage, all the bad feelings she had harbored for this woman. Anger was always the best of helpers.

Yet, what came next left her gaping helplessly once again. No haughty poisonous words, no open gloating, not even a simple reprimand a grownup person would direct at a younger girl. Nothing of the sort. Instead, the woman measured her with an openly amused glance, then proceeded to invite her to partake in refreshments; as expected, an orgy of sweetened cakes and drinks. She wanted to know all about what happened, but unlike Citlalli, she did so with no reproachful comments and no words of critique, not even in her gaze. This would-be high-aristocracy swarming the Royal Enclosure and the Palace, sending their numerous offspring to attend the royal school, needed to be put in their place, the woman had said. Connected to this or that insignificant element of the royal family, boasting an occasional imperial concubine for a grandmother, they kept forgetting their rightful position of serving the Emperor and his immediate family and not trying to conduct his business, deeming themselves a part of Tenochtitlan royalty, free to have their say and dictate to the royal house their views and wishes. Ridiculous! Apparently, Tlemilli's actions in school on that day served to promote the royal house's interests, as far as the haughty imperial sister was concerned. After a while of listening politely, while attacking plates of delicious maize cakes all she liked, Tlemilli gathered that

Noble Jade Doll wasn't regretting the effort of saving her from the slave markets, and that she was to complain directly to her in case of more goading at school. Unbelievable but true!

Since then, she had not been summoned to the princess's quarters, but the school days went on uneventfully, and when she didn't feel like getting up in the morning, no one but Citlalli admonished her and tried to make her attend the lessons anyway. The school authorities didn't even try to reprimand her, let alone discipline in the way the Tlatelolcan *calmecac* would do. No punishment ensued for the crimes of a violent quarrel – an unheard-of occurrence, certainly among the girls of the school – and no discipline matters offered if she appeared later than expected, too many times in her case. The girls made faces but didn't dare to venture anything more telling than an occasional glance, with the poisonous fowl and her big nasty mouth not even at school anymore, or maybe attending some private classes. Tlemilli didn't bother to even think about it. Who cared for the mealy-mouthed sneak as long as her, Tlemilli's, crimes did not affect their possible status in this city, hers and Citlalli's. And with the imperial sister's active backing, it seemed that they were safe now and well set. Even though Citlalli wasn't so convinced, not trusting her past rival and this sudden spell of kindness, suspicious of it. She wasn't happy here in Tenochtitlan, cooped up in their suite of rooms, not daring to come out unless forced. It was as though she had been afraid to draw attention to herself. Sometimes it made Tlemilli worried.

"Why aren't you writing down your answers?"

The priestess's voice broke into her thoughts once again, this time impossible to push away or ignore. The woman was staring at her, her delicately plucked eyebrows raised in an open reprimand.

"I... I didn't hear..." Helplessly, she glanced at the girls as they crouched above their papers, wholly immersed. "What was the question?"

Someone snickered covertly, quite a few voices. The commoner girl Chantli looked up fleetingly, her expression still gaunt, the clearness of her forehead marred with too many creases.

"Look, Tlemilli." The teaching woman's face creased in somewhat similar fashion. "You can't daydream through most of the lesson, then ask for explanations. There are other girls here, girls who spend their time learning and listening. It wouldn't be fair for them to have me explaining it all anew to you and only because you didn't bother to listen before, would it?"

How very polite, reflected Tlemilli, peeved ever so slightly, the reasonable tone and the explanation leaving her somewhat disarmed. It was easier to deal with angered hags, even if angered hags tended to send the rebellious elements to inhale stinging smoke of boiled *chili* peppers a little too often.

"You explained it all many times over," she offered, not wishing to be offensive but needing to tell the truth. "They asked you the same questions over and over again."

A few of the girls glanced up, their gazes having a spiteful quality to them. Stupid fowls!

"At least they asked for a repeated explanation, girl," said the priestess icily, with no attempt to sound patiently reasonable this time. "They honored the effort put into teaching them, the time spent on explaining the details of managing numbers and goods."

To this Tlemilli found nothing to say, sneaking a thoughtful glance at her fingernails instead. Those were dirty and broken in places, catching in the fringes of her embroidered *huipil* in the most unpleasant of ways.

"You must listen to the lesson being taught while it is being taught, girl," went on the woman, still reasonable, to a degree. "Otherwise, you won't be able to manage your own household, to make it work with no faults, with no dissatisfied servants doing their work half-heartedly and the displeased husband who might be quick in reconsidering your status in his house."

"Poor man," muttered someone, generating a new outburst of louder snickering.

Tlemilli stifled all ready-to-pop responses from "shut up" to worse, making a nasty face toward the speaker instead. A feather-headed, chatty thing named Tlazotli, the most outspoken among the harmless element of the class, not truly harmless in her words but managing to get away with an innocent smile and temporary nicer behavior. She had stuck to the commoner girl whenever sent out to do temples' duties as though it was her exclusive right to be paired with this one. Miztli's friend Necalli didn't like that. He said this same crafty Tlazotli used Chantli's good nature and her ability to get the things done. He liked that Chantli-girl a great deal. One could see that from a distance of half a city.

The teacher's frown deepened. "One earns a position of a chief wife not only as the result of one's nobility and birthright. This school is preparing you girls for the important work that is still ahead of you. To manage a large household with plenty of slaves and other serving hands alone, one needs to be able to deal with sums and papers aplenty, to complete tasks of writing down amounts of goods or means of payment, of adding those up or parting and dividing them properly. Otherwise, you will not be able to manage your husbands' households and incomes in a satisfactory manner." This time, the woman's gaze encircled them all, relaying a message. "And you cannot sit with those papers, dividing numbers into groups all day long. You will have to learn to do it quickly, with part of your mind free to deal with other, as important, aspects of your responsibilities."

"Unless one didn't manage to find that fabulously rich, exceptionally patient husband with means," breathed this same spicy Tlazotli under her breath, glancing at her fellow students, two more girls who crouched beside her, working on their pieces of paper, or pretending to do that. Her head jerked imperceptibly, swaying toward Tlemilli, barely moving at all. Tlemilli stared her down as quickly.

"Will you listen this time, Tlemilli, if I repeat the assignment for you?"

She put her eyes back on the priestess, then forced an affirmative nod. Who cared for assignments when all she wanted was to catch this filthy Tlazotli's prettily done braids and pull hard enough to have the empty-headed thing hurled out of the doorway?

"If you have twenty slaves, Tlemilli, and each costs you four cocoa beans to maintain a day. How many loads of cocoa beans would you have to set aside at the end of each moon?" The woman paused. "Write it down carefully, then try to arrive at an answer."

Tlemilli thought for a moment. "How many cocoa beans are to be in each load?"

The priestess's eyebrows lifted slightly. "You think fast." A pause lasted for another heartbeat. "Twenty beans are what traders put in each bag."

"Oh well." She glanced at the light flowing through the partly closed shutters. "Four times twenty loads, then."

The silence that followed had a stunned quality to it. Then it rustled with too many breaths let out at once.

The teacher's eyes grew remarkably wider. "How did you arrive at the answer so fast?"

Tlemilli shrugged, slightly embarrassed. "Twenty slaves multiplied by four beans, then by twenty dawns of the moon." She shrugged again. "Then divided by loads. Twenty beans in each bag, you said."

The woman was still staring. "Can you write it down as quickly?"

She nodded, happy to escape their attention for once. Drawing was never her favorite pastime, but since this note she had sent him from the crumbling Tlatelolco Palace, certain glyphs gained her attraction. He liked that note of hers, very much so! Enough to keep it along with his wonderfully rare puma made of glossy obsidian, the most beautiful figurine she ever saw or touched. He showed it to no one, he had claimed, that puma, but she was allowed to touch it and even hold it if she wished. He kept it in a small bag that never left his side, and yet now her notes were there too, the original and the new ones. It excited him almost as her kisses did, her messages and the necessity to read them, all by himself or maybe with just a little help from her. So she wrote him every time she could, even when they were to meet and wander the Great Plaza together, to talk or huddle and kiss if managing to find dark enough corners to do that. Still she would slip yet another crude piece of paper into his hands before parting, for him to sit and decipher later on. Apparently, he truly didn't know how to read before, just like that old disgusting nobleman

Tepecocatzin had implied, and that was why that other boy Necalli had to peek into her first message – but was she relieved to learn that! Yet now he was making good progress and every newly deciphered message made him glow with pride, beam stronger than the sun in midday. So much so, that she made special efforts to write as simply as she could, to use glyphs that she remembered him understanding or the ones that were really easy to decipher. Anything to make him *that* excited.

"Write it down while I give the girls another assignment." The priestess's voice broke into her musings in time to pull her thoughts back toward the boring numbers, before her mind began composing yet another message to him. Something with numbers maybe. He surely knew how to read dots and flags.

The girls were talking loudly, all at once. Then the priestess's voice took over again. Tlemilli made an effort to concentrate on her charcoal, a long piece but broken in the middle, forcing her fingers to hold it together besides the effort of using it. Nothing to complain about. It was she who had cracked it while being bored by the lesson before. Still, now she had something to do with it.

The commoner girl inched closer, peeking at her paper hesitantly. Tlemilli moved to give her a clearer view, sketching an oval symbol of one cocoa load, the easiest thing to draw, then connecting it to four distinct flags that symbolized twenty numbers each. Four flags, eighty beans. Out of boredom and unwilling to listen to the same repeated questioning and discussions all around, she spent time sketching a glyph of a slave with a flag above, another symbol of twenty, then connected it to four dots with a separate drawing of a cocoa bean, then added twenty *tonalli*-days of whatever moon they were referring to. It didn't matter. Each moon had twenty days in it, every single one of them. Everyone knew that.

"You can copy this thing if you want to," she whispered, motioning the watching girl with her eyes. "But do it quickly. Before she notices." The priestess was busy crouching above the work on the empty-headed Tlazotli, explaining with divine patience. "Before she looks up."

"I can't! She'll know," breathed the commoner girl, aghast.

"Not if she doesn't catch you doing it." Tlemilli made a face. "How can she prove it?"

"By giving me another such riddle to solve!" Her converser's frown held much misery. "She knows I don't know those things."

"You don't?"

The shifting-away gaze was her answer.

Tlemilli rolled her eyes. "It's easy. You just count those dots and connect them or subtract when need be. That's all." She pointed toward her drawing. "See, twenty slaves, four beans. Means four times twenty. Easy. How hard it is to multiply twenty by four? Not hard."

"Multiply?" repeated her companion as though she had said a word of a different tongue, forgetting to keep quiet.

"Girls!" The priestess glanced at them briefly, her frown light, full of suspicion.

"Later," breathed Tlemilli. "I'll show you later. If the litter-bearers are not there."

Indeed, no litter-bearers lingered outside later on, as they had been herded out, conducted through the doorway of their hall, and toward the gates, supervised closely while crossing the schoolyard. Just like back in the Tlatelolco *calmecac*, no contact between male and female students was allowed, surely not on the school premises. The priests running the noble establishment made sure of that; even if out there, it was up to the noble girls' families to have the servants with litters waiting. Tlemilli sneaked a careful glance.

Several boys trained out there under the watchful eye of one of the veterans, huddling in pairs and trios, discharging *atlatls* loaded with blunt darts. Nothing but mid-sized sticks, come to think of it, with no ragged obsidian to crown it. She wrinkled her nose in a certain disdain. Neither Miztli nor his high-spirited friend needed to attend such lessons. They had fought in a real war, had real weaponry stored in Necalli's father's house. This same Necalli never tired of speaking of that.

Her heart leapt, then squeezed in disappointment. No sight of his broad shoulders or back was anywhere around the opening in the fence, neither his nor his friend's. Well, Necalli was away on the mainland, attending an important quest for future warriors, taken along with older boys nearing the end of their schooling. Like back in Tlatelolco. A small twinge of nostalgia came and went away. It was more exciting in Tenochtitlan, ten times more exciting, twenty times more!

"The Emperor is said to visit the construction between the round temple and the Great Pyramid." One of the girls pushed past her, just as Tlemilli slowed down, scanning the open ground one more time. Miztli was not taken on this quest. None of the other boys were. "If my mother's watchdogs are not there..."

"They are, sister, they are." Another one was answering, her laughter as musical as it was faked. This one was observing the schoolyard as closely. "Not a chance of you seeing any of it, unless you managed to talk the Priestess into letting you participate in the round temple's rituals."

"And not even then," contributed another, catching up with the drawing away pair. "The Honorable Priestess would send the commoner girl if there was something to do in the round temple."

It was easy to imagine the faces they made. "Well, commoners know how to work."

Tlemilli pushed herself past them, causing their chatter to cease for a moment. Stupid fowls! The commoner girl had a name, didn't she? And she was good at what she did. That was why the Priestess singled her out and made her work in the temples more than the others. That girl was efficient and she got things done. And she wanted to be a priestess herself, or so claimed Necalli. Even though she couldn't multiply twenty slaves by four beans. The thought made her look around once again, this time seeking the slender form of the fruit of her musings and their gossip.

Outside, the breeze was stronger, bringing along the scent of the much-awaited rain. She sniffed the air, hopeful. A thunderstorm could be a wonderful thing and it would have made it easier escaping Citlalli's maids. Since the violent incident, her sister was punctual at sending servants to pick her up and bring her straight back to the Palace and their suite of rooms. Still, there were ways to avoid that. Necalli and Miztli, with the help of the ever-resourceful Ahuitzotl, had worked out an intricate strategy. But where were they now?

"How did you know all that about the loads, the exact amount of those?" One of the girls, a quiet reticent one, harmless or so it seemed, hovered next to her litter, a large construction with curtains, not an open chair. "I mean, how did you know to divide it all into loads in the end?"

Tlemilli shrugged, busy with observations of her own. Citlalli's servants seemed to be nowhere in sight. What a stroke of luck! "The Priestess said so. She asked 'how many loads' not 'how many beans.'"

"Yes, but..." Her unexpected companion lifted one delicate shoulder, all embroidery and prettily fringed cotton. "I don't know. I seem to miss those instructions, always."

Catching sight of the commoner girl emerging through the opening in the fence as well, Tlemilli moved her head, noncommittal. "It's easy. You just listen to what she says, then divide or multiply or whatever there is to do with those numbers."

A group of boys spilling past the same opening caught the entirety of her attention for a moment, the scrutiny ending with another twinge of disappointment. *Where was he?*

The commoner girl neared them with her typical brisk step. "How did you know—"

"To divide into loads in the end?" finished Tlemilli, making even their aristocratic company giggle.

"Umm, well..." The commoner hesitated. "Yes, that too. But..." She shrugged briefly. "I don't know. How did you do it so fast? You didn't even stop to think."

"What was there to think about?" To smile encouragingly felt called for. "I don't know. Those things are easy."

"Not that easy," said both girls in unison, which made them all snicker again. Then the maids near the closed litter motioned the aristocratic part of their trio in, polite but uncompromising. Which left only the two of them in the alley still full of litters but emptying of those rapidly.

"Let's get out of here. I don't want to get caught by my sister's maids. They are nice but like buzzing mosquitoes; can't be avoided or talked into leaving me alone. But as long as they aren't here..." Glancing at the shadow the nearest low pyramid cast, obstructing the fierceness of the sunlight even if lightly, Tlemilli felt her heart falling at the sight of a small carrier. Citlalli didn't forget! "Oh no!"

"What?" The commoner girl was scanning the open ground between the pyramids as though looking for someone or something as well.

"My sister's litter, it's here." To try and dart into another alley was silly; still, she considered it for a wild moment. Then she remembered what the girls said about the Emperor touring his recent undertaking, a construction of what everyone called a Sun Stone, a huge, marvelously detailed plate of many men's heights, dedicated to Tonatiuh, the Sun Deity mainly, but not only. "Tell them the Priestess told all the girls to attend the ceremony of the Sun Stone."

The girl blinked. "What?"

"The maids with the litter. Tell them we are to tour the Sun Stone, pay our respects like the rest of the nobles."

A glance at the nearing woman, a squat scowling foreigner Tlemilli didn't like in the least, let her know that there was no time. She planted her legs in the cobblestones of the alley, then waited, determined. No, she was not going back to the Palace, not straight away. She had not seen him today at all and this alone was a good reason to detour.

"You are to take us to the Great Pyramid," she said as imperiously as she could, desperate to imitate Citlalli's way of addressing the servants, nicely but in a tone that brooked no argument, not even the slightest. "The Honorable Priestess told us to be there when the Emperor visits the Sun Deity's monument."

"Your noble sister told us to take you back to the Palace, young lady," countered the stocky woman, not impressed.

Tlemilli planted her legs yet firmer. "You will not—" she began hotly, the failed strategy replaced with the customary one. They could not make her go back by force, could they?

"The Honorable Priestess along with the other gods' servants were very clear about our duty to visit the Sun Deity's monument now." The commoner girl's voice rang with this same firm, even if polite authority Tlemilli was aiming to imitate before. "The other girls' litters have taken them to the reverent site already. It would be terribly impolite for us to miss the ceremony, or to be late for it."

Now even the litter-bearers gaped, only two of them. A tiny chair like hers with its skinny cargo did not require more than two men to deal with it.

"Yes," contributed Tlemilli, greatly impressed, sensing their victory. "And if we are late, they all will be angered like never before. And then—"

"But the Mistress told us to bring you back to the Palace," protested the woman, raising her arms helplessly, palms up.

"After the Great Pyramid, you will," informed her Tlemilli, beaming at her companion, answering the commoner girl's victorious smile. "Come. We'll walk there. And you," she turned to the litter-bearers, "you can follow us if you want to. Keep an eye on us and all that."

"But, young mistress!"

The maid's distress was so obvious Tlemilli felt the unwelcome twinge of compassion. "I will go straight to the Palace after that, I promise!" An attempt at a winning smile did not clear the wrinkled state of the troubled woman's forehead. "You can stay close to us and keep an eye. But send them away." She motioned toward the rest of their company. "We can't squeeze into this litter, me and my friend, and it's not like we are going to the marketplace or anywhere." A shrug seemed to be in order. "I'm not up to anything. I just want to see the Sun Deity's Stone."

Her commoner companion was chuckling quietly, and it made her wish to snicker as well, but she kept the fit of inappropriate guffawing at bay, the effort to do so costing her a painful stomach muscle or two. The Sun Stone? But she didn't even hear about this thing before but in passing. Tenochtitlan was in construction all the time, the Royal Enclosure worse than anything, the Great Pyramid's new level and the renovations for the ball court and other smaller pyramids and temples. One couldn't keep track of all those booming hammers and rolling slabs, with the strong dust-covered commoners laying out perfectly round tree trunks, then pulling at their ropes to make huge slabs of stones roll above those, and cloaked engineers running all around, waving their hands in agitation. It was funny to watch those building efforts at the time. She had never seen anything like that in Tlatelolco.

"The Emperor is visiting the Sun God's construction for real, no?" she asked as they began walking briskly, aiming to bypass the ball court on their way to the round temple. A somewhat longer route than retracing their steps along the school fence and then turn the corner of the Earth Goddess's pyramid. Still, they didn't need to coordinate their action. The ball court might be full of training boys even though *he* was rarely sent to the ball training sessions, if at all. He didn't like that game anyway, he had told her once. He wasn't good at it. Not like some other boys were. So if the honorable veteran Yaotzin didn't make him train, then it was only for the best. Still, it hurt to see that the schoolmaster had ignored him so openly on that count. With his exceptional strength alone, he could prove a true talent, no less than that other huge boy that was the best ballplayer in the entire *calmecac* and the nastiest person alive. Or so Necalli and Miztli thought, she knew, even though they never discussed this one, not in her hearing.

"The Emperor was visiting the rest of his building projects yesterday," the commoner girl was saying, walking by with enviable lightness of step, her sandals simple looking, barely adorned, with only one or two shiny knobs to enliven the dull leather, less comfortable than Tlemilli's prettily decorated wear was, high in the heel and around her ankle. "But the Sun Deity's monument he left for another day, because he intended to examine it most thoroughly, they say. The progress and the details."

"Oh, so that's why those fowls were talking about it as though it was a big event," exclaimed Tlemilli, remembering the gossiping girls. "They wanted to go there badly, but their escorts and litters didn't care." Tossing her head high, she smirked. "They won't glimpse much of the Emperor today, I predict."

Her companion smiled briefly. "We won't be able to get anywhere near the Emperor either."

"If there are too many nobles crowding the construction site, we'll hop into my litter and pretend that we are important dignitaries from the imperial wing of the Palace."

The girl snickered, then granted Tlemilli with a fleeting somehow questioning glance. "You *are* from the Palace. There is no need to pretend for you."

"The wrong side of it. Always the wrong side." The smile was sneaking out on its own, impossibly wide. "I always seem to land in the less important parts of the palaces, where they put various unimportant families – advisers and such. Our current suite neighboring the one belonging to some cousin of a cousin of this or that royal family distant member, full of shrill females and babies, and across the flowerbeds there are suites they put visiting dignitaries at. No royal surroundings that." She winked. "It's not like we are living between Axayacatl's wives and their ladies-in-attendance, or Jade Doll's sprawling quarters and following."

"Where do they live?" asked the commoner girl, all eyes now, impossibly round and blinking.

"Who? The Emperor's sister? I told you, on the other side of the Palace's grounds, the prettier side. With huge gardens and ponds and animals in cages. I tried to sneak there once. They say the Emperor keeps caged jaguars there and whatnot. They say he goes to feed them personally sometimes. They say the previous emperor did it all the time, went to feed his animals every day, threw meat to the jaguars and petted them. But Axayacatl is too busy for that, people say. So he leaves it to his servants to make the predators happy. And you can't sneak into this part of the Palace's garden either. There are guards that tell you off if you try to just walk past them."

"Jaguars?" The girl's eyes turned yet rounder, and her unadorned sandals slowed to a near halt. "In the gardens?"

"Well, I didn't manage to see any. I told you. I only heard about it. And they are in cages, locked safely. Or so they say."

The higher wall of the ball court reflected nothing but unusual quietness as opposed to the steady hum reaching them from the opened space behind the round temple, an unmistakable noise of the gathering crowds.

"They won't be training, not on such a day," said Tlemilli, noticing a shadow of disappointment on her companion's face. "Maybe they are out there, sneaking the way we are."

The girl nodded again, her smile nice, even if forced. "Necalli said they may be taken out to the mainland. For something ceremonial, fasting and praying and all that. Out there near the City of Gods."

"Oh yes, the warriors' quest." Hastening her step before the litter and the maid had an opportunity to catch up with them and maybe try to detain her again, Tlemilli made a face. "I heard that he was taken along with some older boys. On the day before, when I heard, I thought he was making it up. Only boys who are about to finish school are going out, just before they become warriors. Or shield-bearers."

"Necalli has already served as a shield-bearer!" cried out her companion, clearly offended. "He has been in two battles already. He has captured a warrior! And weapons too. He has plenty of those stored in his father's house, all his, spears and such."

For some reason, the passion of those words jarred. "So what? Miztli has been to more battles! He even has an obsidian sword now, which they said he can keep as he did capture it lawfully, in a hand-to-hand with a veteran warrior. He is as good. No, he is better!" She flopped her arms in the air, offended as well now. "He is still in school because he is too young to go out there and fight again. And so is your Necalli! Only boys that have seen at least seventeen summers are allowed to leave school and go out there and fight. No fourteen-summers-old *pillis*!"

"Well, I know what he said and he has gone out there on this warriors' quest, and that's it!" The words came out muffled, seeping through the tightly pursed lips. "And he is a warrior already, little summers or not. And he is going to be a great warrior, a great leader! Here in Tenochtitlan, they do appreciate good, promising youths like him and they don't count his summers. Maybe in Tlatelolco, it was different, but in Tenochtitlan, they look at people and their deeds, and not only their ages."

That caught her completely unprepared and she gasped at the

unreasonableness of these claims and accusations, speechless for a moment. "You are talking stupid nonsense, plain stupid nonsense! How dare you? In Tlatelolco, they cared for everything and everyone, and our warriors were the best, and our *calmecac* youths were too!"

The Great Plaza opened before them, crowded to the brim, or so it seemed without the benefits of the elevated ground to assess the situation. A whole lake of onlookers, which never ceased to amaze her, the amount of people in this *altepetl*, their ever readiness to spill out in astonishingly huge numbers.

Still seething over the jab about her native Tlatelolco, now nothing a tributary, reduced to shameful poverty and whatnot – Citlalli related every rumor she heard, even though they could not go out and look for themselves – Tlemilli watched the densely packed backs sullenly, wishing to be anywhere but here. Why did she insist on coming here at all? She didn't need to see yet another dramatic undertaking this *altepetl*'s showy ruler was touring. Who cared for carved stones of enormous proportions? No one but the silly people of this silly side of the island. A glance at her companion let her know that the commoner girl entertained somewhat similar thoughts, even if not connected to her pretentious town probably.

"They are crowding like commoners in the marketplace. Disgusting! We can see nothing in this way."

The glare she received could rival the gloom of the rainy sky. "There are always staircases." Tossing her head high, her companion turned toward the second lower pyramid, picking her step in a telling manner.

Stifling a curse, Tlemilli hesitated, then followed. What else was there to do? And maybe they wouldn't be able to see well from the stairs of that pyramid either; or more likely, maybe they would be thrown from the hallowed staircase by the enraged priests of whatever temple it was hosting. A likelier possibility. Didn't the future would-be priestess know that the pyramid's stairs were no podiums to climb?

However, no one prevented their unobtrusive ascension up only the few first slabs of stone, ten at the most, crowded as those were anyway. No marketplace commoners, yes, but not the noblest audience either. Well-to-do citizens from across the nearest canal, mostly men, dotted with *calmecac* boys aplenty – uninvited observers. The bidden part of the audience congregated near the strangely round pyramid that she could never get used to – who built round pyramids, ever? – with an obvious Quetzalcoatl's temple towering on its top, unattended as well now with the lively activity concentrating below its stairs and to its left, where the shadow of the Great Pyramid was already reaching. There the cloaks of the participating nobles and the litters of the watching ladies created a colorful melee, very pleasant to the eye. Even Tlemilli had to admit that, still brooding over the jab at her beloved Tlatelolco and unwilling to admit anything positive Tenochtitlan-related, not right away.

The Emperor was easy to pick out, his headdress huge, a celebration of coloring, the rest of his outfit glittering, hurting the eye. Unlike Moquihuixtli, the Tenochtitlan Emperor did not use podiums to address the crowds. So much she had learned about this particular ruler through the moon and a half spent here. This one tended to mix among his noble following, not afraid to be overlooked or not listened to. Even Citlalli had to admit that quite grudgingly. Moquihuixtli was not forceful enough, or confident in his words and abilities. He had to work himself up before every public appearance, to prepare his speech and have his closest advisers approve of his words before he used them. She said that he even sought approval and encouragement from her, his wife, and not even the chief one back in the days of Jade Doll's reign.

Did she miss him, a husband of quite a few moons? Tlemilli had pressed once. But in that she got nowhere. Citlalli refused to discuss anything Tlatelolco-related, not even with her. In fact, her sister had sunk into a strange apathy, huddling in their quarters, doing nothing but weaving, going out only when forced to attend this or that royal event, when the servants from the main wing of the Palace came to deliver this or that summons, quite a few lately. Which also worried Citlalli, to an extent, but why, Tlemilli never surmised. Wasn't it good to go out, in style or otherwise? However, Citlalli didn't seem to think so.

"Oh gods, but it is so huge and so beautiful!" exclaimed her companion, shielding her eyes against the glow of the afternoon sun, standing on her tiptoes in order to see better, oblivious of the surrounding people, or so it seemed. Quite a few familiar faces caught Tlemilli's eye, mostly boys she had glimpsed on the training grounds or outside the school fence, when sneaking away to meet Miztli.

Her stomach tightening, she scanned the rest of the stairs with her gaze, encountering nothing but covert glances. He wasn't anywhere around this part of the crowd; neither he nor his friend. Not that it seemed to bother her companion, who was immersed in the view everyone else was devouring, the massive construction near the round temple indeed impressive, so huge, its carvings exquisitely detailed. Even from a distance, it was easy to see how decorated the reliefs in the stone were, how beautifully carved.

"It's Revered Tonatiuh, but not only," the commoner girl was muttering, as though talking to herself. "He is represented by Tlaltecuhtli as well, to remind us of his night journey. So beautiful! And the four previous worlds. Can you see it? So detailed!"

"Yes, it's pretty," admitted Tlemilli reluctantly, her eyes on the glitters of light coming from the Emperor's arms, all those metal bracelets. Miztli had worked with those things once, he had told her, copper and other shining things. He said it was beautiful when melted, beautiful and dangerous, not to near or touch. Again, she searched the nearby steps and pyramids, then the heads that crowded the ground beneath those.

"The Emperor is going to speak. I wish we could hear him here."

"He should be talking from something elevated." Shrugging, Tlemilli abandoned her visual search, concentrating on the orating ruler. He was spreading his hands wide, ascending barely visible steps near the half-finished construction. The Plaza fell silent at once but for some boys down the staircase they occupied. Those were still whispering, snickering loudly, full of mischief.

"We could have squeezed nearer if we came with the servants

and litter-bearers," she whispered, seeing her companion's painful grimace as the girl was trying to catch the Emperor's words with little success. Only the hum of the mighty ruler's voice was reaching them here, this and the giggling of the boys down their stairs. She caught the gaze of one of them upon her, the massive bulk both Miztli and Necalli couldn't stand for whatever reason. For a good measure, she made a face at him, then stuck her tongue out. If they hated him, then so did she. He rolled his eyes and made even a nastier grimace in response.

"I hope the boys are somewhere there and listening," Chantli was whispering again, in obvious desperation. "I want to know what he says."

"Maybe my sister is there among the ladies with litters. We can ask her. She is sure to listen. Even if out of boredom." Then the girl's words sank. "You think they are there?"

A frantic search through the lake of heads didn't help. Those were packed so densely. She tried to penetrate the colorful mass with the sheer power of her will.

"We should have squeezed into that litter she sent!"

The pair of widely open eyes were upon her. "You think they would allow it?"

"Who? The maids? It's not their litter to allow anything." Shrugging, she glanced at the crowded Plaza again, grudgingly. "They might have let us through, if we came there in the litter. They always let litters through." She remembered the warriors with spears, all those Palace's guards, clearing the way for their palanquins. "We can try to make them take us now, but where are they?"

"Somewhere down there." The girl looked at her again, curiously unsure of herself. "Would they let me in too?"

"Of course. Why not?"

"Because she is a commoner and you are the weirdest thing that was ever foisted on this city." The sneering voice broke upon them from slightly below and to their left, accompanied by a spell of heartily roaring laughter. Even before locating the source of it, she knew it belonged to the bulky slab who was staring at her before and who apparently forced his way up in the meanwhile.

"So what are you doing, two pretty fowls, so alone and unaccompanied? There are no cocoa beans to earn here. You should go to the marketplace when the sun sets."

"What?" Incensed by his tone and the sneering expression, let alone by his following, a few other boys, snickering and happy, Tlemilli stared for a heartbeat, not understanding his words but knowing that what he said held nothing complimentary. Also he said she was weird and foisted on his stinking *altepetl* and the other girl was a commoner, yes, but there was no need to throw it into her face like a bucket of excrement after one used it to relieve oneself. "Shut up and go away! We weren't talking to you. It was a private conversation."

Like back in Tlatelolco, local *calmecac* boys and girls were not allowed to mix, of course; still, after close to a whole span of seasons in school, she had seen enough confrontation between pushy boys and weirdly excited giggling girls. In this, the Tenochtitlan *calmecac* was no different as well.

"A private conversation shouted at the top of her voice," the massive bulk of muscle sneered, addressing his words to his followers this time, receiving a renewed bout of chortling. "The weirdest fowl, like I said."

She could feel Chantli tossing her head high, even though it was easy to see her tension, the rigidness of her pose. "Leave us alone."

"Yes, and if you want to see something really weird, go and look at your *nantli*'s obsidian mirror." Tlemilli tossed her head high in her turn. "Also eat something sweet before. It'll help you to cope with what you'll see."

A veteran of many such altercations, she didn't need to spend time groping for insults of that sort. Matlatl's company was a good practice, having an unlimited arsenal of the most poisonous slander to shoot at her and their other half-sisters. Briefly, she wondered what happened to the Lady Perfect. Citlalli said that she tried to save both her and her full little sister back on the burning Plaza, but later on, in Tenochtitlan, they were separated because the scar-faced warrior tried to keep an eye on her, as he had promised, and since then, she didn't know what happened to any of their half-sisters. They certainly were not in the Palace or *calmecac*. But then, where were they?

"Shut up, you stupid Tlatelolcan spoil and a commoners' whore." The angry words brought her back from her reverie to see the bulky boy thrusting his face close to hers, standing a whole stair lower but still almost of the same height. "You should have been sold on the slave market, not pushed into our *calmecac*."

She felt her heart jumping high, like it always did in such cases, her rage splashing in force, faster than the reaction of her mind, the wish to smash her offender, verbally or physically, overwhelming, interfering with her ability to find the correctly squashing words.

"You shut up. They wouldn't even take you, the ugly heap of fat, to the slave markets, let alone manage to sell you there!" Another of Matlatl's statements, concerning possibilities of marriage usually, but it fit the slave markets as well, if the yet angrier expression of the face in front of her or the covert chuckling of the others were to judge by.

"You stinking whore!" he hissed, shoving his face so close she had to move hers backwards unless wishing to smell his last meal or have the remnants of it breathed into her face. It frightened her for a moment, made her wish Miztli were here.

"Leave her alone, Acoatl!" That was the commoner girl, pushing herself between them hastily but speaking calmly, in a surprisingly authoritative voice. "The Honorable Priestess won't be happy to hear you calling noble girls by such epithets." A heartbeat of a mutual glaring had them freezing in this strange pose, all three of them. "Just leave!"

It was easy to hear the gritting of his teeth. "No stinking commoner will tell me what to do," he breathed, then moved away abruptly. "You are not worth spending time on even cursing you."

"Neither are you!" cried out Tlemilli, but the other girl's hand locked around her wrist, pressing it urgently, relaying a message. Still, she couldn't help it. "You are a stink, the worst stink ever!"

He didn't turn back. "Cheap whores, both of you. Go earn half a cocoa bean behind the warehouses of the marketplace. Or do it for free for stinking commoners of this school."

Not understanding too well all this cocoa-beans-earning business on the marketplace corners, she opened her mouth to scream something as nasty-sounding, but the fingers around her wrist pressed again, more urgently this time, hurting.

"Don't goad him, just don't." The words brushed past her ear, whispered hurriedly, relaying much tension. "Let him go." The gentle palm was tightening again, slippery with sweat, making Tlemilli wish to wrench her arm free. "He is dangerous. You shouldn't have… Oh, but you really shouldn't!"

"He was unbearable. So nasty, and insolent, and… and annoying!"

"Yes, yes, but…" The girl brought one of her arms up, pressing it against her own face this time, wiping the glistening beads off her brow. "He is dangerous and he has been quiet after… after…" Frowning painfully, she swallowed, then straightened her gaze. "He has been nasty to the village bo — to Miztli. There was trouble. They ambushed him and, well, it was bad…"

Tlemilli caught her breath. "What happened? When? How?"

"It was before, before you, before Tlatelolco." The white teeth came out, biting the full lower lip. Like Citlalli, this girl was a beautiful sight to look at. There was no way around admitting that. "He beat them bad, and there was this man… Axolin told me all about it. Necalli and Miztli, they wouldn't talk about it, but Axolin told me once. Not long ago." Again, a painful pause. "Miztli beat them hard enough, but Acoatl pulled a knife and it might have ended badly but for that man, the one Necalli served as a shield-bearer in Tlatelolco."

"The scar-faced man?"

"Oh well, yes." This time, her companion's eyes cleared, sparkling excitedly. "That man. Necalli says he is coming here again, with another Texcoco delegation. He hopes to become his official shield-bearer."

"He is too young for that," said Tlemilli absently, her heart still racing, trying to cope with the new splash of acute anger. Did this nasty piece of rotten tortilla manage to hurt Miztli somehow? Oh, but if he did… She felt her fingernails cutting into her palms, the pain nothing, not even a distraction. Oh, but the filthy pile of night refuse would pay. She would make him pay, somehow!

"He already served as a shield-bearer," the girl was saying, as always losing her reasonable way of talking, or rather thinking, when it came to this particular subject. "He should be allowed to join the next war as well."

"What happened with Miztli and that nasty piece of excrement in the end?"

"Well, Miztli beat him hard enough to make this one leave him alone. And that warrior, the Texcocan man, he scared them all too, or so Axolin says. But now," her shoulders lifted helplessly, with little spirit, "now I don't know. He may be plotting something, seeing possibilities, you see? To get to them through us, you or me, or both of us. And we must think what to do, must find a solution, somehow. Without involving the boys, you see?"

"Why?"

"Because, you know, they'll get violent, rush to confront him, get in trouble."

"They can take this pile of excrement easily. Miztli already beat him before, you said. He can make pounded dough out of him, a ground tortilla, a smashed tamale. Anything!"

But the girl exhaled loudly, rolling her eyes in an annoyingly superior manner. "Even if he can do it, it'll land him in trouble. Your Miztli is not a noble with family and powerful relatives to smooth things over for him. He must watch his step, break no rules. And violent rows in school are the surest way to break every rule possible. You don't want him thrown from *calmecac* and back into the workshop or worse, do you?"

For a heartbeat, they glared at each other, then the rising hum of voices drew their attention back to the crowded Plaza. Next to the grandiose undertaking, the crowds were moving, following the Emperor, who had come down his improvised stage, walking among the people again, listening or nodding, preceding his guarding warriors, not needing them in the least.

The sun shone moderately mild now, allowing a better look. In its weakening rays, Tlemilli could see clustering litters, their prettily clad owners sitting proudly, or strolling by, talking to each other. Narrowing, her eyes picked out the cushioned chair belonging to Citlalli, easy to recognize because of its colorful cover, a wittily embroidered cloth her sister had woven with much attention through this last moon of self-confinement. Alone and a little apart, Citlalli did look uncomfortable, watching the Emperor and his entourage, clearly wishing to be anywhere but there. Tlemilli's heart twisted.

"Come, let us reach my sister. We'll be able to stay around and see everything from closer up. No one will try to shoo us away if we are with her."

Her companion hesitated. "Maybe we should try to find your litter and the maids first." However, when Tlemilli grabbed her arm, the girl did not resist, following her down the stairs and into the melee of people and voices.

The nasty foul-mouthed boy and his friends were still lingering on the lower stairs, watching the Plaza. Without the need to coordinate their actions, they both tossed their heads high while skirting around this group. Pleased, Tlemilli stared the grimness of his stare down. Then her attention was caught by the need to navigate their way, and this time, she was grateful for her companion's briskness and skill. But this girl knew her way around crowded places!

"Where did you see your sister? With other ladies in litters?"

Tlemilli just nodded, out of breath and uncomfortable. All those towering backs and shoulders, pressing and pushing, threatening to squash or hurt her were unbearable without his arms around her and his body sheltering, protecting. But where was he? Nearer the round pyramid, many warriors, mostly spearmen from Palace's guard, were milling about, eyeing the crowds with suspicion. Her companion's simple maguey outfit drew quite a few glances, mainly of the beautifully clad palanquins' riders. Tlemilli planted herself closer, then wrapped her hand around the delicate arm.

"We'll find my sister and then—"

"Move away, girls!" One of the spearmen motioned them aside as a group of immaculately dressed individuals proceeded along, surrounding a man in a magnificent headdress, his face strangely unpleasant to the eye even though his features were not disagreeable or repulsive. Only the cold aloofness of his expression was. Tlemilli hesitated, her curiosity welling. There was something familiar about this man. Had she seen him before, somewhere in this Palace or maybe back in Tlatelolco?

A sharp pull on her elbow startled her into nearly jumping. "Don't you dare staring at the Adviser!" a voice rasped, another jolt making her sway, fighting for her balance. Disoriented for a moment, she gasped, then fought to break free out of instinct rather than a thoughtful reaction. The warrior's palm was like a slab of stone, his fingers rock-hard, locked around her arm, uncompromising.

"Let me go!" she shrilled, shocked into panic, oblivious of anything but the need to break free. "Take your hands off me. How dare you!"

Her fists pounded at the man's broad chest even though her mind registered it quite numbly, mainly the futility of it. The warrior didn't even struggle or try to avoid her blows. Nor did the commoner girl's voice overcome the general hum of the others, not this time, her words flowing in a panicky gush, with no authority she displayed with the boys on the smaller pyramid.

In a renewed splash of panic, she kicked. "Let me go!"

"Let her go."

This voice was calm and arrogantly chilly, not reassuring, even though the words it used were. The grip on her hands, both of them by now, loosened at once. She spent a heartbeat on leaping aside, putting a safe distance between herself and her assailant, before trying to understand the situation.

"Who are you, girl?"

The man with the headdress was peering at her with his eyes narrowed dubiously, like a person appraising a bothersome insect, not sure what to do with it – to step on it or to skirt around? It angered her, this dismissive gaze, and the way his lips twisted downwards when his eyes shifted to her companion, who in the meanwhile pressed her arms around Tlemilli's shoulders, supporting.

"No commoners are allowed—" began one of the man's

followers, eyeing the other girl angrily.

"We are no commoners!" She heard her own voice ringing firmly, with enough conviction and strength, and it pleased her despite her heart that was still thundering too loudly, interfering with her ability to concentrate. "We have every right to be here!"

"Who are you, girl?" repeated the headdress owner, impressed into a closer scrutiny, his gaze not thawing but showing a flicker of interest.

"I'm..." She stopped herself before blurting the "head adviser's daughter" bit, forgetting her changed circumstances for a moment. "I..."

Their interrogator's eyes narrowed into mere slits by now. "She looks familiar. Find out who she is." This was tossed toward one of the richly dressed followers, a square man with too many glittering decorations adorning his cloak. "Keep an eye on them until then."

"Tlemilli is a guest in the Palace, invited by the Emperor himself, Honorable Leader." The commoner girl's voice rang with more firmness now, with an appropriate deference. "She is not intruding and her sister is here among noble ladies. We were heading to pay our respects to her."

The man's forehead furrowed with displeasure, then cleared all at once. "Oh, Teconal's daughters!" The corner of his mouth twitched in what might have been a hint of amusement, even though it was difficult to tell, the man's expression like that of a stone statue, foreboding and ice-cold. A heartbeat of hesitation, then the feathers of the imposing headdress rustled ever so slightly. "Let us escort you back to your exquisite sister, girl." Another nod indicated his followers. "It is our duty to be accommodating hosts."

Tlemilli held her head high, but her stomach was churning, turning uneasily, heaving with incomprehensible warning. There was something about this man's expression, something she didn't like. It was as though he had welcomed this opportunity to escort her to her sister, as though he had seen the potential and just pounced on it. But what was this potential? And how was it all connected to Citlalli?

CHAPTER 3

The nobleman who led them now was easy to recognize because of his wideness and a certain heaviness of his bearing. Not a fat man, the Emperor's elder brother was nevertheless glaringly thickset, lacking the gracefulness of movement the rest of his siblings seemed to possess in abundance, the Emperor himself and, most of all, that young rascal Ahuitzotl.

Chantli hid her grin, which always threatened to sneak out when thinking of the little beast. Only this morning she had seen him outside the school opening, perching on the crumbling stones of the wall in his favorite pose of an eagle from Tenochtitlan's city glyph. He was the one to tell her that Necalli was on the mainland now, hastened there well before dawn, a part of the older group of youths that were to journey to Teotihuacan, the City of Gods, and do a ceremonial fasting. Something very important and thrilling; still, it served to dampen her mood for the entire morning, the awareness that he wasn't around and available even for a fleeting peek.

The Emperor's brother was walking ahead, his pace as heavy as his bearing suggested, neither forceful nor springy, yet plodding on, relaying solidness. She remembered seeing him on the night of the ceremonies, before sneaking away with Necalli. Back then, the man looked exactly the same, solid and somehow reassuring; still, the memory of that night served to ruin her mood once again. Why didn't Necalli tell her about that trip to the mainland being scheduled for today? Was it a last-moment arrangement that he didn't know about himself? Two evenings before, they had spent an entire afternoon together, wandering out there on the marketplace and in the better neighborhoods, huddling in snug corners to kiss every now and then. It was such a great day, not ruined even by Quetzalli and her silly banter when they had met her friend back near the workshop, where they had slunk in the end, unwilling to be detected by her father or brothers but welcoming the privacy the nearby warehouses provided. He didn't want her to walk alone after dark, and she didn't want to send him back without a few more of those breathtaking kisses that didn't lose their initial thrill but actually only gained more of it. It was a wonder they both kept wishing to explore but for the usual lack of privacy. Still, even with Quetzalli running into them – not in the most embarrassing of moments, at least that! – this day remained to be most perfect. Yet, now he was on the mainland, and she had to hear about it in a completely roundabout way. A bother!

The crowds kept parting before their escorting spearmen and she forced her mind to concentrate, watching the well-dressed people and their attendants, plentiful in this part of the gathering. Open palanquins, cushioned chairs like the one they escaped near the school opening, or wider constructions dotted the open space that was now enjoying the shade of the Great Pyramid to the fullest, hosting beautifully clad occupants, the comfortably sitting ladies of various ages and girth.

She moved closer to the Tlatelolcan girl, feeling out of place. The previous incident of them taken to be commoners had all to do with her clothing and looks, she knew, not that of her companion. The Tlatelolcan might have been wild and unpredictable, behaving like no girl would have, whether high or low born or anything in between, and no boy, for that matter; still, there could be no mistaking this one's belonging, with her impeccable cotton *huipil* and the colorfulness of her skirt, her sandals closed around her ankles to enhance the walk of a person who had stepped among palaces rather than marketplaces and wharves. There was no way around admitting that. But why was the all-important Emperor's brother escorting them now and why in person?

As though echoing her thoughts, the Tlatelolcan leaned closer.

"Why is he taking us to my sister in person, such an obviously important heap of fat?" The sharp-angled face crinkled with an obvious thought-process. "I saw him in the Palace, I remember that. But I have no idea who he is."

Frightened, Chantli glanced around, her heart beating fast. "He is the Emperor's brother," she breathed. "One of the important advisers and all that. And you should not, you know, call him names." The last words came out so quietly, she wasn't sure she didn't just think them.

One of her companion's pointed eyebrows flew high, arching at an impossibly straight angle. "He was not the nicest to us as well."

And? thought Chantli, fighting the urge to roll her eyes. Even though she came to, actually, like this girl a great deal despite their first misadventures back in Tlatelolco. It was still hard to understand why at times she would behave like a ten-summers-old child or worse. Like young Ahuitzotl, come to think of it. Another dweller of the Palace. Were they brought up differently in those royal enclosures, to think unlike the rest of the world? Necalli was not a commoner, not even close, and yet it was easy to understand him. He thought and behaved in a reasonable manner. While this Tlatelolcan wonder…

"My sister wouldn't come here now but for them forcing her," related the girl in the meantime, chatting away unconcernedly, in the way Chantli had seen her talking to the village boy on several occasions she had managed to glimpse them both, usually after Necalli or Ahuitzotl had made those meetings possible, as before this Tlatelolcan treasure had joined their school, it was difficult to arrange such a rendezvous. Well, of course it was. The Palace's dwellers and their guests were not at liberty to go out and meet *calmecac* students of dubious, or even noble origins. Even though it must have become easier for this pair since the girl had joined *calmecac* herself.

Too busy with her own life and ambition, Chantli did not spend her time monitoring this pair, even though Quetzalli kept nagging with questions, hoping for juicy gossip, most obviously. Still, she had told her friend nothing, feeling obligated to protect

Miztli and his privacy. The village boy deserved that. And his Tlatelolcan girl was not that bad, just wild and as bizarre as in the beginning, yet apparently a good person, reasonable at times. Fiercely loyal too, not ready to hear any slander against her chosen love interest, his more than humble origins or not. That violent assault on Tlazotli's snobbish sharp-tongued friend was a terrible thing worthy of boys and their physical aggression, or rather marketplace fowls tearing each other's hair out; out of place in the noble establishment, with the highest nobility girls and their pretty *huipil*s and sandals. Still, Miztli's Tlatelolcan did not bear any nastiness well, reacting with less self-restraint than the wildest of marketplace women would display. It was a wonder she wasn't kicked out of school right away. They said some high Palace's nobility interfered on her behalf. Necalli said it was Lady Jade Doll again. He said Ahuitzotl claimed that, and the Palace's rascal would know.

"Why would they force your sister to attend?" she asked now, forcing her thoughts to the present and the festive crowd they were walking in now, so much glitter and wealth. "Wouldn't she wish to watch ceremonies and celebrations?"

Her Tlatelolcan companion shrugged. "She doesn't want to go out, not if she can help it."

"Why?"

Another lift of the thin shoulders followed. "She doesn't want to mix with them. I think she is afraid, not sure of herself here yet or something."

"And you?" A richly decorated row of palanquins was placed on a sort of an improvised podium, their occupants chatting with each other, fanning themselves or letting their maids do that, partaking in refreshments served by ever-attentive servants. "You feel at home here?"

"Me?" The girl made a face, glancing at the colorful exhibition briefly, with pronounced contempt. "I don't care. I didn't leave the luxury belonging to the main wing of the Tlatelolco Palace behind. My father's women's quarters are not a place one would miss. You wouldn't like it there either."

"Why?" Her curiosity welled. "You were very much pro-

Tlatelolco back when they competed and shot birds out there on the shore."

"Of course I was!" This time, the sharply outlined face clouded with a flash of anger, then cleared all at once. "It has nothing to do with Tlatelolco. My father had plenty of daughters, nasty fowls each and every one of them. Except for my sister, that is. And now they are all gone. Think about it." A beam. "Now it's only me and Citlalli. Could I have asked for a better life than this?"

Against her will, Chantli grinned, feeling so much more mature and sophisticated. "If not for Necalli and Miztli..."

"Yes, oh yes," agreed her companion enthusiastically. "Miztli saved me and my sister. He is the greatest!" Then the conspiratorial wink replaced the animated excitement. "But he didn't feel obliged to save any of my half-sisters, so..."

"Necalli said that he ran into one of those back in Tlatelolco. He said your sister was busy sheltering a few other girls—"

"Yes, Matlatl!" This time, the beam was dislodged by a tellingly wrinkled nose. "He was guarding her and that littler snake of her full sister, all noisy mess of tears and whatnot. Smeared with plenty of snot, I bet!" The girl snorted disgustedly. "He should have let them be killed or dragged away. He is a good boy, very brave too. He would have spent his time better capturing another warrior or something."

The ridiculousness of those declarations did not dim the glow that was spreading inside her at the mere thought of his bravery. He was incredible, wasn't he, serving as a shield-bearer at the age of fourteen, capturing his first warrior.

"Citlalli!" Her companion's exclamation jerked Chantli from her reverie, feeling her arm being pulled forcefully, still clutched between the delicate fingers. For someone violent and ready to use her fists, Miztli's girl had a surprisingly pleasant touch. "We've been looking for you all over."

The small but beautifully decorated litter stood out among its plainer-looking neighboring carriages, hosting an intricately well-dressed, striking-looking woman who straightened up, then pressed back into her cushions as abruptly, her eyes leaping to their spectacular escort, turning haunted. Curiously relieved,

Chantli glanced at the others, well-to-do ladies of the kind one didn't feel the urge to dart away from their path. To move away politely, yes, but not to flee outright. The memory of her first venture into this same Great Plaza on the day the village boy went missing was still fresh, the feel of being pushed away and into the mud, treated like marketplace rat, even called thus. So much had changed since, and yet... Involuntarily, she glanced around, hoping that the Emperor's mother was nowhere in sight.

"Greetings, Honorable Lady," the Emperor's brother was saying, his voice surprisingly pleasant to the ear, nicely polite, with no fake tones to it, or so it seemed. "It is a pleasure to meet such a beautiful lady on such a glorious day."

"The honor is all mine." The Tlatelolcan beauty straightened gracefully upon her cushioned seat, her nod impeccably cordial, smile matching. She was an alluring woman indeed, her face exquisitely defined, adorned with prominent yet softly outlined features, everything in place as though painted by an artist, generous with his colors and chiseling tools. There was an actual similarity between the two sisters, even though Necalli told her that there was none. It was just that the younger girl lacked the softness her sister possessed in abundance, as though this same artist was in a hurry, carving her out with the same defined strokes, but with no time to soften those afterwards. The image of such a working craftsman made Chantli wish to giggle. Quetzalli's father was a stone worker, and what if the statues he was made to create occasionally came to life and started to walk around, the finished and the unfinished ones?

"Why did your litter-bearers bring your palanquin to such inappropriate surroundings? One can barely see the Great Pyramid from this dismal place." The heavy-set man stood quite easily, his imposing headdress that clearly forced a straighter than usual posture not seeming to inhibit his bearing. "This is not an appropriate accommodation for a lady such as yourself."

"Oh, no, Honorable Leader," protested the noblewoman after the slightest hesitation. "This place and surroundings are appropriate. I have no complaints."

"Come. Let me escort you." His eyes didn't thaw, but there was a hint of something friendly curving his lips. "You deserve a better view, the one our royal ladies are enjoying."

"Oh, oh, I am grateful, but..." The woman collected herself hastily, with a visible effort. "It is a rare pleasure. You do me too much honor, Revered Tizoctzin. I..." Her eyes darted toward them, as though seeking help. "My sister, I can't leave her here. I must..." Another effort of collecting herself reflected in the pursing lips. "Where is your litter, Tlemilli? Why are you walking like a commoner?"

As opposed to her elegant sibling's anxiety, Chantli's companion shrugged with perfect indifference. "Somewhere out there. They lost us." Her wide lips twisted in a snicker. "It wasn't easy to keep up with us and those boys—"

"Just follow us on foot, girl," interrupted the royal man with markedly less courtesy than before. His gaze brushed past the woman's litter-bearers. "Follow." His own followers were motioned as curtly.

Chantli tore her eyes off the woman, who hunched on her cushioned seat, her frown light, dominated quickly. "Come along, Tlemilli, and don't fall behind. I'll send one of the servants to locate your litter."

"We won't." The Tlatelolcan girl's grip on her wrist tightened again, not about to let go. "We'll be quiet and well behaved."

"Who is this?" The noblewoman's forehead creased again.

"Chantli is in our *calmecac*. She is the best student, the future priestess of that school."

Forcing a smile, Chantli glanced around, aware of her lack of belonging, preferring to sneak away. The eyes that studied her generated no warmth. Just a mild interest, exaggeratedly polite.

"I'm not. I just hope to become a priestess when my time comes."

"She knows everything there is to know about temples and such," went on her companion proudly, unaware of the currents. "All the girls want to be paired with her when we are sent to the temples."

"It's not like that." She wanted to bury herself under the beautiful cobblestones, aware of her burning cheeks and the possibility of the important man listening to their conversation.

"Oh." The young noblewoman nodded politely, her gaze sneaking toward their entourage, echoing Chantli's misgivings.

"The pupils of our *calmecac* should not be allowed to run around the Great Plaza as freely, certainly not when the Emperor is touring it," said the headdress owner, confirming their suspicion. "Do not get caught doing it again." The impassiveness of his gaze did not reflect on the sternness of his words. "You are in Tenochtitlan now, young lady, and may become part of the royal family. You should behave with proper decorum and follow your noble sister's example." The eyes shifted back to the beauty in the litter, who seemed to grow more and more uncomfortable with every passing heartbeat. "Your younger sister is a complete opposite to you, Lady, and it is time you paid more attention to the girl's proper upbringing. Back in Tlatelolco, they clearly did not invest in discipline and educational matters."

However, this made the Tlatelolcan beauty straighten up resolutely. "Tlemilli is an impeccably noble girl. She did nothing to deserve reproach, even under the difficult circumstances of her changed life."

Chantli held her breath, watching the broad face of the mighty adviser clouding even if imperceptibly. It was difficult to detect the man's expressions. Still, something changed in the general atmosphere and she felt her own nerves stretching, the urge to run away growing by leaps and bounds.

"We did not sneak away from school," she heard this same discussed Tlemilli declaring, surprisingly quiet and composed, on her best behavior, apparently. "The priestess sent us to that temple upon the round pyramid, and then our litter got lost."

"The Honorable Priestess!" corrected the man icily.

She sensed the girl bridling and her own words began pouring out without restraint. "This is the truth, Revered Adviser. The Honorable Priestess, she might have wished us to help in the glorious Quetzalcoatl temple. It was our duty to attend the temple and see if our assistance was needed. I hope we did nothing wrong."

The contemplative eyes rested on her. "Who are you, girl?"

"I'm... I was honored to be admitted in the noble establishment in order to learn our gods' ways, in order to be of use... of use to our glorious *altepetl* and the royal family."

That came out in a rush, not a satisfactory speech; however, the eyes resting on her changed again, became less dismissive.

"You are the commoner girl my brother put in our *calmecac* before Tlatelolco fell." Not phrased as a question, these words nevertheless held enough interest not to have her stammering all over again. "Have you been connected to the youths our young Ahuitzotl has been using in his attempts to gain attention?"

"Yes, Honorable Leader. Noble Ahuitzotl did honor me with his trust." This came out well enough. She allowed herself to draw in a quick breath.

"Curious." Another thoughtful scrutiny and the man put his attention back to the exquisite occupier of the litter, whose bearers were forced to hasten their steps in order to keep up. "Your sister's proper education will be attended to, Honorable Lady. We can't have a girl of her lineage and connections running loose, disgracing herself."

By that time, they had already reached the tented area where the procedures were calmer and much more dignified, and the glitter of jewelry hurt the eye. Overwhelmed and intimidated not a little, Chantli tried not to gape, grateful for the other girl's continued grip on her arm now, needing it. The litters that dotted the tented space hosted ladies that normally she would be expected to dart out of their way if they happened to cross her path. And yet, now their bearers were the ones to clear the way for the powerful adviser that led their procession.

"He can busy himself with his own education," her companion muttered, keeping her voice satisfactorily low this time. "I'm not running loose. I'm learning in *calmecac* and doing what noble girls should."

Not exactly, thought Chantli, but kept this thought to herself, catching a glimpse of another important-looking group whose path was clearing off as miraculously. By the grandiose construction that, indeed, was easier to observe from such proximity and the slightly elevated ground the tented area was situated upon, she could see the Emperor in his spectacular attire crowned with a headpiece that rivaled this of his brother-adviser in its tallness and massiveness, so many colorful feathers and gems. The other procession was heading their way, a few decorated warriors surrounding a stately slender man in his mid-twenties, walking with marked elegance, sporting less jewelry but inarguably as richly clad.

"Who is this?" breathed Chantli in her companion's ear, as much out of real curiosity as in an attempt to divert the girl's possible outburst of anger. The Adviser was certainly not the man to pick one's arguments with.

As expected, the Tlatelolcan shrugged with one skinny shoulder, still pouting. Suppressing a snort, Chantli concentrated on the passing by dignitaries, whose step slowed considerably, already turning to greet their group and its leader. The tallness and arrogant bearing of one of the decorated warriors caught her eye, bringing the recollection before the actual memory surfaced. Where did she see this man before? As though ready to help, the warrior turned his head, presenting her with the view of the proud profile and the scar that started under the high chiseled cheekbone, to slide all the way down while splitting in an intricate manner, glaring, impossible to miss. The man from the Flayed God's temple, before the Tlatelolco invasion! Oh yes, there was no mistaking this face and this bearing. Chantli took her eyes away hurriedly.

"Texcocans, I knew it!" Her companion was watching the well-dressed dignitary in the warriors' midst, frowning ever so slightly. They must have seen visiting rulers aplenty, those Palace dwellers, even the ones who lived on the wrong side of it, like the Tlatelolcan girl claimed. Did they really have jaguars in cages?

"Are they from Texcoco?" whispered Chantli, leaning closer in order to camouflage her words.

"Oh yes." Her companion nodded vigorously, not yelling her answer at the top of her voice, thanks all the deities for such small mercies. "They have it all over their cloaks. Their Acolhua symbols, that is."

"Oh." Against her will, Chantli glanced at the scar-faced

warrior again, rewarded with the sight of his prominent profile as his eyes seemed to brush past their own entourage, narrowed with customary attention – a warrior seeking signs of possible trouble. Was he afraid his dignitary would get attacked by the ladies in their litters? The thought made her wish to chuckle. "That man with the scar, over there." Moving her eyes alone, she indicated the spectacular warrior as discreetly as she could, hoping her companion would keep it her quietest. "I saw him in Tenochtitlan once, making a sacrifice in the Flayed God's temple."

"Which one?" The unconcerned question made Chantli quail inside. Oh, but why didn't this wild thing keep her voice down? "Oh, that one? Is he Texcocan? I didn't know." Then her voice dropped all of a sudden. "Oh no!"

"What?" demanded Chantli, unsettled, following her companion's gaze that darted toward the litter and the beautiful woman in it. This one still sat remarkably straight, with exceeding dignity and grace, her feathered fan the only indication of her possible uneasiness, not moving at all, clutched tightly in the grip of the long gentle fingers. Her eyes were fixed on the scar-faced man, wide open and strangely alarmed.

"That man, my sister hates him!" The words poured into her ear, gushing and warm, but thankfully quiet. "I didn't know he was from Texcoco; he fought with Tenochtitlan invaders. He is something else, isn't he? He helped Miztli on that night. He was with him all the time and helped him along. So I don't hate him. But my sister does. Oh, very much so!"

"What? What do you mean?" It was difficult to keep up with this flood of unexpected information in the crowdedness and flowing conversations, the customary greetings the two prominent men of two ruling cities were exchanging loud and flowery, the rest of their surroundings watching and listening. The warrior in question was, indeed, looking at the beauty in the palanquin with a somewhat surprised expression, his wariness on display as well.

"He is not a bad man. He helped Miztli." The Tlatelolcan girl kept talking, curiously excited. "And your Necalli too. He will be his veteran warrior when his time comes. His father wishes it so, and of course Necalli himself. I heard him saying it several times. Didn't he tell you?"

And then it dawned on her. Oh yes, the scar-faced Texcocan! The man Necalli served as a shield-bearer back in Tlatelolco, the man he was talking about more often than not, with outright admiration. Chantli caught her breath again, trying not to stare.

"I wish Miztli was here. And your Necalli too. How about we sneak away now? They won't even notice—"

"Why does your sister hate this man?" She watched the Texcocan's lips twisting in a hint of a grin, an inverted one. His head moved ever so slightly, with mocking politeness. The beauty in the palanquin stiffened and the wooden handle of her fan seemed to become in danger of snapping.

"Oh, Citlalli doesn't like him at all. She keeps talking about him. Well, from time to time. If you want to have her ranting for many heartbeats, mention his name."

"What is his name?"

"Tecuani, Miztli says. YaoTecuani."

Warrior Beast? Oh yes, that was a fitting name, and yes, she heard Necalli using it quite often. The full name. With no familiarity of just "Tecuani."

"Why does she hate him?"

The Acolhua dignitary, a surprisingly young man to look at, surrounded by the rest of the decorated warriors and leaders, was exchanging polite platitudes with the Emperor's brother, his voice measured, manner calm, his cultured Acolhua accent pronounced. The scar-faced warrior distributed a few quiet instructions, then sneaked a quick glance at the beauty in the palanquin again.

"He was the one to save your sister, wasn't he?" asked Chantli, recalling Necalli's tales.

The Tlatelolcan girl shrugged, herself watching the conversing dignitaries with certain curiosity. "He saved her yes, but he wasn't nice about it, or so I gather. And he killed our father. That's what she is fuming about the most."

Involuntarily, Chantli gasped, then remembered Necalli's stories. Oh yes, this man did engage in spectacular hand-to-hand, disposing of the Tlatelolcan adviser if he could not challenge their emperor himself. Necalli was full of amusing tales concerning his adored hero's frustrated remarks upon the burning Plaza of Tlatelolco. Yet to realize that this same defeated head adviser was actually father of these two young women made her pause. How did one go about reconciling with something like that?

"And you? Don't you hate him for that as well?"

The wide mouth twisted disdainfully. "No, I don't. My father was a bad man. I'm glad he is not alive to harm me or my sister. Or ItzMiztli." This time, the large eyes flashed darkly. "He was after him, you know? Miztli has a good reason to be afraid of my father. I'm glad he is not alive to threaten him anymore."

The dour frown suited the sharp angles of the girl's face, making it look strangely appealing. Finding nothing to say, Chantli just nodded, taken aback by the carelessly uttered declarations. So much devotion to the village boy! What was it about this one that they all, this Tlatelolcan nobility, unorthodox and wild as she was, or spunky Quetzalli and who knew who else, were losing their heads, behaving outright strangely at times and over a boy that was not that special, not witty or charming, or glamorous, but closemouthed, serious, painfully shy, maybe even boring. What did they all see in him? If this Tlatelolcan force of nature, or even flirtatious Quetzalli, were after Necalli, she would have been angered, oh yes, but at least it would have been easy to understand the allure. But the village boy? No, there was nothing special about this one, and yet her companion just admitted that she preferred her own father dead only because he might have threatened this same much-adored Miztli. A puzzle!

"It is an honor to meet you, Lady."

This time, it was the voice of the Acolhua dignitary that pulled her from her musings, a pleasant, deep, evidently well-trained voice. Stepping out of his warriors' protective circle, the guest stood easily, his smile light, addressing the woman in the palanquin, his head tilted in a perfect greeting, elegance itself. He was a pleasant-looking man, evidently the highest of nobility and comfortable in his status, not artificial or self-conscious. In this, he put even the Emperor's brother to shame. Guiltily, she glanced at their foreboding previous company, noting the frown, light and barely perceptible but there. The man's eyes were fixed on the Tlatelolcan noblewoman as well.

"The tale of your beauty and refinement went ahead of you, but one can see that the rumors did not do you true justice," went on the Acolhua, his smile that of a courtier, holding the right amount of flattery and politeness. The scar-faced warrior, she noticed, was watching the woman again, his gaze curiously intense, as though seeking something.

"It is an exceptional honor to meet the great Acolhua Emperor." The beauty in the palanquin smiled with matching perfection, looking less uncomfortable than before, almost at ease. Her smile seemed to make the afternoon brighter. Even Chantli enjoyed the sight of it.

"The honor is all mine, Honorable Lady." The alleged ruler of Texcoco – but was it truly the heir to the legendary old emperor of refined, aristocratic, cultured Acolhua *altepetl*, the capital of learning, wisdom, and arts? – smiled back, all politeness. Then his gaze returned to the less alluring sight of the Adviser, who just hovered there, neither moved nor displeased. "Shall we proceed, Noble Tizoctzin?"

The heavyset man just nodded, glancing at the woman as though pondering. "I have been escorting the lady to more appropriate surroundings than the ones she has been enjoying." His arm indicated the colorful cushions and other sorts of seating arrangements spread in the shade. "From there, we will be able to join my brother in his tour of the monument."

"Of course." The Acolhua ruler nodded thoughtfully, his previously displayed lightness gone. As he turned to go, his escorting forces regrouped with perfect coordination, moving like one man, following the scar-faced's curt gesturing. It was clear that this particular guard did not tolerate any less dedication than this.

Turning to follow, Chantli caught a glimpse of the woman in the palanquin glancing at the gesturing warrior, taking her eyes away hurriedly, pursing her lips as though challenging, looking ridiculously like her wild younger sibling for a moment.

Curious, Chantli glanced at her companion, but the Tlatelolcan girl did not watch any of it. Straight-backed and looking highly alert, like a small animal sniffing a food offering, she peered at the massive construction, shielding her eyes, her attention undivided.

"Where?" whispered Chantli, amused, certain that the village boy must be somewhere around, mingling in the crowds, even though surely not in their immediate highly aristocratic surroundings.

The Tlatelolcan did not bother to fake ignorance. "There!" The slender arm shot forward, indicating the side of the Sun Stone that was lit by the strongest of lights, its reliefs beautiful, standing out in their play of illumination and shadows.

The Emperor's figure was easy to observe from their new favorable vantage point, the colorfulness of his headdress rivaling the monument itself, the crowding leaders and advisers equally well attired. Surrounding their sovereign, most of them still kept far enough apart to allow a glimpse of another figure that stood out as well, this time for the opposite reasons, the familiar sight of the overly broad shoulders clad in the school cloak, not entirely fitting the respectability of the garment or the rest of the glorious surroundings, pulled on by a smaller figure, another one hard to mistake. Ahuitzotl, the young rascal! But she should have expected something like this.

CHAPTER 4

To stand in the Emperor's immediate proximity was as challenging as ever, stretching his nerves, not too badly, but still. Shifting his weight from one foot to another, Miztli tried to pay no attention to the churning in his stomach, the painful knots that were forming there.

Ahuitzotl was very persuasive, forceful in his arguments – nothing new about that! – arresting possible words of protest before those were born, let alone formed to be sounded. Even Necalli, assertiveness itself, could not override the imperial force of nature, no matter how many counterarguments and even threats he would use trying either to get rid of the younger boy or at least to put him in his place. With Ahuitzotl, nothing worked, save following the young beast, doing whatever he wanted, usually good things, truth be told; useful, interesting enterprises.

Still, this time, Miztli didn't want to get involved. The school day was long and demanding, with too many classes conducted by the priests and therefore pitting him against books and numbers. A large group of older boys readying to become actual warriors was taken out and onto the mainland, to stay there for a few nights in order to fast and pray and do ceremonial things, with Necalli in their midst, an overjoyed addition. For a boy of fourteen summers, it was a huge honor, recognition of a sort. After all, too young or not, the *calmecac* boy did participate in two battles already and in a semi-official capacity, capturing his first warrior on his second try. Unheard of achievements the school authorities clearly appreciated, even if their urge to discipline the unruly *pilli* must have been as great. Or maybe it was the Emperor who made the teachers watch, promote, and challenge the promising boy and let him leave his natural age group.

Well, if that was so, the mighty ruler clearly said nothing of the sort about him, Miztli. Which left them both uneasy and puzzled. They had been together in both battles, after all, their participation sanctioned, to a degree. Especially in the last battle of Tlatelolco. Wasn't he, Miztli, sent there by the Emperor himself, to be a part of the delegation and a bearer of imperial messages? And yet, since the day the neighboring city fell, Tenochtitlan ruler seemed to forget all about his commoner protégé, finding no more use for him. A state of affairs that actually pleased Miztli but not his friend. The *calmecac* boy kept talking about nothing else since the priests told him to get ready for the mainland pilgrimage, as though feeling guilty for leaving his companion behind. Which of course was ridiculous. In *calmecac*, they were supposed to do as they were told.

However, without Necalli, the school day dragged tediously slow, the reading lessons harder than usual, the chores not as swift to accomplish. In one of the classes, Axolin was there to help with the exercise of adding up or dividing multitudes of dots and flags, explaining the rules quietly and helpfully; and yet, that hated Acoatl was there too, toiling with the *amate*-paper of his own, sneering even if quietly, hampering Miztli's ability to concentrate by his mere presence.

Since the fight behind the Earth Goddess's temple, the muscled ballgame star did not try to pick any more fights, but his derision and hatred were there for everyone to see and behold, making some of the boys keep away from him, Miztli, just in case. No one wished to anger the famous bully, no one but Necalli and very few of the others. And Ahuitzotl! This one was uncompromising and very vocal about it, gaining plenty of attention since Tlatelolco war, recognition that his age did not warrant. No one thought to dismiss the fiercely dominant, energetic royal *pilli*, even though Necalli claimed that it was not always the case, that before Tlatelolco, no one had noticed the ten-summers-old or any other young royal offspring admitted to school from much earlier ages than the rest of the city nobles. Apparently, future possible emperors or not, the royal family's youngest members were treated like anyone else, according to the natural hierarchy of ages common to all boys from all walks of life. At fourteen, you paid no respect to ten summers old, just like at seventeen, you dismissed the fourteen summers old. Didn't Elotl back home always try to lord it over him, throwing into his face his lack of two and a half spans of seasons whenever he could not win otherwise?

The smile threatened to sneak out on its own. But would Elotl be surprised to hear about his new life now, the noble school and all the warring, the club from Acachinanco road and the obsidian sword, and the warriors he had killed with it, *actually* killed, and in a real fight, real warring. His brother would refuse to believe it for sure, but when presented with the hard evidence of the weapons themselves, he would have no choice, would he? And Father, what would Father say to that? Would that remarkable man be disappointed? He had wished his son to learn the trade of the metalworkers, after all, to bring the knowledge back to the village probably, to start a workshop of their own. And what would he do with his, Miztli's, newly learned skills of killing people with various weaponry and reading scrolls no one had even seen up close back in Teteltzinco, let alone owned? And yet, Father would let him explain, surely, would let him tell his side of the story. And maybe there was a way to help from his new position of a warrior if he'd become such, to protect their village maybe, or to advance it somehow. They deserved to live better, didn't they, his family and the rest. How to let them know? How to send them word? Even just a short note, like Tlemilli's messages. Could he write something of the sort, tell them about his life on a single piece of *amate*-paper, ask for advice or forgiveness? She would help him compose such a letter, wouldn't she? She loved writing things.

Concentrating back on the colorful melee all around him, Ahuitzotl's grip on his wrist crushing, pulling him along, he fought the urge to reach for the same old pouch containing his cache of treasures, the obsidian puma, the flint knife and her notes, a fairly fat bundle these days. She wrote him every time she could, pressing the densely painted pieces into his hand when they met, or hiding those in the small rock he embedded behind a wide-branched tree in the corner of the school fence. She was so excited when he showed her this new place of hiding.

The tickling in his stomach was back, making it cramp. Her notes were always easier to read, decipher, and understand than schoolbooks and calendars. And she was keeping his messages as well, the pitiful scribble that he sometimes managed to compose, hidden in the sleeve of her *huipil*, close to her heart, she said. He was drawing so well, learning so fast and so easily, she would always claim while pointing out wrongly drawn glyphs, one after another, plenty of those. It was a wonder she managed to understand his scrawling at all. But she always did. Or maybe it was that old magic, her magic. Maybe she was just peeking into his thoughts. He was writing so well, he would end up composing whole books, she had claimed. It was a sentiment that the school authorities didn't echo. Their direful frowns whenever it came to the lessons with books could rival the storm sky at the height of the rainy season. Nothing promising.

"Who cares?" Ahuitzotl had exclaimed only this afternoon, busy dragging him to the emptied courtyard just as the rest of the classes and students were dismissed for good, let out earlier than usual, because of the grand tour at the Plaza, or so they all suspected. "They can make faces and punish you all they like, but you are here to fight and become a warrior, not a scribe. And so am I! I will be the warrior-emperor. Not the poet-ruler like Texcocan snotty emperors are."

By now he had learned that since the Tepanec Empire fell some thirty or more summers earlier and Tenochtitlan gained its independence together with plenty of provinces to rule, Texcoco, another senior partner in the Triple Alliance, boasted to be the most cultured, refined, sophisticated capital-*altepetl*, all learning and libraries and feats of engineering. It was difficult to imagine the things the boys in the school described sometimes, but he tried very hard. They said the Texcocan old emperor, by now dead but not forgotten, had loved engineering so much he had designed water-construction that brought fresh water to Tenochtitlan all the way from the mainland hills, and then went ahead to supervise the construction of the huge earthwork that separated some of the Great Lake's salty waters from fresher ones, at the same time reducing the floods that used to wash over the island too frequently for anyone's peace of mind. They said that through the previous emperor's reign, there were the worst floods in this *altepetl*'s history and that was when the Texcocan wonder of a ruler got to work.

One day, old Yaotzin, the school master and the man who had a habit of entering classes at all times of the day, hovering there and watching, making less diligent students nervous, and maybe even some of the teachers, or so the rumor had it, talked about this wondrous construction and about the Texcoco Emperor's exaggeratedly overstated involvement. Yet it was only thanks to Necalli's quick explanations and then later on Tlemilli's long stories regarding this same history and the Acolhua *altepetl* in general that he managed to understand what it was all about. She had such a funnily disjointed way to relate historical gossip, making faces and gesturing wildly to enhance her story, clearly exaggerating, but he didn't mind. It was the best of pastimes to listen to her and her stories, almost as good as kissing her when they managed to huddle somewhere away from the prying eyes, not as often as he wanted. Necalli would sometimes help them with that, knowing every crack and every corner around the Great Plaza or near the canal, the furthest they dared to go, as she was certainly not allowed to wander away from her royal surroundings.

Still, the *calmecac* boy's help was invaluable, and always timely, not intrusive. He was sneaking away plenty himself, seeking as much privacy with none other than Chantli. It was clear that he was allowed to kiss her as well, however, they never talked about it, for which Miztli was grateful. Too outspoken, his friend sometimes aired aloud too many things, private musings that he, Miztli, didn't wish to even face, let alone talk about. Like that matter with that sharp-tongued friend of Chantli from the night of the fires, so aggressive and full of fire that had nothing to do with burning warehouses, so set on trying to offend him, to make him feel like dirt. Why? Necalli liked to carry on about this sometimes, needling him, Miztli, implying that the girl's strange tendency to verbally attack him whenever he was in sight had to do with her "setting her sights on him," which was the way the *calmecac* boy would put it. One was to answer the torrent of abuse with counter needling, Necalli claimed, with sharp words of his own, putting the cheeky fowl back in her place. Either that or giving her what she wanted. Which was a promising possibility too. And no repeated demands to shut up and leave this matter alone helped.

Every time they were out and wandering the city, he would pray not to run into the spicy fowl, with his inner voice whispering to stay away from such trips at all, but the temptation to join winning sometimes. Also Necalli insisted that he should come along, accompany him and the others as they went around, wandering the marketplace alleys or the smaller plazas and squares, doing nothing in particular, catcalling girls, engaging in their spicy banter. The *calmecac* boy claimed that it was all a part of being in school and that he should get exposed to this pleasant pastime, even if he wasn't interested in other girls than his Tlatelolcan wonder, set on admiring the same old view of the Great Pyramid from every possible angle. The smirk with which he would say that would make Miztli feel his face and the burning wave that would wash over it, but no demands to shut up would work. Like Ahuitzotl, Necalli was a force of nature, to accept or to run away from. Nothing in between.

And yet, this boy was the greatest, most loyal friend he could ever have asked for. So he would tag along when Tlemilli was forced back to the Palace, and those excursions were actually not bad or boring, the other boys just like the boys back in the village, some funny, some dull, some more mischievous than the others, trying to steal tortillas or fruits when there was no need to do that. One time, they ran into Acoatl and a few of his followers, but they were more numerous, so no fight developed, only much mutual name-calling. Other times, it was groups of simpler looking boys from this or that *telpochcalli*, with some pushes and punches involved, but nothing like the night before Tlatelolco fell. Necalli explained that it was unlawful what this same Acoatl and the others did, that if told on in school, they would have been punished most severely.

As though it would have helped him back then, he would reflect, hiding those thoughts, wishing to keep his real feelings to himself. He never went out without the small flint knife the Texcocan man had given him and another one, obsidian dagger like the rest of the *calmecac* students had, this one held openly, on display. And he made sure to be on guard, always, now because of Tlemilli as well. It was with her that they both were exposed to something nasty, another ambush or something of the sort, because when together, they sought to remain alone and unwatched, to do what they couldn't do in public, namely kiss and kiss, and then kiss some more. Still, he could never relax, not entirely, afraid that Acoatl would manage to corner him and this time with her being exposed to the danger as well. A terrible thought.

"Stay here with me and don't dream." Ahuitzotl's commanding voice broke into his reverie, bringing him back to the sunlit Plaza and the noblest of people swarming all around, listening to the Emperor's measured voice, paying respects. "Just remember all those names you used, like Cuauhnahuac and such. Don't forget any of these. And don't get all scared like you always do. My brother isn't scary, and I'll talk to him most of the time instead of you, so don't worry. You just answer his questions and remember what you told me about Cuauhnahuac and that other tongue those others are speaking, in that village of yours where our nobles' villas are. Just tell him what you told me."

He tried not to roll his eyes, cursing himself for turning talkative back in the schoolyard, where this same Ahuitzotl and two other boys made him show them his skill with a sling that the enterprising royal offspring produced like a magician, with just enough style and flair. A real warriors' sling, all crisp leather and sturdy maguey, with a few clay balls to match. Reminded of his hopelessly lost possession back in Tlaquitoc's workshop, Miztli made a face but could not fight the temptation. The schoolyard was so blissfully abandoned, and those fellow students of his so eager and not hostile or malicious, all expectancy, even the royal force of nature.

Careful not to break their limited ammunition, he chose softer targets, certain bushes, and branches of trees. But the clay balls were cracked all the same in the end, because the others wanted him to help them practice, again and again, hitting everything of course but the targets themselves. In the end, Ahuitzotl declared that he, Miztli, would now train them daily, or at least every time they managed to have the schoolyard all for themselves, and then, somehow, he had found himself telling them about his village and how they would make slings whenever they would grow bored, just weaving simple plants and fibers, because if interwoven correctly, everything could make a good enough sling to take down a rabbit or a bird. And then, as expected, Ahuitzotl was demanding to make such makeshift weaponry for them all, the temporarily absent Necalli included, and then more questions made him talk about Oaxtepec and Cuauhnahuac and even some further settlements out there in the west and the south, all of the places he had heard Father mentioning, usually in connection to their relationship with their own region of mining and copper-making businesses, places where people didn't even talk Nahuatl but that other tongue called Matlatzinca by the Nahua speakers.

When queried, he reluctantly admitted that yes, he could speak or understand that other tongue, of course he did. Everyone could speak Matlatzinca, even the traders and tribute collectors. And then before he knew it, Ahuitzotl was on his feet, all agog with excitement, telling them of the petition for help his brother the Emperor received only a few dawns ago from this or that ruler of those same areas and that they must – must! – let his brother know.

Know what? he had asked, taken aback, cursing his loose tongue once again. It didn't matter, declared the forceful *pilli*. This information that he just told them, about alliances of the south, might be important, as was his command of this southern tongue. Axayacatl might wish to learn of this fact. And so here they were, pushing their way into the Emperor's vicinity just as the Tenochtitlan ruler was busy with important matters and people, hoping not to be punished for their temerity. Well, at least that was what he, Miztli, felt. Ahuitzotl was surely not preoccupied with such petty concerns. He had his news to relate, his opportunity to gain more attention, to situate himself in the center of the events again, something he clearly did not enjoy since Tlatelolco fell. A fierce beast!

Miztli forced his thoughts off the impending trial and toward more pleasant, not to say thrilling channels. Was Tlemilli somewhere around, sneaking in these crowds, trying to get a closer look? He was ready to bet his much cherished obsidian sword that she was. Nothing would stop Tlemilli from getting into the thick of it, especially with the rest of the noble Tenochtitlan milling about and all around; not even her sister's litter-bearers and maids. But did he hate the sight of those! Always out there and lurking, ready to accost her and ruin their time together. Yes, she was a noble girl, of preciously noble bloodline and all; yes, her sister was afraid for her and protective now that they had no other family left. Still, he wasn't out to harm her in any way, and Tlemilli said that his lack of nobility meant nothing to her. She kept saying it, all the time.

Yet, it was not what her sister thought, and he suspected that in this, her sister's opinions would be backed by the entire Palace when the time came... Came to do what? He didn't know, didn't dare to formulate his thoughts on the matter. To sneak around and kiss was good, but not as fulfilling as before, not as satisfying. It was hard to just kiss and laugh about it like they did in Tlatelolco. Somehow, it wasn't as funny anymore. And at fifteen, the girls were liable to be offered in marriage, and she was already fourteen, she said, and what if someone came up with the terrible idea of giving her away? The thought alone made his limbs go rigid with fear.

"See that one?" Ahuitzotl was tugging at his hand once again, demanding attention, his voice irritatingly commanding. "Over there, behind my brother, the one who is leaning on that column. Do you know him?"

Squinting, Miztli followed the impatiently waving hand, uncomfortable with the knowledge that it was horribly impolite to point someone out just like that. The man by the wooden works that supported the carved wonder of the stonework underneath it was pudgy, almost square, with his head weighted by a customary headpiece, his jewelry sparkling against the afternoon sun but not as fiercely as the imperial decorations all around him. A few other simpler-looking nobles and warriors surrounded him.

"The short one, with the headpiece?"

A vigorous nod was his answer. "Yes! Do you know him?"

"No, I don't."

His companion regarded him with a frowning look. "You sure?"

"Yes, of course. How could I know him, or anyone else in this crowd? I was to the Palace only three times and only when the Emperor summoned me—"

"Yes, I know that!" Out of patience, the younger boy stomped his foot. "But that one is not of our nobility. He is that petitioning ruler I told you about. He is coming from your lands."

"Oh." He scrutinized the man once again, now mildly curious. Ahuitzotl claimed that some place called Tenantzinco somewhere way behind Cuauhnahuac came to complain about other mysterious towns even further to the west or the south – the royal *pilli* wasn't sure about their locations either – as those were harassing this same Tenantzinco and possibly playing with ideas to defy Tenochtitlan influence in those areas. Still, to claim that he should know the ruler of the city he hadn't even heard about before was taking it too far. All those names were far enough removed from his village and even the neighboring Oaxtepec. Cuauhnahuac alone required close to a day of walking, or so Father said. And he didn't even know there were other towns and cities out there, bubbling with life, speaking the native tongue of his village or something close to it, trying to tie themselves to the might of Tenochtitlan, or on the contrary, to piss it off or make it go away. Away where?

"I thought you would know that one." The royal *pilli*'s forehead creased with displeasure. "You said you knew these names. You said that back at school!"

"Names, yes. But not their rulers. And surely not by face!" In his turn, he glared at his companion, enraged. "I didn't want to come here. You told me to, and you insisted. I never said I have any information that might interest the Emperor. *You* said that!"

The younger boy's glare seemed to be capable of melting copper-powder. He stood it without blinking, reminded of Necalli's similarly spontaneous outbursts, fierce but quick to pass, annoying nevertheless. He was not as quick to relax as they were.

For a heartbeat, only the steady hum of the voices around interrupted the staring contest. Then Ahuitzotl snorted. "You either know or you don't, you stupid thickhead! You can't have it all ways, claim that you know places or tongues, then scream that you don't."

The effort to keep silent, or at least not to let his eyes roll in a telling manner, like Necalli always did, or better yet, suggest this little piece of dung to go and throw himself in the lake became more difficult. Somehow, since the fighting in Tlatelolco, or maybe even earlier, since the night ambush, he didn't feel like reacting in silence to insults or belittling tirades, no matter who their initiators were. In that, he had made great progress, Necalli had claimed, himself amused but for the instances when the bickering was between them. He never failed to answer Acoatl these days, blessing his luck that the notorious bully had muscles but not enough brains to destroy with words, like Necalli or Axolin could. He himself was anything but witty, a painful realization since early childhood, nothing to do with his dramatically changed circumstances. Oh, but how he always envied Elotl his quick wit and the sharpness of his tongue.

Ahuitzotl was still glowering, but as the royal *pilli*'s mouth opened again to deliver more complaints or more likely, direful threats and curses, two neatly dressed servants burst upon them, clearing their way in the dignified crowd, timid but determined.

"Honorable Master, please come."

Ahuitzotl's face twisted in momentary distress before it assumed one of those typical stubborn expressions this boy had in abundance. "Not now. Can't you see that I'm busy? I'm waiting for an audience with my brother, the Emperor!"

"Please come, Young Master. Your august mother wishes you to sit beside her." The leading man was humbly polite but not about to give up. Miztli tried to hide his smirk. Echoes of Tlemilli's sister. Her servants also had to deal with firm orders concerning a potentially unruly charge. However, this time, he didn't care. If they dragged the little brat away, he would breathe with relief and go about his business.

Again, he glanced around, regretting the lack of the elevated point of view. Was Tlemilli somewhere here, sneaking on her own? The ladies in their litters huddled in the shade of the tented area, but he knew better than to crane his neck in order to scrutinize those. Aside from such behavior being completely inappropriate – no one was allowed to stare at the highborn fowls, neither nobles nor commoners like him – both Tlatelolcan sisters did not move in those highest of circles. Tlemilli said that they were lucky to be allowed into the Palace at all, or so some of the Palace's dwellers tried to impress on them. She didn't care for those types and neither did he, even though it hurt to think that someone might choose to look down on her because of her changed status. If only he could do something about it.

"Your mother orders you to follow us to her litter, Young Master," the servant kept insisting, moving to block the boy as best as he could while keeping his voice suitably low. The dignitaries around them paid them little attention, strolling unhurriedly, sneaking glances toward the Emperor, clearly visible from where they stood, talking to a spectacularly dressed warrior, while motioning toward one of the further groups in an inviting gesture. This one contained another magnificent headdress of the highest status. The Emperor's other brother and one of his advisers, Miztli surmised, quailing inside. On both previous occasions when he had met this dignitary, on his first interview in the Palace and then after his first mission in Tlatelolco, this man was either indifferent or outright hostile, hating him and his humble origins, clearly in disagreement with the open-mindedness his ruling sibling displayed.

"I will talk to my brother, then I will come!" declared Ahuitzotl, turning away resolutely, as though certain of his rights, not afraid to be detained by force; yet when the second man reached out, clearly intending to grab their uncooperative target, the young rascal twisted away, darting into the opening between the strolling by groups, unflustered. No Tlemilli this. She would defy her sister servants, oh yes, but not to such an openly rebellious degree. And her sister was no imperial mother. The mere memory of the ice-cold, hideously arrogant woman in the royal chambers made Miztli shudder.

He took a step back, catching the agitated servants' suspicious glance. Were they considering him a worthy substitute? The thought made him wish to laugh nervously, then to take another step away, wishing to be out there, surrounded by less distinguished crowds. Without Ahuitzotl, he truly had no excuse and no reason to be here.

As though summoned by his misgivings alone, a few spearmen decorated and groomed to perfection, their long-reaching weapons sparkling, frowned, then began making their way toward him. His fear splashed in force, regardless of his will or even the possible seriousness of the situation. The memories of the Tlatelolcan Plaza, sun lit and gushing, full to the brim with contesters and watchers, but with warriors and killers as well, welled like water in a river when the heavy rains would make it gush in a forcible flow.

Fighting his panic, he backed away, treading on someone's sandals, murmuring apologies out of instinct. The man he had bumped into, a decorated warrior, scowled at him but let him pass, muttering in displeasure. Another one said something. With the twinge of relief, he left them behind, maneuvering his way more carefully now, but still deeply worried, on the verge of panic.

A large group blocked his way, slowing their step in order to converse with another. Feeling cornered, he changed his direction, only to nearly bump into a litter, a large partly covered affair, to skirt around it desperately, slipping upon the cracked flagstones but keeping his balance, breathing with relief. Of old, he would be running all amok now, he knew, deep down pleased with himself, wondering at the unfamiliar feeling. Was it still Tlemilli's magic that would render him with nicely composed speech, but now was making him think good thoughts about himself as well? She certainly kept thinking him to be one of the warrior-heroes from stories. A wonder of wonders, but it was easy to know that as she never bothered to keep her thoughts to herself.

The warm glow spread anew, and sneaking behind a pile of wooden beams thrown behind the further side of the construction, he wondered again if she was out and around. Her sister couldn't force her back to the Palace, could she? Not when evidently so many noblewomen were invited to tour the Plaza. But for Ahuitzotl's improvised training session, he might have managed to sneak a peek into the girls' hall the moment the priests dismissed their class for good and not only check their secret cache and see if it contained any of her new notes.

"I swear they would never believe it back home, never!"

The words made him jump, not their suddenness or their loudness but the familiar ring of those, the sounds he hadn't heard since leaving for Tenochtitlan more than four moons ago. No Nahuatl this! Whirling abruptly, he caught the sight of two men, simple-looking warriors with maguey cloaks and no spectacular weaponry, standing nearby, leaning against the other side of the same pile, one of them munching on a greenish sprout, again in a most familiar fashion, bringing back memories of his village in force.

"Tell me about it." The second man shrugged, then shielded his eyes against the glow coming from beyond the crowded construction. "We should bring something back, something rare. To prove our words."

His companion exhaled loudly, moving the sprout to the other side of his mouth. "That marketplace! I thought we would get lost there. But for the guides, we would have. So many alleys, and so crowded!"

"But not like that plaza!"

"No, not like that."

For some time, the foreigners sank into their observations, and as Miztli moved to let a group of warriors pass, he couldn't help but remain staring. Who were they? Why were they speaking the tongue Father used sometimes, made sure to teach his sons and remember?

As though sensing his scrutiny, one of the men glanced his way, his gaze narrowing, holding his for a heartbeat. Unsettled, Miztli looked away. Behind the mounting beams and other construction gear, the reliefs upon the nearest edge of the stone were beautifully elaborated, reminding him of the calendar glyphs. He fought the urge to touch them.

"Cuauhnahuac lazy no-goods are missing out. They should have bothered to come with us." Judging by the additional voice, the two loiterers were joined by another. Miztli busied himself with the loose strap of his sandal, kneeling to retie it, seeking the opportunity to linger some more. If only these men went on talking, let him know where they came from. Suddenly, he wished to know that. Cuauhnahuac was not far away from his village and Oaxtepec, hardly a day of walking. Father went there from time to time, when the crops were bad and the rare pieces of green stones were to be exchanged for food or more seeds. Not a frequent occurrence. The longing for home resonated in his chest once again, making it tighten. How were they all out there? Working deep down in the bellies of the hills? Digging more adits? Readying the fields for the rainy season? Worrying about him, maybe; believing that he did well, hopefully. Oh, but they would never guess how well he was doing, never surmise!

"Here you are!" A shadow fell across the cobblestone he knelt on and before he could make out the familiar form or voice, the tickling in his stomach informed him that she found him before he could find her. "Why are you hiding here?"

"I'm not," he said, springing back to his feet, forgetting all about the foreigners. She was beaming at him, all glaring colors and glistening cheeks, like always when running around in the sun. Once upon a time, he remembered thinking that being all red and sweaty did not suit the mysterious sharpness of her face, the goddess of the old stories and scrolls. Now he liked her this way the most. She always looked like that even after the shortest run, usually when they managed to escape her sister's maids and the litter-bearers. Her glaring cheeks were the sign of their success.

"I saw you out there with Ahuitzotl, I and Chantli, we both saw you, but when we ran into this boy just now, you were nowhere in sight."

"I..." He frowned, remembering his momentary fright, then the foreigners. Those were still there, more than a few now, eyeing them with an open curiosity, gaping at her. Angered, he stared one of them down. "Let's go somewhere quieter."

Her chuckle trilled the air. "There is no 'somewhere quieter' to be found here, but we do have to go. Ahuitzotl said you must come back and find him right away."

"Where is he?" The memory of their original quest did not make him expectant. "His mother's servants didn't catch him?"

Her pointy eyebrows arched in the familiar fashion. "What?"

Determinedly, he began steering her away and toward the throng back on the other side of the massive construction where the Emperor's headdress could still be seen, towering in its vividness, wavering above the crowds. The foreigners, he noticed, were still watching them, and for a moment, he regretted the lost opportunity to listen some more. Those Cuauhnahuac people they were discussing, what was that all about?

"What about Ahuitzotl?" she insisted, pressing too close, like was always her custom in the packed crowds since that memorable day on the Tlatelolco Plaza and the shores. Momentarily, he wished the people around them would disappear.

"Ahuitzotl wanted a word with the Emperor, but his mother's servants were as difficult to escape as your sister's litter-bearers."

"I always escape my sister's litter when I want to," she declared smugly. "Always!"

He tried not to laugh. Some things never changed, and this *altepetl* did not change the old Tlatelolcan Tlemilli, not in the slightest, thanks all powerful deities for that. "Not always. Yesterday, they didn't let you get away, not even along that back alley."

As expected, she bridled. "Yesterday doesn't count. They had special orders. Citlalli wanted me to be present in case she was sent for. She said there was much unrest on our side of the Palace, because of the visiting delegations. She was afraid they would force her to be present on this or that audience, like they did a market interval ago. That's why those maids were so persistent." A frown crossed her high brow. "She doesn't want to attend these things, but they don't ask her. Just tell her to present herself here or there. What a lack of manners! Annoying turkeys!"

They didn't do that bad by your sister so far, he thought, but was wiser than to voice such musings aloud. *So what if they want her attend this or that ceremony? They could have sold her away and be done with it, instead of paying for the haughty fowl's upkeep*. But of course none of it could be sounded in Tlemilli's fiercely loyal ears. She would not listen to a word against her adored sister. The arrogant fowl could do no wrong, not according to Tlemilli.

"Will her servants be hunting you down now?" he asked, deciding to be practical about it.

Her slender arm waved nonchalantly. "They can't. She is up there, with the highest of the nobility, watching the Emperor, maintaining boring conversations with his brother, that nasty-looking adviser." Her eyebrows knitted again. "He was actually nice to her, all politeness. Looked like he liked chatting to her. Until the Texcoco emperor came along. Then he began looking angry because the Texcocan was nice to her too. Oh and that man, the scar-faced man Tecuani, he was there too! Would you believe it? He made faces at her and she made faces at him. She hates him so!"

As always, her outburst of information made him blink. "YaoTecuani? Is he here, in Tenochtitlan? Where?"

"Out there." The loose sleeve of her *huipil* waved again, with its previous lack of enthusiasm. "Somewhere around the Emperor, I suppose." Then she caught his arm in hers. "We must go there as well. I promised Ahuitzotl to find you and bring you there."

"I don't think what he wants me to tell the Emperor is important," he muttered, resisting her pull but mildly, reconciled to his fate. Ahuitzotl and Tlemilli combined were a difficult force to withstand.

"What?"

"Things about my village and the towns to the west. Like Cuauhnahuac." The memory of the foreigners surfaced again. They were talking about this same Cuauhnahuac, weren't they?

And in the tongue of the valley of those same western settlements. But he should have stayed to listen, shouldn't he? Especially in the light of Ahuitzotl's nagging.

"What about it?"

He collected his thoughts with an effort. "He said that the delegation from one of those came to ask for the Emperor's help against someone else from this same area."

She wrinkled her nose. "Yes, there were delegations coming from here and there, like I told you. Didn't you listen?" The wideness of her forehead creased again. "But I'm not sure where from. Texcoco, obviously. But the others? I don't know." Her eyes peered at him. "You came from Cuauhnahuac?"

"No." He tried to look elsewhere, wishing to run into Ahuitzotl again now, or anyone else, really. The talk about his village was always a source of embarrassment. She was so naïve about it, asking silly questions, still not fully realizing, or so he suspected. That powerful city of Cuauhnahuac was anything but a village, wasn't it? It was twenty times larger than Oaxtepec, more influential and important by far, or so Father said; with many hundreds of people living there, collecting tribute from everyone, even if paying a part of it to Tenochtitlan in the end. But even the smaller rural towns like Oaxtepec looked down on his village. Everyone did. They were nothing, barely twenty and a half families, paying tribute, struggling not to starve. They were in no position to look down on anyone but the rodents in the fields, and every day in the Great Capital kept sharpening this realization, in no encouraging of manners, not where she or her naivety were concerned.

"Here he is!" The pull on his arm intensified. "The Emperor must have talked to him already. And the Texcocans are there too!"

The colorful crowds near the other edge of the platform did not conceal the familiar figure of the royal boy, flanked by Chantli this time, as pleasant a sight as always, also flushed from the sun, sending a reserved smile his way. Back in the workshop days, she was more open, he remembered, more talkative and nice. Did these august surroundings intimidate her into all this reserve as well?

"Where have you been?" demanded Ahuitzotl forcefully but quietly, conscious of their dignified surroundings. The Emperor's headdress wavered not far away, the powerful ruler's voice heard here most clearly, talking to a group of important-looking men, surrounded by protective ring of decorated warriors. "We looked for you all over. You should have kept close."

August surroundings or not, he didn't like to be reprimanded, not in her vicinity. "You were the one to bolt away."

The boy's eyebrows knitted ridiculously like Tlemilli's before. "I had to, or I wouldn't be here now, obviously! Do you think with your head or your back exit?" Before he managed to open his mouth to protest or say something equally nasty, the boy brought an imperious hand up. "Don't argue. Just come."

He could see both Chantli and Tlemilli chuckling softly. "Don't," breathed Tlemilli into his ear while pulling at his hand once again. "Not in front of the Emperor." He could hear her voice trembling with suppressed laughter and it made the ice in his stomach melt, if only partly. As long as she was there...

"Let us pass," demanded Ahuitzotl importantly when two spearmen blocked their way. "I wish to talk to my brother, the Emperor."

The men exchanged glances. "Where are your servants, young master? And the warriors to guard you?"

"Out there." The boy waved his hand breezily, then pushed his way past them, to be blocked by their spears' shafts deftly. "Let me pass!"

The men hesitated once again.

"Axayacatl!" shouted the unstoppable *pilli*, waving both hands in the direction of the imperial figure.

The Emperor glanced in their direction but did not pause in his speech. Only his head moved imperceptivity, signaling the warriors. The spears' shafts moved away, to create a barrier once the royal boy passed. "The rest of you stay here."

"They are with me!" protested Ahuitzotl, but on this the Palace's guards clearly found a firm enough ground to stand.

"If the Emperor sends a warrior to escort them, they'll be

allowed."

Ahuitzotl's face clouded direfully, but a heartbeat saw him closing his mouth without another protest. "Wait for me here." His words ranged in perfectly warlord-like fashion.

Miztli felt Tlemilli's palm clutching his arm yet stronger, signaling him to keep quiet. Did she think he was going to argue with the imperial family in front of the Palace's guards and in the Emperor's earshot? The thought made his spirit soar for no reason. The warrior-heroes from her stories, did they do such things?

"Why does he want to talk to the Emperor?" Chantli was asking, moving closer to him as well, as though seeking protection.

"He wants Miztli to tell the Emperor things about Cuauhnahuac," said Tlemilli importantly, puffing with pride. He hid his smile as best as he could.

"What's Cuauhnahuac?"

Tlemilli shrugged before he could venture an answer. "A town or a village or something out there."

"A city," he said. "A large important city out there in the west." Then he remembered where he was. "To the south, that is. To the south of Tenochtitlan."

The girl eyed him with marked suspicion, very pretty in her neat sparsely decorated *huipil* and with her hair pulled up in a respectable fashion of a *calmecac* student, a somber one. "What does it want?"

He shrugged in reply, then put his attention back to the Emperor, who was still immersed in his previous conversation with an interesting-looking dignitary, as young as Tenochtitlan's ruler and as impressive, evidently refined and unwarlike, but not insignificant, his garments a celebration of elegance and tasteful embroidery, sitting proudly upon his straight shoulders. Beside them, the Emperor's other brother looked especially heavy, somehow cumbersome, not belonging despite the magnificence of his regalia. Various warriors and decorated leaders spread in half a circle around them, hovering there politely, listening without contributing a word. And so did young Ahuitzotl, standing patiently still for a change, not moving a limb, pretending not to notice dour frowns the Adviser was sending his way. The Emperor appeared not to notice his very existence.

"We should go back to your sister," whispered Chantli nervously. "Or somewhere away from here."

The words that he agreed on wholeheartedly, but as expected, Tlemilli's head shook vigorously. "Ahuitzotl told us to wait here."

He saw Chantli shooting the girl a wondering glance, partly puzzled, partly amused, reflecting on his musings, of that he was sure. Since when was Tlemilli following orders no matter where those came from?

"What? He wants Miztli to talk to the Emperor, tell him important things."

"It's not the time and you know it," said Chantli impatiently, then lowered her voice. "The Emperor will not listen. He is not listening to him now. You can see it as clearly as I do. And it's childish, not worthy of people who want to be taken seriously."

"Oh please!" cried out Tlemilli, not bothering to lower her voice at all. "You are talking nonsense. Important news is important news. You can't delay your say only because it might not be the best time. What if it is too late later on?"

He didn't want to side with Chantli and against her, even though she sounded more childish than Ahuitzotl himself all of a sudden. Still, Tlemilli was Tlemilli, and she would feel betrayed if he took someone else's side, however more reasonable.

"We'll wait just a little more," he said hurriedly, watching Chantli's eyes flashing, her mouth already opening, prepared to return measure for measure. It took him back to his first time in Tlatelolco, trying to will them both into shutting up by the sheer power of his wish. "Until they stopped staring." As discreetly as he could, he motioned at the two spearmen that let the royal boy pass before, their gazes still shooting their way, full of suspicion.

"No, we should stay—" began Tlemilli hotly, but he pressed her arm in his turn, signaling her to keep quiet, not hopeful of the results. Indeed, she pulled her arm away, but before she could say something, one of the men surrounding the Emperor turned to look directly at them, and he couldn't help but gasp, recognizing the scar-faced Texcocan, YaoTecuani, or Tecuani, as the man claimed that he preferred to be called on that night in the agitated pre-war Tlatelolco.

This time, Miztli pressed her arm more forcefully, demanding silence. Such an encounter required the entirety of his attention. In the corner of his eye, he glimpsed another spearman beginning to head their way.

"See, the Emperor is talking to him now," whispered Tlemilli excitedly, her breath warm, tickling his ear. "Of course, we should have waited."

Ahuitzotl indeed was standing straighter now, clearly striving to appear serious and worthy. The Emperor had a smile tugging at the corner of his thinly pressed mouth. Involuntarily, Miztli's eyes drifted back toward the impressive Texcocan, his back again turned toward them, the elaborately decorated cloak flowing down the wide shoulders, proclaiming confidence. What was this man doing in Tenochtitlan? Visiting along with this or that delegation, keeping the dignitary who was talking to the Emperor safe?

"I wonder what—" Tlemilli's breath kept warming his check.

"You, *pillis*, come along!" The curt order did not surprise him as a part of his mind followed the spearman, expecting his approach.

"Where to?" demanded Tlemilli, another expected reaction.

"Come along and hurry," repeated the man, ignoring her while giving him a penetrating look that told it all. *Don't even think of giving trouble.* As though he would contemplate something like that while being in the heart of the Great Plaza and the most noble of crowds. He pressed Tlemilli's arm once again, relaying a message. She was the only one who could cause him to make trouble.

"Where are you taking them, warrior?" This voice was also familiar, deep and authoritative, not needing to rise in order to halt their progress. Miztli felt his taut nerves relaxing at once.

From the closer proximity, the scar-faced man looked as formidable as back in Tlatelolco or in Tenochtitlan on the day after the battle, domineering, not to say autocratic, forceful, full of cold, slightly amused confidence, sure of himself.

"To the tented area over there, Honorable Leader. Where the ladies are." The spearman hesitated. "It's the Revered Emperor's orders."

"I'll take them there. Are they to wait until summoned?"

"Yes, Honorable Leader." Their guard hesitated again, clearly off balance and not knowing how to proceed. "I have orders to—"

"Your orders are changed, warrior." This came out cuttingly cold. "Come along."

They went without a murmur, even Tlemilli. She thought highly of this man, Miztli remembered, talking about him several times, mentioning once that the hardened warrior thought that he, Miztli, could use more self-assurance or something of the sort, had to decide what he wanted for himself. She didn't manage to explain what that might mean exactly.

"So, what are you youngsters up to now?" asked the man conversationally after their perplexed guard melted away, returning to his fellow warriors presumably or going to complain to his superiors.

For a moment, no one said a word. Miztli tried to collect his thoughts that were scattering in the familiar fashion, not missed in the least.

"Ahuitzotl wanted us to talk to the Emperor," volunteered Tlemilli, her hand still in his, but her stride wide, self-assured. No lack of this same desired self-assurance there.

"What about?"

But did he remember such questioning. This man never minced matters or spent time on being polite.

"About Cuauhnahuac," said Tlemilli importantly, evidently not minding the probing.

"Cuauhnahuac?" The man slowed his step and he felt Chantli lurching closer, as though contemplating sneaking behind his back.

"He told us about the unrest out there in the areas where I came from," he hurried to say, hating this mounting misunderstanding. Tlemilli was no better than the royal *pilli* at times. "Ahuitzotl, that is. He said about the delegations coming from the west, asking for Tenochtitlan's help."

"In the south, you mean," corrected the man, matter-of-fact, his expression not changing. "You didn't come from the west, boy."

"Yes, yes." He tried to hide his nervousness as best as he could, unsettled as always where this man was involved but reassured too; a strange combination. "In the south, yes. I just... I didn't, didn't mean it this way. From where I live, Cuauhnahuac is in the west..." Taking a deep breath, he paused, desperate to stop mumbling. "Ahuitzotl wished me to tell his brother, the Emperor, about those areas. He thought this information could be of use."

"Indeed, it could," muttered the man, contemplative. "What did he wish you to tell your emperor about it?"

"I don't know. Whatever would be asked of me, I suppose. Honorable Leader," he added hurriedly, horrified that he forgot to use the title before.

But as expected, the smile quivered again, an uneven quirk of lips, holding an amused, almost mischievous glint. "No need for titles, boy. You are not serving me as a warrior. Not yet." Then the unevenness of the smile widened. "Where is your friend, Tlilocelotl's son? One would expect to see him around as well, up to no good and busy."

"Necalli is on the mainland," interrupted Tlemilli, left out of the conversation clearly for too long. "He went out to hunt or fast or something of the sort."

"He went to pray and fast and prepare to become a warrior," contributed Chantli, another one over her initial fright and unable to keep quiet; not when it came to the *calmecac* boy, evidently.

Their new companion nodded. "About time." Then his face sobered again. "What did the cheeky *pilli* tell you about the southern areas of the other side of our Smoking Mountain?"

Miztli gathered his thoughts hurriedly. "The delegation came from one of those settlements, the cities. They wanted to have our Emperor's help against... against other settlements?"

"This same Cuauhnahuac?"

"No, another town. He used another name, further away to the west. Or the south."

"Tenantzinco? Tollocan?"

He found himself staring. "Yes."

"Which one?"

"Tenantzinco, I think. Its ruler came here to talk to the Emperor, ask for his help." There seemed to be no way around the relentless interrogation. It was back to the night Plaza and the Yellow Water Pond, before his second trip to Tlatelolco – the memories he didn't cherish. "Ahuitzotl showed him to me. Out there somewhere."

"Yes, I know. He is out there still, complaining. I was privileged to listen to his grievances not long ago." The formidable warrior rolled his eyes. "He's a talkative one, eager to sound his undying loyalty to Tenochtitlan and Texcoco. Easy to make this one talk." A derisive snort managed to overcome the general hum all around them, the shaded area dotted with litters and splashing with sounds of female chatter and laughter, bearing upon them, intimidating in its exaggerated luxury. So much glitter and gaudiness. "So how does young Ahuitzotl wish to use you in this matter?" Again, the eyes were losing their amused glint, turning piercing. "What did he want you to tell the Emperor?"

Miztli fought the urge to bolt away. "I don't know exactly," he said, exasperated, not wishing to anger or even just alienate the man. Necalli worshipped this ideal of a warrior, prayed to become his shield-bearer, talked about little else at times. And he was a good man, this mysterious, forceful, inconsiderate Texcocan. After the war in Tlatelolco, there could be little doubt about it. "He wished me to answer questions, that's all. Possible questions, that is. Because I came from those areas..."

To the immensity of his relief, a thoughtful nod cut his trailing off voice in time, before the pitiful mumbling returned. However, now he could feel another pair of eyes boring into him, this one, as expected, belonging to Tlemilli's sister, shifting toward their formidable company, growing yet colder. A quick glance at their escort informed him that the man was returning the gaze, as icy and somehow challenging.

"We'll wait by my sister," declared Tlemilli, evidently missing the currents, the Tlatelolcan woman and the Texcocan man still glaring, refusing to drop their gazes, immersed in a surprisingly intense staring contest. It was as though they had known each other, had had a quarrel only this morning, and were still eager not to let one dominate the other. Miztli shifted uneasily.

"Where did they want you to wait for the summons?" demanded their escort a little too curtly the moment the stubborn beauty took her eyes away, her lips pursed in an uncompromising manner, challenging as well.

"I don't know."

You didn't give that other warrior an opportunity to sneak out a single word, he thought, careful to keep such musings to himself and away from his face.

"We'll wait with my sister," repeated Tlemilli, beginning to clear their way briskly, not about to be led any further. The man gave her an oddly amused, skeptical look.

"Tlemilli, wait." This time, it was Chantli, frowning painfully, troubled. "I think I'd better go. Your sister, and the other ladies, they are not happy with me there. I will see you at school. It's better this way."

Tlemilli's pointy eyebrows flew up. "No, it's not. My sister is not like them! And you enjoyed being there, I know you did." She grabbed the girl's hand impulsively, lovely in her animated vitality. Miztli's heart squeezed and he wished again that the crowded Plaza would disappear, all those commoners and nobles, the pretty ladies with her snotty sister in the lead and even Chantli and the mysterious man of Texcoco, everyone but her and him in the warm pleasant breeze and the soft afternoon sun of the cold moons before the rain.

When he focused, her eyes were upon him, glittering as though reading his thoughts, familiarly mischievous yet enigmatic somehow, promising... what? He didn't dare to even think about it. "Come, please. It'll be pleasant. I promise. Until the Emperor sends for you."

By that time, the tall servant was hovering behind her, waiting with barely expressed politeness. "Young Lady, please follow. Your sister requires your presence by her litter."

"See?" She flashed them a conspiratorial smirk that made even the Texcocan grin, albeit reluctantly. Then he shrugged with one shoulder and led the way, motioning them, including the suddenly frightened servant, to follow. Yet, Miztli noticed how the man's lips pursed and his face turned stony like back in the nighttime Tlatelolco; wary, alert, ready to do battle. Battle with whom? The haughty Tlatelolcan beauty he was forced to save once upon a time?

A glance at the small but prettily embroidered litter confirmed this assumption. The aristocratic lady seemed to be sinking deeper into her cushions, her sculptured cheekbones draining of color despite the fashionably yellowish tint the ointments gave it, her chiseled features sharpening, the shadowed eyes hard, ready, unafraid, indeed, preparing for a battle royal.

CHAPTER 5

The alleys of Oaxtepec were drowning in mud. After the heavy rain that pounded the earth through the previous evening and then the entire night, not only the fields turned into swamps. A multitude of tiny streams ran down narrow pathways between people's dwellings, mixing with fresh earth, carrying it along, sparkling merrily in the occasional rays of the deceptively strong sun.

In this, Oaxtepec was no different from his native Teteltzinco, reflected Elotl, treading the slough, pulling his feet out of the mud that was trying to suck them back in, paying little attention to the process. The journey to the neighboring town, usually a quick run with the sun moving less than half a finger in between, now took twice as long, with the swamp of roads to battle. Still, he didn't regret the effort spent on arriving there. The alternative of staying back home, cooped inside by the unexpected spell of heavy rain along with the brooding, atypically irritable father, silent, tight-lipped mother, and this chatter-box of silliness that was his elder brother's wife was daunting, to say the least. Enough that he had to endure it for two days and nights by now, since the evening the accursed trader had brought his awfully miserable news that didn't make any sense.

Even after two days of brooding, he couldn't find any reasonable explanation to illogical claims. The man had lied, or the Tenochtitlan's metalworker had lied, both filthy pieces of rotten meat, going away with the last of their family treasures, the prettily smooth pieces of green stone, leaving nothing but bitterness and frustration in their wake. No more warm, relatively cozy evenings by the fire, something he didn't cherish that much before but now was missing most acutely. When they were small, it was the best time of the day, with Father and Mother and both of his brothers, tired but fed and cleaned of the remnants from the depth of the earth or the fields, messing around or resting, listening to Father's stories, or their parents' conversations, lazing at the friendly warmth of the fire in the middle of the earthen floor, nibbling on occasional fields' treats, sweet grass or the ear of the early maize. No one was troubled back then. The outside world didn't even exist. Nothing beyond the fields and the hills dotted with adits. No Oaxtepec, no distant Cuauhnahuac, and certainly not the legendary gods-accursed Tenochtitlan that swallowed people and made them disappear, spitting out nothing but confusing stories that didn't make any sense.

Clenching his teeth, he pulled his legs out of the plopping mud with renewed determination, hastening his step, eager to reach the shed in the next parallel pathway to one he tread now before the new spell of rain caught him again, soaking the last of his loincloth and splattering it with more mud, making him look even less presentable than he might be already looking.

Scowling, he glanced at the once-again darkening sky, anticipating dubious gazes or scathing remarks, with him now looking no better than a strange creature out of the woods. Sometimes the people of this town overplayed their importance, pretended to be more urbanized than the despised villages. Even though Tenochtitlan nobles in their villas and their privately tended gardens and fields would not be able to tell the difference, he suspected. Oaxtepec people or the villagers must have looked the same to the mighty conquerors from the mysterious capital-island. Still, it was better to take some snobbery, to fight it off whenever he could, than to stay at home and do nothing of importance. The world was bigger than their fields and their mines and one could not be expected to work those until one died.

Also this time, he had a better reason to join the unauthorized gathering than his regular boredom and restlessness. These people might know something about Tenochtitlan, more than any dweller of Tetletzinco. There were always new faces in those meetings, newly recruited Oaxtepec residents, or villagers from other settlements that dotted their valleys and hills aplenty. Some people were said to bring news all the way from the all-important Cuauhnahuac or the hilly Tlayacapan, which meant that they must have been coming from those western or northern areas. And what was to stop them from bringing word from Tenochtitlan itself? Not of his missing youngest sibling, of course, but maybe some clue, some hint or a lead. If Miztli indeed had gotten involved with the criminal elements of the mighty capital, then word of such activities and people was actually more likely to reach him here, among the frowned-upon element of this town, with their often dubious activities or unauthorized meetings that talked of violence and outright revolt. An encouraging thought.

A gap between lines of tended plots beckoned. To cut through those seemed like a real possibility. It might bring him too close to peoples' dwellings that in this part of the town were clustering together in the strangest of manners, but the opportunity to shorten his way was too tempting. The rapidly dimming light urged him to do so. It felt like dusk was upon them, when his count of time told him that it was not even midmorning, with another tempest bearing on them rapidly, about to erupt.

Stepping over sprouting beans and tomato growths, he didn't notice the girl until practically treading on her, crouched between the rustling greenery, clearly attending to the most basic of needs.

"Don't!" he cried out as she opened her mouth too wide, obviously intending to scream her hardest. On her feet now, she reeled lightly, her skirt partly up, exposing the length of her legs but nothing more indecent than that. "I'm just passing through. I'm sorry!"

"You... you what?" she stuttered, still reeling, but already busy smoothing her skirt, hastily at that.

"I'm nothing," he hurried on, the vision of her legs and the way she squatted there before haunting, interrupting with his ability to concentrate. "Nothing at all. Forget it. I was just, just passing through." Again, his eyes slipped toward the splattered skirt quite against his will. "I didn't mean to..."

"You slimy piece of animal excrement!" A hasty glimpse of her face informed him that she had gathered her senses and that her rage might have been a spectacular thing to watch under different circumstances, not while being a target of it and in the wrong. "You dirty, nasty, disgusting, sickness stricken rat! I can't believe you—"

He didn't stay to listen to more of her shrill cries, even though she presented not a bad view, with her eyes nicely large and shimmering, shooting thunderbolts, and her well defined cheekbones glowing in colors that did not reflect the grayness of the surrounding light. Still, it was her domain, not his, and he was in the wrong, an intruder, a foreigner, not the local of this alley or the neighboring one to seek shortcuts through other people's dwellings and plots.

Hopping over the nearest low fence, he tried not to slip, the splintered wood tearing at his skin, letting him know of its private displeasure. The slippery mud did its best against him as well, but he managed to clamber his way without additional thrashing, leaping over few other obstacles, her screams joined by additional voices rendering his limbs with an extra strength.

By the time he had reached the familiar round shed, its walls made of adobe and not just unvarnished wood, he was scratched all over and splattered badly, out of breath and near panic. Still, his senses made him pause. Drops of rain were splashing heavily all around, bouncing off the previously scattered puddles.

Turning his face toward the gloomy sky, he let those wash it thoroughly, his heart still thundering, still out of tempo. But for the resumed rain! Would these people try to chase him here? Not likely, not in the rain. And it was not like he did something worth chasing, stole or harmed. Stupid hysterical fox! He cursed, then let the rain wash the rest of his body, blessing Tlaloc as he always did. The God of Earth and Rain and Growth rarely disappointed. Even now, this new spell of showers could not have been better timed.

Soaked, but calm again and, most importantly, clean of mud, he made his way toward the blurry shed next to the towering round construction, the place of storage for crops, not the only one around this town. Oaxtepec was not as large and as important as

Cuauhnahuac, but its crops were plentiful, always.

It was darker inside, but he could see squatting people, quite a few silhouettes, at least half twenty, probably more. He pushed his way in with as much confidence as he could muster. The brief silence that fell frayed his nerves badly.

"Who are you?" The question rang loudly, overcoming the hum of the outside showers.

He swallowed. "Elotl, from Teteltzinco."

Another spell of uneasy silence.

"Where did you spring from? And in such weather!"

"It wasn't raining until now."

"Doesn't look like that by the sight of you." One of the men shifted, then motioned him to join their circle. "Make space for the youth. He is the only one from our villager supporters who isn't scared by a few drops of rain."

They moved readily, and he slipped into the indicated place, grateful for the semidarkness that concealed the state of his grazed limbs and the soaked loincloth. Enough that his feet made embarrassingly plopping sounds upon the earthen floor.

"What is going on in your village, Teteltzinco boy?" asked one of the men, the oldest of this local gang, over twenty summers and usually in charge. His name was Metl and, like the rest of them, he worked the fields of his family, until the tribute collectors from Tenochtitlan itself and not Cuauhnahuac as usual came to pick a working force that was to dig irrigation canals for the new fields that were cleared rapidly all over the western hills and the villas of the nobility these days, huge undertaking no one could imagine or understand. Plenty of strong youths were commanded, harming the town's and the surrounding villages' ability to keep up with their regular chores. Not that the Great Capital bothered to lower the usual monthly tribute. Their ambitious undertakings had nothing to do with it.

"Nothing. Nothing out of the ordinary."

"Have you been visited by the tribute collectors?"

"No, not yet. They come when the moon is full, and it's at least five, six dawns from now."

"Will your village have trouble to pay what is due?"

He shrugged, surprised by the interrogation, unsettled by it. What did the general affairs of his village have to do with his willingness to be involved in this or that movement of more discontented among the rebellious elements of Oaxtepec? He was here on his own, representing no one but himself. Not some respectable elder like Father, who was supposed to collect what was due, then try to make the collectors go away satisfied with the amount, usually less than what was demanded. Who could afford to pay some of the luxury items they didn't even know how to produce, feathered headdresses or mysterious cocoa beans no one even saw up close but only heard about? And anyway, he trusted these Oaxtepec people but only up to a certain point. Not enough to tell the tales of ruined mines and how much work it took to repair the damage, setting them back on their workload at least three dawns, maybe more. Or about his missing brother, this same hated island-capital's fault this time.

"Cuauhnahuac sent a delegation to Tenochtitlan," one of the others was saying, apparently not as interested in Elotl's village's affairs as their leader was. "My uncle's wife's second brother said they rushed out in an indecent hurry, intending to reach the Great Lake in a mere few days of walking and before those bastards of Tenantzinco from their west."

"What do they want?" Their leading man's voice hardened.

The chatty informant flinched. "I don't know. I haven't had time to ask that. I only overheard them talking, Metl. I couldn't possibly start asking questions."

"When did they leave?"

"Two, three dawns ago, my uncle says." Hurriedly, the other youth leaned forward, placating. "His wife's brother arrived here only on the evening before. He is sick and seeking healing herbs only our woods are producing."

"They are in Tenochtitlan already, I bet." Metl was not to be sidetracked. "But what would this filthy town wish to say to the filthy islanders and in such a hurry? Why would they undertake a journey in unfavorable weather like that?" He leaned forward in his turn, causing the other youth to flinch again. "Find that out. Everything that your uncle's brother knows. Everything!"

"I will, I will!" The chatty one shifted about, making much noise. "It won't be difficult. That man is talkative and I can offer to take him around, visit one of the villages in his search for a healer. He had accosted both ours already and I don't think they helped him besides plenty of blurry talk. Oh, and while taking his presents, of course. Both did not neglect taking his offerings."

Speaking of being talkative, some traits certainly run in some families, reflected Elotl, mildly interested. He didn't know exactly where this powerful Cuauhnahuac with their tribute collectors was, but the fact that their delegation went to Tenochtitlan jarred. If only he could have approached these people, somehow, talked them into taking him along or at least visiting Miztli's metalworker again, asking more precise questions.

Metl's voice rasped with anger. "Cuauhnahuac will be taking Tenochtitlan's side if it comes to war. I'm prepared to bet my club against such a claim!"

"There must be people like us in Cuauhnahuac as well." The man who said this was thin and stringy-looking, familiar to Elotl from other such meetings as opposed to the one who was chatting about his sick uncle. "Maybe if we managed to connect with them..."

"Our own town is full of traitors as it is," grunted another, a quiet youth of the same age as Elotl was. "Out there in this same Cuauhnahuac, they must be betting that our Oaxtepec is ready to grovel before Tenochtitlan just as their elders do."

"Well, we aren't!" Metl banged his open palm against the earthen floor, getting no worthwhile sounds good wooden planks might have produced. "But we need to be more organized, more forceful in our actions. Otherwise, indeed, outsiders might think that Oaxtepec will do whatever Tenochtitlan or even this same Cuauhnahuac would tell it to." Another punch at the hapless floor was echoed by the thunder rolling above their heads, making the rundown construction rattle. "We must act and not only talk. The canals they make us work on, there must be a way to damage those, to put them out of use."

"How would you do that? Fill it with earth again?" The stringy youth shrugged quite contemptuously, to Elotl's growing disquiet. It was not often that their forceful young leader took an open critique well, certainly not from the closest of followers. There were times when some bigger gatherings on the main square of Oaxtepec got to clashes or verbally violent exchanges. Not everyone agreed on the nature of their grievances, let alone the ways to deal with those. Only on the necessity to do something, to make the tribute collectors leave and not to come back. Also what were they talking about? he wondered. How one dug canals or filled them back up? Like Father's tunnels and mines?

"I don't know *that*. I'm not a stinking engineer from the stinking Great Lake. But there must be a way. And if you don't have suggestions, you better keep your mouth shut!"

A brief spell of silence prevailed, with another round of thunder, more distant than the previous one, rolling by.

"How did you dig those things in the first place?" asked the chatty youth with Cuauhnahuac uncle. "How do they make rivers flow the way they want?"

How indeed? wondered Elotl, leaning forward despite the discomfort of his wet loincloth and hair.

"Like you dig anything else," grunted Metl, still busy staring down his rebellious peer. "I'm not a stinking engineer. They plan how, and we are just made to dig all day long. With bad quality tools! Rotten digging sticks and all that. Not something you would work with, not even your family plot. Good tools they are keeping for their own, slaves and engineers and whoever else that is coming from their stinking island." He frowned again. "There must be a way to make them stop digging, to leave our valley and hills alone."

"If one of us was an engineer, we would know what to do." One of the youths got up, then strolled toward the doorway, peering outside while greeting a few dripping newcomers, shapeless forms on the background of the slashing grey. Some followed him with their eyes, others began chattering between themselves. Craving to check the happenings outside as well, Elotl didn't dare to move, not wishing to draw attention to himself. Metl, he noticed, was frozen in his previous pose, staring ahead, deep in thought. Many gazes were still upon him.

"We can kidnap one of their engineers," he said finally, his eyes narrow, gaze still wandering. "Make him talk, explain things to us. While he is still alive, that is." His eyes glowed eerily, an unsettling sight.

Elotl shuddered, then forced his limbs into stillness. He was not a silly villager afraid of a killing, was he? He would not flee in horror from such a solution. Father was wrong about it, and many other things. They didn't have to tolerate the tribute collectors only because there would always be ones eager to collect tribute. There must be ways to achieve independence and then to keep it against all sorts of warriors and anyone who wished to impose a new tribute upon their villages. Also, there must be a way to find out what happened to Miztli, to reach him and hear his side of the story. Father was wrong about that too!

"This rain is ruining pretty ponds up there in the villas," one of the newcomers was saying, shaking himself like a coyote to get rid of the worst of the water. "It is early for mighty Tlaloc to favor us so."

"What is your news?" demanded Metl, on his feet as well now and peering at the newcomers impatiently. "What did you hear?"

The second man was squeezing his bundled hair. "On the day before this one, our elders received some important-looking visitors from Tollocan."

"Tollocan? Where is that?"

"Out there in the west. Three days' walk, maybe four."

"What did they want?"

The first newcomer looked around wistfully. "Why don't you make a fire? It's cold and wet, and your hospitality can use improvement."

Elotl held his breath, startled by such an openly sounded complaint. And so did the others, he noticed. Metl was not a person to accept an open critique or reproach.

For a moment, the young man's face twisted, but his flashing eyes were the only thing to disclose his fury. When he spoke, his voice rang with unperturbed calmness.

"We cannot afford to be hospitable to our sympathizers, not

yet." His hand gestured widely, indicating their meager surroundings. "When we are successful, it will be different. For all of us." The last words came out pointedly, carrying a clear message.

"Well, you can at least make a fire in this pitiful shed," said the guest, unimpressed. Then he shrugged and left his dripping hair alone. "The valleys out there beyond the western highlands are in unrest and in conflict with each other. The war will break there, and those same Tollocan and their neighboring Matlatzinco are allied and determined."

Still scowling, Metl nodded, then motioned one of the youths. "Go tell my sisters to bring food for our guests." Another heartbeat of hesitation saw him shrugging as well. "Bring some firewood along the way. You two, help him along."

The visitors said nothing, while Elotl breathed with relief, not wishing to be sent away, eager to hear the news. What were those towns and valleys? Where were they, and what was their importance, or how were they connected to Metl and his followers' irritation with Tenochtitlan's presence and rule?

"Tollocan is larger than Cuauhnahuac, and in conflict with Tenantzinco to their south," went on one of the visitors, squeezing the fringes of his loincloth this time. "They said that Tenantzinco's whiny ruler went as far as Tenochtitlan with his complaints."

"Tenochtitlan?" Metl's eyes sparkled. "Do they pay tribute to Tenochtitlan, those people from beyond the western highlands?"

"Some of them pay like we do, some don't." The man made a face, then winked at his companion. "Tenantzinco obviously does. Otherwise, they wouldn't be that eager to involve that rapacious island in their local affairs. I doubt that Tollocan or the other one pays a single maize or cocoa load, or maybe they are just ready to stop paying those. They don't seem to be afraid or fearful. Just like your hotheaded folk, they think that the giant *altepetl* cannot bend them into submission. The records of their conquests do not shadow your plans, do they?"

Metl's scowl had deepened again; still, the young man controlled his temper, obviously trying to impress his guests with anything but a hotheaded reaction, so typical of him otherwise.

"Tenochtitlan did not conquer our valley and hills. Cuauhnahuac was the one to be conquered again and again, but not our Oaxtepec and the surrounding villages."

"We know that, young man." The second visitor wore something close to an offensive fatherly smile. "Still, our town and those same pitiful villages do pay the required tribute, do provide manpower to serve their villas and fields and their engineers to dig new rivers and streams. Conquered or just persuaded, it doesn't matter. We pay and we serve and our situation is not that bad. If we provoke them into conquering us, properly conquering, we may find ourselves with even less means to make our living."

"Or we may find ourselves free of their hateful presence and their filthy demands," exclaimed Metl hotly, this time in a typical way, his fists clenching, ready to come to his words' aid. "There are many of us who feel that way, many who are ready to sacrifice some petty comforts, not to mention our lives, in order to throw the yoke of the rapacious Mexicas. We are many and we are not afraid!"

For a while, silence triumphed. Elotl didn't dare to breathe, cursing the sounds of nearing people that interrupted the staring contest. The youths that were sent for food and the firewood must have been coming back, but even though he was dead hungry, he wished to listen more than that. The newcomers talked well, told fascinating things. Until now, he had heard only Metl and his peers. Never someone as knowledgeable and yet convinced of the opposite views. Why, those newcomers sounded like Father, deliberate and thoughtful and yet unafraid, ready to speak their minds and be challenged for it. Did Father know about those conflicted faraway places they mentioned, Tollocan and another town that sounded like the tongue they had spoken before the expanding Mexicas made Nahuatl into the tongue everyone used these days, even in the privacy of their homes. Still, Father made sure they could speak the Matlatzinca dialect as well.

"How many men are ready to follow you here in Oaxtepec?" asked the first guest while the returning youths poured in, carrying armloads of branches and sticks.

"Many," stated Metl as curtly, not bestowing a passing glance toward the entrance, staring heavily at his challenger instead. "Enough to make a difference." The young man's lips twisted unpleasantly. "Enough for you to come here and consult us."

The newcomer's mouth was twitching in a matching manner, as stony and promising no good. "We brought you news that is important to all of us. It doesn't mean that we approve of your plans any more than we did until now."

"And yet you are here." Metl's lips were nothing but an invisible line.

"To advise you on the developments. To listen to your claims and maybe try to understand those." The visitor's words came out yet stonier. "To attempt coordinate our actions." His wide muddied shoulders lifted in a shrug. "Our people should be united, not divided. We could achieve better results, less tribute maybe, more of the same independence that you crave so. We can achieve that if we are wise. And patient. Not provocative with silly acts of bravery that would bring fleeting glory but would cost our people dearly in the long run."

The youth with the armloads of branches began toiling near the doorway, making a small sheltered fire, careful not to let the flames lick the beams of the entrance, or worse yet, the contents of the shed piled in baskets and jars, maize, beans, green round tomatoes, the precious fields' production, not plentiful in this time of the seasons but enough to warrant its transfer to the nearby elevated construction. When a young man squatting next to him got to his feet, Elotl joined him, wishing to be of help. His chance to partake in the food offering was better this way.

"Make the sparks fly, Teteltzinco youth."

Two flint stones were tossed at him, and it pleased him that he caught both with no effort. To arrange dry grass took him no time. In doing so, he side-glanced two girls forcing their way in, the bowls in their hands balanced with an effort, exuding a wonderfully heavy aroma, their baskets loaded with tortillas. His stomach reacted at once, and so did his heart. It skipped a beat, then tottered, threatening to slip into his empty belly as well.

The girl from the drizzled plots led the way, walking demurely, paying little attention to the gazes that leapt to her and her companion, not all of them interested in the food. Even in the semidarkness of the shed, it was easy to recognize her prominent features, the splattered skirt hiding the length of her legs, but not the way those swayed, temptingly, with blatant invitation. He stared at them for a heartbeat, then took his gaze away, bending above his cluster of dry grass quickly, but not quickly enough. He could feel her eyes boring at him, drilling holes in his skin. Her snort said it all – so much scorn and outright disdain. He doubled his effort with the stones, wishing to be anywhere but here now.

"We don't have to tolerate Tenochtitlan's presence, dig their canals, or work their fields, trying to grow their stupid and useless cocoa beans," Metl was saying, his anger bubbling, threatening to spill out. The pretense of the older and prudent leader didn't hold for too long.

Elotl didn't care, busy thinking of sneaking out and away. If the girl decided to make trouble, accuse him of intruding or worse yet, spying on her while she was attending the private business of making her needs – a true enough claim, come to think of it, even though he hadn't been watching her at all! – he would not be listened to, not him. A wandering youth from the neighboring village, not one of them. And was she one of this same angry Metl's sisters? Oh mighty deities! For if she was, he was done for, absolutely done for!

The grass under his hands long since ignited, the flames running merrily, consuming it. He fetched it absently, to toss into the round pile the others prepared, feeling the eyes of both girls upon him now, their giggles covered but not quite. Outside, the storm piqued, the thunder deafening, drowning their words in its outbursts. For the best maybe, he reflected, sneaking a glance at Metl and his older guests. It would be unseemly to turn violent toward such visitors, and if they kept arguing, it might happen. He had seen the hot-tempered Oaxtepec dwellers losing their temper on lesser provocations than words doubting their more passionate of undertakings.

"Quite a tempest." One of the youths beside him reached for the fire that was already flickering, spreading its much coveted illumination and warmth. Another of those who brought the firewood fed a larger branch to it carefully, watching the flames, making sure they didn't try to sneak along the obstacles that were dotting the earthen floor. "I don't envy you your trip back home, to your gods' forsaken village, boy."

"Teteltzinco is not gods' forsaken, and the way there is easy, no sweat," he retorted, not liking that "boy" bit. They had no cause to be condescending toward him. Their Oaxtepec was no Cuauhnahuac or Tenochtitlan either.

"Would you listen to that one?" The youth who was warming his hands made a face. "If those villagers cared for anything but their filthy fields, they would have been here, helping us, wouldn't they?"

The other one nodded placidly. "Yes, Teteltzinco youth. You people are not very keen on the happenings outside your fields and your holes in the earth. Who comes here besides you? No one."

"My brother is living in Tenochtitlan itself; having a good time there, too!"

"Tenochtitlan?" They cried it out in unison and just as the drumming upon the slanted roof lessened all of a sudden, making their words ring.

"What about Tenochtitlan?" Metl, on his feet now and motioning the visitors toward the girls and their food offering politely, in the fashion of perfect host, looked at them sharply.

"Nothing." One of Elotl's converser's quailed, while the other straightened up hastily.

"The villager from Teteltzinco boasts close contacts there," he explained eagerly. "He says his cousin—"

The piercing eyes were upon him now. "Whom do you know on that filthy island?"

Elotl fought the need to draw in a deep breath. "My brother," he said as calmly as he could, anxious to hide his uneasiness, or maybe even fear.

"Your brother? You said nothing about it before!" That came out menacingly, an outright accusation.

He felt his own anger rising as well. "You never asked."

A new assault on the hapless roof had them growing quiet for a moment. The older visitors eyed him with an open curiosity, having deigned to notice his very existence for the first time. About the girls he didn't even dare to think, concentrating on the glare of their leader, gathering his courage for whatever was coming. To be the center of their attention wasn't that bad but for the wrong timing. He might have welcomed the opportunity to gain some ground with them in this way, but not today, not with the glowering visitors and the angered girls.

"What is he doing there?" In the renewed pause in the storm, Metl came closer. "Next time, tell it all to me before you even enter these premises. Is that clear to you, villager?"

He didn't have to force himself from taking a step back this time. On the contrary, it was difficult to make himself remain still without pouncing on his offender. The familiar splash of anger was near, clouding his senses. "You didn't ask about my family. And even if you did, I don't have to tell you a thing. They have nothing to do with any of it!"

"They have everything to do with it!" There was a growl to the taller youth's voice now, a low, grating, threatening sound. "And you will not talk to me like that again. Is that clear to you?"

He didn't move when the broad features thrust closer, the last words breathed into his face along with the remnants of the chewed tortilla. Clenching his fists so tightly his fingers hurt, he prepared for the first blow, intending to duck, then lunge an attack of his own, knowing where to land his fist, on the side of the head, near the eyes, the punch Father taught them and said never to use unless in the dire need, a punch that he used to a telling effect several times. It would usually leave his previous rivals disoriented enough, discouraging the further attempts to fight, even though Father said such a punch could leave a person senseless.

"Stop that, you two." One of the older visitors didn't move, but his voice rang calmly, overcoming the steady hum of the outside downpour. "If you are so eager to fight, do it after we have left. Until then, show some maturity. If you are nothing but hotheaded boys, all of you, then there is nothing to talk about, nothing at all."

In the corner of his mind, where the red wave splashed not as fiercely, he could feel the others letting out their breath, beginning to move around. Still, his eyes remained glued to those of his possible attacker, a pair of glowing embers, like that of predators at night when camping in the woods, with only the fire to keep you from the wolves if they showed an interest in you. There had been such a night once, with Father and other hunters, and he never forgot the glowing dots inhabiting the darkness and the bottomless fear they brought. Men weren't scary; the predators in the woods were.

"I will deal with you later." The glowering face turned away with finality and abruptness that didn't suit the unsolved confrontation. "Serve the food to our guests!" This was tossed toward the girls, who watched with everyone else, spellbound. He could feel their gazes, not as dismissive as before. The need to take a deep breath became overwhelming.

"Where are you from, young man?" This came from the visitor who did the most of the talking.

"Teteltzinco village." He was pleased to hear his voice satisfactorily steady. The waves of fury were still there, still splashing.

"Oh, the miners' village." The man nodded thoughtfully, his eyes kind. "The rainy season is tough on that business."

He forced his thoughts to concentrate. "Well, yes. There was this tunnel that collapsed only the other day. It was raining on this night too."

"Many got hurt?"

He wondered at the surprisingly well-meaning inquiry. "Only a few." The shivers the memories alone brought were annoying. "No one got killed or buried."

"Good." Another thoughtful nod. "What is your brother doing in Tenochtitlan?"

"Well, we don't know exactly." He stopped himself in time, before blurting out the entire story. It was not these Oaxtepec people's business and back home they didn't know what happened anyway, nothing but an embarrassingly silly accusation that made not the slightest sense. Enough that they talked about it day and night at home now, wondering, arguing, growing atypically angry with each other and everyone – Father and Mother and even Tletl with his stupid crybaby of a wife. Only their newborn had nothing to say on the matter, but it was only because he still didn't know how to talk, was Elotl's grim conclusion, being the only one who didn't say a word about any of that, not after Father's undeserved dressing down on the night road.

"What do you mean?"

He concentrated again. "My brother was sent to Tenochtitlan, to learn the trade of the metalworkers. But he left the workshop he worked at and joined rebellious elements of that *altepetl*. Young people who are not content with that city's way of doing things." Astounded, he listened to the words that were pouring from his mouth, sounding better with every passing heartbeat, worthy and impressive, full of significance. The silence of his audience told him so, their undivided attention. Even the rain ceased to beat on the roof and the ground around their shelter, as though eager to give him an appropriate stage and a background. "I don't know much about these people's activities yet, as it has been difficult to pass word between here and Tenochtitlan, but he promised to let me know as soon as he could. Send word, or even come in person. He takes our towns and villages' interest close to his heart. Like the rest of our family, he cares for our independence and honor."

The trickling of the small streams outside the shed seemed to be the only sound. He drew a deep breath, rethinking hastily what had been said. Could they prove him wrong, flush his lies out? Not unless Miztli came back, and even then. His brother had no ties in Oaxtepec. To the best of his memory, the indifferent piece of meat barely stepped his foot in the neighboring town. A relief!

"Quite a story," someone breathed, then the sounds resumed, of people moving and talking quietly between themselves.

"What did he tell you about Tenochtitlan's people? What is bothering them? Their so-called commoners." A fleeting grin blossomed, to be replaced with the previous piercing thoughtfulness as swiftly. "Your brother isn't moving in higher circles than fieldworkers and fishermen, I presume."

He grinned back, amused by the very thought. "Yes, he is

involved with those who are not happy with what is happening there. He promised to send me word about it all soon."

"How long has he been there?" This came from Metl, still angrily.

Elotl made sure his face reflected nothing untoward, no fear and not too much deference, his anger returning as well. That man was not his father or an elder brother, not even a cousin or anything. Just the leader of the local bunch of discontented hotheads. "About four moons. He left when the last rains were still falling."

The girls were pouring steamy maize gruel into a pair of round bowls.

"Bring more of those," demanded Metl importantly, strolling to squat beside his guests.

The girl from the nearby plots gave her brother a sullen look. The other one shrugged. She was actually better looking than her companion, trimmer and curvier. Still, his eyes kept drifting toward the first one, despite the embarrassing incident. There was something about this fox, something vibrant and spicy.

"Do you know where your brother is staying?" The question came from the second guest, his forehead creased with an obvious thought-process, nodding absently at the girl who had offered him the first bowl.

Elotl cursed his loose tongue for the first time. They were asking too many questions he had no answers to and why didn't they get back to their business at hand?

"More or less. He is moving around, not staying in one place." He shrugged, then busied himself with following the distributed bowls with his gaze. Would he be offered one? His stomach churned loudly at the very thought. "Tenochtitlan authorities are not happy with their group any more than they are happy with yours here. So he is moving around, not staying for them to lay their hands on him in order to drag him to their courts."

Which was not that far away from the truth, he reasoned, his uneasiness returning. He was taking it too far now, getting carried away with stories that had little to do with truth, a tendency that sometimes landed him in unnecessary trouble when he was younger. But he was a man now, not a boy to lie and try to wriggle out of it later on. Those were serious matters. Even though his brother *was* in Tenochtitlan, connected to some dubious elements there, facing this mysteriously ominous thing called "courts," wasn't he? That was what the trader claimed, with these very words.

He answered their gazes with as much calm and presence of mind as he could muster, aware of the girls' unashamed staring. Not so unimportant anymore, huh?

"Tenochtitlan is two, three days of traveling away," the second guest was musing, paying no attention to the cooling bowl in his hands. "Not so far and just as the fields are not needing too much attention." A narrowed gaze brushed past him, then rested on the other newcomer. "We could use firsthand information coming straight from the mighty island, couldn't we?"

"Maybe." The other man nodded, as immersed in his thoughts, his gaze scrutinizing. "The fields can do without you for a few dawns, can't they, young man?"

"They are working tunnels and mines in his village," volunteered Metl, not about to be left out, not this one. "They must be needing him in one of those, if not in the fields."

Elotl fought another wave of fierce irritation down. "The adits are not worked when the rains make the earth unstable. It's dangerous and unnecessary." That came out well. He held his head high, answering their gazes, not averting his. "I can get away for a few dawns, maybe five, six, if the rain continues."

But what was he talking about? What was he offering? He pushed the misgivings away, his stomach churning, head light. Even if the rains came unusually early, here they were, rendering the regular life impossible to proceed with, their work delayed, even for a few days at the most, enough to travel, to do something useful. And hadn't he come here in hopes of finding a clue, some word from Tenochtitlan maybe, an opportunity to hear something that might help them find Miztli or his whereabouts? He did, didn't he? And why couldn't he travel to this same Tenochtitlan himself, look for his brother? It would take him two, three dawns, the important men of Oaxtepec said. Five dawns on his way back and forth, a few more to look around, enough for the rains to hold on, and they could spare his efforts back home. He wasn't that efficient anyway. Father and Tletl could do without him until it became dry again.

Metl was staring at him bleakly. He returned the nasty glare, not about to be stared down. That one was not his leader to render his services or refuse to offer those. He was his own keeper.

"If you think I can be of use in Tenochtitlan, I will go there with no delay," he said, turning his eyes to the eating guests. "I can absent myself from my duties for a few dawns, even half a moon."

They nodded thoughtfully, moving their heads in unison, exchanging more glances. "You are a brave youth. Come with us when we finish here."

The girl from the plots materialized next to him, a steaming bowl balanced easily on her palm, even though it must have been scalding hot. Her gaze held his but only for a moment.

"If you want to add nice gravy to this meal, sneak out in the next few heartbeats." Her whisper was nothing but a breath of air, the swish of her muddied skirt rustling nicely, enhancing her message.

CHAPTER 6

The moment her elder brother Acatlo entered the house, Chantli slipped away and across the alley, rushing for the workshop where her second brother might still be present, or so she hoped, finishing the tasks of the day. Not tidying up, grumpy and in ill-humor, not anymore. The slave boy Father bought after the temple orders brought in plenty of payment, more than they expected, did the tidying up and the cleaning now, thanks the benevolent Flayed Deity for that. It improved the situation at home considerably, as now all males of the house began looking less grim, more approachable.

Not that she wanted to approach them, certainly not Acatlo, but it was still nicer to be at home in the evenings, with no long stretches of heavy silence and grudging glances. Even the visit of the mysterious trader from the south, a man who came to inquire about Miztli or so she had been informed by her little brother one day when she returned from school, the news whispered to her outside and in secret, did not manage to ruin the atmosphere, though it did anger Father at this time, the meeting and the memories it brought along. He had told awful things about the village apprentice, her little brother had whispered, agog with excitement, his eyes sparkling. Real awful things. That the villager had run away, stole, joined smugglers, and was sought by the courts, or committed other terrible crimes.

Horrified, she didn't find enough courage to talk to Miztli about that, even though it happened close to two market intervals ago by now, well after Tlatelolco fell. And yet she wanted to know more before venturing into this sort of talk, to find out who this inquirer was, maybe, or at least what he wanted exactly. An opportunity that did not present itself until now.

The screen shielding the entrance into the smaller shed adjacent to the melting room screeched, interrupting the typical clacking of various tools being moved and the familiar hum of the hissing coals. It was easy to guess that the fires were put out some time ago for their embers still whispered, refusing to let the life in them go. Miztli would always pile the remaining wood inside both braziers, make a fire, then hurry to cover the flames and all the openings in the stone constructions, allowing no air in, thus making the embers good for use on the next day. Father had commented favorably on this technique, careful to do so only when the village boy wasn't around. To the villager, he pretended that he knew all about such ways, of course, and that it was not something special or even favored in the sophisticated Great Capital, but that the uncouth foreigner could use his ways if he wished to do so. How silly. Had Father appreciated this boy, if only a little, let him know how satisfied he was...

She shrugged, then made her way around and into the heat of the outer room, still messed up from the day's work. The village boy was eminently better off now, attending school, en-route to become an elite warrior with an obsidian sword and plenty of good connections, with leaders like the Texcocan scar-faced man looking favorably on him and even the Emperor himself finding him of use yet again, thanks to the ever-resourceful Ahuitzotl. Oh yes, that young *pilli* rascal got his way once again, didn't he? The memories of the afternoon Plaza made her smile.

"What are you doing here?" Her second brother OmeTelpochtli, or just Ome, as he hated to be addressed despite everyone doing this, came out of the melting room, wiping his face with a crumpled piece of cloth, not doing a good job with it. The amount of soot smeared over his nicely broad features was staggering. "Bring me that water bowl."

"Here." She rushed toward the required vessels before being asked. "Was there much to do in the melting room today?"

"What do you think?" he muttered, receiving the bowl with a casual nod of thanks, fishing what looked like an affectionate smile from the depths of his frown. He was a nice person, quiet and reticent, pleasant enough company when not busy trying to emulate his older sibling.

"I thought it became easier after the temple's order and with the new boy around. Where is he?"

"Trying to put the fire out without putting this entire workshop to torch." Blinking the dripping water away, the squat man rolled his eyes in the same movement, an impossible feat. "I have to watch his every step, stay here when everyone is already out and about and see that he doesn't do something stupid until the fire is safely off. And I didn't even begin to teach him how to store the embers in the way the village scum did." His grunt overcame the sound of the stone brazier being dragged over the earthen floor. "The villager at least did his work properly, understood our tongue, didn't need help or supervision. But this one," another eye roll accompanied the new grunt, "this one is useless; skinny, a weakling. If Father wanted a slave to clean the workshop and nothing more, he could have at least bought a creature that understands our tongue properly."

By this time, she began pitying the new boy, indeed a frightened foreigner of an unimpressive size, a captive from somewhere far enough to speak only basic Nahuatl, if at all. Had Father not enough means to buy a better fitting aide?

"You'll manage to teach him with the passing of time, I'm sure you will," she said soothingly, hunting for a clean cloth to offer him from a chest full of lighter tools. "All that the village boy did, this one will do as well."

Skeptically arched eyebrows were her answer. "This one will never manage to lift an empty brazier, let alone a pot full of melted copper."

"Well, yes, but the other things." She shrugged, losing her patience and fast. She didn't come here to comfort her whiny siblings, any of them, even though Ome was ten times better than Acatlo, whose company she avoided as best as she could these days. "Speaking of the villager, who was the man who came asking questions about him?"

He shrugged with as much indifference as she did before.

"Some foreigner. A trader. From his areas. A southerner."

"Oh!" She tried to think it all through. "From his village?"

"Maybe."

"What did he want to know?"

His side-glance interrupted his cleaning efforts if briefly. "Why do you care?"

"I don't," she said hurriedly, busying herself with a hunt after another clean cloth. "I'll bring you more water from the house. You look too dirty to even try to cross the street, let alone head for *temazcalli*."

He rolled his eyes once again, but when she came back running, anxious to have them finish their conversation with no interruptions, he was flanked by the slave boy, a sight of blackened face and limbs, putting her brother's previous appearance to shame.

"Go wash yourself at the lake shore and be back in a matter of heartbeats." To her relief, Ome waved their new company away, then accepted her bowl, not looking angered or suspicious.

"I wasn't asking about the village boy because I care," she ventured, unsure of herself. "I was just curious."

"Sure you are," he said, making a face at her, not an unfriendly one. "You do see him and you do talk to him. It's him who wanted to know. Not you."

For a heartbeat, she found herself gaping. "Why... why do you say that?"

"Because I know it to be truth." His grin was twisting with amusement rather than anger.

"How?" she breathed, encouraged.

"Your chatty friend told me. That pretty one from down the alley. The stoneworker's daughter."

"Quetzalli?"

"Yes, that one. It's good that you are at school and not running around with her anymore. She is keeping bad company these days. If you were still with her, I would have let Father know."

Frantically, she tried to process this information, still stunned that he knew about her dealings with Miztli and that he wasn't angered or intending to tell on her. "What bad company?"

"As though you don't know."

"No, I don't! Like you said, I don't even see much of Quetzalli or Xochi. I'm at *calmecac* and around the temples for half days and more. I have no time for anything else!"

He acknowledged it with a thoughtful nod. "How is it out there in that noble school?"

She collected her thoughts hurriedly, surprised with his curiosity. Her older siblings paid her life no attention until now, not until she angered that brute Acatlo with her connections with Miztli. "It's nice out there, strange and different, but really nice."

"Second Mother says you are aiming to become a priestess."

"Yes," she said, trying to sound matter-of-fact and not like an excited child, hating the hot wave that washed over her face, impossible not to feel, and probably notice too. "But I like learning it. They force us to read and do complicated things with numbers and glyphs on sheets of *amate*-paper. Like Father's writings at the end of each moon."

His grin was again surprisingly light and well meaning. "You'll be doing Father's papers in the end."

"Why not?" She grinned back, then tried to return to the original topic before he lost this rare spell of good humor and easy familiarity. "What is the bad company that Quetzalli keeps? And what did she say about me? I swear I'm not running around here anywhere these days."

"Oh yes, your dubious noble company hangs nowhere around." The frown won again. "Your pretty friend from our alley, on the other hand, can be spotted in the company of the new rough folk that is now crowding certain warehouses and wharves since that looser of the neighboring *altepetl* stopped being the nuisance they always were."

"What new rough folk?" she demanded, fighting the urge to run out and find Quetzalli, knowing that her friend could do silly things, especially now that she must have been angered and offended by her, Chantli's, negligence and the village boy's preference of "weird creatures from gods-know-where," the way Quetzalli kept referring to the Tlatelolcan girl, nagging with repeated questioning, trying to make sure she didn't befriend the "bizarre-looking thing" as well. Which she tried not to, but for what happened today. If Quetzalli heard about their afternoon Plaza adventures, she would explode like a brazier with a fair amount of oil spilled into it.

Briefly, she remembered the Great Plaza, as crowded as on that night before the invasion of Tlatelolco but different, lit by the generous sunlight this time, less foreboding, all festive and babbling. Like an unusually glamorous and well-behaved marketplace on a market day, with nobles being all chatty and less overbearing, especially the ladies. It was fascinating up there among their litters and colorful fans, the haughty royal women not as stiff as one glimpsed them from time to time, traveling along in their litters, waving the commoner elements away.

Well, this time, there were no commoners to shoo out of the way but the servants who were there to take care of the noble ladies' needs. And her, the uninvited element. Oh, but how daunting it was in the beginning! She would have sneaked away but for the Tlatelolcan girl's insistence. Like Ahuitzotl, this one was either extremely naïve or astonishingly open-minded, or both, judging by the rest of this girl's behavior, from her open infatuation with Miztli to her violent misdeeds in school. Such an opposite to her haughtily noble sibling; in looks and in disposition. Could they truly be full sisters? As beautiful as a golden statue, the royal woman was not someone she, Chantli, would wish to spend time with given a choice, but the Tlatelolcan girl kept insisting, thinking maybe that she was doing her, Chantli, a favor by exposing her to the company she couldn't normally meet but by being honored with the status of Palace's maid. Who knew what this one had in mind?

And yes, it was an interesting experience, the noblewomen so beautifully dressed, so polite with each other but only on the surface. It was easy to see their occasional barbs directed at one another, especially when the imperial sister, Lady Jade Doll, appeared. This one did not spend twenty heartbeats there before proceeding to put plenty of noble ladies in their places, some with especially nice, especially poisonous pleasantries, hidden but barely under the coat of exaggerated politeness. Somehow, it became most clear when Tlemilli's sister was addressed, and Chantli couldn't help but to think of two market women about to go for each other's hair but using barbed pleasantries in place of customary curses, their message exactly the same. At some point, she remembered Tlemilli smirking, making faces and rolling her eyes, letting her, Chantli, know that it was all a matter of everyday life.

By then, Ahuitzotl was back, to summon the village boy to the imperial presence, and with good timing too, as at this point, the Emperor's noble sister decided to grace her youngest of siblings and his exotic companion with a conversation, turning amused and almost playful while addressing the village boy, enjoying his embarrassment and his barely coherent answers to her outright impish questions, playing with him. It was strange, this sauciness, and it reminded Chantli of her friend again, the times when Quetzalli would flirt with this same Miztli, embarrassing him into proper impoliteness. And yet this was the highest nobility, the imperial princess; not a neighboring girl from down their alley. It couldn't be that the woman was flirting with the commoner boy half of her age. It just couldn't be.

"Well, it's good that you are in that snotty school now," her brother was saying, chewing his lower lip while shaking his head slowly, as though answering his own thoughts. "If you were still going around with those girls, I would have talked to Father about it. They are up to no good, especially your empty-headed cheeky Quetzalli."

"Quetzalli is not cheeky and not empty-headed," protested Chantli, feeling called upon to defend her friend's honor. "She is just, you know, lively, full of spirit. She gets bored easily. I wish their First Mother put her at school already." Not that this would solve the problem, she knew, but was too loyal to admit that. Quetzalli would have been bored to death in either *calmecac* or *telpochcalli*, or learning to serve in the temples. And yet, her friend was not a bad person, just bored.

He put the bowl down, then wiped his face with the cleaner side of the second cloth. "Not cheeky and not empty-headed, and yet yesterday, she was slinking around the gathering near the old causeway, where Tlatelolcan scum is still operating but now under our local smugglers' command."

"The Tlatelolcans?" She had forgotten all about their conquered neighbors besides the exotic element of their surviving nobility that graced, or sometimes rather disgraced, Tenochtitlan's Royal Enclosure these days.

"Yes, the Tlatelolcans. What do they teach you out there in that noble school? How to sweep an altar and nothing else?"

"They teach us plenty!" she cried out, offended, then made a face, disarmed by the suddenness of his laughter. "You went to the *telpochcalli* of the marketplace. That's no *calmecac*."

"Snotty little you," he said, turning to go.

"Wait!" Springing to her feet as well, she caught him by the doorway, partly blocking his way, feeling confident to ask outright now, because of his unexpected openness. "What did this man want, the one who came to ask about the village boy? Who was he?" His climbing eyebrows made her hand rise in protest. "I'm asking for myself, not for him. He doesn't even know about it. He is in our school, yes, but we are not close, not talking or anything. He is busy with other things."

"What things?" he asked, his eyes clouding in a familiar fashion.

"Many things. He is a good boy and he does well at school, and the Emperor likes sending him on missions. But it has nothing to do with me. He never asked me about the workshop or our family or anything. I want to know it for myself."

"Why?" He was still frowning, his suspicion on display.

"I don't know. I just want to know, that's all. Maybe I'll tell him, maybe I won't. He is a good boy and doesn't deserve the hatred and ill-will of our family."

His eyes narrowed even more. "Do you have a thing for the villager?" he asked slowly, incredulous.

It took her a moment to understand. "What? No! How could you think something like that?"

He made a face, not impressed but looking relieved in a way. "You keep carrying on about that scum's virtues, taking his side against the entire family. One might start wondering." His grin flashed, one-sided and decidedly crooked. "Better that noble *pilli* with a spear than the villager, I say. If you insist on impossible choices, at least that one might be supporting you if you end up with a child. Not like the untrustworthy foreigner with no means."

She was still fighting for breath, too angered to think clearly. "I can't believe you say things like that. I'll tell Father!"

"While explaining why you've been asking about that trader who wanted to know about the filthy apprentice? I wish you well with this."

"It has nothing to do with me!"

"Then why are you asking?"

To stamp her foot against the earthen floor did not make her feel better, only hurt her ankle and one of the toes. Out of old custom, she didn't bother to put her sandals on when at home, even though now it felt strange to go around barefoot. "You... you can't talk to me like that. I'll tell Mother!"

He laughed outright. "Stop throwing fits like a spoiled brat. If I tell you what Father told that man, that southern trader, you will tell me what I want to know about the Great Plaza's gossip."

As much as she wished to scream at him, throw something, then run out, a small voice in her head kept nagging, noting that it was the first time one of her elder brothers took her seriously enough to talk at length and even fish for information that might have been available to her alone. True, come to think of it. It was her who moved in Tenochtitlan's higher circles.

"Why should I tell you anything of the sort?"

"If you won't, I'll tell Father that you are after the village scum and will disgrace yourself with him in the end." He smirked openly. "That'll put an end to your noble school days at once."

"He won't believe you!" she breathed, horrified. But he could do that, couldn't he?

"Of course he will. He is suspicious of you and your *calmecac* activities, not as happy about it as your mother is."

"I'll find ways to get back at you if you do that."

He pushed himself past her, and into the twilight. "Don't push it, little one, and don't become cheeky like that silly friend of yours. Warn that one to keep away from the wharves and the bad company. She is of a respectable family and should know better. And so are you." His eyes, as he turned to look at her, became again serious and well meaning. "That noble *pilli* who angers Father so, be careful of him. I was teasing about the villager, but not about that other one. Don't become heavy with child without him making you his woman. You are not too young to be unaware of those things."

She was fighting for breath again, her fists clenched too tightly to unclench them. "How dare you? I never ever did something of the sort. And Necalli is not like that. He is not after... after pleasures. He is not like that. And so am I!"

The disdainful ring to his snort didn't make her feel any better. "Of course he is. Every man is. Remember that, always, Little Sister." He sobered again. "Just be careful. Don't let that boy have his way with you until he makes you his woman. Even just one of the wives. He won't be allowed to make you his chief wife, but don't agree to become a simple concubine. You are not a marketplace woman to be picked carelessly. Your family deserves better."

The struggle not to pounce at him with the aid of every limb became more difficult.

"About the villager scum," he went on unconcerned, so annoyingly superior she wished a roof tile would fall on top of him, or at least a moderately large stone. "That trader wanted to know about him and Father told him that the stupid piece of meat ran away, which truly did happen. But he may want to contact his family if he has ways to do that. If that trader was asking on behalf of that peasant family of his, which I think he said he did, then they may have gotten a bad story, worse than his true situation might be. It may be better for him to put their possible worries to rest."

She was still too angry to formulate a worthwhile response. "He said Miztli joined smugglers and the courts were after him."

"How did you know that?" Then his smile returned. "Oh, the little rascal told you. He was slinking around the house back then, come to think of it."

That served to put her back on guard. "No, it's not him. I just know."

"You are a lousy liar, Little Sister. But remember, you owe me for this. So when I come to ask questions, be ready to answer those or ask your noble friends for information. Don't try to avoid or evade. Or you are in trouble with Father. Remember, eh?"

He was gone, waving at her carelessly, his palm blackened with soot. Numbly, she stared after him, then shook her head and walked out as well, hesitating, then turning toward Quetzalli's father's house. Oh yes, she needed to talk to her friend and urgently. What Ome said about her was worrisome as well.

CHAPTER 7

The corridor was lit dimly, saturated with invisible slivers of smoke that emanated from one of the torches fastened into the plastered wall. There were several such holders along the length of this passageway, all of them crowned with merrily dancing flames, only one smoking badly.

His throat tickling, holding in a cough, Miztli hurried past it, concentrating on his step, afraid to slip or do something equally silly or embarrassing. Not on these premises. And not tonight. The strangely patterned maguey cloak felt comfortably short, shorter than his school garment and not as nicely adorned, but the lack of sandals curiously bothered him, made him oddly self-conscious of his step, as though he didn't go everywhere barefoot until less than two moons ago. Ridiculous, and yet the current lack of shoes made him feel strange.

"Hurry up, boy!"

A man with a vessel full of glowing coals bypassed him, followed by two more bent down forms. Their cargo was heavier, stone braziers fashioned in the form of coiled serpents. As was his own burden, another stone cask. Well, it had been a while since he carried braziers or tended to such things. And yet, he didn't have to struggle in the way they did. It wasn't as heavy as old Tlaquitoc's massive containers, often with melted metal in it.

Pleased with himself, he straightened some more, then hastened his step. His mission was not to run around these halls, carrying things. The Emperor wanted him to spend time in the quarters allocated to the visitors from the south, to pretend to be a servant, fiddle with things, and try to be helpful while listening to their conversations in case they talked in their native Matlatzinca tongue, exchanging secret observations or other delicate information not intended for the ears of their Tenochtitlan guests. A wise thing to do. How many people who could speak southern dialects were in Tenochtitlan? Ahuitzotl claimed that there were none.

He hid his smile, remembering the brief interview with the Emperor, after Ahuitzotl had managed to convince his august older sibling to give them a few heartbeats of his time. Formidable as ever, the mighty ruler of the Great Capital did smile at him, Miztli, briefly, nodding his acknowledgement, even commenting on the displayed diligence at school as though aware of his progress. Impossible but true. Could the mighty emperor have time to be interested in something like that?

"He does well," Ahuitzotl had confirmed, pushing himself to the forefront, as was his custom. "He can read and write now and do all the rest. But that's not why I brought him here."

The Emperor's thin lips quivered lightly, unevenly. "Why then, Brother?"

"There is this delegation from the south, those visiting foreigners, yes? He can speak their tongue!" This came out triumphantly.

Embarrassed, Miztli busied himself with watching the intricately laid pavement. But why would the Emperor be interested in any of that? The royal *pilli* was so childish at times, so eager to push himself into important happenings.

"You understand any of the southern dialects?" The Emperor's eyes narrowed at him, contemplative. "What tongue do you speak?"

He had to swallow to make his mind work. "Matlatzinca, Revered Emperor. I can speak it. Can understand what they say."

"Where you come from, boy, did they speak this tongue? Your people, your family?"

"No... Well, yes, my father, he taught us this tongue. He said it's our ancestral way... our ancestral way of speaking." To lick his lips didn't help. His tongue felt as dry as a piece of meat after it has been put in the sun to make it good for later eating. "But we don't talk this way. The village, I mean, all of us, we speak Nahuatl, like here."

"And the Oaxtepec locals?" The Emperor's eyes were as narrow as slits and he could feel Ahuitzotl going absolutely still, listening as intently. The eyes all around bore at them, the imperial following keeping their distance, agog with curiosity.

He felt his cloak clinging to his back, unpleasantly sticky. "In Oaxtepec, they speak Nahuatl, Revered Emperor." At least the title came out readily this time. "But they can speak the southern tongues as well, some of them. I think they do, that is. Some people." His voice was trailing off again, pitifully. He paused to draw in a breath.

"Interesting." The Emperor nodded thoughtfully, then looked away. "Stay here, boy, until I send someone to fetch you. You too, little rascal." The narrowed eyes brushed past Ahuitzotl. "I like your thinking, Brother. We'll talk about what you had in mind later tonight. I'll leave instructions to bring you to the Palace. Until then, stay with your protégé. Do whatever the people I send tell you both." A contemplative nod and the man was gone, back to his dignified following and important guests or as richly dressed and important-looking petitioners.

"I told you," breathed Ahuitzotl triumphantly. "He'll get you into spying again. Like back in Tlatelolco."

Miztli just blinked. "But what would he want me to hear or tell? Whom am I to listen to?"

"The southern scum, who else?" The boy's round face brightened with the widest of smiles. "You can speak like they do, but they don't know it, do they? The stupid foreigners will let their tongues run loose. You just wait and see." He shielded his eyes against the glow of the setting sun that was reflecting off the polished angles of the monument dedicated to it quite viciously. "And I'm not returning to school tonight. And you too. Which is the best, absolutely the best!"

Well, it was, to a degree. School at night was not a place he couldn't bear absenting himself from, certainly with Necalli being out and away, enjoying his journey to the mainland, that much coveted pilgrimage to the City of Gods out there in the north. Yet now he had adventures of his own offered, to pass the time without his friend more pleasantly, doing something better than nightly prayers and sacrifice, then slumbering in the sleeping hall, on guard and not entirely relaxed, not with his old-time enemy there, strutting around, throwing nasty remarks occasionally, still having his following. Not as much as before, or so claimed Necalli, but it didn't change the fact that without this same Necalli, he didn't feel safe, not entirely. And then, there was Tlemilli, somewhere here, in this less-prestigious wing of the Palace's grounds, according to her words and her laughter, somewhere where they would place visitors and guests. Even back then on the Plaza, the thought flickered, laden with possibilities. And now here he was, in the same building as her maybe, but disguised as a servant, like back in Tlatelolco, carrying an additional brazier to make the visitors' pastime more pleasurable, to ward off the chill of the evening presumably. But would she laugh hard if she saw him now, if he passed through her suite of rooms by some wild longed-for chance.

"Bring it in, boy."

A pretty-looking maid, all dimples and soft curves, motioned him toward one of the carved openings and the direful scrutiny of two warriors who seemed to be guarding it. Apprehensively, he slipped past them, his cumbersome cargo hindering his step.

"Put it there. In that niche next to the shutters." To his relief, the maid followed him in, motioning toward the indicated spot, businesslike and unafraid.

He crossed the spacious room hurriedly, noting other warriors, standing or squatting in groups, talking between themselves. Many warriors, more than he would assume one needed while visiting the friendly *altepetl*. Of the dignitary from the Plaza, there was no sight.

"Make this one work, then go and take care of the other brazier, in that corner."

Annoyed by her nagging that interrupted his ability to listen to the talking warriors, he propped the stony construction against the wall, then gave the woman a cold look. She answered it with a matching glare.

"I know what do to with this thing," he said, incensed even further. He was no Palace's slave for some bossy fowl to distribute offhanded ordering about.

Her eyes sparked. "Don't you dare to answer me," she hissed, keeping her voice low for the benefit of the guests. It was easy to imagine this one shrilling at the top of her voice. "An insolent brat! I'll let them know about your insolence, boy. Don't you think I won't."

Who cares? he wanted to toss with an equal fury, but the glances from the nearest group of squatting men were almost perceptible, burning his skin. He wasn't here to pick quarrels with annoyingly bossy fowls out to prove their ascendancy, but if the stupid woman kept blabbering, interfering with his ability to listen, or better yet, causing him to be thrown out before he heard anything worthwhile, he would have no one but himself to blame.

To force his eyes away and toward the brazier in question wasn't easy. "I will light this one and then do the same to the one in the corner," he muttered as civilly as he could, trying to listen to the warriors' voices. Some were speaking freely and loudly, but he knew that he needed to hear those who didn't.

"Oh, so now you are ready to comply, eh?" The woman snorted, then tossed her head high, her hands too busy with the tray she carried to plant them in her sides in the typical way of overbearing females. "Watch your step, boy, and come to ask what to do next when you are done here."

When she was gone, he breathed with relief, not sure he would have managed to tolerate more of her bossiness without flaring at her for real. He was no workshop apprentice, not anymore. Even the Emperor said he would be a warrior one day, allowed to go up the Great Pyramid all the way.

"It must be a sacred calendar with some deeper meaning." In one of the cozily lit corners, the visitors were talking loudly, their Nahuatl softer than that of the Capital dwellers, their accent pronounced. He forced his mind to concentrate, his hands arranging the firewood, perfectly dried shortened branches, easy to deal with, unlike some of the wood they would bring to school from the mainland, let alone the bad quality twigs he would have to buy for old Tlaquitoc back in the bad days.

"They said it is, yes. Didn't you hear their emperor talking?"

"When?"

"When he was talking to our Honorable Tezozomoctli." The man glanced at the opening leading to the other set of rooms, quick to take his eyes elsewhere. "I was around and could hear them clearly. He talks well, that man. Like a warriors' leader. Not mincing his words."

"Well, that one has to be a warrior, doesn't he? They are always warring."

To that, the man's peers reacted with various grimaces of consent. Miztli hesitated in his corner, unsure of his next step. These men talked freely, not trying to conceal their words or use different tongues. And while it made it easier to listen to them without being too obvious about it, it left him with nothing but silly gossip and lazily exchanged observations. No special information to report, no secret knowledge.

He glanced at the glowing casks on the other side of the room. The maid wished him to light another one such, but in that corner, no warriors squatted, while near the wall opening, two men huddled close to each other, watching the room gloomily, exchanging quiet remarks. Gathering his excess of the firewood hastily, he headed in that direction, praying the men won't pay attention to his advance.

"Always is the word!" The exclamation of the boisterous warriors in the corner reached him across the room as easily, the loudness of their laughter. "Even with their immediate neighbors. It was a huge massacre, they say, out there on that other island."

"Their marketplace is all that is left from that other *altepetl*, one hears. Our honorable leader will have us escorting him to that famous market for a day of strolling around, buying rare things. The Tenochtitlan emperor promised that."

"As though their own marketplace is not huge enough."

The men by the window were listening to the idle exchange as well, discovered Miztli, fiddling with glowing coals of the other brazier, hoping not to make it flare too high or douse off for good. Other servants rushed past, carrying trays into the inner rooms, piling up plates of steaming dishes encircled by flasks of *octli* aplenty. The bossy maid swept past, directing their procession, too preoccupied this time to accost him again. Thankfully, Miztli busied himself rearranging the perfectly glowing embers, praying that the nosy woman would not remember his existence, not before the warriors by the window resumed their conversation, so temptingly close now, possible to overhear but for their silence. He willed the boisterous group to shut up.

"Get the servants to bring us something to eat as well," some of the loudmouthed loiterers claimed now. "And a mat of *patolli*-game with figurines."

"A round of *patolli* would be a nice thing." This came from the warrior by the window, quiet but easy to understand, the words of the tongue Father used from time to time bringing sudden longing for home. *There must be a way to send them word. They might be worried after so many moons.*

"Not this night." The other warrior, a tall sinewy type, with his hair arranged in an intricate fashion, testifying for taken captives – that much he had learned in *calmecac* so far – shifted, then eased his shoulders, glancing at the darkness outside once again. "The Texcocan was clear about the seriousness of the threat. No idle gossip that."

"Not from this man, yes," agreed the first voice. Miztli didn't dare to glance at them, immersed in his embers' shuffling, trying to make as little noise as he could. They were talking so quietly, while the others kept screaming at the top of their chests, may they fall through the floor and straight into the middle levels of the Underworld. He noticed that he was holding his breath in. The Texcocan? Could it be?

"Surely nothing can happen here in the Palace." The second man sounded as though he shifted again, restless. "When out there maybe, yes. When touring their plazas and alleys. But not here."

"Everything can happen. Everything and everywhere. Cuauhnahuac will pay for this!"

"We don't even know if the threat is real, let alone where it came from." The following pause was heavy, clearly pregnant with meaning. "The Texcocans have a good cause to implicate their old-time conquest, don't they?"

"Why?"

This time, Miztli couldn't help sneaking a glance, rewarded with the view of both men leaning against the windowsill, their eyes on each other.

"Don't know yet. Maybe they didn't like us coming to Tenochtitlan and not to Texcoco. Maybe they wish to invade the southern valleys all by themselves."

However, his companion shook his head vigorously. "They'll get their chance to join, the greedy beasts that they are. Didn't you see their emperor skulking all over this *altepetl*? He came to sniff around, that one. To see what he might be missing."

"The famous Triple Alliance, eh? Yet one hears that they didn't join this last Tlatelolco war. Only the Tepanecs did."

The second man's snort dissolved in the night air outside the window. Miztli held his breath once again, afraid to miss a word.

"There were no worthwhile pickings in Tlatelolco. Only some goods. That greedy island would not let anyone grab a tiny pebble off its shores, let alone to get a foothold, and the Acolhua are always after lands and tribute. Their new emperor is no different from his famous father, all good manners and refinement and pursuing fine arts, but just underneath nothing but greediness and plucking their provinces dry. Two-faced lowlifes."

Another quick glance rewarded Miztli with the sight of the first man's shoulders lifting heavily, as though following a sigh. "Maybe our Honorable Tezozomoctli shouldn't have asked for the help of the Triple Alliance that readily."

A brief silence that prevailed had a confirming quality to it. The servants were back, pouring out of the inner rooms like a procession of ants.

The bossy maid was upon him before he could sneak away. "What are you lingering here for, you rebellious good-for-nothing? Go and make yourself useful in the kitchen houses. You will be in so much trouble when I'm through with telling them what you've been up to—"

"Bring us refreshments!" The loitering warriors' voices cut the hissing tirade short before his self-restraint was tested to its limit; still, it left him more frustrated than before as one of the men by the window shrugged, then went toward his squatting peers while his companion headed into the inner rooms, not waiting for permission to do so.

"Go to the kitchen houses!" were the maid's parting words, and he couldn't help but to return her furious glare, matching in its nastiness, or so he hoped. Then, scooping some of the embers with the help of a pair of wide branches, he made his way toward the third brazier, hoping against hope to hear something of interest coming from the inside room or set of rooms. Was the visiting dignitary there now, sharing more secrets in the tongue of the western valley people? Was he also mistrustful of the Acolhua Texcocans, suspecting their motives or the information they passed? And what was the threat the men at the window were referring to? Cuauhnahuac, so familiar, sounding almost like home while being so far away, but what did they have to do with any of it, the unrest in the west or this delegation he was now spying on? Tenantzinco, a town he never heard of before this noon but now knew all about – its ruler's name and his troubles with even more mysterious Tollocans of the west. This same Tenantzinco came looking for Tenochtitlan's help against the united might of warlike Tollocans and their equally powerful and bothersome neighbors of the city named Matlatzinco, like the tongue they all spoke. So much to learn in one afternoon, to learn and remember. Worse than a lesson on reading or calculating under sternest and most demanding among the *calmecac* priests.

"You, there. Come here!"

It took him a moment to realize that one of the warriors at the far end was addressing him, beckoning with impatience. Startled and curiously jarred, he hesitated, reluctant to leave the proximity of the other room. Could he try and make his way in, maybe when other servants with trays returned? Grab another brazier and claim that he had been sent to supply the room with additional light or warmth?

"Are you deaf? Come over here, you lowly scum!" The warrior who called him before raised his voice. "On the run!"

Blinking, he tried to clear his head, pushing the other room and the possibilities of more information out of his mind with an effort. Admittedly, it was easier to obey a warrior than a shrill maid; it felt more like back in school. He left the brazier alone but crossed the room unhurriedly, curiously annoyed, the awareness of his relative nakedness, his lack of sandals, his lack of rights, however temporary, reinforcing his resentment.

"Yes?"

"Would you listen to this one?" The warrior who had addressed him before seemed to be contemplating the possibility of getting to his feet. "Isn't he asking for a good beating, the lowly scum?"

He swallowed various rude responses that sprang to the tip of his tongue, forcing his eyes down instead, mostly in order to hide the depth of his fury. It was like back in the workshop, bad memories. And yet, the Emperor wished him to be here, to listen and serve.

"Yes, Master." It came out too quietly, obviously forced. He tried to will his mind into working. The strain was too great, making him tremble inside, his mind shrieking, urging him to run out or maybe launch back, to prepare for a possible attack; yet another calmer voice whispering that he was here for another reason, that they had every right to yell at him and call him names, strike him surely if need be, and it was his responsibility to avoid any of it, to be allowed to stay and listen. The tranquility was coming back. "I'm sorry, Master. I don't know what came over me. I should have come right away."

The other warriors grimaced and the man from the window glanced at him narrowly, openly suspicious.

"That's better," growled the original complainer. "Now bring here a mat of *patolli*-game, with figurines and the rest. You have one hundred heartbeats to be back, you filthy dung-eater. Or it'll be a good kick to your backside. It is begging to receive one such now."

He nodded numbly, unable to force any more humbling words in response, his limbs having difficulty obeying him. What was this *patolli*-game anyway? He didn't know, didn't care. To walk away was the first priority, to get out, to escape the mean closeness of these rooms and to think, to make order out of it all.

The barely lit corridor greeted him with its late evening chill, aloof and indifferent, like the rest of these premises. He glanced at its far edge, where he had been led before, carrying braziers. The opposite direction beckoned with its draft of fresh nightly air. His legs took him there without much thinking.

The terrace was vast, moonlit, and utterly deserted. Breathing with relief, he hurried toward its edge, the rustling of the brushes below and the treetops somewhere above calming his nerves. If he climbed or even jumped down, he would be in the gardens, away from this luxurious building's dwellers and guests, on his way back to normality. Just to go over the outer wall, the closest one, like back in the Tlatelolco Palace, and he would be on the Plaza, on his way to *calmecac*, to the familiarity of the evening rites and then the sleeping hall, all ordinary and familiar, a normal life.

A normal life now, he reminded himself, pitting his face against the breeze, letting it cool the burning sensation. This life had not been his until not long ago. Two moons earlier, he didn't even know of the noble school's existence, along with too many other things that now were ordinary and a part of life. And *her* too! Only two moons ago, he didn't know her and she didn't know him, or that Palace that now was her home. Thanks to him. But for his involvement, his persistence of bringing her here and away from the dangers of her native city and family... In the darkness and loneliness of this moon-colored terrace, he could admit certain truths, even if only to himself.

A wave of longing swept him, so powerful he felt like groaning aloud. He had barely seen her today, barely managed to exchange a few words. There was no time, not even for conspiratorial smiles or whispers, not even to tuck a note he had composed painstakingly before this last dawn broke, using glyphs she had taught him and a few others he had copied from an old war account Necalli's father let him borrow for study. There were too many highborn ladies around, their eyes flickering, appraising, some upset, disgusted with inappropriately lowly company, some amused. Like that haughty Lady Jade Doll, this time surprisingly amiable, almost playful, embarrassing with her open attention, the need to maintain conversation with her. She reminded him of that annoying Chantli's friend from the wharves, the stupid fowl he had made the mistake of saving from fire once upon a time. Or so claimed Necalli, always full of jokes and ready to tease when it came to this particular matter. But now the haughty imperial sister was behaving in a ridiculously similar manner and what would the *calmecac* boy have to say about that? Oh mighty deities, don't let Necalli witness anything of the sort. Enough that Tlemilli's no-less-haughty, even if not so imperial, sister made faces when not busy glaring at the scar-faced Texcocan. It was good that the controversial man was there to take this one's attention away. Otherwise, she would be glaring at him, covertly, but she would. Apparently, the annoying fowl still thought that he was a bad influence, not good enough for Tlemilli, out to harm or hinder her, and that after saving her from the horrors of their *altepetl*'s fall, just like he promised he would do. Necalli was always fuming about that. The arrogant fowl must have thought that it was nothing, a matter-of-fact thing, to land in Tenochtitlan Palace instead of a slave market. The stupid turkey!

The voices from the corridor he just left forced him to press against the parapet of the balcony, holding his breath. Faint but distinct. A group of people. Servants, judging by their hushed up yet lively exchanges. He breathed with relief, then thought about the conversing warriors. Not the annoying loiterers but the two men who were talking about important things, using the western valley's tongue, thinking themselves safe from being overheard. They were standing with their backs to the wall opening, leaning against it. Which meant that if someone crouched beneath it, hiding in the bushes that must be adorning the outer wall, one might hear more useful pieces of information. Or maybe what had been said by the nobles in the inner rooms. Those would have wall openings too, letting in the pleasures of the night breeze, wouldn't they?

The ground beneath the small balcony was soft, delightfully grassy. It plopped against his bare feet, bringing back memories of his village in force. Would he go back, given a choice? he wondered briefly. A moon ago, the answer would have been there before he finished asking the question. Now it wasn't. After the fall of Tlatelolco, everything changed – the school, the stepped up training, military and otherwise, learning to read and calculate numbers, dots and flags, getting along with the others, not snubbed anymore and not attempted to be ambushed or beaten, with even that brute Acoatl losing much of his power over the other boys, turning quieter, as nasty but less harmful. And above it all, her, Tlemilli, his private beacon of fire, enticing and sparkling, and never boring or bored, thinking him to be the best of heroes and his kisses enjoyable enough to demand more. But for the chance of finding her here and now, like back in the Tlatelolco Palace!

Clenching his teeth in an attempt to make such thoughts go away, he slunk along the outer wall, trying to calculate. How many paces had he gone along the corridor before reaching that balcony? Twenty? Half of it? Many voices wafted in the air, seeping through various openings, female chatter interrupted with laughter, an occasional child's squeaking. Men were more difficult to pick up in this murmur; still, close to twenty paces of his creeping along the prickly bushes rewarded him with the hum that sounded familiar, to a degree. The voices of the boisterous group? He hoped it was them. Also that they still didn't get any refreshments or that mysterious mat for the *patolli*-game.

A few more paces brought him closer to the peeling off plaster of the outer wall, the glimmering spots dotting the darkness above, promising, just like the voices. Holding his breath, he slunk deeper into the bushes, then froze. The silhouette that darted along the next row of vegetation did so with an enviable confidence and speed. He had had a chance of barely glimpsing it before it was gone, leaving him blinking, his heart pounding in his ears. No rustling but that of the breeze disturbed the night, no other suspicious sound. Had he imagined it? Afraid to move, he waited breathlessly until the floating voices recaptured his attention, his heartbeat calming gradually, allowing him to listen to other sounds besides its wild thumping.

Pressing deeper into the bushes, he strained his ears, a part of his mind still on the night out there and its moving shadows. Who would be sneaking around the Palace's grounds like that? Another eavesdropper? Someone else the Emperor might have sent, or the Texcocans those warriors were discussing, or people from his native far south? They said there was a threat, something that made them worried, a warning coming from Texcoco people or involving Cuauhnahuac. But were they angry with this city out there in the west! Why? And why did it make his flesh crawl, this involvement of a place relatively close to home, to Teteltzinco and Oaxtepec? Maybe it was better that he should not mention Cuauhnahuac while reporting to the Emperor. Not until he knew more, curse the loudmouthed warriors with their stupid *patolli-*game!

As though ready to echo his thoughts, loud exclamations that sounded like a game of luck in progress invaded the night, causing him to resume his creeping, wishing to reach the window in question. Or rather the one beside it. If it belonged to the room he had been in before, then another one might be of the feasting dignitaries.

A silhouette swept across the moonlit patch and he froze once again, breathless. This time, it was a person, a man, unmistakable. Tall and clothed like a warrior; and armed. The outline of the sword with its viciously protruding blades was difficult not to recognize. Miztli pressed against the dampness of the wall, afraid to let his breath out, eyes following another slipping silhouette, then another. For a heartbeat, the third man paused, hesitating at the edge of the illuminated ground, gesturing curtly. That brought his preceding peers back, then, to Miztli's rising dread, sent all three of them straight toward his bushes, in a determined race.

Aghast, he watched them nearing, his limbs heavy, reluctant to obey the panicked command of his mind. When he slid down and into the worst of the shrubs, they were already so near he could feel them, hear the rasp of their breaths. Not an easy feat as his heart was thundering too loudly, roaring in his ears, giving his presence away. There was no point in huddling under the prickly chaparral. They would notice him the moment they came under the relevant wall opening. They couldn't not to.

Their sandals plopped in the muddy earth, not loudly but distinctly, so very close, he felt the tiny drops spraying his hideaway. He didn't dare to move, not even in order to reach for his knife, the *calmecac* obsidian long-bladed dagger tied as required to his girdle, cradled in a simple unadorned sheath. Which of course wasn't there now, when he was disguised as a stupid servant, with no girdle to put any weaponry in, even had he been allowed to do that. However, there was that smaller flint blade hidden in his bag, next to the obsidian puma, tucked there for such occasions, a gift from the wondrous man Tecuani. The thought of the mysterious Texcocan gave him strength, the memory of seeing him just this afternoon, when still at the safety of the Plaza, surrounded by people, having every right to be there. While now...

The men were huddling next to the nearby tree, communicating in whispers. Scanning the dark mass of the building as well, judging by their poses. Reassured, Miztli dared to breathe again, then strained his ears in an attempt to decipher the words they seemed to be exchanging. The wind wasn't helpful, carrying those away. To crawl the length of the nearest cluster of bushes suddenly seemed like a worthwhile idea. They weren't aware of his presence, obviously, and so why not try to learn of their purpose, sneaking around like that, adding to his account of happenings on this side of the Palace.

"—too close and too obvious—" one of the men was whispering, his voice nothing but a rustle, blending with the strengthening wind.

"Here, yes!" rasped another voice, dropping back into quieter murmuring quickly. Miztli strained his ear desperately. "—not here in the Palace—impossible, but—the marketplace—"

Frustrated, Miztli dared to slip into another temptingly dark niche that an intricately trimmed shrubbery created, emboldened by his previous success, needing to know. It was imperative to hear what these men were talking about, to learn who they were maybe. Were they the "threat" the warriors up there were discussing? Would they attempt to climb into the visitors' set of rooms? It was impossible to tell what these islanders or their guests would do. That much he had learned about the mighty Capital so far.

"—just want to know—if this is the right place—" one of the voices kept insisting, as though eager to echo Miztli's musings. "Honorable Tizoctzin told—"

"Would you keep your mouth shut?" demanded the first man, the one who was gesturing before, clearly a leader. Then his voice dropped back to the uncomfortable murmuring. "—stay for a little while—watch—"

Suddenly, they fell silent and Miztli's heart missed a beat once again when the man turned abruptly, peering through the darkness and straight at him, or so it seemed. Aware of his crawling skin, he tried to keep absolutely still, the effort of staying so sapping at his strength, making his limbs tremble. The other two fell silent as well and he knew that they must have an inkling, a suspicion, and that he must do something, spring to his feet and run away maybe, or just keep still and hope they would return to their business at hand. The knife, where was his knife?

While his mind kept concentrating on this less relevant of the dilemmas, his ears picked another sound, that of shuffling feet. Not far away, someone was strolling the path or the open grounds. Lonely footsteps. Light, unconcealed.

His heart, which didn't dare to pound too strongly before, missed a beat as the wild suspicion invaded his mind, the memory of *her* back on the Plaza, edging him off the tented shadow just as he and Ahuitzotl were to be led off and away, after the conversation with the Emperor, whispering hurriedly, promising to find him here, "somewhere around." It wouldn't be hard to find out where the visiting southerners were placed, she promised. It was on their side of the Palace's grounds, the less prestigious one.

He held his breath, remembering how her eyes sparkled mischievously while saying that. And yet now it was not the time, and why would she be coming through the gardens and not the inner corridors, unless there was another building here or anything.

His mind didn't spend time analyzing any of it. As the rustling of the footsteps stopped, then resumed momentarily, his eyes caught the movement from the grouped silhouettes, one of them slipping away and back toward the lit patch, and then his body was throwing itself up and over the bushes, his legs completing the leap, landing on the other side, breaking into the wild run, avoiding the collision with the shadow that rushed to intercept him but barely. The man tried to grab him nevertheless, but it became increasingly easy to escape the gripping fingers and then a badly directed punch, the muddy ground too slippery, favoring his bare feet and not the sandaled ones of his assailant. A shove of an elbow enabled him to break free, leaving his rival staggering, clutching into no more than his inadequately tied cloak, the other silhouette bearing on them, in a hurry to join the fray.

Not staying to retrieve his temporary garment or make sure his opponent went down sprawling for good or not, he sprinted toward the sounds coming from beyond the path and the vast flowerbeds that adorned it, the rasping of the man's breath and the higher pitched squeaks strangled but full of fury, so familiar, bringing back the memories of the warring Tlatelolco in force.

Having no plan and no clear idea, he collided with the darker mass of their struggling limbs, trying to make sure who was who before attempting to do something about it, his thoughts rushing like mad squirrels, senses on fire, screaming danger, knowing that the other men were surely hot on his heels and that he had no chance against the three of them, experienced killers or spies, or whoever they were.

Indeed, the man who had intercepted her, held her expertly from behind and across her torso, pinning her hands to it while paying no attention to the flurry of kicks with which her legs were assaulting his. His other hand pressed firmly against her mouth, arresting plenty of screams, of that Miztli was sure.

He didn't spend his time observing them any further. To throw his fist forward in order to crush it against the man's temple its hardest was child's play this time, not an effort at all. Her assailant stood at such comfortable proximity, as though waiting for him to display his skill. For a wild moment, he wished Necalli was here to see it. Then the torrent of her outcries burst out unrestrained, and he was busy catching her, struggling not to let her follow her captor's fall. The man went down so quickly, so decisively!

"Keep quiet!" he managed to hiss before his pursuers were upon them. Not quick enough, he turned to face them, lurching as though drunk on *pulque*, with her still in his arms, struggling to maintain their balance too, as nimble as always but as clumsy, the impossible combination belonging only to her.

Sensing the nearing fist, this one armed with lethal obsidian, of that he was sure, he twisted away, moving them both in a desperate attempt to avoid the contact. The other shadow was upon them as well, and he fought not to let her go against the wild pull and her funnily strangled squeak, then found himself doubling, gasping for breath, a fist that crashed into his belly doing so with accuracy and force, much as his own did to the man that had dared to assault her before. The thought alone had him throwing himself in her general direction, guided by the sounds of struggle, disregarding his own attacker for a moment, needing to make sure. But for having his *calmecac* gear and the knife now!

Avoiding another punch, or maybe this time an armed fist, a likelier possibility, he collided with the man who was attempting to restrain her, driving his shoulder into the broadness of the outlined back with force before absorbing the anticipated blow but somehow twisting away from the worst of it, kicking with all he had, his knee connecting with some flesh, hurting it but not enough. His pursuer was as relentless, single-minded in his determination to get him as quickly and probably as silently as possible, that much was clear.

As his fist connected with this or that limb again, not nearly as efficient as the first time, a blow from behind sent him sprawling. Disoriented, he tried to push the muddy earth away, struggling against the fierce yank that had one of his arms twisted cruelly, pulled backwards amidst a spectacular outburst of pain. Combined with the uncompromising push in his back, it pinned him to the ground, frustrating any thought of resistance, let alone an actual deed.

Frantic with attempts to breathe against the assault of the fresh earth, he could hear Tlemilli yelling, the ferocity of her protests familiar from the warring on the Tlatelolcan marketplace, cut short by a hissing tirade, surprisingly efficient. In the corner of his mind, he wondered what made her shut up so readily, then the worry for her exploded anew and he tried to break free once again, successful only in making his agonized arm pushed yet higher, the damp earth strangling his cry, mercifully at that. Tlemilli's words were still there, typically gushing but quiet; half pleading, half threatening. It was easy to recognize that tone of hers.

"Check on Cipactli," rasped the voice above, very close and as carefully quiet. "The girl won't do anything stupid, or that one gets his arm broken for good before the rest of him follows suit." He could hear Tlemilli gasping, but this time, he kept as still as he could, desperate to gather his senses now that he knew she was not in immediate danger. *Who were these men?*

As though willing to echo his thoughts, his captor shifted, leaning closer or so it seemed, his knee pressing worse than before, threatening to break his back as well. "Who sent you? Tell me quickly or your arm is going out of your shoulder."

Before he panicked again, knowing that he could not tell a thing, certainly not the identity of those who sent him, aware that there were ways of forcing the truth out of him even if he managed to deal with the fiercest of pain – her presence changed it all, didn't it? – the earth stuck in his face became a blessing. What could he tell them when choking in the mud, barely able to breathe, let alone talk coherently? To mutter something inaudible helped. His capturer seemed to understand the situation as well.

"Don't you dare to move a limb, girl," he demanded, relaxing his grip if not the pressure of his knee. "Who are you and who is he?"

He could hear Tlemilli gulping loudly. For a heartbeat, nothing but the rustling of the other man's footsteps or other sort of activity not far away interrupted the peacefulness of the night. Even the nocturnal insects paused in their chirping, and only an owl hooted somewhere behind the artificially forested vastness.

"Cipactli is out cold, maybe dead." The other man's whisper barely disturbed the silence. Neither did his footsteps. If not stretched on the ground, with nothing to do but to listen intently, he might have been startled, reflected Miztli, unable to fight the renewed wave of panic, the urge to break free at all costs.

The knee rooted into his back deeper and his arm was pushed back up again. "Stop that, you filthy lowlife! I'll be breaking you into pieces anyway. Don't make me start right away." A brief pause brought a measure of relief in the pressure again. "Help me turn him over."

"No, please, please don't hurt him!" Tlemilli's voice shook, unbecomingly loud, turning back to whispering hastily. His heart went out to her. She sounded so frightened! "He did nothing, nothing! You can't break him, please! He is not, not anyone you think he is. He came to meet me here... out here. I asked him to. I told him! He was just doing what I ordered him to. You can't—"

"Shut up," demanded the first man. "Stop blabbering and try to make sense." When he shifted, Miztli forced his cramped muscles not to react, the sudden relief in the pressure promising, to be used when his chances were better. Would she manage to keep their attention for long enough to have him do something about it? "Who are you, girl?"

"I'm... I live here in the Palace," she said in a firmer voice, clearly filling with hope just like he did. It was easy to predict her way of thinking now, her reactions and sometimes even deeds. Despite their current situation, a warm wave splashed in his chest, pushing the rippling panic away. There must be a way to escape these people, somehow.

"Isn't this the wild girl the Revered Adviser just—" began the second man, but the first one cut him off angrily.

"Keep your mouth shut, Tecolotl! Don't you think—"

"Don't you flare at me," burst out Tecolotl as angrily, the hissing of his voice shaking the darkness. "You are not my superior. Only Cipactli and as long as he is out..."

By this time, the man who had pinned him to the ground was shifting again, as though deliberating the advisability of leaping to his feet, his knee still there but hardly pressing, neglecting to secure his arm in as hurtful position as before. Putting it all into one concentrated effort, Miztli shoved himself sideways, disregarding the blinding pain and the way his arm was slow to cooperate as he rolled onto the same side, shaking his assailant off and into the damp earth. But for the man being less on guard! Before he could as much as try to straighten up, they both were upon him, pinning him back to the ground, their weight crushing, smothering him into a new bout of panicked resistance.

Oblivious of reason, the pain in his shoulder blinding, the earth hard against his back, hurtful as though against him in this too, he squirmed madly, kicking with every limb that moved, slamming his forehead into a briefly appearing face, bereft of any reasonable reaction. When the pressure was gone, he clawed his way up, anxious to see where the danger was coming from, berserk with worry.

Tlemilli was scrambling back to her feet as well, his senses informed him before his eyes did, throwing herself at him, yet before getting busy with an attempt not to go back sprawling from the sheer power of her drive, his eyes took in another shadow darting toward them, more bodies littering the ground, at least two more in addition to the one he had punched before it all started.

"Quick!" breathed the newcomer, while Miztli was busy fighting for balance, Tlemilli's hands clinging to him, hurting with the desperation of their grip.

Still disoriented, he blinked, then realized that his previous assailants were on the ground, one of them moaning lightly, trying to move. The other was just a heap of limbs, like the one they called Cipactli, lying at some distance, stirring now as well.

A hand grabbed his shoulder, pulling with force he found difficult to resist for the moment. "Quick, you stupid cub! Both of you!" Turning away, the man beckoned impatiently, clearly expecting no argument, welcoming none.

The memories surfaced, indefinite but there. Again Tlatelolco, but this time the nighttime *altepetl*, preparing for war, not engaged in one such yet. Could it be? Tlemilli's hands were pulling as well now, and in another heartbeat, he found himself running, his legs not very steady but doing their best, following the faintly outlined silhouette, turning into another pathway, then another.

"Climb this. Quick!"

The wall was massive but not high, hardly over his own height. Hoots of several owls and other night birds reached from across it, bringing memories of home. He pushed those away, concentrating on the challenge. Tlemilli, she needed to be helped across, and his shoulder and arm were still on fire, yet an attempted move did not make him wish to scream in agony like before.

The noise of the hot pursuit neared. He could hear it most clearly, oh yes, the plopping of the warriors' footsteps faint but not their voices. No clandestine sneaking around, not this time. The man hopped up the dark mass of the wall as though it wasn't there at all. One moment beside them, scanning the darkness; the next already up, perching on the edge, motioning impatiently.

Tlemilli tugged at his arm again.

"I'll push you up," he whispered. "You just grab the edge…"

She nodded readily, and despite his hurting arm, it turned out surprisingly easy to haul her up the slippery stones, because the man atop it joined the effort, catching her easily, putting her over it as though she had no weight at all. The other rock-hard palm was already grabbing him by his good shoulder, pulling with equal decisiveness.

In another heartbeat, they were over the obstacle, panting. Or maybe it was just him, having a somewhat harder time keeping up with the resumed dash toward the darker shapes of various low constructions, his face still caked with mud, having difficulty letting air in and out through his clogged nose. Even so, he could not help but notice the heavier odor that enveloped them now, like that of the fields in midday, quite a stench. Also the sounds. No fields but a forest those. The distinct growling somewhere between the farther constructions had his stomach turning with fear.

"Here."

Another wall was blocking their way, but this time, the man led them alongside it before diving into a narrow opening, a crack in the damp stones. The growling grew stronger, joined by other distinctly forest sounds, squeaking and grunting, and an occasional howl or a bark. To press Tlemilli closer while slowing his step seemed like a necessity now. She reacted by pushing herself into him with yet greater spirit.

"Don't linger. The warriors will track us here as easily," tossed the man, then slowed his step as well, beckoning them toward the wider path, where the moon was reaching with more generosity. "Now quick. Tell me what you were doing out there. Both of you!"

Beyond the alley, the stench was getting stronger, and so did the noises. That low growling! Miztli tried to organize his thoughts. "I... we... we didn't... It's not what it looked like. I was not..."

"Stop stammering this silly nonsense." The man came closer, not threatening but as always intimidating by his mere presence, his face just an outline in the faint moonlight, the scar glowing eerily, enhanced by the dark shadows. "Why were these men so determined to make you talk? What were you doing under the Tenantzinco delegation's window?" The generous mouth quivered in a familiar grim amusement. "Don't try to talk your way out of it, boy. We have little time before the Palace's guards arrive, hot on the heels of the intruders who made so much noise sneaking around forbidden grounds." The man shook his head, his lips still twisting. "I will not be here, providing them with answers, and neither will you two stay. But before that, you will answer my questions." Now the grin was gone, replaced with a granite-like cutting voice. "I will not resort to the ways of those who captured you before – wish I had a few heartbeats to spend on asking *them* questions! – but I do expect honest answers from you. You know you can trust me not to misuse your information. I think my worth was proven enough in the past."

Miztli's head was reeling and he wished to have a moment of respite, just a few heartbeats of being alone and thinking it all through. The scar-faced man, oh, but he should have expected something like that, shouldn't he? To pop out of nowhere, saving his life, *once again*, then demanding answers, wishing to know what their emperor was up to and what his enemies were up to, diving into the thick of it with no visible reason, no plausible explanation, eager to learn it all. Why?

"Those men worked for the adviser." Tlemilli's voice startled him, reminding him of her presence. She was again tucked in the crook of his arm, so snug and belonging, he forgot her existence for a moment. "They wanted—"

"Tenochtitlan's adviser?" The scar-faced man cut her off forcefully, his voice grating the darkness. "The Emperor's brother Tizoc?"

He could feel her tensing, and his arms moved her away and behind his back, acting out of instinct, as became their custom. "Yes, they talked... they mentioned the 'Revered Adviser' and..." The memory of their blurring voices, the way they floated somewhere above and behind his back, drowning in the aroma of the fresh earth and his fear and helplessness and pain, made him nauseated. He swallowed hard, yet the level eyes, flinty and hard and in control as always, helped for some reason, gave him strength. "I don't think we can know for sure that it was the Emperor's brother, who sent those men to... to do whatever they were supposed to do out there..."

"Yes, they were this same 'adviser's' men," insisted Tlemilli, stepping forward and away from the protective screen of his arms. "I saw them earlier, escorting that man. Back on the Plaza, that is. One of them, the one who was... who was holding you," now it seemed to be her turn to swallow, "he was with the adviser, the Emperor's brother, back on the Plaza. I remember his voice. He spoke strangely, and he looked the same."

Her words brought the wave of dread back, but the scar-faced man was busy squinting at her, his attention undivided. "What did they say back in the gardens now? Word for word!"

He could sense Tlemilli bridling and it brought his equilibrium back, a semblance of it. "They wanted to know who sent me. They kept insisting on knowing that." To draw a deep breath became a necessity. "And yes, one began talking about the adviser, but the other one shut him up quickly, before he could tell more. He kept insisting on knowing about... about the identity... the identity of those who sent me."

"And who are they? Tell me quickly. We don't have time." The pitch-black vastness behind the wall they had climbed was still alive with distant shouting. And so was the darkness ahead and all around, disturbingly vivid with a life of its own, from hooting owls and other night birds of prey to growling he didn't even dare to think about. If back home now, he would be anxious to find a shelter or at least make a really big fire.

"Quick!"

The Texcocan's hand once again locked around his upper arm, rock-hard, yanking uncompromisingly. Not daring to resist, Miztli made sure to hold Tlemilli as comfortably as he could, relieved to feel his arm reacting properly now, aching but not as badly as before. So maybe it wasn't broken. He thanked all benevolent deities for that.

The smell grew worse as they progressed, half creeping half running, following their forceful new leader's example. The Texcocan was sliding along, half bent and as silent and sure-footed as a predator on a trail. A hair-raising sight. The low rumbling and snarling all around didn't help against the illusion. Was this man a shape-shifter, the mysterious *nahual* one heard about only in stories? And what was this place?

"Oh gods, it's where the Emperor keeps his jaguars and pumas," breathed Tlemilli when a sudden roar had them jumping aside, even the fearless Texcocan. "I can't believe it!"

"Keep quiet and talk only in whispers," was the laconic response. "We don't have much time." Pausing well away from the dark forms of the sheds on both sides of the path they were walking, the man shook his head, his chuckle soft, caressing the night. "Don't lean against anything and don't come close to these bars and screens. Stay in the middle of this path and if we are forced to run or walk away, keep to the middle of the pathways until the stench lessens."

"Why?" asked Tlemilli, pressing against him in force like back in Tlatelolco, but at the same time sounding curious and unconcerned.

"Think for yourself, girl," grunted the Texcocan. It was easy to see the outline of his wide shoulders lifting in a brief shrug. "Exploratory paws can squeeze through those bars, always ready to pounce. Or just to explore. Neither will be pleasant to you, I can promise you that. They see perfectly well in the darkness, those magnificent creatures. And they are watching, believe me on that." In the faint illumination of the moonlight that sneaked here as though reluctantly, Miztli watched the man's hand coming up, touching the scarred side of his face lightly, contemplatively, the fingers running alongside the invisible-now sight, outlining it. *Could it be?* he wondered, his mind painting vivid pictures of those "exploratory paws," massive, sinewy, crowned with terrible claws, striking fast, retreating before finishing their work.

"I didn't mean that," protested Tlemilli without her usual passion and force. "I meant, the stench. Why did you say we can wander around freely when the stench goes away?"

"Because then you have obviously wandered far enough from those cages and ponds." The man snorted loudly, then shook his head again. "Enough silly chattering. Tell me what your emperor wanted you to do. Why did he send you to wander around his southern guests' windows? And do it fast, boy. Do not anger me into deciding not to help you out any longer."

Behind his back, something was sniffing the air noisily, spreading more stench. Miztli forced his body into stillness, his instincts screaming, urging him to break into a wild run, no matter where or how. "The Emperor did not tell me to wander under those people's wall openings," he said slowly, trying to gain time.

Was there a way to avoid telling it all? Could he try to do that? This man was so mysterious, so obviously set on the course no one seemed to know or understand. Even Necalli admitted that his admired hero must have plenty of hidden goals and purposes, something he wasn't ready to share with any of them. Should have seen his worshipped veteran now, slinking around Tenochtitlan Palace like a jaguar on a hunting path, spying after spies, knowing where and when and maybe even why, asking questions to missing answers, not even trying to camouflage those with made-up excuses. And why would he? How many people dared to say "no" to such a person?

"Where did he tell you to 'wander' then? Inside their rooms?"

In the strengthening light of the moon that decided to pour its illumination generously all of a sudden, breaking free from the surrounding clouds, it was easy to see the man scanning him with a piercing gaze, his lips quivering, forming again the familiar inverted grin. "Dressed as a serving boy and all that? I see." The arching eyebrows climbed high, replacing the grin. "Why did he have to use you for such a ruse? Doesn't he have enough real slaves to do the listening? What is so special about you, boy, to force you into a disguise you can't even manage, let alone make look convincing?"

For some reason, the words along with another skeptical scrutiny sounded outright offensive. He was not that insignificant, was he?

"He is special, very much so!" As expected, Tlemilli was the one to take offense on his behalf, most readily as always. "He is the only one in the entire Tenochtitlan who can speak the southern people's tongue and no miserable slave or servant can fight like he does or understand what is said enough to bring the important information and not just stupid gossip. No one can do this but him!" Rearing like a ground snake about to strike, she leaned forward, unafraid and oblivious, looking magnificent, all fire and flames. "No one can do what he does, no one!"

"All that, eh?" The Texcocan's expression was wavering between skeptical disdain and a grudgingly appreciative amusement, a sight to behold. "Well, first of all, keep your voice lower unless you wish your highly admired hero back upon the ground, beaten for information." The amusement was gone, replaced with a matter-of-fact frown. "So you speak the southern tongues, boy. Which one? Matlatzinca or something more Chichimec?"

There was no way around it. "Matlatzinca. The tongue that they speak in the western valleys."

"I see." The wide lips were again twisting in a grudging appreciation. "Your emperor is a resourceful man." A glance in the direction they had come from wiped the amusement off once again. "What did you learn eavesdropping on those people? Tell me quickly!" The hard eyes were upon him, piercing. "You don't have a reason to mistrust me, boy. I didn't let you down before. Do not anger me by trying to evade or hide what you know. It isn't wise to do that and I do expect a certain loyalty from you."

For some reason, the words made him ashamed. This man was so good to him, back in Tlatelolco and now, anything but harmful, even if his ways were forceful and his goals unclear; maybe dubious, yes, but not from his perspective.

"They are afraid that people, killers or someone, would try to harm them, or maybe their dignitary. While here in Tenochtitlan. Not in the Palace but on the streets, marketplace." For some reason, he found it easy to remember the warriors back in the smoke-filled room, their quiet but urgent voices, the words that they used. "They thought that some people may wish to interfere..." Suddenly, the newly gained confidence evaporated all at once, shattered by the memory of the words regarding Cuauhnahuac and this same man's native Texcoco, the implied greediness on the Acolhua Capital's part.

"To interfere with what?" The question shot out sharply, not about to let him get away with muttered excuses. "What are you trying not to tell me now?"

He fought the urge to take a step back, the man suddenly a threat, leaning closer, openly dangerous, menacing. As always, it sparked a wave of acute resentment.

"I tell what I remember, and I don't—" he began hotly, but a low growl cut his heated tirade short. Coming from behind their backs, it made his body throw itself away and toward the opposite bushes as the icy wave cascaded down his spine and his arms shot forward, grabbing her on their way, his mind seeking routes of escape.

In the now-generous moonlight, the bear looked monstrous, rearing on its hind legs, huge paws propped against the wooden beams, leaning on those heavily, making them tremble. The grotesquely wide nostrils were sniffing the air, spewing foul odor. Or maybe it was the dreadfully dark mouth, such a fetid crevice, a putrid abyss. Tlemilli let out a strangled cry and he pressed her tighter, his mind amok, calculating their way out, finding none.

"They say those cages are mighty strong." The Texcocan was

still out there, standing in the same pose as before, in the middle of the pathway, seemingly unperturbed. His hand rested easily on the hilt of his knife, drawn already, yes, but not thrust forward; just ready. As though a knife would help against such a monster. "Like I told you two before, you better stay in the middle of the alley. There is no telling what is observing you from those bushes you are trying to dive into, carefully caged or not."

That brought Tlemilli out of the panic-stricken stupor faster than he, his mind momentarily refusing to cooperate, resisting her pull back toward the well-swept ground but only for a moment. The grunting, quieter but as vicious, was indeed coming from the other side of the shrubs, where a lower construction spread into the darkness, enlivened with several glowing dots, more than one pair, as though ready to back the warning. This one was more familiar, bringing memories of various hunting parties he had been taken on from time to time, thrilled and excited and safe with Father, protected by fire that would last them through the night and keep the wolves and coyotes at bay, nothing but those same glowing dots in the darkness.

The Texcocan shook his head, then motioned toward the darker patch of an open ground, safely removed from beams and sheds and their menacing snarling. Squeezing Tlemilli so tightly, he was afraid she would not manage to breathe, Miztli followed, this time with no hesitation. It was safer with this man around. There could be no argument about it. And if the forceful warrior wished to know what he knew, so be it. He didn't care. The Emperor didn't say not to share his knowledge with anyone but him, not in so many words. He shuddered, then took his thoughts off it all, pressing her tighter, feeling the fluttering of her heart against his chest.

"This place is amazing and terrible." Her whisper tickled his ear. "I wanted to see it, but now I just want to be away from here."

As though echoing her words, the Texcocan slowed his step. "It must be magnificent to tour in the full light," he muttered when another low growl evaporated in the darkness, coming from their left, a clear warning. "They don't have such a collection of wild animals out there on the Tlaloc Hill outside Texcoco." Then he froze all of a sudden, looking like a prowling predator himself yet again.

How did one capture such things, that huge bear or growling jaguars, to place them in those strange constructions that would not let the animal escape while putting it on display? wondered Miztli, fighting the urge to run away from another low growl. But this one must be a jaguar, or maybe his namesake, a puma, and but for the darkness, he might have managed to see it, to watch safe and unharmed. A wonder! If only they had a torch, even just a burning stick to look for a moment.

As though answering his thoughts, a bright dot sparkled not far away, flickering between the darker shapes, then another. At the same moment, the Texcocan's hand locked around his arm once again, pulling hard.

"Up there!" the man breathed, charging up the pathway with his typical single-minded resolve, waiting for no confirmation. Not that Miztli thought of arguing, understanding too well. The moving lights meant only one thing. The Palace's guards! Clenching Tlemilli's arm in his turn, he pulled her along, surprised by her continued cooperation. It wasn't like her to just follow, but then who would wish to stay in such place all alone?

"Here!" The hiss of the Texcocan wafted in the night breeze, quiet but forceful, his silhouette changing direction, darting toward what looked like more solid darkness.

"Not again," panted Tlemilli, clearly recognizing this or that sort of a barrier that needed to be climbed as well, but he pulled her on, determined not to fall behind. This man was their only chance, and she needed to be delivered back to her sister safely. Why did she have to go out sniffing around at the first place? It was wild and very Tlemilli-like; still, she was taking it too far now and, without her, he mightn't have gotten in trouble in the first place, come to think of it. Still, as always, her mere presence reassured him, gave him more power.

"I'll get you over it. Come!"

The Texcocan reached what looked like a wooden fence and was motioning impatiently, difficult to see in the fading moonlight but clearly looking toward the flickering spots. Those were moving rapidly, multiplying like dots on the sheets of *amate*-paper back in *calmecac*.

"Keep quiet!" This came as a low growl, silencing Tlemilli's loud panting. The man's eyes were on the nearing lights, but his senses were probing, Miztli knew, reaching behind the wooden barrier, trying to recognize the dangers it hid. His own ears reported unsettling trickling and splashing, as though a considerable body of water was lying in this heart of the city, with deadly creatures inhabiting it. *Ahuitzotls?* The cold wave was back, washing his entire being with a most primitive dread.

"Come!"

To his immense relief, the scar-faced man did not jump the obstacle but burst into a run alongside it, not waiting to make sure they complied. Pulling Tlemilli along, holding her tightly while feeling the wild pounding of her heart again, he listened to the hooting of the owls that were now again dreadfully close, greeting them from the darkness they headed into, warning not to proceed, maybe. Oh, but they needed to get away from this place!

"We'll go over this one." The Texcocan paused for a mere fraction of a heartbeat, scanning a new barrier that sprang to their left, this one made of solid stone, more visible but not by much. The stench coming from beyond it was as heavy as back by the caged bear.

Miztli shuddered again, then hesitated, watching their self-appointed leader shooting another look in the direction of the moving lights now coming from their right, then leaping up the new obstacle as though it was just a few palms high. Which it wasn't, not even near. While part of his mind was busy contemplating how to haul Tlemilli up and over it before their only chance of escape disappeared in the foul-smelling darkness, a slight noise made his nerves prickle worse than before. Something wasn't right behind the dark mass, and when the Texcocan's impressively wide yet lithe silhouette vacillated, poised upon the slippery stones yet leaning slightly, clearly readying to pull her up and help her over, he hesitated for a fraction of a heartbeat, reluctant to let her go.

"Hurry up, for all the small and great deities' sake!" hissed the man, then stopped abruptly.

When he came tumbling down, head first, in most ungraceful fashion, it had Miztli watching in breathless stupor, not understanding any of it, least of all the force with which the man managed to do that, flying quite far, slamming against a tree at least half of ten or even more paces removed. A hiss familiar from their Tlatelolco adventures had another object cutting the darkness, bringing him out of the paralyzed stupor.

"Stay here," he cried out, pushing Tlemilli behind something dark, either a beam or a tree; he didn't know, didn't care. "Don't move!"

The Texcocan shoved himself up drunkenly by the time another wild leap brought Miztli to the man's side, his senses screaming danger, expecting an attack of whatever was assaulting them. Another missile flew by, planting itself in the bark of the tree the man was clawing for support, wavering badly, clearly disoriented. His hand, when it grabbed Miztli's shoulder, locked around it brutally, in a crushing grip.

"Over there... the shrubs," he heaved, veering badly, leaning on his new support with all his weight, or so it seemed, making Miztli struggle to stay on his feet at all. "The dark... We need to get there... In the darkness..."

Which was a sound, good idea, reflected Miztli numbly, noticing Tlemilli's silhouette rushing toward them, slipping next to the Texcocan but from the other side, clearly trying to help, hindering their step even worse. The footsteps of the people from the other side of the wall were almost as distinct. He registered it without thinking, his mind clearing all of a sudden, becoming ice cold, calculating.

CHAPTER 8

Elotl succumbed to the urge of sneaking out and away the moment the locals who came to guide them into the vast crammed-to-the-brim wooden construction began bidding their farewells.

The more respectable elements of their delegation had left long since, taken to homes of various locals, presumably, to smoke pipes or gorge on crispy tortillas and talk in a flowery roundabout way. He speculated on that briefly, mainly on the aspect of crispy tortillas. However, at the time, the semi-darkness of the huge building that stretched to too many paces felt like a safe haven. Even among the remaining people, five other men of various ages, clearly experienced travelers as opposed to his non-existent expertise in wandering distant towns and hills, one could feel a certain sense of relief and lessening tension. They all greeted the opportunity to stay out of the gushing, crammed, brimming streets of the sprawling *altepetl*, even if for a little while.

Fascinated and barely over the shock at the impact of their arrival, Elotl had huddled at the far corner, momentarily relieved to be away from the strikingly wide avenue laid with stones instead of flattened earth. It felt strange under his feet, unnatural. Who were the people who went to all this trouble of polishing stones, then laying them out for everyone to step on? How many were they? Must be twenties upon twenties, but why? And then there was the crowdedness. But he didn't even imagine that so many people existed in the entire world of the Fifth Sun, let alone would bother to gather in one place, one island, however huge, flood its stone-covered avenues, gush like leaves in welling streams after days of rain on the wet season, busy amidst the most overbearing clamor, such loud noise and commotion.

On their journey here, they did pass through quite a few towns, each one larger and more impressive than Oaxtepec, with a lively flow of people coming in and out through the more and less well-kept roads, rushing to and fro. Yet it was nothing like the movement near the shores of those endless bodies of water, first between the lakes called Chalco and Xochimilco and then the hills facing the Great Lake itself, grayish-blue in the rays of the high-noon sun, teeming with canoes like a puddle under a leaves-shedding tree. An incredible sight!

He had had a hard time trying not to gape, and the sensation did not disperse now, half a day later and in the heart of this impossible hubbub, so many people and buildings and streets, all running around or sailing, people by many twenties, boats by the same count, so many his eyes began aching from the attempts to count and his legs from walking those broad strips of land that miraculously stretched over the entire lake, or so it seemed, all hurried, busy, jostling and pushing their way, at home in this impossible tumult.

Even now that the sun had gone down to the Underworld, the clamor did not subside, reaching them through the open shutters and the partly uncovered roof, assaulting their ears and their other senses, the smells nauseatingly rich, foreign, making his stomach churn. The brief refreshment the Oaxtepec delegation was greeted with did not last for long enough to feed all of the new arrivals, certainly not the unimportant elements such as foreign youths tagging along for an unclear purpose. The two men from Metl's shed made themselves clear but only to him. He was to find his brother, learn of his connections, meet these possibly discontented Tenochtitlan denizens and sound them out, then to report back home. The rest of their delegation was to present themselves at the place they called the "royal enclosure," somewhere near that island's magnificent pyramid that towered all the way to the sky as it looked from the distant shores, where, according to the gossip, the great island's mighty ruler lived and launched his conquests from. A hair-raising place, surely. If only he had been allowed to accompany that delegation all the way!

Forgotten in his far corner, he watched the locals who came to guide them here, bidding their farewells, diving into the noisy darkness with no hesitation, unafraid. It made him envious, to a degree. One needed to gather much courage to navigate one's way in this gushing river of people, to know where to go or even how to do it without being trampled on or at least jostled badly.

His fellow travelers were busy talking, making themselves comfortable, fishing blankets and remnants of their foodstuff out of their bags. He had none of this. The hastily rushed afternoon back in Oaxtepec three dawns ago saw him starting on his first far-away journey without any due preparation, no useful items packed, no edible goods; not even his talisman, the perfectly round green stone he had found in an old mine once and kept all for himself against the chance to barter something without family knowledge should the need arise. It never did, but the green stone was so beautiful, so smooth to the touch that he kept it close by, reassured by its presence, calmed by it. Yet now, even this reminder of home wasn't there. A bother!

His stomach rumbled again, empty since the moldy tortilla and a piece of dried meat he had been given on the evening before, a humble fare. The rest of their party ate almost as sparingly; almost but not quite. He was an unwanted addition no one knew or cared about, or bothered to talk to. A good turn as far as his dubious semi-secret mission was concerned, but not so good when it came to his general state of wellbeing. Three dawns of trudging along with no one to talk to and nothing familiar to focus on wore on his nerves. Alone but not, surrounded by people he was supposed to follow, yet on his own – oh, but all this was challenging, testing his willpower, frustrating. He had never been so alone in his entire life.

The draft from the partly shut wooden screen beckoned, bringing in noise and smells but also the freshness of the breeze, its pleasant chilliness. He slipped toward it almost against his will, mainly to busy himself with something, anything, an action as opposed to the depressing inaction, his envy at his fellow travelers' annoyingly lively chatter. The paved ground did not feel strange under his bare feet, not anymore. It was actually pleasant to step on the warm smoothness of those stones. He fought the urge to go down and see those more closely, to touch the polished wonder with his hands. Were those the roads his brother was walking? Did it feel good to him, natural? And where was he, anyway?

A quick glance around informed him that the flow of people had actually lessened compared to their previous walk through the wideness of this alley. Still, the darkness did not banish this *altepetl*'s dwellers into their homes like it would do to his fellow villagers. Not even near! Quite to the contrary, the moon shone brightly, unrestrained, aided by torches some passersby carried, good quality torches of the sort one would be glad to take down the mine, evidently well oiled and wrapped in a thick piece of cloth. Many such lights danced in the distance, where the dark forms of the cane-and-reed huts seemed to retreat, giving way to some brighter surroundings.

His legs took him forward without much thinking. To ease into the stream of strolling people turned out to be surprisingly simple. A woman with too many baskets loaded upon her hefty arms jostled him but moved away without a comment. And so did a few others, murmuring about clumsy foreigners but not challenging in an open way.

Concentrating on his steps, he walked on, pretending confidence he didn't feel, knowing of the importance of such a display, learning all about it from his early days in Oaxtepec, mingling among the snotty toughs of that town, anxious to be accepted but not as a poor villager. Any display of misgiving was bound to put him down and where he actually belonged. It must have been working the same here in this crowded monster of a city. It had to!

Holding his head high, he walked on, trying not to gape, a resolution challenged when the moon and torch-lit square opened before his eyes, as large as a field of maize or cotton, spreading everywhere, teeming with people. The clamor was back, a deafening noise. His stomach as tight as a clogged mine opening, he chanced an open scrutiny, hoping against hope. Would Miztli be somewhere around, walking this vastness, hurrying to reach some place? There seemed to be plenty of youths of his brother's age, congregating near a strange-looking elevated construction behind which sounds of trickling water were so clear they overcame the buzz of too many voices talking at once, coming from everywhere. Involuntarily, he drifted closer, pushed out of the way by a rushing by group of older people, their cloaks dusty, hair pulled into a neat bun.

"Watch your step, you stupid lump of meat," one of them called out but didn't pause when Elotl returned the furious glare, not stepping aside even though they all had passed by already. The brief gesture of the man's upper arm was difficult to mistake. He contemplated returning it, then put his attention back to the chattering youths and the other congregating people, some of them drinking from flasks, others kneeling in groups, tossing stones, clearly playing or gambling. In Oaxtepec, there were plenty of elders who did this, drank *pulque* and played bean games. Not in such numbers, yes, but they did. Again, he wondered if his brother might be somewhere around. The trader said Miztli was mingling with bad company, criminals and such, but where were the monstrous city's criminals hanging? Not upon such lively inhabited square. And yet it was night or close enough to it. Weren't respectable locals retreating to their homes at such a time? In Oaxtepec, they certainly did, not Metl or his followers but others who were looking for no trouble. Even though he rarely stayed around the neighboring town so late, having a long enough journey back home always ahead and waiting.

"Not now, Ollin."

Next to the stone construction with water in it, a good-looking, generously endowed girl was pushing a youth with disheveled hair and a crumpled loincloth away, pouting openly, not angered for real.

"Get your filthy paws off me!"

The youth that ridiculously resembled Metl in the wideness of his cheekbones and the sharpness of his chin grunted something, then went back to his efforts of getting under the girl's prettily adorned *huipil*, greatly concentrated. She slapped his seeking hands away, then put her attention to the nearby group of men in undecorated cloaks that reminded Elotl of Oaxtepec's well-to-do folk one would glimpse while sneaking toward the town's main square, strutting along, looking down their long noses, their fancifully flowing cloaks putting them far apart from the commoners working the fields.

Forcing his head higher, he strolled closer to the strangely walled pond, making sure his back was as straight as it could be, proclaiming his right to be here and stroll wherever he wanted. The girl with the groping youth pushed her persistent admirer away once again, then gave Elotl an indifferent look while squinting against the glow of torches that came from the wooden beams of the fence on the other side of the open ground. By now, it was overflowing with loudmouthed boys of Miztli's age, silly youngsters full of agitation, boisterous pieces of work, spelling trouble. He made sure his knife hung loosely in its sheath, within easy reach.

The cloaked men regarded him with a suspicious glance of their own, some of them, but were quick to divert their attention as another clamor burst from behind the other side of the strange pond, a steady hum of a large body or maybe just many feet walking at once, greatly coordinated. It made him think of warriors he had glimpsed once when still a small child, walking the road behind their fields, terribly sure of themselves and unstoppable, progressing loudly in their strangely clad feet, dangerous in their togetherness. Suddenly worried, he tried to see through the flickering darkness. And so did the rest of the crowding locals, he felt, his uneasiness growing. Only the youths by the fence were shouting as loudly, their waving hands a distraction, annoying in their persistence.

The cloaked men stirred and some of them melted into the darkness, while the girl with her horny admirer displayed rising interest as well, pushing the youth away once again, this time clearly meaning it. Which he didn't take well. Even from a relative distance, it was easy to see the strength with which his hand locked across the girl's upper arm, spinning her around as she began stalking away, still interested in the cloaked men. Against his will, Elotl began walking in their direction.

"Out of the way!"

Instinctively, his feet made him leap aside from the path of another group, this one tightly packed around a sturdy construction that looked like some sort of seating arrangement and seemed to be hovering in the air, propped by several stout-looking men. Like the nobles passing through Oaxtepec on their way to their villas one sometimes would glimpse but without such heavily armed escorts.

Hurriedly, he took another step back, bumping into two men and a woman with baskets, who muttered angrily but did not take their eyes off the approaching warriors and the hovering seat. Unsettled even further, he pushed his way past them, then, seeing the opportunity, sneaked along and toward the crowded fence, sensing the measure of safety there, at least by putting distance between himself and the strange party. The boys lining the wooden planks were still talking loudly, most of them streaming in through the narrow opening, paying the procession across the square little attention.

The good-looking girl, he noticed, was still having a hard time against her single-minded admirer, pinned to the pole of the fence, struggling to break free with what looked like an honest effort now, her fists flailing, trying to reach for her attacker's eyes, having not much success against the expertise of his grip. A few of the youths watched with certain interest, shouting encouragements but for what side, it was difficult to tell.

Elotl didn't hesitate. "Leave her alone!"

To grab the youth's shoulder and yank hard wasn't easy. He did so with all his power, aware of their audience and his lack of sheer physical strength, not anywhere near his brothers' league.

"What are you doing?" cried out his victim, turning to stare and looking genuinely baffled for a moment. His face was a study of changing expressions, from bewilderment to open suspicion to anger. "You stinking piece of rotten meat!" The anger won, obviously. "Go away! Take your rotting carcass elsewhere, you walking pile of excrement. Run away to the hole you crawled from."

"Leave the girl alone," repeated Elotl, feeling at an acute disadvantage, especially at the face of this same curvy fox's reaction, who was staring at him with as much bewildered hostility as the rest of them, not trying to thank him for his gallant intervention, or at least to run away in tears, like any decent girl he knew would have done.

The youth drew himself together with an admirable swiftness, his hand darting toward his side and the nicely wide waistband adorning it, coming back armed with an impressively ragged dagger. "This is the last time I'm telling you to go away, you stinking foreigner. Run back to your stinking fields and do it fast."

His embarrassment evaporated at once, pushed away by the wild flare of temper, reacting likewise to lesser insults than that. "Shut your stupid mouth, you stinking heap of excrement! Go away yourself before I make you do that!" The knife, tucked in the small bag attached to his loincloth, slid out readily, always kept within easy reach. He wasn't new to this sort of confrontation, knowing the type. Plenty of those in Oaxtepec, among Metl's followers and some others. The youth indeed did not make him wait.

"You stinking provincial, you'll regret it!" he cried out, pouncing to close the distance, but halting abruptly at the sight of the poised dagger, a good, fairly long obsidian Father presented him with during the last rainy season. The youth's own shorter blade was evidently of somewhat lesser quality. "This is your last chance to run away, you stinking peasant corpse."

"Not as stinking corpse as you will be in another heartbeat," retaliated Elotl, feeling better by the moment, encouraged by the outburst of chuckling coming from the watching boys. A side-glance informed him that quite a few of those and the girl were still there, watching with keen interest. Yet, the nagging worry was there, spoiling the excitement that always preceded fights. What if those fence-sitters decided to reinforce his rival, to back him against pushy foreigners and their "stinking fields"? His rage splashed with renewed strength. But how dared they? And how did they know?

"Shut up, you filthy piece of foreign excrement," his rival cried out, making no effort to close the rest of the distance. "One more word and you will be cut into so many pieces the cleaners will have to scrub you from the pavement and walls."

He allowed himself to roll his eyes, feeling better than he had in days, since leaving Oaxtepec. "Stop chirping and get on with it." To let the knife slide gracefully between his fingers felt good. He did this with relish, catching it most easily back in the firmest of grips. There was plenty of time to practice this through the boring evenings back at home and it was obvious that the rotten piece of meat wouldn't attack, not without serious backing.

Carefully, he shot a quick glance, making sure none was available or readily offered. Also it gave him an opportunity to check possible routes of escape, just in case. There was a commotion at the far edge of the fence, but on the other side of the square, all seemed to be as lively as before, with the grim warriors and the hovering seat gone. The girl was glancing in this direction too, but before he turned back to his skinny rival that was nothing but words, he saw her eyes returning to him, flickering with amused, slightly derisive interest. How annoying! But they were all looking down on him, worse than back in Oaxtepec even. The wish to use the knife after all welled.

"You better—" began his rival once again, then his eyes shot toward the fence's commotion that seemed to be nearing, following a figure wrapped in what looked like an especially long cloak, or maybe just a vast piece of material, it was difficult to tell. The forcefulness with which it bore upon them had Elotl's spell of confidence disappear all at once. As did the skinny youth's next step. Without spending more time on glancing around or throwing more of his filth Elotl's way, he turned on his heels and fled around the fence's corner, swallowed by the darkness of what looked like another pathway or alley, gone as though he had never been there at all.

The rest of their observers did not stay to watch or comment on any of it either. As though swept by the sudden gust of wind, the sight of their short cloaks disappeared in the opposite direction, along the fence and the opening that was swallowing the rest of their peers earlier. Bewildered, Elotl just stared.

"What is happening here?" demanded the darkly cloaked apparition, seemingly a man with his hair surrounding the blank oval of his face in what looked like a single mass, greatly foreboding. "Answer now!"

Involuntarily, he tried to back away, the rough poles cutting into his back, blocking the way of retreat. The darkness that swallowed the skinny coward before beckoned.

"Who are you, young man, and what are you doing by this school? Whose knife is it? Are you permitted to carry it? What school do you belong to?"

Overwhelmed by this flood of strange questioning, he shifted toward the route to safety, but the frightening man moved with surprising agility, blocking his way, towering there like a menacing creature straight from the Underworld, an ominous presence.

"What school do you belong to? Or what workshop? Are you allowed to carry weapons? Give me this knife!"

The scrawny hand came out, as dry and as wrinkled as a ground snake after moons of no rain, *poisonous*. Horrified, he pressed into the planks of the fence yet harder. His knife? No, he could not, he would not...

"He is attending the *telpochcalli* of the marketplace district, next to the second canal, Revered Priest." The girl's voice penetrated the rising wave of panic, clear and beautifully calm, ringing with encouraging confidence. "My second cousin removed, the nephew of our First Mother, is attending this school together with him. They are allowed to carry knives, all of that class's pupils."

A momentarily silence prevailed; a heavy, menacing soundlessness. A heartbeat passed, then another. The voices from behind the fence reached them but faintly, not as lively as those carrying from the rest of the animated square. It was difficult to believe that the boisterous boys might be somewhere behind those wooden beams. Not the shouting, laughing, dangerously babbling lot. Yet, if the scary man came from in there, then there was no wonder. Numbly, he reflected on it, clutching his knife tightly, his palm slippery, back awash with sweat.

"Who are you, girl?" grunted the man finally. "How are you

connected to all this?"

The curvy fox lowered her head demurely. "I will be honored with attending this school soon, Honorable High Priest. My sister has an honor to be guided by the priestess who is teaching in this establishment."

"Who is your sister?" The questions kept coming, as hostile as the ones shot at him. Elotl dared to sneak a glance at her, grateful, even impressed. She was a brave little thing, all things considered.

"She is..." This time, the girl's speech faltered, turned halting. "She is attending this school and she has nothing to do with this other *telpochcalli* boy. I just mentioned it... I just—"

"What are yours and your sister's names, and what is your father's trade. Answer quickly!"

Now Elotl felt outright bad. "She has nothing to do—" he began, but the cloaked man's glare cut him short.

"Hold your tongue, young criminal!" It came out like a lash. "Your turn to answer questions will come soon enough."

In the corner of his eye, he could see the girl shifting, as though about to burst into a quick run. He didn't blame her this time, contemplating the same, the merciful darkness to his left beckoning again, possible to charge through but for the need to extricate her from the same predicament. He couldn't possibly leave her to the mercies of the scary man, some sort of an official, not just a bully, clearly. It was because of him that she became implicated. Somehow. It was still difficult to understand it all.

"Answer me, disobedient child!"

"The stone worker," she sputtered. "My father is the stone worker from our district's *calpulli* and..."

The hubbub of the square was rising again, with a new procession of torches winding its way around the stones of the water construction. Accompanied by powerful voices that demanded the crowds to disperse yet again, it drew the attention of their interrogator as well, and as the man turned his head, Elotl saw their chance. Grabbing the girl's arm, he darted into the shimmering darkness, where his previous rival disappeared in a likewise fashion, trusting his instincts rather than any rational thought, doing what he always did the best, following his senses, unless under the crumbling ground. He shivered, then pushed the memory aside.

Not surprisingly, the girl followed, her footsteps as rapid, resonating against the warm stones. Her wrist felt soft against his fingers, delightfully smooth. Briefly, he reflected on it, then pulled them both into a pitch-black breach that spread to their left, a pathway or maybe just an opening into someone's patio. The feel of breaking bushes made him suspect the latter.

For a heartbeat, they listened, keeping absolutely still, inappropriately close but not caring, worrying about the cloaked man. Then the girl pulled away abruptly.

"Don't you dare touch me!" In the pitch black darkness that surrounded them now, all he could see was the mere outline of her, still temptingly curvy. "Keep your paws well away!"

"I'm not pawing you," he muttered, at a loss as to how to proceed, having difficulty recalling how they got there but knowing that they should be running on fast. "That man, he was mean, as harmful to you as he was to me. You couldn't stay to face him."

"Oh, yes?" Her hands thrust against her clearly silhouetted hips, in a warlike fashion of girls that never bode well to a man, not in his experience. "Well, it was because of you that he became incensed with me. You were the one to pick fight with Ollin in the first place and it was silly of me to try and help you out at all." In the renewed flicker of moonlight, he could see a small frown crossing her prettily round face. "You could have run like he did. To stay and face the *telpochcalli* priest was more than stupid. Even for a foreigner with nothing but a worn-out loincloth and no sense, you should have—"

But by then, he had had enough. "I helped you out, you stupid snotty fox," he cried out, forgetting to keep quiet. Her speech, even if vicious, was delivered in satisfactorily hushed tones. "That skinny rat had his paws all over you and you had no chance of getting away from him, you wimpy incompetent gutless squirrel! Without me, you would be enjoyed out there in front of everyone by now, way before that cloaked man came and he would be yelling at you just the same, and you would be quivering and answering all his questions, your father's name and all that. You are *that* pitiful!"

Her eyes were huge and still growing rounder as he spoke and that did not help to mend his temper. On the contrary, it made him feel somewhat guilty and thus caused his rage to flare yet fiercer. She had no right to make him feel like an uncouth barbarian from the hills. He did nothing to warrant that.

"What are you staring at me like that for?" he demanded, disregarding the need to lower his voice, this entire day of continued humiliation, let alone the stupid ridiculously pointless journey, culminating here, in this stinking dark alley, with nothing to do and nowhere to go but to tread back to the stinking warehouse and dismissive glances of his would-be companions, or worse yet, to crawl back home, like a kicked coyote with his tail between his legs, begging forgiveness, back to the mines and the fields and the stupid boredom, hoping to live down this folly of his one day.

She was still staring at him, her nicely dimpled chin quivering.

"What do you want? Go away. Run before you get *pawed* once again."

Her footsteps rang with appropriate hurry, swallowed by the darkness in no time. For a moment, he just stood there, then crashed his fist against the nearby stones, wincing with pain but not caring. It was all just too much.

Unwilling to follow her course of flight yet afraid to risk retracing his steps back to the troublesome square, he hesitated, then felt rather than saw the approaching shadows. Quite a few, progressing with no aid of a torch or even the moonlight that did flicker weakly but not on his side of the dark alley. His sanity returning, he calculated fast, his ears informing him that those people were walking briskly, his senses translating it into a confident walk, not something one would wish to confront in the dark corners of the city one was a stranger to. Look how the girl called him a naked foreigner with no sense. The fury splashed anew, then subdued. The nearing people were more important by far, clearly a danger.

Clutching his knife tighter, his back against the bushes,

contemplating, he found himself clawing his way through those before his mind managed to decide on the proper course of action. Like always, it was better to trust his instincts, even though what worked in Teteltzinco or Oaxtepec might not be as handy here, in this monstrously crowded inimical place. No wonder Miztli did not fare well here. No, he must not leave before finding out what happened to his brother.

A cozy patio with short rows of vegetables dotting it greeted him, surprisingly calming, ridiculously similar to their own back home. It looked deserted, but he knew better than to linger, even in order to get his bearings. Not now. The dwellers of the house adjacent to this patio might not take his intrusion well. As in sophisticated Oaxtepec, people liked no strangers roaming around their patios and their vegetable plots. The memory of Metl's fiery sister surfaced. Such a tempting-looking fox, spicy, delightfully dangerous, taunting with her looks, promising. It would be a thrill to hold this one close, to exchange a fleeting kiss and some groping around. She looked as though she meant it when she said to come visiting when he was back from Tenochtitlan.

On the other side of the prickly mess, there seemed to be another patio, smaller and more neglected, lined with uneven rows of sprouting green. Here the moonlight reached more easily, and while it allowed him a better look to try and find his bearings, to determine a possible direction, it was exposing him dreadfully, leaving him open to any wandering or prying eyes.

A concern that proved relevant the moment he reached the next yard, as neglected as the previous one but not abandoned. A small shadow, nothing but a skinny underfed child crouched in the middle of it, staring at him, as wary as a surprised forest rodent. Elotl tried to slam his mind into working, his panicked gaze noting that another mess of prickly bushes hovered only a few leaps away. Even if the child screamed like Metl's sister did when he had jumped on her doing her needs in between the sprouts, he would be out and away before the rest of the indignant family showed up, and this time, he wouldn't be lingering around any nearby sheds, to be recognized later on in the most embarrassing of manners.

"Don't scream!" he breathed loudly. "I'm out of here. Leaving."

To his astonishment, the child reacted by bolting away himself, leaping toward the same bushes he was intending to accost, diving into their not-so-very tender embrace with the swiftness of a squirrel, surprisingly sure of himself. Blinking, Elotl stared for another heartbeat, then followed the example, giving himself to the mercy of the prickly branches that of course made it their business to tear at his skin.

Spilling into a new narrow pathway, hedged by a dark mass that looked too solid to be another prickly barrier, he glimpsed the skinny shadow scrambling back to his feet, pouncing toward him instead of away, planting a very sure kick at his side, hardly painful but vicious, followed by another. Not as sure of his own footing as yet, having emerged out of the inimical shrubs' clutches, Elotl wavered, grabbing a scrawny limb that assaulted him, whether to steady himself or to initiate a counterattack, he didn't know. Which resulted in a struggle of unexpected proportions, the boy wriggling and kicking with true determination, biting and even slashing something tiny but sharp. A knife? The moonlight was pouring more generously here, but it still did not allow a worthwhile look.

Stifling the most direful curses that threatened to burst out on their own, Elotl struggled to keep the little rat at arm's length, knocking the knife out of the bony hand, absorbing more kicks. The boy's feet were small but rangy, their angles painfully sharp.

"Stop it, you filthy piece of stupid meat! One more kick and I'll knock you senseless!"

A better directed hit was his answer, accompanied by another attempt to break free. He shook the boy hard, his rage sudden and difficult to contain. "You filthy rat!"

Surprised with his own determination not to let his prey go – but what did he want from this one? Answers? Answers to what? – he twisted to avoid another kick, then heard rather than felt a nearing presence. People were walking the dusty stones, coming up the pathway, talking rapidly, in hushed tones. More than a few pair of feet again. Elotl didn't fight the urge to bolt away. In this huge, strangely violent *altepetl*, such a reaction seemed to be the only wise course.

To his surprise, the boy, as free as a bird now, instead of bolting in another direction, or maybe even toward the newcomers, did the only unforeseen thing, namely followed him up the narrowing alley, then darted aside and into the solid wall of bushes and stones. Out of an instinct rather than a thoughtful reaction, Elotl changed his direction too, a quick glance informing him that there must be an opening there, a dark gaping crack. No chance of squeezing through.

He glanced at the road, then leapt toward another dark mass of scattered stones and beams that blocked the rest of his way, diving under their dubious protection, near panic again. No, he didn't want any more encounters with the irrational locals, neither grown people nor youths set on threatening but not following their threats through, nor unreasonably foul-mouthed foxes and little rats who attacked like crazed forest cats, sporting knives and using them with no hesitation.

The muffled voices floated in the darkness, reaching him before the silhouettes did. Holding his breath, he listened to the pouring words, quiet and urgent, rushing like a current in a narrow passage.

"Don't even think of running away with it, or any other such silliness. All the stones in there are counted. Every single one of them!" A brief pause that ensued was loaded with clear meaning. "One missing trinket and you will be begging for mercy, to be put to death quicker than it'll happen."

"Yes, yes," the other voice hurried to interrupt, its trembling pronounced. "It will be delivered as it is. Of course it will!" The nervous gush rose in volume. "Tlatelolco is easier to move through now. I won't be detected this time. I swear!"

"You better!"

Another bout of rustling had Elotl catching his breath once again. They were moving. Nearing his dubious hideaway? Sweat rolled down his back and his forehead, soaking his hair. To reach for his knife became a necessity. If only he wasn't crammed in here so awkwardly, tucked under a wide beam and a few crumbled stones, twisted between his own limbs, in the most helpless of positions. Would he have enough time to uncoil when discovered, to defend himself somehow, or run away, or put up a decent fight?

The voices dropped to mere whispers, muffled by the rustling of the stones above his head. Showers of small gravel came next. He didn't dare to breathe, or hope, for that matter, but for a wild moment, the temptation to follow these men over the breakage surfaced. There must be a secret passage there, or maybe a place of hiding.

The shuffling of the now-lone footsteps brought him back to reality, still weak with relief. They were leaving; by different routes, but they were. All he had to do was to wait, then follow the same alley rather than climb the stones above as one of the men did. Was that the one threatening, or the one who was so very afraid, promising to succeed no matter what?

Unable to fight the temptation, he peeked out, catching a glimpse of a figure rushing away, passing the moonlit spot next to which he remembered the little rat disappearing into this or that crevice of the crumbling wall. As though brought out by the sheer power of that memory, the slim silhouette darted out and into the darkness as well, as soundless as a forest creature, indeed something feline, an ocelot cub.

Half expecting to see it assaulting the drawing away man in the way it had happened to him, Elotl slipped out as well, feeling as though on a hunting trail, all senses and danger, proud of his own soundless walk. Boring this *altepetl* was not; anything but. For some reason, it made his mood improve by leaps and bounds. Even the memory of the curvy fox from the square was not annoying, not as badly as before. She was unreasonably ungrateful, yes, and yet so nice looking, with such a promising spark. But for the opportunity to run into her again, preferably under better circumstances.

The steady hum of the lake was back, soothing his nerves. Like on the accursed square, the shore was clamorous and well illuminated, crowded with too many people, walking or rushing or talking in groups. Again, he wondered if the dwellers of the huge island slept at all through their nights.

The man with the bag was still clearly visible, his obvious hesitation and fear, pausing to talk to a group of huddling people, nervous and ill at ease. The skinny boy was around as well, slinking after his "prey," following like a coyote on a fresh trail of footprints, probably aware of his Elotl's presence as well. He didn't care. Who could prove that he had a connection to any of that? Near the shore, people seemed to be more reasonable, not seeking to pick fights.

The illusion that shuttered fast enough as he walked into a better lit spot next to the wooden planks that seemed to be plunging straight into the dark water, hosting people and canoes with baskets, the strong odor of fish emanating from those, causing his stomach to react in a violent manner, bringing his hunger back in force.

"What are you sniffing here for?" a hill of man demanded, his massive shoulders and arms buried under too many baskets lining those, balanced in a miraculous way.

"Nothing," declared Elotl, fed up with people challenging him wherever or whenever he went into the open. What was wrong with them all? "I didn't tell you something or bump into you or anything!"

"Watch your tongue," the man growled, stepping closer, planting his feet on the pavement as though intending to root there forever, like a mighty forest tree. "Skinny foreigners like you would do better keeping their tongue between their teeth or they will be assisted in that."

Against his better judgment, Elotl refused to move, or better yet, to sprint away and back into the safer darkness. There was plenty of space to bypass him; he was not in the way of this rude fisherman stinking of his catch. His knife was again sleek in his sweaty palm.

"Thief! Thief!" The yells erupted from the shimmering darkness, where groups of people were congregating, and where the nervous man from the dark alley went. "The dirty cub! Stop him, stop him!"

Startled out of their staring contest, Elotl glanced away. The fisherman, even if huge, was too overloaded with his cargo to be considered a real threat. Still, he kept this one in sight while sneaking a peek toward the continued agitation, surprised to see the fearful carrier of the bag with mysterious stones he was not to lose or else charging after none other than the skinny rascal that was sprinting away, running as though the entire army of the Underworld creatures were after him, eager to sample the taste of his flesh. Which wasn't anywhere close to this; still, the nervous man from the alley seemed to be closing the distance, aided by a few others, as eager to win the race.

The skinny thief might have been a fierce little thing, but a runner he was not. Even from a certain distance, it was easy to see how badly out of breath he was. The small bag was clutched in his gaunt palm, swinging together with its frantic sway. For some reason, it made Elotl feel bad, thinking of his brother running from this or that gang of criminals or rather the warriors eager to take him to those mysterious courts the trader was talking about.

Without thinking, he darted out and toward the boy and his chasers, seeing the little thief's eyes widening, halting abruptly, then changing direction of his flight, a desperate maneuver. It made his skinny limbs wave wildly and his chasers close the rest of the distance, gaining on him, victorious. When Elotl collided with the one leading the chase – not the bag's owner or rather a carrier, but another sturdier-looking type – it seemed to take everyone by surprise, even the culprit himself, who in the meanwhile went down sprawling, absorbing one hearty kick after another.

"You stupid lump of meat," cried out the man Elotl collided with, fighting for balance himself, having an upper hand as opposed to his victim. "Use your eyes, you stinking foreigner!"

Elotl pushed him away with enough force to have the man going crashing down, putting it all into his initial shove. When lacking exceptional physical strength his brothers possessed in abundance, one has to do with swiftness and viciousness of the very first attack. His experience taught him that much.

Not waiting for his first victim to recover, he planted his fist into another man's belly, then pushed him away using his shoulder and his own body's drive. The boy was struggling back to his feet in a surprisingly clumsy fashion, and, seeing a momentary opening, Elotl grabbed the grimy shoulder and partly dragged, partly carried him back toward the planks and the temptingly quiet darkness behind those, wondering why he had been doing it at all.

CHAPTER 9

To fight the waves of the deep, primitive terror that permeated her entire being turned out to be next to impossible when the darkness filled with distinct growling, closing from all around as though eager to swallow them and eat them alive.

It was one thing to listen to stories and revere jaguars, those legendary beautiful lethal creatures, capable of killing a warrior with one sweep of a mighty paw, one bite of powerful jaws, one monstrous roar and cry. In Tlaco's stories, it was thrilling and wonderfully dangerous, delightfully hair-raising, tickling one's senses and possible fear. However, in the nighttime reality of Tenochtitlan Palace and its forbidden grounds, there was no thrill and no excitement. Only terror and dread, and this all-prevailing panic, the urge to run somewhere, anywhere, away from the growling and the stench. But how stinking this place was!

"Don't come near... near the cages." The Texcocan's voice rang faintly, weak but reassuring, familiar, promising safety, a ridiculous combination as the man could barely walk, let alone lead the way. Still, she knew that he would know what to do if any of the prowling creatures would spring out of the surrounding darkness, to devour them all and tear them into pieces. The wave of panic was back, pushed away with an inhuman effort. Miztli needed her help, and so did the Texcoco man he had half carried, half dragged along, propped against his wide shoulder, stifling groans.

Earlier, after the failed attempt to go over the wall and the ensuing attack by whoever was pursuing them, the scar-faced man looked dead, crumpled on the ground he had hit with such a loud thud, lying there in a dark pile of limbs. It had taken her a few heartbeats to find her bearings, to try and understand what happened, why Miztli was pulling her so roughly, shoving her behind a cluster of foul-smelling beams with none of his usual tenderness and consideration, disappearing into the darkness almost as quickly, leaving her alone amidst nearby splashing and monotonous squawking, the smell so foul, so revolting, coming from behind those same rotten planks. Immediately, she panicked, not thinking twice before charging into the same dangerous shadows, to find them struggling, trying to progress into some thicker darkness. To leap forward and nearly crash into them seemed like the only thing to do, but when she propped up the wavering man from the other side, Miztli seemed grateful. Not that it helped. Her grip caused the man to utter a funny groan, then collapse back onto the ground and stay there, this time an inanimate form.

"Is he dead?" she had breathed, her heart thundering, racing madly as though trying to drown the noises, not all of them belonging to other than human creatures. The night breeze was soft, bringing along words and rapidly exchanged sentences, drifting closer and closer.

"I don't know," panted Miztli, putting his ear to the man's chest in what looked like a surprisingly practiced manner. Then the old resolute firmness, familiar from their running around in the war-torn Tlatelolco, flooded in and his silhouetted shoulders straightened decisively, making her feel better. "We must get away from here."

The wounded was stirring, murmuring incoherently. Relieved, she let out a held breath, then watched Miztli getting to his feet, straightening with an effort, his shoulder propped against the Texcocan's side once again, taking most of his weight, she knew, hauling his charge up despite mild resistance.

"Careful!" was their rewarding hiss, cut short by an anguished groan. "Stop that! Let go, you stupid cub!" This time, the wounded did manage to put up a fight that resulted in him wavering, standing on his own momentarily before going down again, caught halfway by Miztli, both of them swaying precariously, the man's cry tearing the night, animal-like, fitting in these particular surroundings.

"We must get away from here," insisted Miztli with matching forcefulness, getting an upper hand. They were still upright, in a somewhat better position now, swaying but not looking as though about to go tumbling down, not again. "We must go. Now!"

The man grunted, then motioned with his head. "Come from the other... the other side..."

And suddenly, she knew what the problem was and before Miztli resumed his attempts to argue or pull by force, she sneaked under the wounded's other arm, trying to prop it up as best as she could. He was so tall and so heavy! Then Miztli seemed to understand that he had been pulling from the wrong, the wounded, side, and in no time, the crushing weight was off her and they stumbled away and into the dangerously alive darkness, vibrant with foul-smelling sounds, dotted with invisible eyes, focused on them hungrily, of that she had no doubt.

And now here they were, still in this grunting and growling, away from human voices but not reassured by their temporary escape. The Palace's guards would come sniffing around, hot on the daring intruders' heels, and what would they tell if caught? What could they tell? Oh, but Citlalli would be furious, angered for real. More than she must have been angered by now? Back from the royal reception she was forced to attend by the vile adviser's servants sent to deliver the invitation – an aggravation in itself – and probably worried sick by her, Tlemilli's, absence. Oh Coatlicue, mother of all gods!

"Stay here, in the middle... the middle of the path," repeated the Texcocan, wavering but holding on, clearly trying not to lean on Miztli, who was panting loudly himself, not very steady, gasping for breath. "Keep close together."

As though she needed the reminder. But for this man, she would have been in Miztli's embrace all this time, pressing the closest, less terrified and unprotected than now. Bother this! And where was this man wounded? How seriously?

Another growl, this one so close she could smell the warm breath of the creature emanating from the darkness to their right.

To throw herself into Miztli became a necessity. His arm squeezed the breath out of her, wrapping around her with much force while he struggled to stay on his feet anew. She didn't care. Neither the needs of their wounded companion mattered at this point. Only the nightmarish darkness with its bloodthirsty sounds and eyes.

"Keep away from the bars!" The Texcocan man staggered toward the darker shape of what looked like trees or bushes and was leaning against one of the trunks heavily, catching his breath. "We keep... keep going forward..."

She could feel Miztli pulling her along with much force. "Lean on us," he said firmly, in a tone that brooked no argument. "Tlemilli will support you from the other side. Do it now!" The flickering of the torches in the darkness they had left before could not be mistaken, plenty of dots dancing in the night, heading in their direction. "Come! There must be a wall there, another fence."

This time, the man didn't argue or even comment. A heartbeat of hesitation, and she felt his movement, the anguished effort, the suppressed groan.

"Let him lean on you. Support him from the other side." Miztli's hands pushed her along with little ceremony. "Careful of the wound."

The urge to flare at him, to tell him go and distribute his orders elsewhere, welled, then died away, cut by another low grunt, this one coming from their left and slightly behind. A different sound. She felt her scant body hair raising.

"A puma," muttered the Texcocan, leaning on them heavily, partly dragging along, partly leading, clogging her nostrils with an odor that brought back her dying Tlatelolco in force, this mix of sweat and blood, such a disgustingly sweetish stench. "They keep them closed at night... they must. They wouldn't let them out like that. Not on the Palace's grounds."

The words did not reassure, not this time. Neither did the shudder that rocked his body, then another. Was this man afraid? No, it couldn't be. Even under such circumstances, even like now...

"There would be a fence somewhere out there." Miztli's voice rang with its previous stony firmness, reflecting no hesitation and no fear. "We will reach it and go over it."

This time, she didn't feel like offering an argument. Bettering her stance against their charge's ribs, his formidable palm locked around her shoulder, digging into it as though trying to crush it, she concentrated on her step, the blinding darkness oppressive; no protection there but only a threat, the moonlight so faint, barely able to light the shapes of the surrounding vegetation among the darker masses of fences. To think of what was behind those made her stomach turn to jelly. The night was alive with rustling and grunting, full of careful movement, pierced with an occasional mournful howling or snarling. Weren't they better off waiting for the people with torches, eager to punish them for intruding or not? The voices were nearing rapidly, very sure of themselves, reassuring in a way. They had light and weapons and knowledge of these inner gardens and paths, where to go, how to escape.

"Maybe we should..." she began, then swallowed hard, feeling them veering, leaping away from a louder noise, a sort of an intense hiss that originated from between loosely placed beams that blocked their way, sounds of trickling water accompanying it, resonating in a strange way. At the same time, several voices and the shuffling of sandaled feet burst upon them from the darkness they had barely escaped, ominous in their confident loudness. The Palace's guards knew that their prey could not escape them. Secretly, she welcomed their advent.

"Over there," breathed the Texcocan, pulling them in the opposite direction with a surprising strength, as though regaining his old vitality and power. "Quick!"

Not to squeeze through the crudely cut planks was not a possibility, as Miztli's arms were already pushing her ahead, their touch as always encouraging, overcoming the doubts. He could not be caught sneaking around the Palace, running away from the guards. Imperial mission or not, he would not fare well at the hands of their captors, let alone their wounded companion.

As though eager to strengthen her resolve, a mournful howl made the voices out there subdue for a moment. It echoed among the dark trees, answered by another lone mourner. The spirits of the Underworld? She felt her legs giving way, her chest unable to get even a small gulp of air.

"Wolves!" Miztli's breath was warm upon her cheek, his hands gripping her again, so very welcome, protective. The aroma of burning oil was mixing with the rest of the stench all around now, the flames dancing in the air, small lakes of light, not friendly or promising.

She stared at the dark forms behind those, afraid to breathe or move or even think, for that matter. The people upon the trail they had left seemed to freeze as well, listening. Nothing was left but the lively darkness, continued splashing to their left, an occasional low hiss, other warbling that did not belong to the birds, of that she was sure. That and the thundering of Miztli's heart resonating against her body, so very close, the only reassurance, thumping loudly enough to give them away. Why wouldn't the warriors drag them out already, away from this terrible place, anywhere but here!

The howling ricocheted again, then something swished, landing in the vegetation beyond the trail, making a rustling noise. Two of the nearest flames came to life all at once, darting after it. In another heartbeat, she felt Miztli pushing her ahead and into the grating darkness, away from the lights but in the wrong direction. That splashing and hissing; no, she didn't want to know what it was.

To resist his push didn't help, however, as she began digging her heels in, determined to slow their progress if not to stay where they were, the rasping breath of the Texcocan burst upon them from behind the darkish silhouette of something elevated; maybe a crate, maybe a platform. Leaning against it with his entire body, his good arm supporting his stance, presumably, he had only his head to beckon them with, indicating that they should come behind it, or maybe climb it; it was difficult to tell. Behind their backs, the voices of the warriors merged into a steady hum, not drawing nearer; a relief.

"Over there, quickly!" The man's voice was nothing but a breath of air, so quiet she wasn't sure it wasn't her imagination that put those words out there.

To follow his staggering figure wasn't hard. He was wavering like a marketplace commoner drunk on *pulque* she once saw back in Tlatelolco, such funny gait. Trying not to snicker, she felt Miztli propelling her ahead before leaping back toward the wounded, propping him up once again, careful to do so from the correctly unharmed side this time. Good for him.

She glanced at the resumed splashing sounds, smelling the pond now, heavy with its typical watery aroma, worse than her favorite pond in the Tlatelolco Palace, not the one with ducks and fish. Was this pool full of similar creatures, hence the splattering? Before the question formed fully, her eyes caught the sight of something moving in what looked like thicker vegetation, stirring ever so slightly, like a log that suddenly came to life. Momentarily paralyzed, she watched it, her instincts screaming danger, her limbs refusing to comply with her frantic mind's pleas. The long shadow moved unhurriedly, walking rather clumsily on its fat short extensions for legs. *Cipactli*? The legendary crocodile from the calendar and the stories?

In the glow of the nearing torch, it was easier to see its ragged ungraceful form, the outline of the giant jaw, just like in books, so disproportionally big, even if not opened as yet to show the razor-sharp blades for teeth, a multitude of those if the books were to be believed. In the middle of her overwhelming dread, she felt Miztli's arms clutching her again, while the Texcocan man's voice rasped somewhere nearby. "Go, go now. Run! Up there, up the incline. Now!"

Then his arm shot up and forward, a knife just a silhouetted extension of it, separating at once, shooting toward the torch and the man who held it, his attention on the crawling monster as well, seemingly transfixed. The intense low hissing, familiar from their earlier meddling here, tore the darkness again and again, but as the torch wavered and fell, flickering weakly upon the damp ground and next to its suddenly sprawling holder, it changed its tune, became more ominous. Then the monstrous *cipactli* was leaping forward with surprising agility, running rather than crawling, his short legs pushing hard, and as another yank had her hauled away and up the incline, she could swear that the giant jaws were opening, showing terrible blades for teeth, larger and more numerous than on any painting, sparkling dully, liked ragged obsidian.

"Up there... behind the shed," rasped the Texcocan, running as fast as they did, or so it seemed, having no trouble keeping up, not this time. "We climb... climb this thing." Then he stumbled over something and would have gone sprawling but for Miztli leaping forward, catching his shoulder while still clutching her upper arm tightly, somehow managing to balance them all without slowing their step, or at least without stopping for good.

Her dread retreated at once. The images of the opening jaws and the man beside the smoking torch, fluttering weakly, at the mercy of the dangerous monster creature; all those didn't matter as long as *he* was here, keeping her safe. Keeping them all safe!

Abruptly, she freed her arm from his grip. "I'll help."

The wounded was staggering badly again, but when she slipped her shoulder under his arm, revolted by the renewed odor of wet stench but not caring, he leaned on her readily and their progress became easier, in a way.

CHAPTER 10

The new alley was broader and abandoned, sleeping quietly as appropriate for this time of the evening. Elotl glanced at the sky. Was it past midnight already? The boy by his side nudged him with his pointy elbow, indicating the nearest patio.

"There. Plenty of *chian* there, and beans and tomatoes."

Elotl pushed the skinny joint away. "I'm not going to steal their food," he muttered angrily, wondering how he got involved in this continued misadventure when all he wanted to do was to walk around, see what this "capital of the world" was all about, look for his brother or his possible whereabouts. A simple thing to do, back home or in Oaxtepec, but apparently not so simple when it came to the busy monster of an island, so huge and sprawling and buzzing, so full of people and goods and violence, everyone unreasonable and quick to take offense, either snobbish or obnoxious or just outright nasty. The warriors and the carriers of the seat, the girl and the filthy type who kept bothering her, the man of authority with a cloak and this skinny street rat, just an underfed child of little summers but as vicious as an angry opossum, attacking when thinking threatened and with a knife of all things, running away, then stealing from someone, robbing the man outright, then turning all helpless, sprawling right there on the planks of the water construction, with his chasers ready to harm the little thing if not to kill and he, Elotl, left with no choice but to intervene, fight those who he managed, then run away, carrying the stupid culprit along, he and his loot, that bag the man from the previous pathway was told not to lose or else. What a stupid predicament!

Back at the clamorous shore, he didn't think it all through. The men were brutal and unreasonable, set on hunting down the pitiful thing they should not. Whatever his crimes were, the boy looked in dead trouble, and the thought of his brother lost here in this monstrous place, maybe as helpless and hunted, made him act with no logic or forethought, and now here he was, stuck in another dark alley, freezing in the strengthening wind, soaked after thrashing in the shallow water under some massive construction where the boy, back businesslike and efficient, had made them hide. Back then, all he wanted was to get away from it all, return to the huge wooden building and the indifference of his temporary fellow travelers, relax and think without the need to run and fight and escape again and again.

"See? Over there. They have no fence there, nothing!" The rapidly whispered words brought him back from his unhappy musings and into the moonlit darkness, the wind not as cutting as back by the shore but still freezing cold, his loincloth soaked, clinging to his skin. "Their beans are the best now, the tastiest."

"I'm not stealing their food," repeated Elotl angrily, hating it all, the wind and the cold and the brightness of the night and his unwanted company with no principles and not even the most basic morals, looking a neglected child but acting a corrupt ruffian, a true storage room rat. "Just go on, find that old man who would get those stones off you, like you said he would, and be off."

"But you are hungry too," protested the boy, his eyes widening in genuine puzzlement. "You said so yourself."

"I'm not going to faint the way you did. Or steal!" he added pointedly, forgetting to keep quiet.

Momentarily freezing, they listened, but the random noises and calls coming from behind various patios lining the dark alley did not change in volume or frequency, the shouting erupting from the dwelling they had been watching ringing with stridency, enlivened by different female voices, all shrill with real viciousness.

"I'm not going there," he repeated more quietly, moving away from the unpleasant touch of the grubby elbow. "Don't count on me feeding you in this way. Just get on with your previous scheme of getting rid of the stones. I can't wander about with you for the entire night."

The boy's eyes were huge, out of proportion with the gaunt scrawniness of his face, nothing but bones and stretched skin. "Those stones aren't yours."

"They aren't yours either," retorted Elotl, making a face in response to the fiercest of glares. "You keep forgetting that I was there before, way before you got your stupid skinny behind into so much trouble I had to save it from getting a real beating."

"I did not—" began the boy hotly, looking as though about to spring to his feet and either attack his offender or sprint away rather fast. The second thing he would have done with no delays, knew Elotl, but for his limp. Somewhere in the melee of the shore, the little rascal must have twisted his ankle or maybe broke something, as later on, their way out of the water under the massive construction and up an intricately looking incline was marked with plenty of awkward jumping on one leg. Otherwise, he wouldn't have seen the filthy rat and his precious loot anywhere nearby by now. On that he was prepared to bet the last of his meager possessions.

"Stop yelling and get on with your search of that old man," he said tiredly. "I get one stone for saving you and carrying you all the way here. And that's it. From then on, you can limp away with your loot all by yourself."

"But the beans," insisted the annoying little thing, frowning against the shimmering darkness of the patio in question. "We need to eat first. It's more important. The stoneworker has plenty of fowls to grow things, and no sons at all. Just useless girls," he related, as though after a thought. "That's why they are screaming. They always do."

More shouts indeed emanated from behind the peeling adobe of the nearby opening in the wall. Elotl made a face. "Eat from what you get for the stones. It must give you twenty meals or more. This bag looks plump enough."

"Twenty meals?" repeated the boy incredulously, his eyes again widening beyond proportions. "Twenty beans or more?"

"Maybe even twenty and a half," said Elotl, suddenly amused, feeling old and sophisticated, not such a familiar feeling since reaching this over-crowded island. "With not only beans but some nice cobs of maize thrown in. And a good cut of a deer, all fat and dripping." His stomach reacted to his own words a little too noisily, painting pictures he didn't care to imagine. Father carrying a whole dripping doe on his massive shoulders, or a huge bag made out of skin belonging to the hunted creature, holding in already cut meat and fat.

"What's 'cut deer?'" asked the boy, frowning. "Why is it wet?"

"What?" He came out of his reverie, noticing that across the thinly lined bushes the doorway of the house they had been watching screeched, pushed aside with too much force, spewing out a figure that looked familiar, in a way. The shrill yells poured out together with it, unrestrained now.

"Go away, why not? Go and do what decent girls don't! It'll be so like you to end up on the marketplace, painting your teeth black and offering yourself for one cocoa bean at the most."

"Leave me alone, you stupid bag of bones!" cried out the girl, her voice unmistakable, bringing memories of the crowded square back. "You'll be there faster when Father sees you for what you are and throws you out." The rest of her words trailed off in a bout of noisy sobbing.

The boy by his side lurched as though about to run away, but when no more figures sprang out to mar the relative peacefulness of the night, he froze again, barely breathing. Elotl held his breath, calculating his own ways of escape. That stupid fowl! Why was he running into her again and again, and under the silliest of circumstances?

His unasked-for accomplice relaxed visibly, and actually snickered while the girl's outlined figure stomped past their hideaway, then picked up something, throwing it against the peeling wall. Her panting breath tore the darkness.

"One can think she is with one of her lovers," the boy related, then winced as the object of their observing whirled in their direction.

"Who is there?" she demanded, not frightened in the least, her hands already on her hips, in a painfully familiar fashion.

"Don't yell that loudly," retorted the little rascal, peeking out as nimbly and as carefully, like the forest rat that he was. "They'll hear you in the house and throw you out once again."

"No one threw me out, you stupid little monkey," snorted the girl, coming closer, yet actually lowering her tone. "What are you doing here? Stealing beans again?"

The boy limped out of their hiding, leaving Elotl to crouch there all by himself and contemplate his possibilities. To bolt away and across the road was tempting, especially since the bag with stones was still in his possession, something the skinny thief seemed to forget for a moment. Before that, he was all wariness and narrowed glances, even when weak and reeling in the shallow water, unable to walk properly, attempting to snatch his loot back. Again, it made him wonder about the contents of the stolen parcel, its worth and amount, remembering the green stones Father paid the trader for information on Miztli and sometimes for other things, seeds in the times of bad harvest or quality tools, outstandingly sturdy anvil or hoe, good scrapers made of antlers or bones. How many such instruments could the stones from this bag buy? Would it make Father forgive if he brought such treasures back? His stomach tightened painfully.

"You get us some of the beans and I'll give you a pretty green stone in return," the boy was saying in ridiculously grown-up tone, as though flirting. "I have plenty of those."

"In your dreams, you stupid little baggage," commented the girl, moving a pace ahead and so blocking his way of escape, even if inadvertently. "Who is with you?" She was next to him before he managed to decide whether to spring to his feet or not, towering momentarily, having a clear advantage. Her eyes were mere slits, clearly visible in the unhelpfully brightening moonlight, widening rapidly. "You again!" she breathed, then pursed her lips. "Why are you following me?"

"I'm not," he said, jumping to his feet a little too hastily, scratching his limbs against his previous cover's prickly touch. "I didn't... It's just a misunderstanding!"

"Like back on the plaza, huh?" Her nicely defined eyebrows

flew up in a perfect accord with the downward curve of her mouth. "Harassing me, then yelling at me, but now following me here, and with the help of that filthy little thief Azcatl. I wonder what the *telpochcalli* priest I saved you from would say to that. Or our neighborhood's court!"

Her chin was jutting forward in a warlike fashion, and her hands did not leave the support of her hips, a very pretty picture but for the wave of fear that washed through him at the mere mention of those mysterious courts. Was this how Miztli ended up with such things being hot on his heels? A wild look at the dark alley let him know that it was still quiet, moonless enough, promising safety. However, a leap over the low bushes became hindered by the annoying boy who threw himself in his way, catching his leg and clinging to it, frustrating his dash for the freedom and from the unreasonableness of it all.

"Get off me," he hissed, trying to shake off the little pest without the need to hit him hard. Panicked as he was, he had still enough lucid thinking not to wish to hit the skinny bag of bones that had had his share of violence through this evening already.

"He is trying to get away," breathed the boy, still careful to keep quiet, his hold on Elotl's leg turning painful, not relaxing despite the violent shaking. "Don't let him!"

To this, the girl reacted by lifting her eyebrows yet higher.

He tried to peel the persistent thing off using his hands, the reason for the insistence dawning. "Get off me, you stupid cluster of bones. I'll give you your filthy bag. I wasn't trying to get away with it."

"What bag?" asked the girl readily, frowning at the sound of the screen being pushed away back at the darker mass of the house. "You are making so much noise, you stupid boys!" Then toward the doorway, and the strident voice inquiring as to her whereabouts or rather the nature of her company. "I'm here, enjoying the quiet. All by myself. Leave me alone!" Her head jerked sideways, indicating the alley he was trying to reach before. "Quick. Get out, both of you."

Obediently, the little thief sprang to his feet, hobbling away and across the bushes but not before making sure that he, Elotl, did the same. He snorted silently, then noticed the girl following, squeezing through in one gracefully flowing movement.

Once back in the dimly lit pathway, the hum of the voices reaching out, coming from different patios, calming in a way, she hastened her step, then halted in front of them. "What bag do you have?"

Involuntarily, Elotl glanced at his unasked-for company, hating himself for doing this. The stupid boy was not the one to decide on their loot.

"Nothing! There are no bags or anything," declared the boy promptly, looking exaggeratedly innocent.

"Yes, there is a bag, a stupid bag that this stupid thing stole," said Elotl firmly. "And since then, I'm stuck with him. And I want to get out of it."

"What's in it?" asked the girl briskly.

"Stones. Some sort of stones."

"Let me see." Her hand shot forward so vigorously, he felt like taking a step back along with the accursed bag.

"Don't show her," cried out the boy, then fell silent all of a sudden, like an animal, all ears. The voices of people were dim but very sure of themselves, progressing up the alley, heading from the same direction they had come earlier, the flicker of their torches unmistakable, more than a few.

Perturbed, Elotl listened, the yank on his hand familiar by now, to be expected. Out of an instinct, he resisted, fed up with it all. If those people were still on their heels, persisting on sniffing them out even in this quiet neighborhood, then he wanted to have nothing to do with it, not anymore. He had enough of his own troubled dilemmas to face, to think the things through, to start the search for his brother. If those filthy courts that were after Miztli began chasing him as well, he could not help but make things worse.

The girl was still there, blocking their way. "They are after you?" she inquired, matter-of-fact.

"Maybe," he said, resisting the attempt of the boy's grimy hand to snatch the bag once again. "Stop that! If those people are still after you and not about to give up, then we are better off giving them this thing back."

"No, we are not!" cried out the boy hotly. "It's not their—"

The figures materialized out of the darkness, the lights they carried flickering in the strengthening breeze, their poses like those of hunters on a forest path, alerted, ready to pounce. Elotl's instincts took over once again. Shoving his companions into the darkness of the bushes they had emerged from, he froze, praying that they would keep as quiet as forest mice, or even quieter. The skinny thief did not worry him, but the girl was a wild thing, unreasonable, unpredictable, obviously greedy, the worst of company for such situations.

The silhouettes with their torches stopped their progress and grew silent, scanning the night. He didn't dare to take his eyes off them, resisting the pull, this time of a pleasantly soft palm, the insistence of its fingers. Only when their touch disappeared, he became aware that his companions weren't there anymore, leaving nothing but rustling shrubs in their wake. The wave of panic splashed with renewed force. Like back in the dusty alley beyond the square, it welled, then turned to anger, the resentment helping, guiding him into the whispering darkness, hot on their heels. They were creeping alongside another cluster of vegetation, this one supported by a semblance of a fence with no densely placed planks. The men in the alley were talking again, in urgent whispers.

Here.

The girl motioned toward a new barrier of shrubbery, this one higher and better kept, her nicely outlined back and hips disappearing there promptly, without waiting for them to catch up. The street boy dove after her eagerly, his hobbling creating too much noise. Hesitating, Elotl listened to the sounds of possible pursuit, then followed into their new hideaway, crossing another patch of an open ground, this one not cultivated but rather scorched, littered with too many objects, pieces of stone and broken pottery, sharpened tools and anvils like back home. The voices at the alley grew in volume.

In there, motioned the girl, leading their way across the crowded yard and into the dark opening. *Keep quiet,* the finger pressing against her lips related. The wave of heat that greeted them took Elotl by surprise, reminding him of home again. The flames maintained near mines were made to rage their fiercest, not like the other fires, for cooking or warming or lightening one's evening.

"What's in there?" he whispered, sensing the heat coming from another opening, this one narrow and uninvitingly suffocating.

"It's none of your business," whispered the girl angrily, leaning back toward the outside, clearly trying to listen to the voices from the alley. "Hush!"

He gave her tilted back a murderous glare, then glanced around once again, taking in the smallness of their new hideaway, just a storage room, clearly, crammed with objects and discarded breakage like back in the courtyard. The boy was curling next to the opening and their new savior, catching his breath and listening at the same time, ready to act upon his ears' report. Elotl made a point of drifting as far away from them as he could, peeking into the scorching room, this one bigger, dotted with glowing stone constructions like those near the mines indeed, even if significantly larger.

"What's in that bag of yours that they are so eager to catch you?" demanded the girl once the voices grew fainter, drifting away along with the breeze. "If you won't tell me, I'll catch up with them and give you away. Both of you!" The last phrase was shot toward the boy, with little to no compassion.

"Nothing," began the little thief hotly, but the girl's shooting toward the doorway brought him back to his feet as well. "Wait, it's not... nothing important. Just a few stupid stones. Wait!"

"Show me," she demanded uncompromisingly, then turned toward Elotl. "Give me the bag."

For a fraction of a heartbeat, he just stared, taken aback by her bossiness even more than incensed by it. Did she truly expect him...

"If you don't give this thing to me," she repeated, moving again as though about to head out and away. "I'll—"

He darted for the previous opening before his mind decided what to do with her threats, blocking it with his body against her charge for the freshness of the outside, pushing her back roughly enough to have her stumbling, not meaning to do that. Her squeak of surprise tore the silence, and but for his instincts that made him grab her on her new dash for freedom while pressing his palm against her mouth, she would have barreled her way past him, leaving them on their own and again on someone else's property, this time a house or a hut, even if seemingly uninhabited.

"Stop it," he rasped, pressing her tighter against her intensified struggling, her limbs pleasantly soft but having their sharp edges. "I'll let you go if you promise not to scream or run away. Promise!"

She squirmed some more, then ceased, her body warm, delightfully trim against his limbs, not helpless or sagging, not conceding, ready go back to attacking him again and yet expectant, in a way.

"Don't scream and don't run out," he reminded her, releasing his grip, confused more than alarmed, not trusting her in the least and yet needing to let her go. "Or I'll make you regret it. If those men find us because of you, I'm telling them that you are with us, have been with us all along."

"You wouldn't dare!" she hissed, pressing against the opposite wall, still too close for his peace of mind, the hut so small and crammed, the other opening glowing like the passageway into one of the Underworld's levels, promising nothing good. "And no one would believe you anyway, an uncouth, filthy, naked foreigner smelling of excrement. Just look at you; you are nothing but—"

"Shut up," he told her, too tired and spent to take offense. "I told you not to scream or else."

The boy in his corner was snickering, watching with his eyes open wide. "You can't betray us now. He'll make you regret it."

"Shut up, you filthy little monkey!" she demanded, but in a remarkably quieter tone. "Keep your stupid mouth shut tighter than a turkey's back opening."

The colorfulness of her last expression made Elotl wish to snicker as well. He forced his thoughts off her nicely glowing cheekbones, enhanced by the semidarkness, sharp and soft at the same time. "Stop cursing and answer my question. What is this place? Do you know who lives here?"

"Lives?" Her lips curved derisively, while her eyebrows knitted into a single line. "It's a workshop, you man of wisdom. No one lives in workshops, unless weird people or strange foreigners. Are you a peasant from a faraway village?"

"Shut up!" he flared, hard put not to push her against the wall or do her any other harm. "It's none of your business where I'm from." The use of her own phrase came in time, made him feel sophisticated, to a degree. Still, he wished he knew what this "workshop" meant, why people didn't live in such places. Was it a storage room, like the one they were storing maize and other foodstuff at? This hut was crammed, yes, but with objects, not food, and who would build a special place to store tools? Even in Oaxtepec they didn't do this. Or maybe they did. Metl held his meetings near their customarily elevated granary, a sort of a shed that no one seemed to live at.

Her eyes were boring at him, gleaming with fear, the tears clearly near, glistening. It made his anger well like back in the alley behind the square, hating himself and this entire situation. Clenching his teeth, he drew away a pace, then another. If she bolted out, then it was too bad. He couldn't guard her every step.

The boy drew closer, looking ready to take his place at watching their unexpected prisoner. As though he could stop her, a skinny limping heap of bones that he was.

Elotl drew his breath in through his nostrils, wishing to be anywhere but here. "Whose workshop is it? Where is the owner of this place?"

She pressed her lips tight and said nothing, watching him from under her brow.

He wanted to groan aloud. "Oh, go away. Go and report us to anyone you want to, the courts or those people or whoever. Get out of here!"

"You can't let her—" began the boy, but he waved him to shut up, then turned his back on them, trying to force his mind into thinking. The annoying fowl would most likely be scampering off now, back to her home and her shrill family members hopefully, and not those mysterious courts. And was it not the best course to throw the bag with the accursed stones at the boy and leave this entire mess as well, try to find his way to the people he had arrived here with and rest, sleep, think, figure out what to do?

"Where did you get that bag? Whom from?" the girl was asking quietly, addressing the skinny thief.

Still there? wondered Elotl numbly, refusing to turn back. The discussed bag burned his clenched fist. Slowly, he brought it up, undoing the string, trying to see through the darkness. The stones felt good, perfectly smooth against his touch; cool, delightfully slick, rolling upon the coarseness of his palm, not fitting. Five oval forms, different sizes, one darker and larger than the others.

The girl was beside him again, peering into his open palm. "Where did you get this?" she breathed, leaning yet closer, not trying to reach for it.

Ready to close his palm in case she did, he shrugged. "He stole it. Snatched it from some stupid fellow who was told to deliver it to some marketplace somewhere, or else. I bet this other man is now in real trouble."

She shot him a narrowed gaze. "Tlatelolco market?"

He shrugged again.

"Yes, Tlatelolco, those losers," contributed the boy, hobbling closer, in an obvious hurry. Ready to defend his goods, reflected Elotl, partly amused, pitying the little thing against his will.

"Show me that leg of yours."

The boy regarded him with a suspicious look. "Give me the stones back."

"After we are out of here. *Safely.*"

"Where were you going with this?" inquired the girl briskly, still immersed in the study of pretty stones.

"To some stones worker or something like this." It felt silly to shrug on and on, so he motioned with his head, non-committal. "He said there was some fellow like that around."

She looked up, openly startled. "My father?"

"He *is* a stoneworker," cried out the boy defensively. "You always brag about it."

"It's a different kind of stones, you stupid monkey." Her

laughter rang without mercy. "My father doesn't buy or sell precious stones. He works regular stone into tools or utensils, or statues. Did you really think he would buy those things from you, stolen as well? How stupid is that?" She snorted again, even louder this time. "Tlaquitoc would have bought some of this from you sooner, to put into his pretty earrings and bells. But my father? What a thought!"

"Who is Tlaquitoc?" asked Elotl, mainly to calm the spirits, with the girl growing too smug and carelessly loud and the skinny boy changing colors and expressions in no promising manner, preparing to scream his hardest, or so he suspected. "Can we go to him now and get rid of those stones?"

She rolled her eyes tellingly. "We are in his workshop, you bright man of ideas. And if you want to go to his house out there across the alley and offer him stolen stones, go ahead. I'll be watching with interest. And from a safe distance." Her smugness faded under the direfulness of his glare. "You wanted to know whose workshop it is. You yelled at me plenty about it before. So here you are, among all this copper that is yet to be melted."

"Melted copper?" he repeated, feeling silly and not even angered as he felt he should be. "Where?"

She made a face. "In there."

To glance in the direction of the narrow opening and the heat it radiated didn't help.

"This metalworker Tlaquitoc, my friend's father, he melts his metal powder in there," she went on explaining, talking slowly, like to a child or a stupid person.

He didn't care. "A metalworker?"

Now they both were staring at him.

"Answer me!"

"Yes," she let out even slower, openly puzzled, not condescending like before. "Why?"

He tried to make his mind work. "Does this man... does he have someone, a boy he teaches or something like that? A boy that used to be here, I mean..."

Her face was twisting in an already familiar grimace. "He has boys to slave for him, not to teach. Like that annoying apprentice.

Or the new one that he actually bought this time, a skinny little thing, looking worse than Azcatl." Wrinkling her nose, she shot a glance at their unimpressive company. "Maybe you should have come and worked here instead of sneaking around the streets, stealing things. He might have bought you for a time, when the villager scampered away."

"What villager?" interrupted Elotl, his hope splashing anew. "When did he scamper? Where?"

She grimaced again. "It's a long and an annoying story and we don't have time for any of this. If old Tlaquitoc finds you here, either he or any of his sons, the overgrown brutes that they are, you are both done for. So just decide what you want to do about those stones." Her face was a study of goodwill, widely open eyes, nicely pursed lips, an overplayed innocence. "If you give me one of the stones, that nicely round one, I'll bring you to that old healer woman, behind the marketplace main alley. She buys things like that. Stolen goods, you know. Maybe she'll give you some nice cocoa beans for your trouble."

"The old healer?" cried out the boy, grimacing as though he had bitten into something unripe and bitter. "The one from the stone house? She is nasty; she won't let us in!"

"You, she won't let *you* in," declared the girl smugly. "But she will let me in and in a hurry. You just wait and see!"

He tried to force his mind into dealing with the problems at hand, his thoughts still racing. "There are more metalworkers in this town, no? I mean, not only this man?"

Now it was the girl's turn to grimace as though she had bitten into a green tomato instead of a red one. "Can you think of nothing else now? And did you just call Tenochtitlan a 'town'?" Her snicker was too loud, despite the reassuring silence, with no whispering voices to disturb the darkness of the night out there. "Where did you come from to call it that?"

The skinny boy joined her in her quiet but healthy fit of laughter. Elotl felt like slapping them both. "Just answer my question!"

"Which one?" She giggled, eyes dancing, enjoying herself, annoyingly attractive, all sparks. "About boys working here? Or about other boys working in other workshops around this 'town'?"

The wish to slap her or at least to yell at her grew. "If you don't—"

The voices burst upon them with disturbing suddenness, seemingly out of nowhere, a flow of firm, confident words. His heart leaping madly, he charged toward the heat of the narrow opening, pushing both his unasked for accomplices ahead of him, not thinking it all through. The confidence of the nearing footsteps was disturbing, sending his mind into panicked fits.

CHAPTER 11

Pressing his fingers to his eyes, Miztli fought the urge to slide down the wall he slumped against and drift away and into a blissful oblivion. The tiredness was bad, overwhelming, and his head pounded as though twenty clubs were having at it from the inside, all viciously heavy and made of the best polished wood. The lack of stench from the bizarre place with wild animals was of no help, because the thin but undeniable odor of blood and sweat was still there, brought along together with them, to more resentment of the elegant owner of these quarters. The thought alone made him wish to stay thus, with his eyes closed, protected from dark glares.

"You can't do this, you just can't!" repeated the woman in a frantic whisper. "You must be insane even to think about it, Milli! How could you? And after wandering out there and at night, again in the most dubious company, reverting to your old ways. You made me sick with worry! You can't—"

"Forget it, Citlalli. Stop it! It's not the time. Please! We need your help, you must help us!" Tlemilli's voice climbed, then dropped back to as dramatic a whisper. "You know about those things; I know you know. You told me that yourself! You can dress wounds, I know you can." Sneaking a glance between the protective screen of his fingers, he caught the sight of Tlemilli leaning forward, her tones still hushed but forceful, curiously dominating. "Just take a look at his wound. It won't implicate you in anything, I promise you. Please, Citlalli, please!"

Her hands pressed to her chest, pleading, her expression irresistible, that mix of guiltily pleading smile. This was how she had made him turn around and go back and into the warring Tlatelolco, leaving the relative safety of the war-torn shore behind, he remembered. There was no logic in her plans of saving her sister, no sense. Still, she had pleaded in exactly the same way, cute, mischievous, determined, not denying her own lack of reason and rationality, not claiming anything but just urging, offering temporary solutions to irrelevant smaller details, leaving him with no option to say "no" or to take her away by force, powerless against her determination. And here she was again, now demanding unreasonable things from her haughty sister, the aristocratic lady in her prettily decorated set of rooms, her night *huipil* looking better than a celebrative dress on the most important ceremony in his village; such a highborn, scandalized oh so thoroughly mistress, so deeply horrified, shocked, and yet proving powerless, already succumbing to the great willpower that her younger sibling had in disproportional abundance.

The smile threatened to sneak out despite his bottomless exhaustion and discomfort, the fear of being here in one of the Palace's buildings again, uninvited and unbidden, after making such a mess of a relatively simple mission. The new wave of dread splashed, then died away. It was not the time to think of what the Emperor wanted from him. There were more important things to worry about. Like the bleeding Texcocan, now slumping against the wall, weakened into half consciousness, his face pale and lifeless, usually so vital and forceful but now just a mask with no colors applied to it. Or like Tlemilli's determination to have her haughty, aloof, openly hostile sister's help in any of it. Or like the mess they must have left behind in the part of the Palace's gardens that the Emperor clearly cherished and invested in, now dotted with upset animals and at least two dead or badly wounded warriors, and the rest of the royal guards searching, combing those grounds, eager to catch the intruders. Oh, but they had been in the heart of monumental trouble and so far yet from relatively safe ways of escaping even the most immediate danger.

Unwilling to face the arguing sisters, he knelt beside the wounded, busying himself with supporting the sagging back, relieved to see the movement of the chest, barely visible but there.

When back between the cages of growling jaguars or howling wolves, even near the pond of the terrible water creature, the man was still leading, still in control. Wavering, yes, bleeding, putting a great effort at staying upright or keeping an eye on them and their dangerous surroundings, coordinating their actions, thinking of their next move – a leader, like always, a jaguar on the trail, not to be sidetracked. A reassuring presence in the most hopeless of situations, like back in the nighttime Tenochtitlan and Tlatelolco, on the night before the invasion. Unless not on the same side. A possibility Miztli preferred not even to think about. May all revered deities keep him and Tlemilli safe from *that*. And Necalli too. But did the *calmecac* boy worship this man!

And yet, after the desperate flight from the terrible pond and the monsters inhabiting it, with the torches of their pursuers dancing far enough to reassure, the Texcocan began wavering badly, sagging against him, Miztli, too heavily, making it difficult to progress. The forceful man had barely said a word, but by then, Tlemilli had taken a lead, recognizing their new surroundings near the side of the Palace where their original troubles began, declaring that they had no choice but to go to her suite of rooms and have her sister take care of their companion's wound. It was right there across the trees and the flowerbeds, she insisted. A short walk, no sweat. And even though both Miztli and their formidable but half-conscious leader reacted with vigorous protests to this, she had prevailed and so here they were, with the now barely conscious Texcocan and this same haughtily hostile sister, the most aristocratic of ladies, the former empress of Tlatelolco, still wooed by the highest of Tenochtitlan nobility, witness the happening upon the Great Plaza only this afternoon, appalled and about to turn them in.

"The ointments, Citlalli... How about this ointment you made me smear on that cut I had on my arm," insisted Tlemilli, her words gushing worriedly, pressing. "You must have something of this smelly cream left somewhere around. You must!"

"Those smelly creams are made fresh when needed, Milli," grunted the noblewoman, bestowing a dark gaze upon her unruly sibling, shaking her head. Then the resolution flooded in. "Go out there and keep an eye on the entrance. Make sure no maids are tempted to check on our wellbeing tonight. Not even Tzintli."

"But you'll need my help..." began Tlemilli hotly, then changed her mind. "We will keep an eye on the outside, I and Miztli. Just call for us when you need help. We'll—"

"*He* is not staying with you!" hissed her sister with sudden passion, sounding ridiculously Tlemilli-like but for opposite reasons. "Get it out of your head or I will make sure to notify the Palace's authorities without delay while locking you in here until you have come to your senses!"

Tlemilli's gasp tore the suddenly still, suffocating air and even from his uncomfortable spot upon the floor and in the meager light of a single torch, he could see her eyes growing into enormous proportions before narrowing with radiant fury.

"You can't treat me like Father did, so get it out of your head too!" cried the girl out, leaning forward as though welcoming the confrontation, looking magnificent in her passion, again a painting of a war deity, beautiful in her strangeness. Despite his own mounting resentment at her sister's continued scorn, he felt his heart increasing its tempo, swelling with pride. She was not a simple human being, she just wasn't!

Then his attention snapped back to the wounded, who stirred all of a sudden, shuddered violently, then began to struggle into an upright position, muttering uncomprehendingly, his eyes open but blank, unblinking, frightening in their single-minded resolve. That brought the sisters out of their furious staring, and as he strained to support his charge without letting the man harm himself by an outright springing up, he could feel them both dropping beside him, relieved not to be left alone in it. But it was frightening, the wounded's mindless thrashing.

"Water!" breathed Tlemilli's sister. "Bring water." Then she was on her feet and gone, not waiting for her instructions to be followed.

With a good case, apparently. As he struggled not to let the man fall, he could feel Tlemilli frozen by his side, not helpful in the least.

"Hold him still!" The owner of these quarters was back, her

flowing hair striking him across the face, her perfume too strong, overwhelming, making him wish to back away. The flask she brought made a hollow sound, banging against the stones of the floor. "Hold him!"

He clenched his teeth tight, the drops of water refreshing, sprinkling him as well. The straining body relaxed a little, sagged against his arms, making his own struggle not to let go more difficult. However, by this time, Tlemilli was by his side again, helpful if only with her mere presence.

"Drink," the noblewoman was murmuring with surprising softness, insistent but patient. "You must drink. Like that, yes. Careful. Small gulps." It was as though she was guiding a child, holding the flask to the twisted face, supporting the back of the wounded's head with her free arm, astonishingly gentle. "Yes. Good. That's enough for now."

The man choked a little, then sagged against Miztli's arm, making his struggle to maintain his position yet more difficult. Still, he felt his relief welling, watching the eyes of the Texcocan focus, gain a semblance of normality, cloud momentarily, then snap back to reality again. Their concentration was painful as he peered at the woman who was still leaning close above, the flask ready, her other hand still supporting, wrapping the wounded's nape gently, in a ridiculously embrace-like fashion. For a moment, Miztli felt like snickering aloud. They looked like lovers from stories, the wounded fighter and his beloved. Tlemilli was barely breathing by his side.

"You are safe," the woman was whispering. "But you must keep quiet; must let me examine your wound."

The Texcocan nodded, his lips colorless, just an invisible line, the rest of his face looking no better, such a gray mask.

"Good." The woman sobered, straightening up briskly, leaving them with more weight to take on. "Move him to the mat by the torch." She didn't even deign to look at him. "Tlemilli, bring one of the mats, but put something on it, a cloth, a dress you don't mind throwing away. We can't have blood staining it." She was speaking rapidly, as though to herself. "You, boy, carry him there, then bring more water. There must be another flask in the outer room. Which won't be enough, so you may have to run out and fetch more."

Overwhelmed by this flood of words and instructions, Miztli pushed his resentment away, busy maintaining his balance as the Texcocan persisted in his attempt to straighten up all by himself, clearly intending to make his own way toward the indicated spot, not wishing to be carried. Good for him. He was not about to offer an argument or sacrifice more of his pitifully meager remainder of strength. Also, it was annoying how this woman kept giving him haughtily spoken orders. She did think him to be no better than a slave, didn't she?

"What are you doing?" she demanded again, looking at him with obvious fury. "I told you—"

"He wants to walk by himself," he muttered, desperate to remain patient. For Tlemilli's sake!

"I'm good," groaned the Texcocan. "Can... can walk... where needed..."

She pursed her lips, then busied herself with poring through a wooden chest stuffed with clothes aplenty, displeased with them both, as it looked. "Milli, take the torch out of its holder and hold it as I tell you."

Tlemilli seemed to remain the only one unaware of the currents, happily ignorant. Done with spreading a prettily colorful cloth over the rustling reeds of the mat, she leapt toward the flickering torch as though it was her only chance to snatch it.

"Take the flask and go to the kitchen areas," went on her bossy sister, bestowing him with another ice-cold look. "Bring back two more, all full to the brim."

"Where do I get those things?" he demanded, helping the wounded to make himself comfortable upon his new seat and against the wall, in a hurry to turn around and face his adversary. For that was what this woman was, an adversary, or worse yet, an enemy. She hated him no matter what he did for Tlemilli. "Will there be no one to ask me questions?"

Her perfectly arching eyebrows plunged to create what looked like a single line. "Think of something, an explanation. You should be bright enough to do that!" Her words rang like pieces of copper thrown against a stone floor.

"I'll fill the flasks," volunteered Tlemilli, this time quite hastily. "I know where the servants bring refreshments from." Her own eyebrows straightened as direfully. "And how should he know where the kitchen things are? He is not a slave here. You keep forgetting this, Sister. He is a warrior, a *calmecac* pupil, a future leader and all that. Why do you keep forgetting it?"

The other woman rolled her eyes and said nothing, but her face wore the color of a storm cloud, curiously adding to her beauty rather than taking away from it. Grudgingly, he was forced to admit that, wishing with all his being to declare her ugly and never see her again. But for the opportunity to take Tlemilli away from it all, somehow – this Palace and most of its denizens!

"Just hold the torch for now, little one," said the woman finally, kneeling next to the wounded, armed with a cloth and the disputed flask, peeking into it dubiously. Her hand rested upon the crouching man's back, the unharmed side of it, surprisingly gentle and soft again. "Please, be patient. It will probably hurt."

Probably? wondered Miztli, eyeing the man's crumpled cloak, most of it nothing but a mess of mud and dried blood, all stiff and reeking, pinned to the body underneath it quite tightly, the viciously short shaft sitting there as though belonging, ominously firm. It was scary to imagine himself in the Texcocan warrior's place. Mesmerized, he watched the woman's fingers pulling at the sticky material, trembling but nimble, as though knowing what to do or how. She didn't touch the protruding piece of polished wood at all.

"I will use your knife, if I may."

Was this a ceremony at the imperial court, to be talking like that, asking for permissions? Tlemilli was breathing noisily by his side, clearly too fascinated to mind her torch, which was tipping precariously, about to start dripping into the mat, risking putting them all on fire. Hastily, he took it away from her, encircling her shoulders with his free arm out of habit, in case she needed it. No frivolously inappropriate thoughts, not now, even though she was as lovely and enticing as ever, more so after the mutual adventures out there among the terrible animals, snuggling against him readily, such an encouragingly familiar warm presence, making up for her sister's cold treatment and more.

"Give her your knife," muttered the Texcocan, glancing up briefly while straining to turn his head, his eyes clouded with pain. "The flint... the small one... it'll work the best."

Nodding hastily, Miztli tried to hide his apprehension, releasing Tlemilli's shoulders while searching through his bag, the flint knife this man had given him once upon a time never taken out or put to use, not until now. Shuddering, he hurried to offer it to the woman without making his torch drip.

A few more heartbeats passed. He felt Tlemilli shuddering as well, pressing into him with much force. Her sister's hands trembled as she tried to cut the stiff pieces of cloth off, not nicking the skin underneath it by a miracle, or so it seemed. Twice the small blade brushed against the ugly dart, and each time the wounded pressed into the mat he crouched upon, leaning on his knees and elbows with too much force, burying his face against it as though about to bite the raw straw. Finally, the part of the impressively massive back was on full display, crisscrossed with muscles and mud strikes aplenty, smeared badly, swollen around the protruding shaft, angrily red.

"I must... must wash... wash around it," mumbled the pretty noblewoman, losing most of her previous sincerity and aplomb. The gaze she shot at them was haunted, pleading for help.

"I think you better pull it out first," ventured Tlemilli as haltingly. "It must be pulled out anyway, mustn't it?"

The woman gave her another pathetic look. "It must be cleaned first," she insisted, reaching for the flask and the large piece of a cheerfully patterned cloth, grabbing those as though afraid they would try to dart away. "It must. There is too much dirt all around it. And it's... it's not good. It should be cleaned first." The last sentence came out firmer than the previous ones, ringing with conviction.

Why? wondered Miztli, glancing at the wounded, who was still crouching but sagging perceptibly, as though welcoming the respite in the treatment too. Yet, when the woman's delicate fingers reached for the angry mess, much less assertive than her words indicated, rubbing the swollen skin as lightly as they could, trembling badly, he shuddered, then shot into an upright position, not helping their improvised healer in the least.

"You must, must stop moving," cried out the woman, too loud and clearly not caring, her voice trembling, out of control. "I can't... can't like that..."

She jerked away and almost tripped on her own prettily embroidered skirt when her patient finally managed to straighten, wavering on all fours, looking like a predator about to charge. A hunted, hurt predator.

"Citlalli!" breathed Tlemilli, darting toward her older sibling, encircling the shuddering shoulders in her arms, protective.

Miztli found himself leaping toward the wounded. It was clear who needed help here. Not the spoiled haughty woman about to cry.

"I can't when you move," Tlemilli's sister whimpered, clutching to her younger sibling quite willingly, clearly needing her support.

"Stop messing with it," hissed the Texcocan, his voice contorted, not a familiar sound at all, reminiscent of the low growling from the forbidden area they had managed to escape. "Just pull the damn thing out and be done with it! You can torture me later if you want to, you stupid fowl. But now just pull the damn thing out!"

Surprisingly, the aristocratic woman did not take offense at such an address. On the contrary, her shoulders straightened and the soft whimpering subdued. "Lie down," she ordered with remarkable firmness. "Lie down and stay still."

But her difficult charge did not comply. Wavering on all fours and looking grotesque in his smeared half nakedness and his bizarre pose, partly crouching, partly turned, head bent to one side, trying to face them, unable to do so fully. His face was a contorted mask, with his eyes the only feature alive, shooting thunderbolts, wild and not completely sane, not anymore.

"You, boy, you pull the damn dart out," he rasped. "Just yank it hard and pay no attention to anything else." His breath hissed, drawn forcefully through the widening nostrils. "You, girl, get me something to bite into. Anything. Like a piece of wood or cloth or anything. Quick!" Another painful pause. "You, be ready with that cloth of yours. Press it hard to the wound after he is done with that dart. Be ready with more cloths, if you don't want to have blood all around your pretty rooms." Another breath was drawn in convulsively. "Just do it quickly, boy. Don't dawdle. Pull hard and be done with it. It's nothing to be afraid of. It's just a stupid dart."

The tirade died away as abruptly as it burst out while its originator sank back into his previous crouch, clearly having wasted the last of his strength. Miztli shuddered, feeling the silence almost physically, knowing that it was up to him now, no one but him. A fleeting glance at his companions confirmed this conclusion. He drew in a deep breath.

"Tlemilli, get what he said; something, anything..." An urgent scan brought immediate results. "That thing."

To dash toward the tray with flasks and small dishes took him no time, the large wooden spoon looking promising, satisfactorily sturdy. He grabbed one of the cloths Tlemilli's sister still held in her lifeless hands, wrapping the improvised instrument in it, somehow knowing that for the sake of the wounded's teeth, the device for stifling down screams had better be softer than raw wood, however smoothly polished.

"Here!" Dropping next to the curled-up man, he offered his improvised tool with enough force to catch his wandering attention. "Just bite into it. And if you can... lie down, on your stomach, that is..."

The man nodded, then moved obediently. He tried to pay no attention to the odor of blood and the torn flesh, glaring so viciously, not belonging, obscene.

"Tlemilli, hold the torch. Bring it closer, like that, yes." She obeyed him as readily as the wounded did, and it reassured him, gave him courage to reach for the bloody mess.

The touch of the raw flesh was revolting, wet and slippery, no chance of getting a good grip. He closed his mind to the man's suffering. It had to come out; brutally or not, but it had to. Otherwise, it was needless torturing, like the man said, prolonging the inevitable, a cruel deed.

His fingers locked around the slippery shaft, dug in with conviction. The sound of creaking wood did not distract him, even though he knew that those were the man's teeth gnawing into the wrapped spoon, trying to crack it up. The gurgling that erupted from the depth of the wounded's throat reinforced the conclusion. He pushed his welling nausea away, forcing his fingers to dig deeper in search of a better grip, feeling the edges of the cutting point, somehow knowing that he was doing right. The body under his palms was convulsing, struggling to push him away. He leaned on it with his entire weight, fighting not to let the slick obsidian escape the tips of his fingers, digging deeper yet, getting a better grip.

The torchlight was dancing wildly, but the lack of proper illumination did not bother him, his instincts trusting his senses and not the eyes now, letting him know that Tlemilli was half lying against the wounded too, helping to hold him in place, or trying to. Her sister seemed to join the struggle as well. He paid them little attention, his fingers claws, locked around the razor-sharp edges, disregarding the pain where those cut into his own skin, not hesitant or uncertain, yanking their hardest, not about to give up.

The limbs underneath him were thrashing with real force now, but as he slipped, his fingers did not let the barbed edges go, and the dart was still there, clutched in his bleeding palm as he struggled not to let the wounded roll onto his back as well, holding the tormented body with the last of his strength, his heart racing. In another heartbeat, the struggle ceased, but his mind took a few more moments to understand, blinking the sweat off his eyes, trying to get a grip.

"The cloths!" He could hear Tlemilli's voice, ringing with urgency. "He said to press them, not to let the blood..."

With an effort, he pushed himself up, still clutching his barbed spoil, afraid to let it go. The wounded was slumping on his side, sprawling helplessly, clearly wandering other worlds, blood trickling upon the tiles of the floor, marring their purity. It wasn't pulsating wildly, as he half expected to see, and it reassured him, remembering that man in the mine two rainy seasons ago, with the blood gushing out of his severed limb, convulsing and spouting, as though in a hurry to drain off. He blinked to make the terrible vision go, then dropped back beside the wounded.

"Cloths. Give me those cloths!"

The royal woman didn't move, frozen in her petrified staring, but Tlemilli reacted at once, tearing the colorful pieces out of her sister's nerveless hands.

"Press them to the wound," she breathed. "He said to press and not to let go." Not bothering to surrender him her catch, she knelt beside the crumpled man, shoving the wet piece to his ravaged shoulder so strongly, he shuddered and came back to life with a groan. By that time, the royal woman stirred from her untimely stupor and hurled herself straight into her former brisk efficiency, carrying the flask she didn't let go all this time for some reason, rushing to bring a cup from the same reed table he had snatched the spoon earlier from, supporting the wounded's head, making him drink while succoring him gently, her words a thread of soft soothing rustling.

Miztli blinked the sweat from his eyes, then forced his palm to unlock, staring at the intricate patterns the arrowhead left there, crisscrossing lines, dripping red, crimson and glaring as opposed to the darker mess that was smeared upon it and belonged to the wounded.

"It's still bleeding!" called out Tlemilli, keeping her voice satisfactorily low this time. "What do I do?"

He forced his attention back to her, remembering how she was beside him all this time with the torch and while he struggled to hold the wounded in place, and before, in the darkness with animals and back in Tlatelolco.

"I'm so glad you are here," he whispered, shifting back toward her, fishing around after another piece of material to replace the dripping one. The raw mess of the Texcocan's shoulder was terrible, but the blood still didn't pulsate out of the torn wound and again he remembered the man from the mine and breathed with relief.

Obediently, Tlemilli moved when he motioned her to let him

examine the wound. "Of course I'm here. Where should I be?" she murmured, her lips twisting in her typical one-sided grin.

He shrugged, then put his mind back to the wounded, who was choking on his water now, struggling to hold it in.

"Tlemilli," breathed the imperial woman. "Go out there and see that we are not disturbed. I think I heard noise. The servants, they may hear us and try to come in and see what is happening. We made so much noise!"

"Why me..." began Tlemilli, then changed her mind once again, the sounds of the outer screen being moved catching the attention of them all now. "I won't let them in!" As nimbly as only she could be at times, the girl sprang up and rushed away, carrying their only source of light along and into the shimmering darkness of the outer rooms.

"Give me the knife," groaned the Texcocan, but the owner of these quarters put a calming finger upon his lips, relaying it all in one elegant gesture.

The darkness prevailed along with the silence, disturbingly heavy. Holding his breath, Miztli tried to listen to the possible sounds, voices, maybe arguments, maybe shouts and demands. It was such a wild night and what was to stop the Palace's guards from coming here, having done scanning the dark outside, figuring the route of the culprits' escape or, gods forbid, their identity? An icy wave splashed once again, freezing his stomach, and he didn't fight the urge to jump to his feet in order to rush out and after her, if for no other reason than to be there and protect her, do *something*.

Cold fingers locked around his arm, almost familiar in their pleasant smoothness. "I'll go and see what it is all about," breathed Tlemilli's sister, on her feet as well now and lacking in trembling. "Stay here, look after him." Before the murmuring of her words died away, she was gone, swallowed by the semidarkness of the opening.

For another heartbeat, Miztli didn't dare to let his breath out. The sounds of the night filled his straining ears, the breeze from the outside rustling in the bushes, the chirping of the night insects, the distant hum of occasional voices – which ones belonged to

Tlemilli? The wounded was stirring, and he dropped back to the floor, feeling the man's groan coming out, impossible to stop. His hand groped desperately, locating the turning face, pressing against the gaping mouth, strangling the dangerous sound in. The ensuing struggle took his attention from his immediate worries, the man weakened by his condition but still fiercely strong.

"Quiet, please. We need to keep quiet!" he breathed in desperation, having an upper hand but not sure for how long. "Please!"

The struggling limbs relaxed imperceptibly, giving him hope.

"Please," he murmured again. "We must keep quiet. It's only because of that... only because..."

"Get your hands off my face." The words were spat into his palm, easy to guess. Still, he breathed with relief. The Texcocan was back, fully conscious, enough to grow angry over such an insolent treatment or to appreciate the danger they might have been in.

Carefully, he backed away, then tried to listen to the voices again, a part of his mind on the wounded, aware of his struggle to achieve a more upright position, appraising the risks. The people out there would hear them now, most certainly, especially if the man attacked him for his previous insolence.

A whisper that disturbed the darkness shortly thereafter confirmed his misgivings. "Give me your knife."

"What knife?" he murmured, playing for time. The voices from beyond the opening were clearer now, poured in softly, female voices but more than just two.

"Any knife!" The exasperated note in the whispering voice was too pronounced to miss. "Whatever sharp tool you have closest."

He didn't like the idea of parting with the small flint again, his only weaponry under current circumstances, however, it was neither the time nor the place to argue and the Texcocan was always a decent man. He wouldn't try to appropriate his possession or attack him with it.

"Good." He could feel the man nodding, taking hold of the offered weaponry while leaning against the wall awkwardly, with one side of his body, clearly drained of strength once again. How were they to make their way out and away? wondered Miztli, his head pounding worse than before, refusing to deal with new hurdles. This night, oh but it was too much and what would he say to the Emperor when asked what had been overheard in the suite of the Tenantzinco dignitaries? Nothing concerning this man surely, none of his presence or involvement, but then how was he to explain any of the happenings? And all this, provided that they managed to escape now, somehow.

"Help me up." The urgent whisper made him nearly jump, sunken too deeply in the helplessness of his musings. "Quick."

He couldn't find enough strength to argue. If they made too much noise and were caught, well, it was too bad. And maybe Tlemilli could not be implicated now, safe in those cozy, prettily ornamented quarters, a rightful place for her to be. Again, he listened to the voices, noting the silence. No one talked out there in the other room or the corridor beyond it.

The man's rock-hard hand was clutching into his shoulder as though trying to break its bones. Even so, the wounded wavered too badly, and but for Miztli's further support, he would have gone crashing back down, of that there could be little doubt.

"There must be a wall opening here..." murmured the Texcocan as though talking to himself. "There must be—"

"In the other room. I saw one on our way here. But we came through the corridor and the doorway."

The grip on his shoulder tightened, then relaxed. "We'll try that outer room now that it's empty. Give me—"

A struggle to progress on his own was not crowned with success. Anything but! As badly as he tried to clutch the man without hurting his ravaged back, they both ended up still upright but crushed against the wall, gasping for breath.

"We'll wait... a little..." declared the Texcocan, sliding down and back into a sitting position. "Pray to any deity you want that your girl managed not to let her imperial sister give us away."

"She won't!" It came out too loudly and he pressed his palm to his mouth, afraid to squat and relax as well, wishing there had been a wall opening here, even just a small crack to squeeze through. Tlemilli would understand and he would find her tomorrow after school and explain. The thought of school served to dampen his mood even worse. They must be furious with his absence at this time of the night, well after midnight rites.

"Sit down, boy." The Texcocan's voice rustled softly, unexpectedly warm, like a breath of a summer breeze. "Relax and gather your strength. You spent too much of it too, I bet." An ensuing pause held even more coziness. "I thank you. For everything. For carrying me instead of bolting away, for pulling that arrow out, for being there and doing everything right. You are a worthy jaguar cub. Or rather a puma cub, eh?" His chuckle held nothing but amusement and not a hint to the pain and exhaustion he must have felt. "We'll hope that your girl and that pretty sister of hers manage to help us out and away. No uselessly haughty royal fowls. A surprise."

"Tlemilli is not like that," he muttered, embarrassed to no end, grateful for the darkness that concealed the burning of his face, the unexpected praise so genuine and honest, so matter-of-fact, yet more precious because of that. Did this man truly think him being worthy, not useless and clumsy, scared out of his wits? "She... she isn't a spoiled royal fowl."

A light sway of the outlined head was his answer. "Maybe not your girl, but the Tlatelolcan royal wife came out as a surprise. I must admit that." He could feel the man's exhaustion enveloping him, almost tangible. "Get one of those cloths she used, the biggest you can find. She won't like all this blood all over her walls. She won't be able to explain... in case she decides to go on being decent." As Miztli rushed back toward the bloodstained mat, he could hear the man muttering, "We'll wait for them to come back for a few more heartbeats, then try the other room and the wall opening in it."

CHAPTER 12

The terrace was small and cozy, more of a balcony, a fenced platform, overlooking the gardens rustling not far below. An easy jump, a familiar one. This was where she had gone out earlier, when Citlalli had departed for the imperial dinner, after fretting about inadequate clothing and footwear for all eternity, or so it seemed. The former imperial chief wife, Tlemilli's sister, did not wish to appear at Tenochtitlan Palace's royal quarters looking less than perfect, even if to attend such an event was not of her choosing. The sudden and forebodingly official invitation after a whole moon of living in the Palace as an invisible guest and after the previous bout of attention from none other than the important adviser, the Emperor's elder brother no more and no less, was unsettling and worrisome. Even Tlemilli understood its significance. The adviser might have a wife, or maybe several such, but what was to stop him from wishing to enrich his collection? Citlalli's blood was impeccable, her looks and manners outstanding, her record at being an imperial spouse already impressive. In addition, she had no protective family, no influential relatives to negotiate or even refuse on her behalf. Should the Emperor give his agreement, the stocky, cold, disagreeable noble might get his way if he wished to espouse the highly eligible Tlatelolcan spoil. Tlemilli got shivers even just thinking about something like that.

Citlalli had kept carrying on as though nothing happened, but beyond her sister's perfect composure, Tlemilli could see how unsettled she was, maybe even frightened. The way she snapped at the maids when they offered one disregarded *huipil* after another, one pair of less than perfectly fitting jewelry or shoes, let her know how upset her sister was, despite the efforts she made to behave as though all was well.

Her heart going out to her beloved sibling, she tried to stay out of the way, knowing from the last moon's experience that sometimes her fiercely expressed opinions and support were nothing but a hindrance. Her ideas were not good in such a situation, and anyway, nothing bad had happened as yet. And in the meanwhile, she had her own evening to think about, to plan and scheme and try to think of ways to join Miztli on his new spying mission. Between his hastily whispered reassurances and Ahuitzotl's chattiness, she knew that he would be here in the Palace tonight, spying on Tenantzinco visitors, commissioned to do so by the Emperor himself. Oh, but did the Tenochtitlan Emperor appreciate him! Her thoughts kept jumping from her sister's predicament to her private plans for the evening, and thus the preparations for the imperial feast passed without her getting in Citlalli's way. One good turn. The moment the decorated litter sent for her sister in a special order departed, she had bolted for the outside as well, before the remaining maid who was busy seeing the important lady off was back to try and keep an eye on her. The little terrace provided ample opportunities to slip away without being noticed.

And here they were again, on the same terrace but together now, with so much happening in between that her mind refused to even try to think about it. The forbidden animal gardens and the beasts inhabiting it, the wounded Texcocan, as brave and forceful, but weakening so rapidly, with only Miztli's strength and quick thinking left to carry them out of this terrible place. She didn't doubt *his* ability to save them once again, but it was a relief to reach the safety of their quarters, where even Citlalli turned out to be less difficult than expected. By the time they had staggered in, stinking, smeared, and wavering as though drunk on *octli*, she was already there, claiming that the feast ended early when it most obviously didn't. However, there was no time to call her sibling out on a puzzling lie, as the wounded man needed a treatment and only Citlalli could be trusted to know what to do.

Even though at some point she remembered that her sister hated this man, not forgiving their father's death or some other possible misdeeds, whatever they were. Citlalli's reaction to the impressive Texcocan was a little too passionate, too feisty for a simple grudge of a deed done in the middle of war. Father was not a good man. They both knew it, and they didn't miss him in the least.

"It's down that alley and then to the left, yes?"

Miztli's words tore her from her reverie, bringing her back and into the blissful freshness of the night, away from the closeness of the inner room with no wall opening, enveloped in the heavy aroma of blood that permeated it; such a stench! The wounded, groggy and weakened by pain, kept directing their healing efforts, even though Citlalli had tried to make him shut up and let her do the cleaning all by herself, with the help of their pitiful remnants of water and cloths. However, her patient had other ideas. *Octli* was better at washing open wounds, he claimed, at cleaning off the worst of the dirt. A strong, well-brewed *octli*. Not a watered down version of it that was sometimes served in noble places, especially if ladies were involved. The remark that made Citlalli glow with indignation, her eyes sending thunderbolts her unasked-for charge's way. But of course the forceful man had his way and so here they were, on the quest to get *octli* without alerting the maids, who already were sniffing around, trying to see what was wrong with the noble ladies to generate so many strange noises. It wasn't easy to get rid of the inquirers. Without Citlalli's help, she mightn't have managed.

"Just tell me what alleys to follow," repeated Miztli, his voice as quiet as a breeze, his elbows propped against the low parapet, peering into the darkness. Not in a hurry to storm it, it was easy to see that. Well, she was not in a hurry to let him go.

"Yes, all the way down that alley, then by the pond with the splashing water you'll see those buildings, one story, small things. You can't mistake them. They look like commoners' dwellings out there by the marketplace. Back in Tlatelolco, I mean. It's easy to recognize them." A glance at his pursed lips made her feel bad. "I'll come with you!"

"No!" He stirred back to life with a start. "No, no. You can't.

You shouldn't be out there. The guards..." His hand locked around her wrist, pressing with urgency, rough and slippery with sweat, but oh so very pleasant to touch, so reassuring. "Tlemilli, you promised! Your sister, she will be furious. And she will not help Tecuani. She said so herself!"

"She will go on helping us, you silly. You know she will. She is just nagging because she thinks she is my mother and father and all responsible grownups combined." To catch his arm in her turn proved to be even more pleasant, to press it with her free hand. "You may not find those kitchen houses, or they may not let you in, or give you what we need. Citlalli said it's imperative to get water as well, not only that *octli*. Why is this man, the Texcocan, so insistent about the *octli*? Will he really be pouring it into his wound?"

His face darkened perceptibly. "He'll have to drink some of it as well when we'll be heading out," he muttered, his grimace easy to see in the uninterrupted moonlight, smeared with mud and blood like war-paint, bruised too but not badly; handsome despite it all.

She fought the urge to reach out and kiss him. It wasn't the time, was it? "Come, let us hurry."

"No, Tlemilli, I'll find it. You can wait for me here if you want to. Tlemilli!"

His attempt to recapture her arm did not crown with success. She pushed it away easily while sliding over the low barrier, an exercise practiced so many times. "Are you coming?"

He glared at her from above, then slid over the parapet too, slipping upon the muddy ground, fighting for balance, if momentarily. "You are wild!"

Pleased with herself, she made a face at him. "And you are not much of a jumper."

His grimace held it all, and then they both were snickering, trying to stifle the inappropriate guffawing down.

"You *are* wild!" he breathed, then caught her in his arms, pressing her tightly, possessively.

Forgetting their purpose, she snuggled against his familiar warmth, not bothered by the smell – she must have smelled as bad

– or the lack of clothing on his part. Even when dressed like a slave boy, with nothing but a loincloth, now muddied and torn in places, and not even shoes, he looked nobler than many, breathtakingly well built, not a servant but a warrior, a mighty one.

When his lips sought hers, she reacted most readily, loving the kissing since that very first time back in her Tlatelolco Palace. It never surprised her, never made her wish to pull away. On the contrary, of late, when huddling in those not-very-well concealed corners of the Great Plaza or behind the school fence, it felt as though they could do more; could, or maybe even should, do something wonderfully wild, something they weren't allowed. She was not far from the age of being eligible to be given away in marriage, and why couldn't it be him? Citlalli would not even hear about it, she knew, would never allow for something like that to happen. And probably the rest of this royal house's dwellers, those who would be deciding her fate when her time came. But it didn't matter. She wasn't about to be given to anyone but him, to let anyone else touch her in such a manner. Not in the least. Not even if the wellbeing of the entire world of the Fifth Sun was dependent on it. It could go down, flood, or fall apart like the previous four worlds as far as she was concerned, if this was the price of not being given to anyone else. Even the Emperor himself, if he was silly enough to decide to have her. Citlalli could have imperial husbands, if she didn't object to that. The thought of Citlalli made her somber.

"We need to hurry," she whispered, breaking from the magic of his lips, her skin nothing but goose bumps, the shivers most pleasant, unsettling in their intensity, following his palms that were holding her strongly, sliding down her back and beneath her *huipil*, spreading shivers and magic, frightening in its intensity. The realization made her push him away in fright.

His arms did not let her go, not readily. Tense and dominating, they pressed her, squeezing the breath out of her, and for a moment, she fought him for real, the sudden awareness that it wasn't in her power to break free frightening, sending her mind into panicked resistance. When his grip lessened, after how many heartbeats she couldn't tell, as her heart was racing madly, in a wild tempo, she tried to jump away, but now it was her body's turn to betray her, as instead of pulling away, it swayed forward and back into his arms, leaning against him, clinging to him with complete disregard of her initial struggle for freedom. His arms embraced her again, most readily, but she buried her face in his chest instead of offering it for another kiss, as was their custom, needing to catch her breath, desperately unsettled but not knowing why.

He was breathing as heavily, his chest rising and falling against her cheek, his embrace full of tension. "We must... must go and look... look for those kitchen houses," he muttered, beginning to ease away.

She busied herself with scanning the ground under their feet.

"Come," he motioned, not daring to touch her for some reason.

A shrug seemed to be in order. Another spell of heavy silence prevailed.

"You want to go back? I can, can lift you back there... so you would climb—"

"I'm coming with you," she stated, surprised by the firmness of her own voice, the authoritative ring to it. "Come!"

He followed without a word and she blessed the darkness of the pathway as it wound itself toward the trees and the thicker vegetation adorning its edges. The burning of her cheeks would be less noticeable there, allowing her to raise her head and look forward. In the corner of her eye, she could see him as immersed in the happenings upon the cleanly swept pathway. Was he as embarrassed as she was? But why? It was she who had acted strangely, beating at his chest like a frightened child, hadn't she? How stupid! And why did she do it? The hot wave was back, washing her face all over again.

"It's at the end of this alley and then to the left," she hurried to say, the silence unbearable, wearing on her nerves.

He didn't even nod, strolling beside her like a slab of stone, a walking statue. Her anger splashed as forcefully as her embarrassment before. So she acted silly, so what? What right did he have to make faces, to lapse into offended silence? He did stupid things too sometimes, didn't he?

"You are ugly and annoying when you are like that," she informed him, not bothering to keep quiet. "I hate you when you make faces."

He shuddered visibly, which made her feel better. Statue alive, at least that. "Be quiet," he breathed. "They may be all around. Searching and all that."

Who cares? she wanted to say but didn't. The Palace's guards, oh yes. What if they were still around and searching? He did look like a runaway criminal, and so might she. Well, a dressed criminal, in her case. The thought made her wish to giggle. Then the resentment returned. He was watching the darkness, alert and listening, looking everywhere but at her. Annoying turkey!

"If you are so afraid, you can go back. I'll get the water and the *octli*. I know where it is." She snorted loudly. "In the meanwhile, you can sit in my sister's rooms and shake with fear all you want."

His grunt barely disturbed the night.

"What does that mean? Talk like people do. Can't you do even that?"

"Stop that," he said stonily, his voice quiet and very low. "Stop talking nonsense. Go back yourself if you want to, or stop talking stupid things."

She felt the air escaping her chest at the bout of fury that took her. What a rotten piece of meat that boy was, stupid filthy rotten lowlife!

"How dare you?" she cried out, the abruptness of her halt causing his steps to cease too, at least that. "You are just a piece of stupid rotten loathsome disgusting—"

His hands were grabbing her shoulders, making her sway with the forcefulness of his pull, dragging her off the path and into the bushes, the dancing lights at the far edge of it not gaining her attention, too busy trying to understand. Did he just assault her? She fought him fiercely, with the aid of every limb and her sharpened even if partly broken nails – Citlalli's servants never managed to make those grow satisfactorily, not with her continued running about – but he was so much stronger, his grip on her mouth strangling, making the panicked fear return.

"Quiet, Tlemilli, quiet," he breathed, his hands straining to hold her, uncompromising, his words barely there, penetrating the wave of fear together with other sounds, voices and footsteps coming up the path he had dragged her off of. With an enormous effort, she forced her mind to concentrate on those, still struggling but with less determination.

The people walking the alley were nearby now, enough passersby to make plenty of noise. She pushed his hand off her face but didn't try to break free anymore, aware of the danger. There were warriors out there, easy to tell apart from the servants, their voices loud and firm, words forceful. Softer female tones interweaved melodiously, laced with laughter. Some of the men guffawed in an uninhibited manner. Daring to peek out, she saw their backs, one of the warriors pulling a figure in a skirt closer, making her sway and giggle. The others' comments grew in volume.

He was nothing but a frozen statue, barely breathing by her side. Over her initial startle, she snuggled against him, feeling safer to do so, wishing to be near. What came over them before? It was wrong to bicker and fight. And why wouldn't she wish to enjoy his closeness, his touch? But for his quick reaction, they would have been spotted, asked for their purpose, challenged maybe, connected to their misadventures back in the place of the animals.

"They are gone," she whispered, peeking out again, then glancing at him carefully, unsure of herself.

He nodded stiffly, not looking back at her.

"We go on now?"

"Yes."

"Miztli!" She caught his arm as he began easing out of the bushes, her heart squeezing at the way his eyes darted toward her, dark and guarded, troubled, openly gauging. "I'm sorry, I didn't mean to yell at you or hit you. I was just surprised. And you were acting weird. And I didn't like it. I hate when you become like that, not talking and not friendly. I like you when you are serious but in a good way. Not like now." It was getting silly, her helpless chattering and the hurt in his eyes tore at her. "Well, I don't mean to say that I don't like you like now too and that don't want to be friends anymore. I just... I just want you to be back, the real you, you know. Not all quiet and angry."

He was looking away again, at the darkness of the ground under their feet this time. "I thought you were mad because... because of that kiss," he muttered. "Because of how it was..."

"No!" she cried out, then lowered her tone hastily. "Why would I be mad about that?" But as she said it, she knew that he might be right. There was something wrong with that kiss back under the terrace, and yes, it was then, come to think of it, that their quarrel had started. "That kiss, it has nothing to do with it. You got mad and annoying, so I got mad too. The kisses are good, always. Unless they make you mad and annoying." It came out silly again, but this time, she could hear him snickering and it made her feel better at once.

"We need to hurry now," he said, his smile fleeting but there, that familiar shy, bashful smile she loved so much. "They must think we stayed to drink this *octli* all by ourselves and are now snoring drunkenly or swaying and giggling out there."

Snickering in her turn, she followed his lead, letting his hands guide her out of the bushes without allowing too many of those to tear at her clothes and skin.

"Did you ever taste *octli*? Did you try to drink it once?" It was good to snuggle against him as they began walking up the once-again dark pathway, the flickering lights and the voices gone, dissipating out there for good, or so she hoped.

"Yes."

"What? When?" To try and peer at him without moving from the safety of his embrace was difficult, so she settled for a quick peek. "No way! You are lying to me."

His smile was impossible not to hear. "No, I'm not. Necalli's father lets us drink when we visit his house. He says future warriors must know how to handle this beverage, must learn to get used to it." He fell silent for a moment. "He is a great man. Very wise, very good, and kind."

She remembered her first night in Tenochtitlan and the crippled warrior with the reserved smile and crinkling eyes. "He let you drink *octli*? I can't believe it! I want to try it too!"

He chuckled softly. "Steal a gulp from that flask we are supposed to get now." His arm pressed her tighter. "But ladies don't drink such things. Only warriors. And elderly men."

She found nothing better to do than snort, incensed that he did something she wasn't allowed, not even by stealth. "I know what the law says. Everyone who drinks *octli* in public gets punished, unless they are old men. Or warriors. Or nobles. But not in public. So you are not allowed to drink it out there any more than I am."

He shrugged indifferently. "It's a nice drink. Necalli likes it."

"I bet he is not enjoying any of it now out there, in the City of Gods."

"Oh yes." His smile was again easy to guess. "And no food either. They are fasting and all."

"Why didn't they take you along? Aren't you attending the same classes?"

His shoulders lifted again, abruptly this time.

"They should have, you know?" she went on, sensing his disappointment. "You are as good as him and better. You are already a warrior. That school is a waste of time for you, and the Emperor knows it. No wonder he keeps giving you important tasks and missions."

"Which I keep messing up," he muttered, growing tense against the touch of her limbs again. "I have nothing to report to the Emperor. Nothing! Just silly gossip from some filthy visitors' quarters and a terrible mess to explain."

"No, it's not..." Helplessly, she searched for something to say, something positive and encouraging, something that would make him feel better. "It got complicated, yes, but there must be a way to bring the information you were supposed to. We can go back there where you were supposed to spy, see if they are still awake and gossiping. Or maybe the Texcocan, YaoTecuani, maybe he'll find a way to help you out. After everything you have done for him, he owes you, you know. And he'll know what to do. He always does. We'll talk to him when we get back and maybe—"

"He is barely alive to help me drag him out and away from this place, Tlemilli!" He cut her off with a surprising lack of consideration, obviously angered again. "He has been doing some unauthorized spying of his own, this man. And it went horribly wrong. Because of us! He is not in the position to help me, or even himself, at this point. And I don't even know how to smuggle him out of here before he is discovered. It'll be up to me, not him. And I don't—" Abruptly, he fell silent, his frustration cresting, seeping through his touch, reaching her.

For some reason, it made her feel stronger, more sure of herself than ever. "We'll deal with it," she said firmly, pressing him with her arms, both of them around his torso, hindering their progress. "We'll deal with it all, get this man out and safe and unharmed, provide the Emperor with the information he wanted from you, get my sister from the vile attention of the adviser. We'll deal with it all, I promise you, and it will be the easiest. You'll see."

He stopped and was peering at her in wonder, holding her tightly, with both hands, just like she did, listening with his breath bated. In the resumed moonlit that the fork in the path they had reached offered, it was easy to see his expression, so much wonder and almost childlike expectation, as though she had been the best of orators, as eloquent with her words as Citlalli was. It made her legs go weak.

"We'll wriggle out of this mess, you'll see. The Emperor will not be disappointed and the Texcocan man will value you more now, like he values your friend or even more than that. He has seen your worth this evening, and he will not forget. He'll help you out if you need help."

The palanquin was upon them before they managed to notice its progress, coming from the second alley, preceded by only a few servants and maids. Catching their breath, they froze, not daring to move, the rustling shrubs offering safety, so near, so out of reach.

"Move away," demanded one of the men at the forefront of the small procession, not a palace's guard judging by his attire, or rather the lack of it, but an authoritative enough individual. "Off with you two, stupid slaves!"

For a heartbeat, Tlemilli found herself staring, bereft of words, the prettily curtained seat the sturdy litter-bearers carried gaining the immediacy of her attention, such intricate patterns, like that of Citlalli's litter but larger, more lavishly decorated. A noble person for sure, royalty. The "slaves" bit, she didn't try to process yet. Was this lowly person addressing them?

Miztli's hands were pulling her away again, but for some reason, she found herself resisting, needing to see who the rider of the palanquin was. Suddenly, it was imperative to do that. The outline of the figure behind the flimsy curtain moved, displaying a light, slightly familiar grace. A woman, for certain.

In spite of herself, she leaned to see better, but the men who had barked at them stepped forward, accompanied by another two, all of them solid and bulky, impressively well muscled. "Are you deaf? Move away, you dirty pieces of human waste!"

She could feel Miztli growing again as rigid as a stone statue, and as his arms pushed her behind his back, firm and uncompromising, she glimpsed the curtain moving, pulled away by a pair of long elegant fingers. The burly man shoved him with little success, and was now raising his hand with an unmistakable manner; however, before he could attack or Miztli react – she knew he would not be struck down, not him! – a cold voice dominated the night.

"Leave them be." Then, in a quieter, more amused tone, "Come closer, both of you. Here, where the light is." The elegantly groomed hand motioned at them, then at one of the men. "Bring your torch here and hold it."

There could be no mistaking the voice; still, she could feel Miztli hesitating, growing yet tenser, while her legs pushed out and forward, acting as though on their own accord. Here in Tenochtitlan, Jade Doll was not an enemy.

"Who would have guessed?" In the general moonlight aided by the flickering torch, it was easy to see the familiar chiseled features, cold but not inimical, not like back in Tlatelolco, derisive in a bearable way, the full lips twisting slightly, pulling up at one corner, climbing down at another, in an almost conspiratorial grin. "I thought you were done with doing mischief, girl."

She felt curiously comfortable to grin back in a likewise fashion. "I'm not doing mischief. We have a good reason to be here."

"And what reason is that?"

"Well," she glanced at Miztli, hoping for help, but he still stood where he was, beside the man who was set on pushing him away, both of them frozen forms, watching intently, "we needed to get something. To bring it..." There was no need to complicate it all by mentioning Citlalli, who still couldn't stand this woman. "The thing is, well, I can't tell what we are up to, but it is nothing inappropriate. We were doing nothing wrong."

One of the litter-bearers shifted, causing the grand seat to waver ever so slightly. "Careful, you imbecile," called out the woman, frowning at those who held her in her elevated position, hovering above the ground on the strength of their arms alone. Must be tiring to do that, reflected Tlemilli briefly, following the woman's gaze that now shifted to Miztli. "Come here, boy."

His reluctance was impossible to miss, even in the semi-darkness. The way he moved his legs, so unwillingly, even though his back was exaggeratedly straight and his bare chest thrust out, his head high in an obvious attempt to appear confident. Her heart went out to him and she didn't fight the urge to step back in order to stand by his side. He never liked or trusted this woman, did he?

"So," said the princess, measuring him pointedly. "Running naked around palaces yet again, aren't you, boy?"

She heard him drawing in a sharp breath, growing more rigid than before.

"He is not naked. He is wearing a loincloth and the Emperor himself made him come here like this!"

The elegantly outlined eyebrows climbed up. "Did he?" Then the uneven grin returned, ignoring her once more. "Keep serving my brother in unconventional capacities, don't you, boy? What did he ask you to do this time?"

Again, it was easy to feel his hesitation, his uneasiness coming in waves, like ripples of breeze.

"He can't talk about it, he—"

"Let him speak, girl. He can do it for himself, can't he? Inform me about the secrecy of his mission, or share the details of it if I ask him to do so. After all, I'm not an outsider with a questionable past but a member of the royal family, our powerful ruler's full sister, an elder sibling at that." The coldness was back, and the haughtiness. "What are you doing here, commoner boy ItzMiztli? What is your purpose, slinking around the Palace's gardens at night and in questionable company?"

This time, he drew himself together before she could burst out with indignant protestations and claims.

"I'm serving our Emperor, Revered Princess. He wished me to be here and do his bidding and I..." The phrase that began so well faltered momentarily, and she heard him drawing in another sharp breath. "He did not wish me to talk about the nature of my... my mission, but if he would have allowed it, I would have told you. I would have been happy to tell you all about it, that is. Revered Lady." The last combination was added hastily, as though an afterthought. Still, she marveled at his unexpected eloquence.

"Not badly spoken." The imperial lady seemed to value his speech as well. "You certainly learned a thing or two since our first meeting back in Tlatelolco, boy. Good for you." The full lips quivered in an inverted grin again, unsettling in a strange way Tlemilli couldn't explain. As did the woman's gaze that slid over him, as though assessing, measuring openly, with a sort of a grudging appreciation. "You do surprisingly well, commoner boy from a gods' forsaken village. Making the right moves, nurturing the right friendships, gathering an interesting following among our noble even if somewhat eccentric elements of the Palace."

The glittering eyes shifted back to Tlemilli briefly, leaving her staring, blinking in puzzlement at the obvious, if chilling, derisively offhanded challenge that brought back the forgotten sensation of being back among her numerous half-sisters and the perpetual nastiness of their competition and needling. Was this woman trying to pick a fight with her? She tried to make her mind work.

"Well, it's late and we don't have time for a proper talk I wish to have with you, young commoner. Pay your respects to me tomorrow, when the sun is..." The perfectly smooth forehead creased momentarily. "When the sun has passed its zenith by a finger or two. A servant will come to fetch you when it's time. Be punctual and follow without delay." Again the eyes rested on her, this time with only slightly cold condemnation. "And you, young one, should not be wandering outside like a serving maid getting quick pleasure with handsome boys. This is not how the noblewomen of Tenochtitlan conduct themselves. Your sister should teach you better manners, or at least keep an eye on you. When she slipped away in the middle of the imperial evening feast, some thought it to be glaring impoliteness. My brother Tizoc certainly wasn't pleased. However, now I can see that she might have good cause to worry." The royal head shook lightly but tellingly, making the beautiful diadem sparkle against the moonlight. "To keep an eye on an unruly thing like you must be challenging. The Tlatelolcan Head Adviser and his women certainly did not make a good job out of it." The smile that stretched the quivering lips did not hold any more coldness. "As you can see, I do not forget favors and good deeds. However, you should not test my or everyone else's patience; even that of your glorious sister. I bet she did not condone your running around with commoner boys at night, even though but for you and this same commoner, she wouldn't be here, enjoying the life of Tenochtitlan Palace in the first place." A shrug. "Follow my palanquin, girl, and after we reach my quarters, you will enter it until it delivers you back to your side of the Palace."

The curtain moved decisively, signaling the end of the improvised interview. Overwhelmed by too much information and demands provided in one tirade, Tlemilli opened her mouth to argue this or that point – just who did this woman think she was to order her about like that? – when the idea struck, too brilliant not to consider it. The palanquin, was she going to get this spacious carrier all for herself after its rider was delivered to her royal quarters?

Miztli was still holding her tight, not about to remove the protectiveness of his arms. She leaned at him hurriedly, seeing one of the maids separating from her fellow litter's followers, clearly about to supervise and make sure the new orders were obeyed.

"Get the water and *octli* and go back to Citlalli," she whispered hastily, liking her new idea better with every passing heartbeat. "I'll arrive there soon and with this big pretty litter. Wait for me there and tell Citlalli and the Texcocan to be ready."

"What?" His stare was almost funny in its bewilderment.

"We don't have time. Just wait for me there. I'll explain when I'm back. It's the best idea ever." His eyes were so round, it made her laugh and wish to kiss him right there and then, regardless of all the scandalized eyes. "You look so funny. Just wait for me in Citlalli's rooms. Don't do anything silly until I'm back." The palanquin was drawing away, dissipating in the darkness despite the flickering torches the servants carried. "I must hurry. You just go back and don't get caught."

He was staring at her back with the same baffled wonder, of that she had little doubt, standing in the middle of the path, helplessly lost. However, there was no time for any more talking. To catch up with the disappearing procession was the first priority. She waved him to go on without turning back.

CHAPTER 13

When the man's broad form blocked the narrow entrance, Elotl knew they were done for all over again. It was bad enough to cram in the airless, annoyingly sultry, sweltering room dominated by a pair of stone braziers and little else, huddling next to the girl and the skinny little thief, aware of her presence more than he wished to be under the circumstances, embarrassed to no end.

The groaning and the silly thrashing of the pair outside in the storage room that they had managed to escape in the nick of time, before it had been invaded presumably by the owners, went on for some time. Or maybe those were intruders like them, seeking privacy to get quick pleasure. Their strangled groans and cries sounded so silly, embarrassing, enhanced by the occasional giggle the girl next to him would stifle with less success than the rest, echoed by the silent guffawing of the little thief. They seemed to be amused rather than embarrassed. The realization that made him even more furious. But did they have no basic decency, those dwellers of the great city?

"Don't!" he hissed when the little boy crawled closer to the opening after a muffled thud followed by another had their curiosity piqued, clearly wishing to see better. "Stay here!"

"Don't you want to see it too?" breathed the girl into his ear, washing his senses with the smell of well-cooked beans, not an unpleasant odor but for their predicament and his fury with her. "They are doing it against the wall, I bet. Poor girl."

"Shut up," he muttered, fighting the urge to catch her and shake her hard. Besides the beans, she smelled disturbingly delicious, something musky and sweet, or maybe spicy. The thought of how her lips would taste invaded his mind quite against his will.

"You shut up," she said sharply, then gasped, but it was too late to take the exclamation back. The thrashing in the outer room stopped and before another heartbeat was over, the broad silhouette of a man, this one not skinny or underfed, bore upon them, blocking the narrow opening, making it look smaller than it was.

"What's the meaning of this?" he demanded, not keeping his voice low. No intruder this one, oh mighty deities! "Who is in there?" The man's charge forward had him nearly stumbling over the crouching boy, but the scrawny rat, clearly a veteran of many such situations, wriggled out of the massive hand's reach, shooting for the outside with an agility of a true rodent, his damaged ankle forgotten. A squeak of surprise from the woman who was still out there followed the hurried rustling, but by that time, Elotl was already up, grabbing what looked like a strangely shaped hammer, a satisfactorily heavy object, comfortable to handle. To be armed with a tool like that made him feel infinitely better, finally in control after the insanity of this entire evening.

"Drop the annealing hammer!" demanded the man angrily, aborting his new charge in midair, but not retreating, not clearing their way out. "You filthy thief, drop it before you get hurt."

"Let us out and I won't hit you with it," retorted Elotl, taking a step forward, pleased to see the man retreating a step in his turn. "And I won't be taking this thing with me. We didn't come to steal. It's all just a misunderstanding."

"Didn't come to steal? Then what did you come to do here?" The man's eyes darted toward the girl, narrowing, then widening with surprise and then an open fury. "Quetzalli! You filthy little whore, how dare you bring your lovers into our workshop?"

Elotl found himself staring, speechless for a moment.

"What?" The girl gasped, then straightened up like a maguey string that was coiled too tightly. "How dare you call me that? I didn't! How dare you?"

"Oh yes you are, you little piece of loose upbringing. Everyone knows about you and your running around with the new

Tlatelolco smugglers, doing all sorts of inappropriate things. Is this one of them, the filthy Tlatelolcan?" The fleeting glance Elotl received caused him to stiffen with rage as well. "How dare you sneak into our workshop for filthy groping around?"

To that, the girl reacted with an unexpected and quite a pitiful gulp, losing her fighting spirit, all of it and at once. "I didn't," she whimpered. "It's not like that."

Elotl felt his rage escalating to new levels. "Stop talking to her like that," he demanded, stepping between them, his hands gripping the unfamiliar handle with enough force to make them numb. "You were the one to get quick pleasure, not us. It wasn't us that was doing all this groping out there. Stupidly noisy groping!"

This time, it was the man's turn to gasp, but in no pitiful way. "You filthy vermin," he breathed fiercely, in a surprisingly quiet voice. "After I'm through with you, there will be nothing remaining to drag into the courts, or to be of use to that loose fowl. The mess you will end up to be, not even our district's court will sentence for breaking into my father's property or touching our tools."

It was an effort not to back away from the man's advance, a stocky piece of rotten meat, with plenty of muscle if not height. Elotl bettered his grip on the wooden handle, seeing where the round stone tip would be hitting, on the side of the head preferably, against that line of the eyes, not too high yet not too low, to eliminate the possibility of missing. As always, in his case, the first hit was the one to determine the outcome, even though the heavy tool was an unexpected benefit.

The man's eyes were glowing like embers in the nearest brazier. Elotl considered charging himself to get it over with. To freeze in the same pose was turning unbearable.

"Don't!" The girl moved so suddenly, he almost wielded his improvised weapon at her. "Wait, both of you. Please!" Her voice rang surprisingly steady as opposed to her previous whimpering and she spread her arms wide, stepping toward the furious owner, half demanding, half pleading. "We really did nothing wrong, Ome. You must believe us. People were after him and

Azcatl, that little thief from the marketplace's second alley, beside the Tlaloc temple, remember him? So I helped them and we rushed here to escape. They were combing our alley, the people who wanted to catch them. We had no choice!" She took another step forward and now stood directly in front of the man, talking in a breathless rush. "But they are gone now, so we can go, leave, never bother you again. You forget that you saw me here and I'll forget that I saw you. I will never tell Chantli about you and that woman out there. I swear!"

"You will not be allowed to come near my sister!" spat the man fiercely, proving to be immune to her veiled threats. It was obvious that they knew each other and that she was hinting that his right to be here now was as questionable as theirs was, or at least close enough to it. "And I don't care if you tell anyone about me coming here at night, in any company I wish. It's my father's workshop. I'm allowed to be here. Unlike you!"

"Your father will not take your coming here to have pleasure with loose women kindly and you know it."

"You little whore! When *your* father hears about you sneaking into our workshop to enjoy men, he will be disposing of you quicker than—"

"No, no, you can't tell him anything like that. Please!" Again, the whimpering pleading. She was losing her spirit so easily, that girl. As easily as she was regaining it, or so it seemed. Elotl felt like following the example of the skinny thief by running out and away from it all. "Please, OmeTelpochtli, please! You can't! It's nothing like that... it's not! I didn't, didn't do anything of the sort..."

Their accuser was glowing too happily again, with too much smugness. Elotl tried not to succumb to the new wave of fury.

"Look, both of you," he said as reasonably as he could, his voice satisfactorily calm but his hands still gripping his improvised weaponry with too much force, trembling lightly. "Let us leave and go each our own way. Your girl is still out there, you know, probably wondering." He motioned toward the narrow opening. "You better go calm her, and in the meanwhile, we'll leave and will not show up again ever." The man was eyeing him darkly, yet his pose was not of someone ripe to attack, not anymore. Taking a deep breath, Elotl took a step back toward the braziers, placing the hammer next to the nearest one, careful as though it was made out of brittle obsidian. "Here, the hammer is back, and we are off." He motioned the girl curtly, praying she would listen and wouldn't add a word while scampering off and toward the outside. "You can forget we ever existed."

"You talk like a cheap soothsayer on the marketplace, man." Unimpressed, their accuser moved a fraction, letting the girl pass, curiously affable all of a sudden, or at least tractable enough to talk, the splashes of his previous fury seemingly gone. "I may let you two go, but you will explain to me first what that was all about. Come to the shed." The curt sway of the head invited Elotl to follow the girl's example. Numbly, he did just that, still ready to fight, with his fists if need be. The people of this island were changing too fast, all of them, not always for the best.

In their previous hideaway, the girl named Quetzalli was standing in the company of another, a plump tousled thing of an indefinite age. Even the scrawny thief was still there, hovering in the doorway, ready to bolt away. Elotl rolled his eyes, aware of the man following in his footstep, his danger signals still up.

"What is it?" the disheveled fox demanded, timid and daring at the same time. Was she like the girl he had spent half an evening with, changing from reckless bravery to the worst of cowardice in a matter of heartbeats? "What is going on?"

"Shut up," was the man's laconic response, not angered but matter-of-fact. He seemed to be of the same age as Elotl, actually, or maybe just a little older. His eyes did not linger on the women or the hovering boy but turned back at him, piercing hard. "Now tell me what it is all about and do it quickly. If my brother or father join us in this, you are done for, this time for good. They aren't as patient as I am, or as tolerant of foreigners. Not after that little piece of filth, the apprentice. So tell it all fast and be off. Who was after you and why? Why did Quetzalli say you had to hide here?"

Again, the mention of the "little piece of filth apprentice" sent his thoughts scattering. "Who is that apprentice? Was he a boy who worked here?"

"What?" His interrogator's eyebrows jumped up. "What do you know about this one?"

"Nothing. What do *you* know about him?" This came out stonily, in a threatening growl. He didn't care. It was all about Miztli, it was! The metal-melting workshop, the apprentice who got away while making them all angry. It all added up! But where was his brother now? What happened to him? "Tell me where this boy, this apprentice, is now, and I'll make it worthwhile for you." The feel of the bag the little thief had stolen reminded him of Father paying their rare family treasures to the greedy trader that brought them nothing but bad news. Father's stones were small and ragged, nothing but fractured green pieces compared to the slickness of the polished treasures the bag in his hand held, as large as birds' eggs and as glossy. "If you tell me where this boy is now, where I can find him, I'll give you a good green stone. A really large one."

"You can't!" burst out the girl called Quetzalli, finding her tongue again and in the worst of timing as always. "You can't give him those stones for the stupid village boy."

He paid her no attention, gauging his adversary's reactions, sorry for leaving the hammer back in the inside room now. To spread the contents of the bag upon his palm took him no time. However, as they all leaned to examine it, even this same spirited Quetzalli, he felt his body as tense as an overstretched bow, ready to react to the violence should the angry man decide to reach for it, to try and take the contested pile of wealth by force – a fair possibility. If it came back to fighting, the hammer would have been handy, even if just as the means to deter.

"Where did you get those trinkets?" the stocky owner exclaimed, blinking as though trying to clear his vision. As he leaned closer, Elotl closed his palm, stepping back hastily, preparing to dart aside.

"It doesn't matter. Tell me about that boy who worked here, all that you know, and I'll give you one of the stones."

"You can't!" cried out the girl and the skinny boy in unison this time.

Elotl concentrated on the man, whose eyes were now mere slits, same as his lips, pursed dourly, reflecting an angered thought process. "What do you want to know about this piece of human waste?"

"Everything. What he did here; why was he kicked out; where is he now – everything!" He didn't take his eyes off the furious mask, readying his right fist to lash out, glad that the stones were clutched in his left palm, not in the way of his meager means of defense. "I need to find him. If I'm successful, I'll bring you another such stone."

"*I* know where to find him!" cried out Quetzalli-girl, stepping closer as though about to try and snatch his treasures as well. "You want to know his exact whereabouts, you pay me. Not him. He doesn't know a thing."

That threw him out of balance. "What? How?"

"How? I got to see his ugly face over and over since Tlatelolco fell. Too many times to count and none of them pleasant!"

"Where?"

"Give me a stone. The round one!"

"After you've told me!"

"No, before!"

The silence around them deepened, then broke with hurried footsteps, trampling the grass of the small yard with disturbing confidence. The scrawny form of the boy darted for the faintly outlined opening, clearly shooting for the freedom of the outside, an attempt that did not crown with success. The roaring voice and the sounds of violent struggle brought the skinny wrestling limbs back, held quite contemptuously by an exceptionally large silhouette that put the other indignant owner of this workshop to shame.

"What's the meaning of this?" demanded the newcomer, holding his dismal captive with one outstretched arm, like a hunted coyote cub, while eyeing them with startled surprise. "What is happening here?"

"Nothing," said their previous accuser readily, in the same tone the girl Quetzalli had used before, as though eager to convince, to display the possible innocence of their intentions.

"I'm sorry this silly squabbling woke you up, Brother. It's our sister's friend, that silly Quetzalli. She came here to me asking for help. And maybe I'll help her, yes. She is a good girl, and Chantli's friend. You go back to sleep. I'll deal with it. Did they disturb Father's sleep as well?"

The last phrase came out a little too hastily compared to the entire performance. Elotl tried not to chuckle, still clutching the stones, ready to bolt for the outside in case of a renewed attack. Against two bulks like that, united or not, he had no chance, his self-respect and desire to prove himself notwithstanding. Still, it was amusing to see the first man reversing roles with the spunky girl.

"You may have disturbed Father's sleep as well with all this squabbling and shouting," grunted the second man, eyeing them darkly while still clutching at this struggling spoil. "What's with this marketplace dirt? What deals do you do with such scum, Brother?"

"Nothing untoward," stated the first man firmly, holding his head high. "I'll see them out. You go back to sleep. Chantli's friend needs to be taken home. And her friend as well." This time, the casual nod indicated the other woman, puzzling Elotl but only for a heartbeat. The dubious fox and more than a dubious tumble in the workshop was clearly not something this man wished to share with his family members. "I'll be back shortly." As the larger owner was still holding the kicking boy, his younger sibling put a reassuring palm on his shoulder. "Go back to sleep, Brother. You have a difficult day behind you. Father would need us both wide awake and rested tomorrow. With the order of the marketplace temple..."

The girl was by his side again, a warm, uncomfortably enticing presence. "Don't you dare give him the stones!" The murmur of her words made his ear tickle. "I know where that good-for-nothing apprentice is, with whom he is running, and where he spends his time. Ome doesn't know a thing. Just let him get us out of here and away from Acatlo. He is an awful man."

"The big one?"

"Yes." She nodded eagerly, squeezing past the intimidating

forms of both brothers, the skinny thief still held by the first one, out of sheer spite, was Elotl's angered conclusion. The other girl slipped away hurriedly, bypassing them and pushing him with her plump elbow in her haste.

Elotl hurried after them both, his heart beating fast. Could it be that he would actually find Miztli, hale and healthy and unhurt, running all over this city, even if hated by everyone around? What did this cheeky local fox have against his brother? She said she had met him plenty of times and none of those encounters were pleasant. But it did not make any sense. What could ever-agreeable, likeable Miztli do to this one? Or these people he had worked for? Well, there were always ways to piss off someone you worked for; there could be no argument about it. Whether family or strangers, one could be caught lazing around or doing things unsatisfactorily or wrong. Even though it was difficult to imagine Miztli doing badly. The annoying piece of work did everything he touched well, in the mines or the fields or around the house; even when taken to hunting trips, he and his unerring sling. So maybe it wasn't Miztli they were all hating so. But if it was another runaway apprentice that pissed everyone off, then where was his brother? Still alive? Well? Unharmed?

"How does this boy look like, the one who worked here?" he demanded, catching Quetzalli-girl's elbow when the other one paused as well, peering into the darkness of the workshop's yard and the voices that still poured out of there. "Tall? Broad? Like a really huge slab of stone?"

In the renewed stream of the moonlight, it was easy to see her grimacing, rolling her eyes in an unmistakable fashion. "Yes, he isn't the smallest thing alive. Not as huge as Acatlo, but not as skinny as you or other people. Ball players look like that, or slaves they bring to build pyramids and other things. All muscle. Girls went crazy about him, some really silly fowls, Tlatelolcan brood. He is still stuck on that bizarre thing, Chantli says. She is in the Palace now, living as though nothing happened. Should have been sent to the slave markets, if you ask me; her and her loose, lusty sister. But the stupid villager saved her and now he is stuck, feeling obliged to be around that ugly stick. As though anyone would let him have her, with all that royal blood flowing inside this ugliness and whatnot."

The man from the workshop bore down on them, alone again except the scrawny form of the street boy hobbling beside him, trying to keep up. Elotl breathed with relief, taking his mind off the confusing jumble of information with an effort, disappointed yet also grimly amused. There could be no doubt that nothing of it had anything to do with his brother, not a word of this city's high circles' gossip. The close-mouthed, ever-shy self-conscious Miztli involved in the affairs of the Tenochtitlan royal family, saving princesses or courting after them? That was beyond a joke, a funny story to share back home, when he did find his brother and managed to bring him home safely. There would be plenty of laughs concerning this misunderstanding, however, it didn't help him now at all. If not that person everyone hated and gossiped about, then where was the actual Miztli?

"You owe me for this, all of you," hissed their last would-be rescuer. "Acatlo would have you, naked foreigner, in the court of our district first thing in the morning, tied and thrown in the workshop in a very uncomfortable position until it happened. And you, Quetzalli, would be now facing your own father and hasty marriage somewhere nasty and away from here." He brought his hand up as the girl began protesting, silencing her. "Now, we don't have time. Let me pick one of the stones and be gone wherever you were all going."

In the freshness of the outside and away from the closeness of the workshop, Elotl felt infinitely better. "I promised you one stone for the information on your former worker, but it seems that this girl knows more than you, and it's the wrong person anyway." He didn't take a step back as the man swayed yet closer, threatening again, but his bunched fist was prepared to put it all in the first blow, missing the hammer from the room with the braziers yet again. "You helped us, yes, just now," he added as a concession, appreciating the man's self-control in not launching an attack in order to try and take the loot by sheer force. Come to think of it, this one wasn't a bad man, decent enough through the entire interaction back in the metal-melting place. "But it's not worthy of one whole stone. If we could split it somehow, exchange one of those for something else, I would have given you a part of its worth."

"You want to get rid of those stones anyway," said the second girl, speaking for the first time. She had smoothed her hair and her clothes and now looked more presentable, not as pretty or as well dressed as the other one but passably nice.

"What do you mean?" demanded her admirer, who until now did not display much fondness of the woman he was caught making love to.

She shrugged with less spirit than before. "Just what I said. From what they told, those are stolen goods, easy to find. Those are precious stones, very expensive. Whoever it was stolen from would be looking for them."

Elotl shifted under their gazes that went toward him, appreciating the argument but not liking its implications. What she said made perfect sense! "The boy got it from some skinny frightened type." Now it was his turn to shrug. "He was supposed to deliver it to some people in that other town, whatever it's called."

"Tlatelolco?"

"Yes."

Now it was the skinny street rat's turn to shift as uneasily. "He was nothing, that man. Just some stupid brute from some stupid alley."

"But they chased you already," contributed Quetzalli-girl, atypically quiet for a change. "They know what you look like, both of you."

Elotl found nothing better than to shrug with pretended indifference. "I can deal with them, but," another shrug seemed to be in order, "we do need to split some of those stones' worth anyway. Between some of us. So..."

"The healer woman!" cried out both Quetzalli-girl and the little thief in unison, but the man from the workshop waved his arm to shut them up.

"Where would you get rid of such things?" he inquired, shooting a narrow glance at his girl, assessing her with some interest.

She looked anywhere but at her man or any of them. "The healer woman of the stone house, yes. Behind Tlaloc temple. She'll have enough cocoa beans to buy this pile and more. And she won't be afraid to do that, to keep such costly things. She has plenty of bullies to keep her house safe."

"Will she let us in at this time of the night?"

For the first time, the girl's strangely colored lips twisted in a sort of a hinted smile. "For such stones, she would accept anyone and at any time of the day or night."

CHAPTER 14

The litter-bearers did not argue with the Texcocan. They didn't even pause to look back before bolting away and into the merciful darkness, in a hurry to reach more respectable parts of the city, probably on the run. Miztli didn't blame them. Too tired to give it even a passing thought, he moved to the wounded's side, ready to offer his hand or a shoulder as a prop, in the way they had grown accustomed to moving through this wild, insane, terrible night.

"Not yet," said the man curtly, motioning him to stay where he was, himself leaning against the beam of the nearest stall, utterly exhausted. The corner of the two alleys and the small square their crossing created hosted nothing but crudely made stands, now empty except for an occasional wooden crate or an overturned basket piling at this or that corner, in a neat arrangement despite the night breeze tugging at it.

It always amazed him, the exceptional cleanliness of these streets and alleys at night. On the last moon's frequent excursions all over this sprawling giant of the city along with Necalli and some of the others, he had witnessed whole armies of slaves busy with brooms and baskets, clearing leftovers of each clamorous day, scrubbing the capital of the world clean. It had something to do with night deities, Necalli had told him, the obligation to keep the streets spotlessly tidy for the night. Well, deities or not, it was definitely a pleasure to walk along those swept polished cobblestones, not busy picking one's step, fighting not to let one's feet be sucked into puddles and traps like back home.

"Give me your shoulder."

The curt words brought him back from his musings and into

the chilliness of the night and the reality of their challenging situation, with the wounded man he admired more and more with every passing heartbeat wavering badly, struggling to stay upright on his own, a difficult feat now that the litter Tlemilli had managed to organize by pure magic was gone, sent away in no uncertain terms. *Why?* he wondered numbly, not daring to ask. The Texcocan man knew what he was doing, always. There could be no argument about that.

"It's not far from here," repeated the wounded as though reading Miztli's thoughts, leaning on the offered shoulder heavily, washing his senses with the intense aroma of blood, fresh and stale, mixed with sweat and *octli* aplenty. His cloak was literally dripping, and Miztli suspected that more was soaking in. That gap in the man's back, it must be still oozing blood or other strange liquids. The *octli* he was made to spill into it, to rub into the raw flesh that both women refused to even come close to, did nothing to calm the bleeding. If anything, it seemed to work to the opposite effect, making the gaping wound glare even more angrily. He shuddered at the mere memory.

"Hold on, boy. It's really not far," commented the Texcocan in a stronger voice, straightening up a little, making an obvious effort to walk on his own. "Wish we could use that litter your girl managed to pluck out of the thin air so neatly. It's been of a great help."

"Why didn't we?" muttered Miztli, not wishing to spend his dwindling strength on idle talk, yet curious, his closemouthed companion's sudden spell of chattiness too tempting not to explore.

He could hear the Texcocan snort faintly but poignantly. "You tell me why. Do you ever think with that head of yours, or do you use it only for eating?" An impatiently drawn breath tore the air, hissing. "Do you really think that the Tenochtitlan princess's litter-bearers should know whom they took out of the Palace just now, and where and for what reason?"

Miztli was hard put not to grind his teeth at the familiar snapping. "Tlemilli paid them to take us out and to ask no questions while doing so. They didn't ask a thing. They don't know who we are. They didn't even see your face, and mine is of no importance to anyone."

"I wouldn't be so sure about that, jaguar cub," muttered the man, leaning on Miztli more heavily again, his exhaustion and pain almost tangible, seeping through from his entire being. "The Emperor singled you out too many times not to have the Palace dwellers' eyes upon you. And anyway, it would be too easy to track our steps from any destination we would be arriving. Those litter-bearers have eyes, even if they were paid to do this side work and keep their mouths shut. They won't be so quiet tomorrow with dawn, unless no one asks them questions, and maybe even without additional inquiries." Another noisy breath came through the widening nostrils, impossible not to hear. How could he be still on his feet at all? wondered Miztli, his heart going out to the brave man despite the previous telling off. "Think more broadly, boy. Never trust people, especially those you pay to do something for you and then keep quiet about it. They'll do it as long as it suits them. Never for longer than this. And it won't be in accordance with your plans or priorities."

There was merit to this statement. To ease his own fatigue, Miztli concentrated on thinking it all through. "She paid them to take us out. She didn't ask them to keep quiet about it, but it's obvious that they would do it. Their mistress may get really angered if she knew that they did this without her permission. So it's in their interests to keep quiet about it, isn't it?"

The chuckle that trilled the air not far away from his ear had a fatherly sound to it. "Not bad thinking, boy. And yes, in some way, it is correct to assume that those people might wish to keep their mouths shut not because of your girl's cocoa beans but because their own good and wellbeing is involved." The arm leaning upon him became heavier. "It's... it's a long subject to preach about when both of us are barely keeping on our feet. But... Well, let's just say that it would be for their own good and not only ours that these men cannot disclose our current destination... the house we are heading to. It's... it's not far now. Just another crossroad. And a few of those patios to pass." A groan escaped the pursed lips, not amused or fatherly, not anymore. "She is well off... that healer. You'll get to relax and eat and rest for the remainder of this night as well, jaguar cub. You'll see..."

But to get to such a heavenly place already! "Why are we going there?" began Miztli, bettering his grip on the man's torso, trying to ease his struggle even though his own limbs were trembling now, about to refuse to support him.

"Healing, to begin with." Another chuckle had a softer quality to it. "Your girl and her sister are remarkably nice ladies, surprisingly resilient and open-minded – no surprise in your girl's case – but healers they aren't. For me not to bleed to death or tumble down the first Underworld's level with rotting a back, I'd better—"

Another crossroad opened before them, lit generously by the moonlight, swept as cleanly as the previous one, yet not as quiet or abandoned. Voices floated at its far end, unmistakable shouts accompanied with drunken laughter.

"Here," breathed the man, steering them both toward a narrower pathway that was glaring darkly to their left, wavering but holding on clearly on the sheer strength of his willpower.

His heart breaking into a wild race, Miztli followed, pausing to reach for the flint knife, back in the small bag, the only encouraging possession for now besides his talisman. But did he miss his weaponry, the sword and the club stored in Necalli's father's house, or at least his lawful dagger, the one he was allowed and even required to carry like all *calmecac* students of a certain age were. It was left along with his cloak somewhere there in the Palace, when he had to change to the serving boy's clothing, or rather a total lack of those.

The embarrassment was back, haunting. It was hard to believe that there were times when to go everywhere dressed in nothing but a simple loincloth felt normal, appropriate. These days, he felt naked walking like that, even when disguised as a servant. Certainly when facing Tlemilli, or worse yet, her haughty inimical sister, the high lady, the former imperial wife but now a refugee living here in this Palace thanks to him, and his friends' and Tlemilli's efforts, come to think of it. Yet the haughty lady cared nothing for his bravery, his achievements, his efforts to do well at school and not only in military training, his loyalty to Tlemilli, his readiness to do anything for her. They all must be thinking him to be unworthy, beneath her and the nobility of her blood and upbringing, even Necalli and his father, even this man beside him, a noble of Texcoco with his mysterious connections in the wild Highlands across the mighty Smoking Mountain. The Emperor certainly, with all his businesslike lack of snobbery or pretense, his readiness to promote promising youths, but probably up to a certain point. If he dared to ask for Tlemilli when older and having plenty of brave deeds behind him, captured warriors, weaponry, and other enemy regalia, would they all think him to be unworthy? Would they laugh in his face and send him to fight in another war, to serve them and this city in ways that fit certain peasants from gods' forsaken villages, those who had enough skill to be of use as warriors and not simple slaves carrying braziers, never good enough for better than this?

His stomach was churning bitterly, filling his mouth with bile. She was the only one who thought him worthy, truly worthy; the only one who gave him purpose and courage and strength and eloquence of speech – her magic! – the will to go on and excel, in training with weapons, yes, but also in deciphering glyphs, understanding what those said when combined together, even in difficult books or symbols of numbers. Another important challenge to best, according to Necalli, if one wished to be a leader and not just a warrior, responsible for the organization of campaigns, for counting and dividing supplies and spoils and other details of complicated war enterprises.

Necalli believed in him too, the true friend that he was. But the rest didn't. Or was he just tired and overwrought to think such silly thoughts? And what did the princess, Lady Jade Doll, another haughty piece of work want from him? Why did she demand that he pay her a visit when in the Palace and reporting to the Emperor? It didn't make any sense, and the woman was acting outright strange, measuring him with her eyes in a way that made him feel dirty and naked – which he actually was – exposed and somehow defenseless, a small rodent at the hands of a smug well-fed jaguar and at its lazy mercy. Even Tlemilli was startled. He could see it most clearly, the way she was staring when the high-born fowl was talking to him in this nearly flirtatious way. It made him think of various dirty remarks Necalli would have brought up had he been there, like back with this annoying friend of Chantli, the temptingly curvy Quetzalli and her habit of talking to him in a provocative manner. Necalli never tired of bringing it up and it was a mercy that he didn't see the haughty princess behaving with similar silliness, playing some strange female game. Thanks all gods, Tlemilli and Chantli were nothing like that!

The repeated thought of Tlemilli made him feel better. When she had arrived back at her sister's quarters with the haughty princess's litter, puffing with pride at the neatness of her solution of leaving the Palace in the easiest of ways, even the redoubtable man of Texcoco had to agree that there was merit to this idea. With the aid of a flask of *octli*, he, Miztli, had managed to steal from those same kitchen houses they didn't manage to reach in the first place, the man was spent, exhausted with pain, able to offer little help in carrying him out and away. Even Tlemilli's sister, horrified at the very thought of using Lady Jade Doll's very own litter, had to agree in the end, bringing forth a whole handful of prettily smooth, already peeled and out of the hull, cocoa beans the nobility used to pay in the marketplace with. That made the litter-bearers agree, albeit reluctantly. But were they relieved to be allowed to bolt back for the Palace only halfway toward the marketplace and the wharves!

He forced his mind to concentrate, listening to the voices that were dying behind their backs, dissipating in the darkness. In the narrow pathway, there was not enough light to see even his own limbs, let alone the man he was supposed to take care of. He hastened his steps, trusting his instincts, ready to reach out and catch his staggering companion should the wounded lose his balance and fall. *Where were they?*

Just as the silvery light began glimmering ahead once again, symbolizing the end of the cramped passageway, another outburst of voices assaulted their ears, this time not drunken and not merry, anything but! The familiar rasping shouts, thuds of blows being delivered or exchanged, strangled cries out. They froze in their tracks.

"Get him! Don't let him get away!" yelled someone as frantic footsteps broke in their direction, echoing against the stony pavement. "Get him!"

Miztli felt his back breaking in a bout of sticky sweat, the memories powerful, more than a moon old but still there. *Hold him!* But did he remember that cry, and the nauseating wave of panic that followed, the helplessness of the fear.

Without thinking, his feet took him forward, resisting the pull of the rock-hard hand that locked around his upper arm, arresting his progress with surprising strength considering his companion's weakened condition. For a moment, he fought to break free, then his mind cooled and his ears returned to absorb sounds, now louder scuffling, screams and yells, the thump of a fall, a rasp of heavy breathing.

The fingers wrapped around his arm fastened painfully, their signal clear. He clenched his teeth against the sounds and the memories, appreciating the man's wisdom and reasoning, yet unable to just listen and wait. The yelp of acute pain that erupted, followed by another, a more desperate howl, made his stomach turn almost as painfully.

"No, please," a voice screeched. "No! Please! It's not me... it wasn't me... It was stolen... No!"

A brief spell of quieter hassling resulted in another voice demanding, "Stolen how?"

The moaning of the assaulted man went on for a few more heartbeats, stopped by resumed beating, then more pleading, more disjointed responses and mumbling, more questions being barked. The handle of the flint knife was slick in his palm, about to slip away, sweat covering his back, more threatening to drip into his eyes. The stony fingers held him with uncompromising firmness, not trembling or moving, radiating no signs of life. Did the man of Texcoco possess no feelings?

"The stones... I did not... they were stolen... " The assaulted man was babbling, rambling incoherently now, not pleading with his assailants anymore. "It was not... I was not... The filthy thief, the boy, and then some foreigner, naked peasant... they ran and we almost caught them... people around, they helped, tried to help..."

The flow of words became even less coherent, although no more sounds of beating or torturing came. The people who wanted some stones or the information surrounding their obvious disappearance were listening avidly, not talking between themselves and not even moving. How many were they? He tried to figure that out, feeling the Texcocan, nothing but a stony statue in the darkness, and yet obvious in his undivided attention, listening as avidly. It was easy to conclude that.

"The foreigner... he helped, helped the thief... that little piece of garbage Azcatl, he always steals, like the rat that he is."

"What foreigner? What did he look like?" someone demanded.

A sound of shuffling feet generated a yelp, then more pitiful whimpering. "I don't.... never saw, never! He isn't... isn't from here, he isn't... never saw..."

"Whom were you supposed to give it to? Where?"

More sounds and shrieks. "Tlatelolco! The marketplace... the marketplace... where they build the new market, the huge market, where they broke the plaza and buildings and warehouses and everything... Please!"

"Get him up!" More scuffling and stirring resulting in plenty of whimpering, this time clearly of fear and not outright pain, let them know that the interrogation must have been coming to an end. "Take him away and across the causeway. We'll see if they've got the stones."

"Unless the thieves tried to get rid of it here. Wiser to do that." Another voice that didn't say a word until now tore the darkness, low and concentrated, as though pondering.

"Where would they go? The old healer? Xochitl?" The first voice was already drifting away, sounding less concerned.

"Where else? Those stones are worth a fortune."

"Then we'll split it. You two, go to the old witch's house, watch it—"

The Texcocan yanked at his arm so suddenly, Miztli found himself shuddering, as though awakening from a dream, while the rock-hard fingers slipped, releasing his arm, yet not before yanking at it once again, relaying a message. He obeyed their command out of an instinct, accustomed to following this man's lead. Retracing their steps along the dark passageway turned out to be more difficult, the need to keep absolutely quiet challenging, stretching his nerves, the screams of the interrogated man still ringing in his ears, gone by now but not from his mind.

Back upon the moonlit crossroad, the Texcocan didn't pause. A curt motion of the man's head motioned toward their original destination, reeling as though drunk on *pulque* but determined, his face a grotesque mask with no colors applied to it, the sharp cheekbones protruding, lips pressed into near disappearance. Not daring to offer his propping services, Miztli followed close by, ready to catch the man should he falter for good. *How far were they to go now?*

Not very far, apparently. Bypassing the bawdy group they had originally tried to avoid, drawing none of their attention thankfully, they dove into another dark pathway that must have ran parallel to the one they had managed to escape, then another. Before reaching the faintly lit edge of it, the Texcocan wavered, and clinging to the nearby pole for support stilled for a moment, his rasping breath the only sound to tear the darkness. By then, Miztli felt like clinging to another beam of this same faceless fence as well, if not sliding down and into the dusty stones. The clubs inside his head pounded so loudly he could barely hear the sounds around them, the chirping of the night insects, the faint voices coming from the shut screen of the adobe house behind the fence, the drunken laughter of the men on the crossroad. The thought of the brutal criminals ready to beat people into telling them whatever they knew was the only one to keep him upright for now. Echoes of the Tlatelolcan wharves. And they even mentioned that other city, they did! The marketplace that was now being expanded and rebuild, and some criminal activities around it. Did the downfall of this annoying *altepetl* change nothing?

"Give me your shoulder," grated the wounded in the voice he had difficulty recognizing, so low and strident, barely there. "It's not... not far now. The end of this alley. The big house. Stone, not adobe."

He forced his limbs into obedient moving, swaying under the renewed pressure of the tormented body, the Texcocan's entire weight now upon him, or so it felt.

"If I can't... not there... can't be of use," the rasping mutter went on, panting. "Passed out... You don't try to get in. Wait... wait for me to come back. Try to wake me up. Don't try to get in. She has trained... trained slaves, servants. They shoot well, use clubs. Don't try to sneak in. Make me come around again."

Despite his exhaustion and the wish to arrive somewhere, anywhere, in order to just sit down and rest, Miztli shuddered. Not again! No, he could not deal with any more shooting or chasing, not tonight. He needed a heartbeat of respite.

"Here!"

By the densely placed poles of what looked like a palisade, branches interwoven thickly enough to create a protective screen, the man paused again, reeling in an attempt to straighten up and see better, but thankfully all there, his mind not wandering other worlds. For a moment, he fought for a more independent position, then, successful, cupped his palms around his mouth and shouted something Miztli did not understand. Was it another tongue? Too spent to try and listen, he let the man repeat his cry. Then again. By the time the light behind the palisade flickered, then moved, at some point accompanied by the screeching of a wooden screen being shifted, he felt like giving up for good, lying there in the street and falling asleep, letting whoever wanted to do whatever they wanted with him.

The blur of the inner patio swept by, enlivened by a pair of torch holders and not only the moon. He didn't care. A flight of stairs, challenging those as the Texcocan was again practically lying on him, spread across his shoulders, leaning with his entire weight; then inside, an unpleasantly cold room, then another. Helpful hands relieved him of his burden, but it took him many more heartbeats to focus his vision and even this came with an impatient demand to move out of the way. The woman who said it didn't even look at him, waving her hands at the others, at least two more men and a young scrawny girl, all eyes and disheveled hair.

"There, put him there, on that mat. No, closer to the fire. Make the fire stronger. You, bring more firewood and a pot to boil water. The smallest one. You, little Ayotl, go bring my tools. Hold the needles above the fire. Use pincers, like I did yesterday. Remember?"

The frightened girl nodded, then scampered away. The men followed.

"You, boy." This time, the bossy woman seemed to be addressing him. "Come here. In a hurry. You aren't hurt, are you?"

He shook his head numbly, crouching next to the Texcocan, who lay on the cluster of mats face down, like a dead body. "Is he..." His own voice croaked like a half broken jar dragged over the floor, ridiculously ugly. "Is he?"

"Stop mumbling. Lift him while I cut off his cloak. What happened to him? Was he stabbed?"

Resigned to the renewed struggle with the heavy limp body, Miztli tried to make his mind work, feeling the reaction, the trembling bad, interrupting his ability to do as the woman said.

"Relax, young man," he heard her saying in a kinder voice. "You two are safe for a while. Whoever was chasing you cannot get in here."

"No one was chasing us," he mumbled, struggling to put the man down without letting him fall, the remnants of the stiff soaked cloak already off, revealing more of the gaping wound, not as large as it looked back at Tlemilli's sister's room, with only a pitiful torch to lighten their view, but so angrily red and glaring, a mess of raw flesh. "I think no one saw us arriving here. He sent the litter-bearers off. Away from here. Not anywhere near."

The woman leaned forward, inspecting the wound. "I trust Tecuani not to bring his troublesome connections or enemies anywhere near me or mine," she muttered as though talking to herself, inappropriately amused. "This boy knows how to sniff around without getting in trouble. Worthy of his brother, that one. I wonder how he managed to get shot. Not like him to let a silly dart do him so much harm." Shaking her head, she motioned at the girl, who had returned in the meanwhile, hovering with indecision. "Put the tools here. Carefully!" The sharp cry made not only the girl but even Miztli himself jump. "Now bring me the small pot if the water boiled there already, and put another one on, the larger vessel. With plenty of water, yes? I don't need to elaborate on everything, do I?"

The girl disappeared out of Miztli's view.

"She is not the brightest," murmured the woman, her frown brief but unmistakable. "Yet one can't throw such thing out, not at her age. Back on the streets, she will be used in no uncertain ways." A soft snort accompanying the words relayed it all. She did regret her own kindness. For the first time, Miztli dared to sneak a glance at his new hostess. A generously wrinkled face was again bent above the inanimate Texcocan, curiously good looking, appealing in a way. She was old, like all healers, but slender and well kept, her hair lavish, glittering with the dark of glassy obsidian, gathered loosely with a pretty string, her eyelashes strangely long and thick, her lips well defined, glistening red. Her robe was loosely tied, hanging in elegant folds, fitting for a much younger woman, certainly not a respectable old healer. Miztli tried not to stare.

The girl, a small skinny creature of an indefinitely young age, placed a pot with bubbling water, then rushed to organize ominous-looking tools, razor-sharp curving bones and other things he didn't care to think of their purpose.

"Bring the white ointment, and do it on the run. Then pour some of the sap into a bowl and warm it until your finger can barely stand its heat. Quick, little one. In a matter of heartbeats!"

The wounded was stirring, groaning ever so slightly. "Poor boy," said the woman with a laugh and not a hint of compassion. "He should have stayed in the other worlds until I finished. Hold him still!"

The last order was clearly meant for him. Miztli took a deep breath, then pressed the shuddering shoulders back down, forced to struggle against the immediate reaction, the man again unexpectedly strong for his weakened condition, fighting the enforced confinement.

"Please," he heard himself whispering, afraid and anxious, spent, on the verge of giving up. Did he dare to force this man down, time after time? "The healer, she is taking care of you. You must stay like that. She told me to keep you like that. You must let her take care of your wound. It looks bad, really bad."

The woman came to his aid unexpectedly. "Stop making trouble, Tecuani," she demanded curtly, adding an offhanded push to Miztli's desperate efforts. "Lie still and don't move a limb. Not until I tell you to get up. Don't even dare to breathe deeply. Lie absolutely still."

Not making sure her curt orders were being obeyed, she knelt comfortably, nimble and again too graceful for her obvious age, snatching one of the curving bones, treading it with a coiled sinew, businesslike and completely absorbed.

"Don't move a muscle," she repeated when the needle was threaded and a piece of cloth fished out from the smaller bowl where the water wasn't bubbling anymore. "What did you put into this wound to make such a mess out of it?" she murmured, beginning to rub it after pouring some of the warm liquid into it, causing her patient to freeze in a tormented convulsion. It was easy to hear the grinding of the man's teeth, such a strident, helplessly harsh sound. Miztli felt his own palm pressing against the slippery shoulder with force, this time not to hold but to encourage, at least a little. How painful it must be! He watched the needle nearing the swollen flesh, piercing it with no mercy. The body under his arms convulsed again.

"Hold still," repeated the woman curtly. "Not long now. It's not the worst of it. People deal with more terrible wounds. Yours is nothing. That dart or an arrow or whatever it was didn't even go deep, not enough to damage something of more importance than your stupid hide, jaguar beast. You have nothing to complain about." It was as though she was enjoying it, testing his strength and endurance, curious as to the outcome. Miztli wished they hadn't come here.

A glance around let him know that the room was empty now save for the girl, kneeling next to the fire, stirring something in another small bowl, her face puckered in painful concentration. It was easy to recognize this expression and it made his stomach twinge with compassion, the memories of his first moon in Tenochtitlan welling, the inhuman heat of the melting room, the endless load of work, from way before sunrise and into the dusk, the perpetual displeasure and admonitions, the loneliness. Had it ended not so very long ago? Less than two moons. He shuddered, then put his attention back to the spread wounded and his continued torment.

"Two more stitches," the woman was saying, replacing the thread on her needle-like tool of torture. "To close it well. We don't want any bad things setting in there, do we? Not after all the harm you already did to this wound. What did you pour in there? A chocolate drink?"

"*Octli*," groaned the Texcocan, tensing all over again as the razor-sharp tip pierced another torn tissue. "They say it helps. Helps to clean. Something about this drink. Kills the rot."

To this, the woman nodded, a smile tugging at her lips. Were they painted with something? wondered Miztli numbly. There was a layer of something on them, the color and the glitter.

"It depends, you would-be healer. If the *octli* is strong and well brewed, it may help, yes. *Pulque* can be of more help; they always brew it to make it as strong as they can. *Pulque* and *octli* are the same thing, even though your aristocratic friends would not admit it." She snorted softly, good-naturedly. "So where did you get shot? In the Royal Enclosure, I bet. Only the highest nobility would have spare *octli* to pour into people's wounds."

The Texcocan grunted something noncommittal.

"The youth will tell," said the woman with curt laughter. "He looks scared enough."

The flickering eyes brushed past him before returning to thread another strand, briefly appraising, making him feel naked again. Like back in the dark Palace's alley and the haughty princess in her curtained seat, demanding that he pay her a visit on the next day, promising to send her servants to escort him. Why? What would the notorious noblewoman, the Emperor's sister with her Tlatelolcan history, wish to tell him or hear him telling?

"Don't look so frightened, boy," the healer was saying, done with the needle and tossing it aside, her fingers nimble, tying the last strand around the angry red edges, wiping the seeping blood away. "I won't be demanding a payment for taking care of your master, even though you are certainly a good-looking thing, deliciously well built and so very fresh and innocent. And wild. Ah, what a temptation."

"Stop that, Xochitl," called out the Texcocan, stirring as though about to try and fight his way back to his feet again. "Leave the boy alone. He is not to be harassed. Or used! Take it out of your head."

Done with the last tie, the woman snorted softly, unperturbed, her amusement spilling, a disquieting, somewhat chilling amusement. "Back to giving orders, are we, YaoTecuani?" Her lips were twisting again, but in no generous fashion this time, with very little mirth. "And what are you going to do to reinforce your stern words now, tough warrior? My slaves here are strong and trained with weaponry. And many. Enough to subdue one beaten wounded and one untrained youth; to do whatever I like with them *both*."

Before he had time to get frightened some more or think of reaching for his meager weaponry – the flint knife, where was it? – the body under his palms jerked upwards like a rearing snake about to strike, pushing him away, making his hands slip. Crouching on all fours, wavering but holding on, the wounded thrust his face into the squatting woman's startled features, causing her to sway backwards and almost topple over.

"Don't you even think of crossing me," he hissed, terrifying in his animal-like fury, looking grotesque, his face twisted hideously, dripping sweat, his back trickling a strange mix of liquids, his straining limbs shaking. A cornered wounded jaguar, the most lethal creature to irritate into attacking. Miztli felt his heart coming to a temporary halt. A clacking of fallen pottery told him that the girl by the fire did not fare any better. "You betray me and you are dead! And so are your sons, *both of them*. And their brats too. *Slowly!*"

The healer drew in a sharp breath, then pulled herself together with an admirable swiftness. Her eyes narrowed into a pair of slits, her lips – a matching line. "Is that so?" she drawled slowly.

The wounded didn't waver in his strange half squatting, half crouching position, his eyes widely open, as opposed to the slits of his opponent, shooting lightning bolts. "Yes, it is, Xochitl. And you better remember it, always!"

Another heartbeat of laden silence passed. He could hear the pouring in footsteps, and this time discovered enough presence of mind to find his knife, apparently still there, already clutched in his sweaty palm. To spring back to his feet was not an effort, to face their new possible attackers, all armed with clubs, five in all. His eyes counted them briefly, with no emotion, then took in the pile of firewood, good sturdy branches among those, a possible help. He calculated his way toward it in the same unemotional way, trusting the Texcocan to deal with the most dangerous adversary, the woman, putting her out of his head.

The silence lasted for another heartbeat. Then their hostess's voice broke it, ringing with its previous light amusement. "Wild beasts, both of you. What a pretty show."

He didn't dare to turn back in order to look at her, but the poses of the armed men relaxed all at once.

"Lie down, you wild thing. I still need to smear the ointment over that ravaged back of yours. If anything of it is left to smear. You scared my girl into spilling it, you violent brute. Is there anything left in there, little Ayotl? Did the bowl get broken?" The girl, on her knees now and near tears, was trying to pick up the fallen vessel, unsuccessful on that score, not with those badly shaking hands of hers. "Help her, boy! Don't stand there and just stare in that ready-to-fight stance of yours. You can go back to guard your master after you've been useful to him otherwise, wild cub that you are."

"He isn't my slave or servant," grunted the Texcocan, this time in a normal voice, clearly calming down enough to do as he was told, namely lie down and let the healer get on with her treatment. How fast they were all changing! "Leave him alone, woman. That boy has nothing to do with any of it."

Miztli forced his legs toward the frightened girl, who flinched and looked as though about to bolt away at his impending approach.

"Spin your tales to someone more gullible," the woman was saying, her amusement obvious, on full display. Which caused the hovering men to relax even more; still, they didn't retreat or let their clubs down. "It's a curious choice to pick out of our city's slums and you never brought any escorting youths along, never let anyone accompany you in the more shady among your dealings. Does it tell me this young foreigner is someone of importance, to be ready to deal with in the future? Or did you just change your lovemaking preferences into your older age, eh, jaguar beast?"

At the last phrase the girl, who until now crouched in the same ready-to-bolt position, not attempting to help him pick the bowl but just staring with her eyes wide open and terrified, snickered as though against her will. Miztli felt his face bursting in all sorts of glaring coloring. But did this woman just imply...

"Keep your mouth shut, Xochitl." The Texcocan didn't move, sprawling on his stomach, letting the healer examine his wound uninterrupted. Clutching the bowl with the remnants of the glistening ointment tightly, Miztli hurried back, feeling safer by this man's side, much safer. "You can think of nothing else, woman, and the dirtier the thought the happier you become." The man's voice was coming muffled, his face tucked into the woven cover of the mat, beyond concern now. "Tell your slaves or your lovers or whoever those brutes are to go back where they came from. It's getting crowded here." He squirmed when the warm ointment touched the raw flesh with no gentleness, then grew still once again. "And leave the boy out of it. He has nothing to do with anything. He just happened along. I shouldn't have brought him here, yes. I was not thinking clearly. That stupid wound was killing me. The worst possible location and timing and everything. There were more stupid moves I made this night, woman. But you will not hear of it. Trust me on that."

Her body was trembling with laughter, the fringes of her embroidered robe – no *huipil* that! – falling aside, revealing more than Miztli wished to glimpse. He busied himself with squatting back in his previous place, daring not to touch the wounded due to the woman's dirty hint, impossible not to understand despite the Texcocan's surprisingly placid response. To be near this man felt safer. The rest of this house and its dwellers were too unsettling to trust. And how could the formidable warrior lie so relaxed now, after the uttered threats and the violence of his own previous response? The skinny girl stood next to him warily, leaning forward, clearly ready to receive the bowl back.

"Turn over," the woman commanded, pressing a clean-looking cloth to the smeared mess of her patient's shoulder. "I'll tie it loosely for now, but before you go out, we'll make it tighter, to keep the bandage on. You can't run around sporting this sort of a cut, if at all."

Obediently, the wounded rolled over, causing the girl to lurch back quite a few paces, frightened again. The woman gave her young apprentice an amused look. "Go fetch the root of *hoitzitzilli*, girl. Put it in the pot and let it simmer for a while. It is boiling already, so we won't have to wait long." Shaking her head, she moved away, easing her shoulders and suddenly looking old and worn out. "You and your troubles, you wild beast. I swear I will have nothing to do with you in the future. Your brother knows I don't owe him that much."

The wounded was struggling to sit up, too busy to pay the surprisingly genuine words any attention. Miztli rushed to help, relieved at the displayed prowess and spirit. The man still looked ghastly, like back on the moonlit crossroad; however, to have him up and about was good, reassuring. He didn't want to stay alone in this place any more than in the night street full of violent criminals eager to torture people for information. *Calmecac* and his friend, Tlemilli and the Palace seemed to be days of walk away. Would he manage to return in time for the morning lessons? Would the Emperor send for him? Would he be angered with his lack of worthwhile information to report, with only pieces of silly gossip the Tenantzinco escorting warriors were engaged in? He couldn't even remember the silly things they said, something about going to the Tlatelolco marketplace, but what? He closed his eyes against the welling dread.

"Drink water until your brew is ready. That'll give you some of your strength back," the woman was saying, herself sounding deep in thought. "You can stay here for the night, you and your mysteriously good-looking fiercely-loyal no-slave." He could feel her eyes boring at him again, and was grateful for the protection of his own closed eyelids, however temporary. "Bring that one some well brewed *pulque*." This time, her voice rose, clearly addressing someone located further away. More servants with knives and clubs? Her chuckle shook the rustling silence. "A strong drink, one that would be worthy to put in people's wounds."

"Bring me one such as well." The Texcocan's voice rang with encouraging firmness, the traces of the man's typical spells of grimly light humor in it obvious. "We both earned that for our night's misadventures." The bantering tone disappeared. "You may receive another visit tonight, this one of no old friends or acquaintances."

The woman shifted with abruptness, and opening his eyes in time, Miztli saw her narrowing her gaze toward the Texcocan. "Who?"

"Your local thugs, nothing to do with me and my activities." The man's good shoulder lifted in a one-sided shrug. "On our way here, we detoured through quite a few dark alleys and patios, and in one, they were beating up some stupid whiner who managed to lose a bunch of precious stones. The last we heard them, they intended to put an eye on your house, knowing where people go to get rid of goods that cost more than a handful of cocoa beans."

"Who were they? How many?" The words shot out with no more playfulness, like darts from *atlatls*.

"It was too dark to see." The man shrugged again, leaning against the wall awkwardly, sparing his wounded side a hurtful contact. "Can they get in, or rather, fight their way in, those local thugs?"

The woman snorted, then motioned the girl, who seemed to be falling asleep near the fire, curled around herself like a small animal, dozing off. "Keep stirring it, you lazy bag of bones. I'm not keeping you here to let you get your healthy night sleep. Bring this pot here. I'll see if it's ready." Her grimace was one of acceptance. "You better get your strength back if we are up to an attempt of robbery. My servants are good and always have someone out there on alert. But who knows? If those stones are what I think they are, half of Tenochtitlan would be now on the lookout for them, plaguing my patio, stupid lowlifes that they are."

"Who was paying for what services?" inquired the Texcocan, wrinkling his nose against the smell as the girl staggered closer, wavering under the weight of the large pot she was carrying, holding it in her sticklike arms by the sheer power of her will, or rather, her fear, as it looked. The memories of the blazing containers with melted copper surfaced again, pushing him up and to her side, snatching the steaming vessel without thinking. It was not even scorching hot, and not that heavy, but he hated the climbing eyebrows of the older woman, the crookedness of her spreading grin. The girl gasped before jumping quite a few steps away, keeping a safe distance.

"Bring it here, you courteous youth." The healer motioned him closer, rising to sniff at the pot's contents, dunking the tip of her finger in it. "Put it back on the fire. It's not nearly as bitter as it should be. You, little one," another motion of her head brought the girl from her safe hovering, "you go and tell Tlacatl and the rest to spread out in the patio and by the gate, keep an eye out for intruders. Tell him to be very attentive or else." The woman grimaced, then shrugged with acceptance. "They should take care of this scum. The thieves and the possible interceptors." Cupping her palms around her mouth, she shouted toward the disappearing back. "Tell Tlacatl to come here, while the others spread. And bring that *pulque*, little one. Our guests certainly deserve a gulp now."

"Those who bring the stolen goods better be let in," commented the Texcocan quietly, running the back of his hand over his eyes, his exhaustion on display once again, clearly visible in the frightening pallor and the way he sagged against the wall, his forehead glistening in the dancing flames.

The woman eyed him narrowly. "Yes, they will be. Tlacatl

knows his work. He is a good boy. Not as good as you, Acolhua Highlander, but good enough." She got to her feet with an effort, her walk not as perky as before, relaying tiredness. "That drink will keep you nicely alive, well into the next dawn, maybe. The root of *hoitzitzilli* is powerful and rare. Long-distance traders bring it by special request. A costly thing too! You may want to compensate me for that."

To Miztli's growing embarrassment, the wounded rolled his eyes. "I'm not your commoner from this stupid *altepetl*'s slums or a peasant from out there, touring this island, all awe," he muttered, shifting to find better a position. "Spare the litanies about the costs of the medicine for those." He shifted again, then snorted, frustrated. "The damn wound!"

"It'll give you much trouble yet before it's over," informed him the healer, a certain amount of satisfaction to her voice. She dipped her finger into the simmering brew again, the fire under it weak, barely adequate. "Almost."

"Tell me about the stones. How are they connected to Tlatelolco? And the visiting Tenantzinco folk." The last phrase came out softer, poignantly sweet.

He saw the woman tense, then lift her shoulders with exaggerated indifference. "How should I know? You must have drunk some of the *octli* the aristocratic no-goods were pouring into your wound."

"Oh yes, I did," confirmed the wounded as sweetly as before. "Even when I listened to that scum out there, discussing those stones and what it was supposed to pay for. That *octli*, it certainly enhanced my hearing abilities. And that Tenantzinco delegation, pah, such provincials, no subtlety, rustic manners, wishing to tour the renowned marketplace of this recently conquered—"

"Enough!" The healer's slender arm jumped up, making her lavishly embroidered sleeve sway in a pretty manner. "Talk politics at such a time of the night, wild boy. No wonder you don't have a wife. You would bore her to death, the poor thing. Certain Texcocan princesses, eh?"

Her adversary's eyebrows began climbing up slowly and very suggestively, yet at her last phrase, his face darkened and his eyes flashed. "Don't!" he said curtly, in the voice that made Miztli shiver. "Go back to the point, woman. Tlatelolco, Tenantzinco, the stones. We don't have a whole night." His gaze shifted suddenly, focusing on Miztli. "You, jaguar cub, go in there, find that girl, the little apprentice. Tell her to arrange a good wash up for you and some new clothes. Certainly a cloak. Bring here two of those, for both of us." His eyes returned to the healer woman. "I'll pay you for two cloaks if they are of a good quality. Tell your apprentice to cooperate. While they are away, we'll talk."

His tone brooked no argument, had Miztli dreamed of offering one. Even the spicy woman said nothing, just stirred the brew, then tasted a drop of it from the back of her palm.

"Go in there, boy," she said with forced lightness that fooled no one. "Tell little Ayotl to do as Tecuani said. Don't hurry back, both of you, and don't even think of listening by the doorway."

As though he would dare to do something like that. His tiredness welling, Miztli forced his limbs into moving, crossing another narrow opening, finding himself in a smaller room with mats and cushions aplenty. A draft of breeze from the outside beckoned. He put his face against it.

"What are you doing here?"

The sharp exclamation made him jump, even though his senses told him that it was the skinny apprentice before his darting eyes took in her scrawny form. She was standing at the doorway, gaping at him.

"The healer, she sent me here," he said hurriedly, afraid that she would start screaming. She looked as though contemplating this possibility. "She told me to find you. She said I'm to tell you to help me. She said that, I swear!" To bring his hands forward, palms up, seemed like the right thing to do. She lurched away even so. "I swear I'm not lying. You can go in there and ask her. I'll wait." To reinforce his words, he moved away from the doorway, leaving plenty of space for her to pass without chancing too close an encounter with him.

"She told you to find me?" she repeated, incredulous, not moving a limb, like a small animal facing a dangerous one, afraid to draw attention.

"Yes, she did. She said you are to give us cloaks. Me and the Texcocan man. Honorable YaoTecuani, that is. And she said we are to stay here, for a while, while they talk. They needed to talk. In privacy, that is." But why was he telling her all that, that small, terrified child? She probably couldn't even understand. He cursed his clumsiness once again, that annoying stuttering. With dawn, he'd have enough opportunities to stutter when facing the Emperor with his nonexistent information on the Tenantzinco delegation he spent almost no time listening as he was supposed to, while getting in wild trouble that had nothing to do with it. Oh mighty deities! But maybe this same YaoTecuani could help him, tell him something about those Tenantzinco people he was clearly interested in as well. Oh, but he would be better off staying and listening.

The girl was still studying him, with less fright than before. "The Mistress wanted to talk in private, eh," she said all of a sudden, a crooked grin twisting the thin line of her lips. Then her eyes sparkled with open delight. "Come." Her skinny arm swayed as though trying to draw half a circle, disappearing in the semidarkness of the outside along with the rest of her.

He stared for a moment, then, refusing to think it all through, followed, the softness of the breeze beckoning again, inviting to escape the suffocating closeness of the crammed room.

"Here." She was signaling with her entire body, motioning toward what looked like a large container, as high as half of a man standing upright. He dove behind its readily offered cover, grateful.

"Up there." She signaled again, indicating the towering wall, its plaster dark, peeling off in places. There was no wall opening there; still, the voices floated alongside it, coming from somewhere near the ground, as though people crouched on the floor, determined to talk in uncomfortable positions. He recognized the healer woman's tone, its typical derisive amusement. How so? A glance at the girl told him that she was listening avidly, all ears. Ill-at-ease, he did the same.

"I'm not involved in it as heavily as you think I am, you nosy boy," the woman was saying, a touch of pouting, almost flirtatious complaint to her voice. "The Tenantzinco delegation is of no interest to me. I have nothing to gain or lose from its safe stay here in Tenochtitlan, or from our Emperor's eagerness to go out and conquer more southern towns and lands. This foolish ruler of Tenantzinco thinks he'll gain Tenochtitlan's support and thus will subdue his troublesome neighbors with no sweat or investment, but it will not be this way. You know it and I know it. And your brother up there in his beloved highlands knows it too." A soft chuckle interrupted. "I can see why this delegation's current wellbeing worries you. Your brother wants Tenochtitlan busy and up to its neck in various wars and campaigns out there in the south, away from his side of Smoking Mountain, away from Huexotzinco and even this troublesome Tlaxcallan so-called confederation. Don't they call themselves this way these days?"

Another soft chuckle enlivened the night. Then a brief silence followed. Of the Texcocan man's voice there was no trace as yet. Miztli held his breath, momentarily worried. Whom was this woman talking to? And was the Texcocan all right, not harmed or rendered powerless in any other way?

"You are too well informed for your professed disinterest." When the man spoke, his words rang strongly, to Miztli's immediate spell of relief, and they held none of the previously displayed, slightly challenging, somewhat typical male superiority that characterized the Texcocan's attitude toward their current hostess and benefactress until now. "And you do know about the attempt to silence that Tenantzinco delegation, or at least to prevent their demand to make Tenochtitlan involved. Those stones have everything to do with it." The last phrase came out icily in the quietness of this back of the garden.

"You are in no position to demand answers from me," retorted the woman with none of her previously flirtatious tone either. "Whatever you were trying to achieve, you failed. Those stones, the payment, or Tlatelolcans, or the visiting foreigners with their silly requests; they will all go on doing whatever they were supposed to do while you will be stuck here or elsewhere, recovering from nasty wounds, with the boy you are dragging along for some reason helpless without you and your guidance.

You will not recover in time to do something in this particular play. And you are not in the position to demand answers from me. My life is of no interest to you. You are not your brother!"

Another bout of silence prevailed, through which Miztli felt the girl nodding sagely, as though satisfied with her mistress putting the pushy stranger in his place. As though anyone could best YaoTecuani. He fought the urge to run out and back into the fire-lit room, just in case. The man was wounded, and that woman was nasty, dangerous, evidently highly unscrupulous and not to be trusted.

The Texcocan's laughter interrupted the night, soft and sharp and again unbearably superior. "Don't discard me that quickly, Xochitl. You may be surprised with what I can do even in such an unfavorable condition. Or what that boy can do, for that matter. You would do better keeping us both on your side, woman. Your history with my brother has nothing to do with it." He paused again, evidently to gulp something. That brew the woman was making for him? But what was their history? Why were they fencing like enemies and old friends at the same time? And who was this man's powerful brother even the nasty Tenochtitlan healer was afraid of? Must be the same highlander leader Necalli's father kept mentioning with affection and respect.

"You are as insolent as you always were, boy," said the woman, her sigh loud, holding an open grudge. "You never knew your place, and your brother kept encouraging you instead of curbing your insolent strike, like they did back in Texcoco. One wonders why you still live in that snotty *altepetl*, or anywhere around our 'lowlands.' Unless all you care about is spying for your brother or working to keep the might of Tenochtitlan from reaching toward his domain. They will, one day, you know? And not so long from now." A pause prevailed again, accompanied with a nasty glare, of that Miztli was sure. "After they are through with the south, maybe, eh? A few more spans of seasons and our warriors will be besieging the passes of Smoking Mountain and the other one, crossing to war on Huexotzinco and then Tlaxcala, taking them all."

"Shut up," was the Texcocan's tired response. "It's hard

enough to keep your medicine in without vomiting it all over your prettily swept floor. Your nastiness doesn't help my self-control." Another pause, more comfortable than the previous ones. "It won't happen and you know it. Not as long as my brother is in charge of the matters up there, being listened to and obeyed even by the Tlaxcala hotheads."

Surprisingly, the woman's laughter shook the darkness, its affability spilling. "With him up there and in charge and you sneaking all over our *altepetl*s, making sure they are keeping busy and elsewhere."

In the next ensuing pause, Miztli felt the girl moving, motioning him to follow her out, urgency to her gesturing. Hesitating and wishing to hear more, he caught her hand, but she wrenched it away violently, bolting back toward the moonlit patch of the patio and the dark opening, still clearly visible from their hideaway.

"What about those stones?" the Texcocan was asking quietly, as though returning to the boring discussion he was forced to conduct somewhat against his will. "Was it a payment to the Tlatelolcan brood of killers or troublemakers for hire? The previous scum of their wharves and shore smugglers? The escorting warriors of the Tenantzinco dignitary certainly thought so, even though they didn't know how much was paid and in what way."

"Tenantzinco visitors seem to be exceptionally well informed, unless the information came from the locals – or the visiting Texcocans! – who wished them to know."

The girl reached the open ground, then paused, turning back and motioning once again, in an impatient gesture. Still hesitating, he took a careful step, then saw a shadow slipping from the shrubs of the fence, pouncing at the girl, grabbing her roughly, shoving her unresisting body into the stones of the wall, making some plaster fall. Appalled, Miztli charged at them as fiercely, his anger overcoming his common sense. She was just a child, a defenseless skinny frightened child at that! And she didn't struggle, but only whimpered weakly, protesting something.

Reaching them in a similar leap like that of her assailant before, he pushed the bulky man away using both hands and the drive of his body, putting all his might into the violent shove. As expected, his rival went crashing down, but as Miztli dove after him in the fashion he imagined the Texcocan would do, pinning his momentarily disoriented victim to the ground while attempting to wrench a heavy club from his hands, the man squirmed wildly enough to push him off and away, then mounted an attack of his own, his fist crashing into Miztli's side, taking his breath away. He retaliated by kicking sideways, then pummeling his own fists into whatever limbs came into its reach.

The bushes around rustled with untoward urgency, sprouting more slinking shadows; of that he was sure. He could hear the girl whimpering somewhere above, pressing to the wall most likely, useless and scared. Tlemilli would have been waving this or that club by now, kicking at his possible new attackers or screaming at them. A wave of acute longing swept him, and scrambling back to his feet, he grabbed the nearest lying object, a plate or a bowl, judging by its roundness and its weight, feeling better for being armed, even if questionably. The man he assaulted was groaning in the dust, struggling to get up as well. He kicked him back into sprawling, but the girl's whimpering calls penetrated his mind, even if partly.

"No, no, it's Ixtli... You should not... you can't..."

Two more silhouettes appeared upon the shadowed mass of the fence, disappearing down the darkness of the bushes as quickly.

"Who is Ixtli?" he rasped, turning to face their possible attackers. The man's club he tried to get at the first place, where was it?

"He works, works for the lady... he is not..." Her mewing was outright annoying.

"And those men?"

In the corner of his eye, he could see her shaking her head most vigorously. At least that. Were those the men the Texcocan was warning the healer about? But she said she sent her own men to watch for them, to spread out and... There was no time for any such musings. Glancing at the man he had beaten into temporary harmlessness, he saw the discarded club rolling in the dust, temptingly close.

"Get that!" he tossed at the girl, turning away in time to duck an attack of another club, this one held expertly in one of the intruders' hands.

The swish of the polished wood resonated in his mind as he threw himself sideways and away, while hurling his improvised missile, aiming for his attacker's head. It made a hollow sound breaking against the side of its intended victim's face, seemingly not causing much damage, yet making the renewed attack slow down.

Two more shadows popped from behind the thick shrubbery near the fence, hesitating as though not sure as to how to proceed. Hectically, he darted back toward the opening, determined to retrieve the club from the girl's hands before the man who attacked him got his bearings, or his friends came to his aid. Where were the other defenders, the men the healer had sent out in order to protect her courtyard? They could not be so stupid as to mill out there in the front patio!

The girl and the club were gone. Blinking, he stared at the doorway, then, acting rather on an instinct, darted inside as well, determined to find the Texcocan, no matter the reason for it. He could not be expected to fight the invaders all by himself, with no weaponry and no help. It was not his house, not his business or people or friends. Except the man of Texcoco.

Inside, the clamor was as lively, more so with shouts and footsteps of running feet as opposed to the silent skirmishing out there. As he burst into the main room, two men rushed to intercept him, taking him by surprise. Panic stricken, he fought their hands, which tried to pin him against the inner wall, slamming his shoulder into one of the attackers, yet losing his balance as another man's fist brushed against his ear, making it ring. Scrambling back to his feet despite a fierce kick, then another, he heard the Texcocan's voice roaring, overcoming the annoyingly droning buzz that seemed to fill the entire room.

"Stop that, you stupid pieces of excrement! He is not the intruder, you lousy good-for-nothing would-be warriors."

The blows stopped, but not the buzz. Afraid to fall once again, Miztli grabbed the nearest beam, steadying himself against the wild sways of the room. The Texcocan was swaying too, standing on his own but with as much difficulty, waving the attacking men away, yelling at them his hardest, with whole gamut of colorful curses to help his gesturing along. When the man finally turned to him, he was a sight worth seeing, one of those grotesque statues from old books or some of Tenochtitlan's temples, carved body smeared with all sorts of hues like war paint, face colorless, twisted with rage, coated with as generous amount of liquids. Miztli fought against the urge to giggle stupidly. It all was truly too much.

"How many intruders are out there?" barked the man, not amused in the least. "How many did you hurt?"

"I... three, I think there were three men..." He tried to collect his thoughts, the monotonous hum in his ears retreating, replaced by pulsating headache. He could see his last pair of attackers being waved on and toward his previous battleground. "I hit one, but I don't think... I don't think he was hurt, not seriously. I..."

His eyes leapt across the room, taking in the woman, standing in the opposite doorway, yelling toward the front patio, her expansive robe fluttering in the wind, falling down her shoulder in a strangely inappropriate manner, although she could not mean anything of *that* sort. The girl was trembling in one corner, curled around herself like a small animal, hugging her knees. Of the club he had told her to fetch there was no sign.

"I should go out there. There was this club. And that first man. He might be not... not one of them. She said his name was Ixtli. He is still out there, I think."

The Texcocan's good arm flew in the semidarkness, arresting the gushing flow of words. "Relax, boy. You'll run out of breath." The familiar flicker was already there, twinkling in the well-spaced eyes. "Come. We'll see what they are up to out there in the back. Xochitl's men will take care of any possible frontal invasion. Stupid fools!" Snorting, he caught the doorway's pole for support, swaying but holding on, as determined and unstoppable as always. "Not to check the gardens beyond the house? Ridiculous!

This woman hires the wrong men and for completely wrong merits."

Back in the backyard, the commotion was nearly subdued, with the defenders overcoming the sneaking in intruders who clearly did not count on such outright fighting back. The man Miztli attacked first, the one who assaulted the girl, was on the ground again, this time mounting someone, a struggling form, his fists pounding.

"Stop that," commanded the Texcocan, his voice ringing with undivided authority, overcoming the tumult. "Hold him still. Is he alive?" He didn't move from the support of another doorway's column, clearly not up to a feat of walking around on his own, not yet. "Disarm him, then bring him inside." Squinting against the moonlit landscape of several wandering men and a few still ones, he frowned. "How many were killed or got away?"

"No one got away, Master," replied one of the men hurriedly. "One of them I killed myself. And this one," he kicked another sprawling form, "this one seems to be dead too."

"Bring in the one who is still alive," tossed the Texcocan, motioning Miztli to follow him back in. "And keep him this way. I need him to answer questions of mine. Hurry!"

"What about the wild boy?" called out one of the men, hurrying after them obediently. "Is he with you?"

"What do you think?" grunted the Texcocan, leaning on Miztli's shoulder in already a familiar manner while storming the main room once again. The sounds of more footsteps and the dragging of their captive's feet followed them as duly. "Use your eyes and your heads next time before you attack people who are guests here. You couldn't have missed this boy coming here with me!"

"He attacked me!" cried out the one called Ixtli, his face looking the worst indeed, livid with bruises and grazed skin. "And he was huddling with that filthy little Ayotl, eavesdropping or doing whatever other dirty things!"

The girl, still curled in her far corner, uttered something between a gulp and a cry.

"He attacked her... I didn't know," muttered Miztli, quailing against the wondering gaze that turned to him momentarily, its twinkle pronounced, the arching eyebrows completing the picture.

The healer woman, who strode back into the middle of the room as well in the meanwhile, chuckled. "What a cavalier." Then she sobered as well. "Stop loitering in that corner, little one. Go inside and bring two cloaks. And *pulque* with some food. Whatever is ready to be eaten, even just dry tortillas with fruit. Be quick about it!"

The girl scurried back to her feet and fled, looking relieved. Uneasily, Miztli followed the Texcocan, perturbed by the piercing glance the man gave him before turning to stroll toward their captive. Eavesdropping, oh, but they did this, they did!

The intruder, bleeding already and smeared in all the dampness of the garden's soil, was struggling with yet more spirit, spitting curses. However, with the approach of the stern Texcocan, he grew quieter, backing away, nearly toppling into the fire.

"Tell me all you know and do it quickly." The Texcocan did not spend his time on idle talk or any roundabout questioning, kneeling awkwardly before the spread down prisoner, bringing a long vicious-looking dagger out in a barely perceptible movement. "Talk!"

The man's eyes glazed and he let out a gust of quick breath as the knife pounced toward his face, hovering a hairbreadth away from it, poised to attack.

"Did you break in here because of the stones?"

The eyes blinked frantically as the man's tongue slipped out, licked his cracked, muddied lips. "I... we... no—"

The knife didn't hesitate, not even for a heartbeat, slashing down and across the smeared cheek and the gaping mouth. "Talk or your eye comes out next."

By this time, the man was screaming in an ugly high-pitched voice that made Miztli wish to shut his eyes and his ears together. The ragged obsidian pounced again, nicking the eyelid.

"No! No, please! I'll tell, I'll tell!" The interrogated captive was babbling, saliva dripping down the side of his mouth, mixing with trickling blood, fresh and glaringly red, enhanced by the flames, glimmering strangely. "The stones, yes, they were stolen. Some stupid boy stole them, and the foreigner. That filthy Tetl couldn't keep them, but he got what he deserved. And the stones, they are watching, watching the streets. They'll get the thieves, they will!"

"Where were the stones heading to? To pay for what?"

"What? Pay? But I don't, don't know... No!" Another scream and an outburst of incomprehensible gurgling followed the renewed movement of the knife. Horrified, Miztli watched the ragged obsidian pressing, the face underneath it just a jumble of features, distorted into inhumanness, smeared and bleeding and bubbling hideously. "Yes, pay pay! Pay for shooting... shooting. Just a little arrow or dart. The Tlatelolcans, they can... still strong on their, their side of the island. They can handle, can handle... no problem with shooting, but need to recognize, to know whom. The stones... the stones to be delivered—"

Suddenly, the tormented body shuddered, then went still, its straining limbs dangling, not twitching or struggling anymore. The rustle of a breath let out of a few throats at once shook the smoky air. Miztli felt the ring around his own chest loosening.

"He is still alive," said the Texcocan, reaching for the threatened eyelid, pulling it away as though wishing to peer into the interrogated man's thoughts. "And he knows plenty. Good." Awkwardly, he straightened, propped on his good arm, the one that held the interrogating knife before, his face again study of colorlessness. "Get me something to drink. That *pulque* your nosy little apprentice was supposed to bring."

The healer woman made a face, then shouted toward the inner doorway. "He knows more than this, oh yes," she added thoughtfully, eyeing the mess of their captive with the detachment of a metalworker checking on the vessel with melted copper, measuring. "We'll get good information out of him. Tlatelolcan scum, eh? Keeping our Tenochtitlan criminals out of their business. Interesting! One would have thought..."

She shook her head, then looked up in time to frown at the hurrying girl, loaded with cloaks adorned with witty patterns, and a tray with flask and cups upon it. The crisp material felt good upon Miztli's shoulders, surprisingly fitting.

"Serve our honorable guests a cup each and do it quickly." Then her gaze focused on the Texcocan, another one sunken in his thoughts. "What about the fools who stole the stones? Simple marketplace scum? Or something more heavily involved?"

"Only one way to find out." The Texcocan curved his lips, then shrugged with his good shoulder. "Send your men to watch those who are watching the nearby streets. If they run into the stones' current holders, then they are just stupid thieves involved in something they have no chance of handling. Either way, you have a good chance of laying your greedy hands on that treasure. *Again!*" he added pointedly, giving the woman a poignant look. "You are another one who knows more than she is telling. Those stones and their destination are not foreign to you. Anything but."

The woman grinned back, unabashed. "If you don't need their help in handling this screaming mess any further, I'll send them all out now." Her eyes brushed past Miztli, then lingered, focusing. "How about the boy?"

"No, he stays here. He needs to rest and gather his strength. When—"

The racket broke out most suddenly, coming from beyond the front patio and the alley behind the fence, impossible to mistake – yells and shouts and heavy objects falling. The Texcocan straightened abruptly, on his feet but wavering, his face grimacing with pain, draining of the last of its color.

His heart off to a wild tempo, Miztli leapt to his side, while the rest of the men in the room jumped to their feet as well, grabbing their weaponry, their eyes on their mistress, a bizarre sight. The woman nodded curtly, generating their quick exodus, but for the one called Ixtli, who was directed back toward the inner doorway.

"Leave your club here," called out the Texcocan curtly. Again, his tone brooked no argument, and none was offered. "Get the club, boy." Miztli rushed to obey as well, feeling infinitely better at being clothed and armed at long last. "Go out there and see if those no-goods need any help." The wounded's eyes held his. "Be careful and remember what you've been taught."

CHAPTER 15

The men pounced upon them out of nowhere, attacking like hungry wolves in the night forest, with no restraint and no mercy. One moment they were walking the now-blissfully-deserted streets, hidden by the helpful darkness, in a hurry but watching their step, hopeful. Then, in a matter of heartbeats, it was again back to running, fighting, shoving or trying to escape, like this entire evening since his arrival in this accursed violent and overwhelmingly bubbling city. But was he tired of it all!

Jumping to avoid the swinging fist that was aiming to reach his belly, armed with something that looked suspiciously like a knife, Elotl slipped, then fought for his balance, intuitively reaching for the girl, pushing her away from the harmful touch of the suspected weapon. However, another pair of arms tore her from his unsteady grip, and then he became too busy resisting the shove of another body, this one disturbingly strong, pinning him to the cobblestone of the ground that they somehow reached by now, interfering with his ability to breathe.

Squirming wildly, he managed to free his legs, which were for some reason pinned as helplessly by someone else's fallen body, or so his instincts told him, kicking some bony limbs away, then flexing his knee enough to sink it into his original attacker's side. It eased some of the pressure, but the man's hands were upon his throat already, wrapping around it and squeezing hard, taking his attention away from this temporarily achieved advantage.

To strain his neck's muscles became the first priority, a lesson learned back home in Oaxtepec brawls. Panicked thrashing about never helped. One was wiser by making it harder for the strangler to achieve his goal, by resisting where it counted, by playing for time and seeking opportunities to hurt one's opponent elsewhere. The stranglers' concentration tended to be on their hands alone. The last moon's brawl with Metl's rivaling faction taught him that.

His own fists pounding, legs kicking, attention on his neck's muscles and the need to push the dread at the supply of air that lessened with every heartbeat away, Elotl squirmed as best as he could, jabbing his knee into temptingly unprotected legs, trying to do damage, any damage. His knife, where was it? Back in its sheath, when he didn't have enough sense to take it out and carry it openly while walking these dangerous streets? How stupid!

The night began blurring, dotted with surprisingly pretty flashes of color; still, he didn't let the rising dread prevail, straining his throat, doubling his attempts of assault, incensed with some additional blow his lashing out legs received, then another. When something heavy landed upon them, he wanted to scream with frustration; however, it made his rival squirm, then groan, and the fingers pressing into his throat slipped off, if momentarily. Enough to give him a most blissful moment of respite, his own fingers claws, reaching for his rival's girdle and the unvarnished hard wood attached to it as though certain of its existence, as though knowing beforehand. The sweaty hands were grabbing his throat again, but this time, their attempt was short lived, cut by a groan as his own hand slashed at the man's side, cutting with relish, already drawing away to return as eagerly, as quickly.

In another heartbeat, the swirling colors retreated, the night returning to black again, and he didn't need much effort to push the strangling hands and the heavy body attached to those away. The squirming man did not put out any resistance, busy screaming into Elotl's ear instead. To roll away from it all became a necessity; even though he wished he could just lie there for a moment, relishing the sweetness of the night air, gasping to get more of it.

The shrill cries of the girl drew his attention, familiar in their viciousness. But didn't she yell at him with as much venom sometime before? Lurching from another pair of trampling feet, he forced himself up and into the slashing darkness, the knife of his former strangler still there, clutched so tightly he could not feel his knuckles anymore. The girl was still screaming, struggling to break free from a pair of hands that held her firmly across her chest, but a shadow pouncing at him took Elotl's attention, and he had hardly enough time to avoid the touch of what felt like a club rather than a simple fist brushing against his shoulder, making him sway.

Leaping aside, he spent a heartbeat slashing at the hands that held the girl, liking his new weaponry, even though it was a relatively short curving knife with chipped edges. It cut as well as Father's razor-sharp dagger, and the man who held the girl cried out, then pushed her away, lashing out but missing, giving Elotl a tempting opening to strike with his newly acquired weaponry once again.

Which he might have done but for the persistent club pouncing at him, this time sending him sprawling from the sheer drive of his own leap aside. The cobblestones met him with their hurtful eagerness, becoming familiar since entering the accursed city. He rolled away but was not fast enough to avoid the vicious assault of a thick-soled sandal that sent him back down amidst a spectacular outburst of pain. Another kick made him fight for breath, drowning in his own gasp of agony, but by that time, he found neither strength nor presence of mind to resist the yank that pulled his head up, then slammed it against the same accursed cobblestones. He was too busy trying to breathe.

"Where are the stones?" someone rasped, a low distorted voice. It was as though his new assailant was speaking from below the lake's surface.

"I don't know what you are talking about," shouted the girl in her typical annoyingly high-pitched shriek that also sounded as though coming from below plenty of water. "We don't have any stones. We didn't even see any! Please!"

"Shut her up," was an unsympathetic response of a different more distant voice, this one actually sounding clearer. "Search him. And that other one. And the fowls. Where is the other one?" Which brought the screams of the one called Quetzalli up to an even more annoying volume. "Shut up, you stupid rat!"

Nauseated by the blood that was filling his mouth rapidly, Elotl struggled against the hands pinning him down mainly in order to spit the bile out, even though a certain concern for the girl did enter his mind, to a degree. These people were vicious, nothing like the rivaling factions out there in Oaxtepec. No one was that eager to kill their rivals in Metl's surroundings, or so quick with action without plenty of threatening words to begin, and often to end, brewing clashes as well.

Another bout of footsteps shook the pavement as rough hands tore at his loincloth, peeling off his much cherished sheath with the knife, pausing clearly to examine it, then throwing the ragged obsidian away. There was no mistaking that sound clattering upon the dusty stones. Abandoning the outright struggle, Elotl tried to wriggle closer to the dying away clatter, hoping against hope. The treasures they were looking for might keep them busy for a while, giving him chance to reach for his knife.

"The stones!" cried out the nearest voice, asserting his wild assumption. "I think it's—"

In another heartbeat, the pressure disappeared, but not in the way he anticipated. Anything but! The violence was again all around, shouts and kicks and thuds of landing blows or falling bodies. Rolling aside in time to avoid being trampled on, Elotl pushed the pavement away, groping his way up the stones he was slammed against earlier, feeling the girl's presence rather than seeing it, another one seeking this kind of support, he was sure of that.

"Run," he groaned, the words slurred, ridiculously clumsy in coming through his swollen mouth. "Run away. *Now!*"

She mumbled something as incomprehensible and actually hurled herself at him instead of following the sensibility of his words. If the buzz in his head wasn't as loud or as confusing, or his limbs so awkwardly irresponsive, he would have attempted to follow his own advice as well. As it was, he wavered and nearly went back down again, clutching the crumbling stones for support.

Only to tumble back down nevertheless as another silhouette

crashed into them both, his scream throaty and unbearably distorted, such low gurgling. The girl was somewhere underneath, preventing his renewed attempt to roll away with her limbs that were twisted with his, and she was screaming too, in that familiar way that made his head wish to explode or crumble inside like a mine in the shifting earth. When another form landed beside him, rasping for breath but at least not shrieking outright, he was grateful, his mind registering the familiarity. The man from the workshop? Was he still there?

"Are you good?" he grated with as much previous difficulty at letting words out, his mouth on fire.

"No," breathed the man, sounding surprisingly calm. "Help me up."

Easier said than done. Elotl tried to wriggle away without hurting the girl in the process.

"Where are the stones?" demanded someone, an unfamiliar voice. A flurry of dull-sounding blows accompanied by whimpering cries followed. "Where is it?"

More mumbling somewhere up there, then more blows and screams. Halfway up and almost successful, Elotl heard someone exclaiming triumphantly, "Here, I got it. The same bag, would you believe it?"

Amidst a new outburst of loud activity that this time involved more busy rustling and moving about rather than mere beating of various protesting forms, Elotl pulled the girl up after him, then tried to do so for the workshop man, achieving no results. The man was heavy and his groan of pain tore the darkness.

"What to do about the rest?" asked one of the newcomers, a burly man of a surprisingly clean exterior as opposed to their previous assailants. In the renewed moonlight, it was easy to see that.

"Kill them too," tossed another, a well-dressed-looking individual in a flowing short cloak and a club grasped confidently in his hands. "Stupid thieves."

"No, please!" yelled the girl, back to an annoying high-pitched howl that made him wish to close his ears and run away. Was that her intention? If he was her attacker, he reflected randomly, clutching the captured knife that was still in his numb palm with all his strength, he would have left her alone for certain. As it was, his eyes followed the man who stepped forward, wielding his club with professed ease, as though enjoying himself, probably the case.

To hurl his own body at her assailant if sideways seemed stupid, but he had no other options. It knocked the silly girl off her feet once again – didn't she have any sense, this one? – but his knife managed to slash at the hands that clutched the attacking cudgel, feeling the impact, the disgustingly wet sound of tearing flesh. To stay on his feet became a challenge once again, as his ears absorbed the anticipated thud, that of a club falling softly, rolling upon the cracked stones.

"You filthy rat!" bellowed the man, throwing himself at him, weaponless and not caring, his hands dripping blood that was actually pulsating quite strongly from one of them, glittering darkly in the silvery night. "You nasty piece of Tlatelolcan excrement!"

Himself not as agile as before, Elotl spat the blood from his mouth, his anger blinding, beyond care. "You nasty, filthy, dirty piece of human waste," he yelled, doing his best at planting his fist at his attacker's belly, the knife not there anymore, but none of his concern as well now. It was just too much, all of it, and that "kill them" instruction was the lowest form of cowardice, of nastiness, of lowliness itself. "You are beyond any respect, you dirty cowards. You—"

As they went down together in a mess of limbs, he knew he was done for, trapped again under a heavy body, the broad hands already going for his throat in a familiar fashion, showering him with sprinkling blood, his own as viciously determined, fingers claws, tearing at whatever they managed to grab. No more attempts to strain his neck's muscles to prevent strangulation, no more careful seeking for the opportunity to reverse the happenings, nothing but the need to hurt, to beat and injure and make them all suffer. The filthy pieces of cowardly meat!

Another pair of feet darted towards them just as he managed to sink his knee into his attacker's ribs to a telling effect, the muffled groan like most beautiful music, resonating with triumph. The man's grip was weakening, slipping off, yet the force that hauled him up had nothing to do with their struggle, of that Elotl was sure. To a degree, it disappointed him; however, the possibility to lie there for a moment and gulp the chilly air was bliss, even though his nose and mouth did not cope with the renewed flow too well, both clogged and on fire.

"What are you doing?" cried out someone, then another voice. His attacker was apparently too weak to protest with more than incoherent groaning, sprawling not far away as it seemed, thrown onto the cobblestones without care. "What in the name—"

"Keep away!" barked someone, a painfully familiar voice, yet doing so in a completely unfamiliar fashion, as stony and hard as a piece of granite from the mines. It was as though Father was there, materializing out of the thin air, to face this Tenochtitlan riffraff like he did occasional robbers or some unjust tribute collector from Oaxtepec, trying to take more than they were supposed to. Did he pass out and was now dreaming? "Don't step any closer!"

Blinking, Elotl tried to see better, having not enough strength to prop himself on his elbows, his vision swaying, annoyingly blurred. The silhouette of the man half turned to their group, half to their recent attackers stood proudly firm, unwavering, his cloak swaying in the night breeze, the club held in both hands, protruding with much confidence, promising death. A warrior? If it wasn't so painful or disgustingly bitter, Elotl would have gulped, disbelieving what his mind was insisting upon, his eyes at odds with his ears, remembering the voice too well. How could he not?

Then the girl broke into sobs, rushing ahead while throwing herself at their rescuer with violent determination, clutching to him with both hands. "Miztli!" she screamed. "Miztli, you must help me! Please! You must, must make these men stop, you must! We did nothing wrong, I swear we didn't do anything. I swear!"

His brother pushed her away quite roughly, sinking to his knees next to Elotl, thrusting his face so fast and so close it made his nausea soar into a near uncontrollable level. "You good?" he rushed, this time in his familiar anxious, hesitant speech. "Are you hurt? Wounded? Where? What... what are you doing here?" His hands groped Elotl's shoulders, pulling him up, hurting.

"Get your hands off me," he groaned, trying to wriggle free from the stone-hard grip, unsuccessful on this score. "Let me up, you crazy piece of dung. I... I was looking for you and where was I supposed to do that? In filthy Cuauhnahuac or around Smoking Mountain?" His mouth was still feeling as though full of fluffy cotton flowers from the fields near Oaxtepec, the words coming out more coherently even if as hurtful as before. The girl was standing very close, wide-eyed, and the wounded man from the workshop, by now propped on his elbow, gaped as though the spirits of the Underworld materialized out of the thin air, full of purpose that couldn't be anything but bad. The two of the men who attacked their attackers drew closer as well, one kneeling next to his bleeding comrade, the other staring in a narrow-eyed way.

"You know them, boy?" he demanded, openly indignant.

He could feel Miztli tensing. "Yes, I do," he said with his previous unfamiliar firmness. "And if something happens to any of them, YaoTecuani will have your skins for it!"

"The man of Texcoco?" repeated the kneeling man, looking up sharply.

"Yes! And now go away. Take the stones and your wounded back to your mistress." But did it sound strange to hear his little brother doling out orders like that, sounding very much Father-like. Miztli, of all people? Elotl couldn't help but gawk in appreciation.

"And you? What shall we tell Honorable Tecuani?"

"I... I'll come back later. I have other things to do. I'll come back later, I promise." That sounded more like the Miztli he knew. Elotl fought the need to laugh stupidly. But was it all so incredibly bizarre! Miztli, of all things, coming up in such a crucial moment, like in the tales of the storytellers, rescuing them in a spectacular fashion, looking changed, unrecognizable, giving orders to violent scum, then turning back to his halting way of speaking when pressed and unsure of himself, sounding like a boy half his age in the best of cases.

The hysterical laughter was near, difficult to hold in. He grabbed his brother's wide shoulder, always rock-hard with muscles but now seeming twice as broad as before, thrice as hard. "Help me up, you wild coyote."

That made Miztli's worriedly puckered face break into the widest of grins. To call him drubbed *coyotl* instead of proudly noble *miztli* was his way of making his younger sibling angry since they both could remember themselves.

"Ome is wounded. He is bleeding all over!" called out the girl, who apparently in the meanwhile had enough sense to check on the workshop man. "You must help him. He is bleeding!" Again, her voice was climbing up to annoyingly high levels.

Miztli tensed all over again. "OmeTelpochtli?" he repeated, narrowing his eyes at the sprawling man. "But... how?"

The workshop man grunted something, then dropped back to his back, clutching his side with both hands. "Of all things," he muttered, beginning to struggle back to his feet in his turn, much less successful on this score. Elotl felt his worry returning.

"He needs to see a healer," whimpered the girl, not attempting to help the wounded but kneeling there in touching helplessness. For some reason, he felt bad for her.

"Weren't we on the way to see one?" he asked, finding it easy to stay upright with his brother's sturdy support, such a surprisingly comforting feeling, Miztli's shoulder so solid, his hand propping his, Elotl's, back in an astonishingly practiced manner, as though all he did was to carry wounded. Did he? Thousands of questions swarmed his mind, but he pushed them away, concentrating on the problem at hand. "How badly is he hurt?"

"I can hear and talk, you know," grunted the injured, answering Elotl's question even if inadvertently. "I don't know if it's bad. It's bleeding, but the pain is bearable. If I don't move, that is."

"Where did you get stabbed?" inquired Miztli in a surprisingly cold, openly hostile voice.

"In my side somewhere," grunted the man with matching

animosity.

"We were on our way to see the healer woman, yes," hurried to put in Quetzalli-girl, as though trying to pacify both sides. "Truly! We were on our way there."

As though that explained it all. He remembered the accursed stones, glad to be rid of those, for good or so he hoped. Their last attackers did take this treasure, didn't they? And where were the skinny thief and the other girl?

"The healer is here, yes." Miztli's tone didn't warm, growing more reserved and unfriendly with each uttered word. "But she is pissed with you more than anyone. She will be helping you into the Underworld faster than doing the healing for you."

"Why?" They called it out in unison, he and the girl.

"You were the ones to steal those stones, no?" grunted Miztli, glaring at the girl and the wounded. "How stupid was that!"

They stared at him in momentary disbelief, and while Elotl felt like joining his current companions in some vigorous protest – just who did his little brother think he was to tell them what to do, whether it was something stupid or not! – the silhouettes of their previous attackers bore on them once again, rushing back down the alley.

"You are told to go back now, boy," shouted the first one, nearing them quite determinedly yet with a certain amount of wariness that was difficult not to notice. Was he afraid of Miztli? Somehow, Elotl did not suspect any other case for their apprehension, returning to eye his brother's club, still held most firmly in his free hand, ready to be of use. "YaoTecuani demanded that, and the Mistress as well. Need help with the wounded?"

He could hear Miztli letting out a held breath. "Don't make any trouble," he said quietly, addressing them but looking away, not taking his eyes off the approaching men. "It'll be all right. I'll... I'll make sure of that."

CHAPTER 16

The fire was flickering with renewed vigor, made stronger by a whole pile of dry logs, sending tongues of flames as though trying to burst free from the restricting borders of the surrounding stones. Warily, Miztli watched the healer motioning the apprentice girl, shaking her head. Tlaquitoc's son was spread on the mat previously occupied by the Texcocan man, already a mess of blood, water, and other dubious liquids, now reinforced by more dripping discharge. Face crumbled and colorless, the squat man was doing his best not to squirm or probably cry out in the face of the treatment, the healer probing inconsiderately, pressing all around the bloody gash, causing more crimson trickling to come out.

Shivering, Miztli looked away in time to see the apprentice girl pushing a bowl full of clean water toward Elotl, who was squatting next to him, curiously calm – the calmest of them all, surely – despite his face being a mess of swollenness and crusted blood, his lower lip like those of old statues of some ancient deities, disproportionally huge. He was talking strangely because of that; still, it was impossible to mistake his brother's voice back there in the dark alley, however improbable it all was, his favorite words of curses always including "cowards" in them.

Oh, but how lucky it was that he came there in time, could interfere and make the healer woman's cronies stop and listen. It was like a dream, a sort of a nightmare with a good ending. It was still impossible to take it all in. Elotl? Here? Coming to Tenochtitlan, looking for him according to his own words tossed out there in the darkness, when they all didn't get over the first shock as yet.

Unable not to, he reached out and touched his brother's arm, making sure that he was real, not the fruit of a feverish illusion. This day was bad enough without the proof that he was losing the last of his sanity.

Elotl's eyes flickered at him, curiously unharmed, considering the condition the rest of his face was in, radiating a beaming smile. A wink completed the picture before his brother went back to the bowl, washing the crusted blood off his cheek and his lower jaw obediently, as instructed by the healer before.

"When do we get to sneak out of here?" he whispered, rubbing his chin with little consideration to its condition, as though unconcerned with the pain, like a healer taking care of someone else's wounds. "I can't become all soft and brotherly with them watching." Indeed, the eyes of the two men the healer instructed to stay in the room for reasons unexplained but obvious did not waver from them. "And I'm still to hear how you got to all this, the cloak and the club, to strut about like those nobles of Oaxtepec, eh?" The push of the elbow was careful, but there, reminding him of Necalli. Oh, but how he longed to talk to his brother, to ask about the family, and yes, tell about himself – not all of it, but the most, the wonder of school and about noble *pillis* like Necalli and Ahuitzotl, and the warriors' life, and maybe even about Tlemilli, well, just a hint maybe – but it wasn't possible, not in their current surroundings.

"Later. When she is done, maybe. When the Texcoc—when Honorable YaoTecuani tells her to let us all go."

A glance at the Texcocan reassured him once again, the man still crouching near the fire, tired and spent and again frighteningly pale but as formidable and straight-backed as always, unyielding, a person in charge. It was good to know that this warrior was around and aware, not about to be fooled by the dangerous healer's once again semi-amused affability from the beginning of their visit, before her house came under an outright attack. There was no cause to trust this woman. Anything but. However, the Texcocan knew how to handle her, even when wounded, clearly still in a great deal of pain, exhausted and not at his best, not if it came to an outright confrontation. What hold did he have over the nasty witch?

As though reading his thoughts, or probably just sensing his scrutiny, the man shifted his gaze from the merrily dancing flames, glancing up briefly, then motioning with his head. "Come, jaguar cub. Help me up. We'll stroll the front patio; check it for possible intruders."

The healer woman snorted softly.

He could feel Elotl tensing by his side, losing some of his nonchalant humor. "My brother, can he come with us? He won't... won't get in the way."

Eyes back on the fire, the Texcocan shook his head. "We won't be long. He'll be safe here until then. All of the newcomers will be, won't they, Xochitl?" The last phrase came out somewhat menacing, relaying a clear message.

"If you don't take long and promise to take them all away," grunted the healer, losing her previous amused affability. "And pay for this one's treatment. He needs to be stitched and watched for extensive swelling. Not to mention the brews he'll have to consume, plenty of medicine. That is not a harmless wound he got. He is lucky to be alive at all." The wounded flinched but said nothing, and Miztli could not but admire the man's courage however strongly he hated them all, this entire family except Chantli. Tlaquitoc's second son was not as nasty as Acatlo, not as eager to sneer and put down or slap with too much force. He would actually keep to himself most of the time; still, he was the part of this household, the part of the bad times in the melting room and the attempted deceit of forced slavery. He pushed his rising anger away.

"I'll be back in no time," he whispered into his brother's ear. "This man, he can be trusted. But only him. Not the healer. She is dangerous. She is..." He tried to think fast. "Just stay here until I'm back and do nothing. Don't draw her attention to you or Quetzalli." A quick glance informed him that Chantli's saucy friend didn't entertain any silly ideas like talking or moving, curled next to Elotl, all eyes and pallor, atypically quiet. What was this one doing in the middle of it, and why with his brother? The memory of the incessant needling and teasing, and that evening when she talked nasty to Tlemilli surfaced, to be pushed back as determinedly. It was not the time. "Just keep very quiet, both of you. She is busy enough with the filthy piece of excrement. Let her stay this way."

Elotl's glance held a measure of puzzled wonder this time. "What do you have against them? Or they against you?" he added shrewdly, with the most crooked of smiles.

"Nothing," grunted Miztli, hurrying after the Texcocan, who managed to rise to his feet without outside help, walking quite steadily considering his previous condition, his ointment-smeared and still cloak-less back glistening. "Just wait for me here and keep quiet." He didn't like the idea of leaving Quetzalli alone with his brother, not this gossipy quarrelsome fowl. What did she manage to tell Elotl until now? Nothing good, surely.

Outside, it was darker and colder, the dawn not far away, making the night thicken as though reluctant to yield its previous victory. The Texcocan leaned against one of the inner poles of what looked like a shrine, a small stone construction in the form of a round bowl, guarded by four beams and a makeshift roof of woven branches. Miztli eyed it with uneasy interest, tired beyond measure, craving to be back in *calmecac* and safely asleep, having nothing but morning lessons to look forward to, the regular life.

The regular life?

His gloom kept descending, making him wish to crawl into the darkest of corners and curl up there, forgotten. The regular life was his village, or even Tlaquitoc's workshop, the melting room. *Calmecac* and a life of a warrior, noble *pillis* and priests and books full of glyphs he still could not decipher but a few of those, training with all those wonderful weapons, reciting proper rites and ways to worship deities, adding and dividing numbers, huge numbers that only a glyph or two could describe; oh, but all this was no normal life but a glimpse into something, a place he belonged only as long as the Emperor thought he was useful there. But he let the Emperor down this time, made a mess out of it all. An unforgivable failure a man like Axayacatl would not tolerate or give a chance to correct somehow, if there was a way to correct it.

"There is not much of the night left, and we both can use a little sleep before facing the dawn's challenges." His formidable companion's voice rang with surprising tranquility; affable, calm, matter-of-fact. Soothing, in a way.

Miztli just nodded, unable to concentrate enough to generate a reaction, any reaction, not knowing what to say.

"It'll all work out in the end, boy. No need to dive into all this gloominess because of one rough night." The palm landing upon his shoulder was warm, giving off its strength, a friendly, trustworthy pat. "You think too much, jaguar cub. Always did, didn't you? But you can't survive this city or the life that you were thrust into with such an attitude. Not a chance, boy." The rough fingers pressed his shoulder strongly, almost painfully. "Take my advice on it. Think through what I say and don't discard it with pretended politeness. Listen to my words, then decide for yourself. It is your life, after all. But I'll tell you something. You've been given an exceptional chance, something your fellow villagers from out there in your southern nowhere cannot fathom, cannot even try to imagine in their wildest of daydreams. And yes, this is a demanding life you are leading now, and not an easy one for a boy with no family to back him up and no connections. And yet, it is a thousand-fold more satisfying, more rewarding, more promising – for your descendants as well – than a regular life of a regular commoner. Even if you have to work harder and face more challenges than your peers of that noble school, even your friend Necalli. Now this boy is not looking for an ordinary life of an ordinary *pilli*, and yet his challenges are nothing compared to yours. Yes, everyone's life is easier than yours for now, and still it is better than what you have left behind. I'm prepared to bet my sword and my decorated shield on it, given to me by our old emperor for deeds I do feel proud about." The rough palm landed on Miztli's back again, with much force this time. "To cut the long tirade short, take my advice. Enjoy this life of yours; take each day as it comes. Don't brood and think about what you did wrong or what could have been done better; who will be angry with you or why. When the Emperor is pissed, deal with it, but in case he won't be, why brood about it now, why drive yourself mad with the thoughts of it? Deal with the troubles as they come. Plot and prepare, yes, certainly. But only if you can do it. If not, leave it at that and worry about the troubles only when they come." The flashing smile was sudden and astonishingly open, transforming the weathered face, making it look younger and unarguably handsome. "Think about my words when you have time, even though I just told you not to think too much. I must be getting old to start preaching to youths in such fashion and under completely inappropriate circumstances. So let us get back to what I want you to tell me or do before Xochitl sends her spies out to overhear what we've been talking about."

Blinking, Miztli tried to force his concentration back, mesmerized by the tranquility of the voice and its friendliness, the kindness of its words. But the man was so wise, so well meaning. So worthy of listening to! He searched for something to say, anything. It would be so impolite to just nod in response, wouldn't it?

"Now, first of all, what about this miserable bunch of would-be thieves? Is that beaten-up youth really your brother? Do you have any more family in this city?" The crisp businesslike leader and a man of dubious goals was back, speaking curtly, demanding answers.

Miztli drew a deep breath, still under the previous spell, the anxiety and gloom splashing near, yes, but not overwhelming, not anymore.

"Yes, Elotl is my brother and, no, I have no more family here in the city. Not to my knowledge, that is. I didn't know he was here. I truly didn't. He said he came looking for me, but I didn't have time to ask more, not yet. I... I hope we are allowed to talk, a little..."

The Texcocan nodded curtly. "What is his connection with the stabbed commoner and the marketplace fowl?"

"I don't know. I... I'll ask him that, and I will let you know. The moment he tells me."

Another curt nod made him feel better again. The man believed him. And why wouldn't he? Still, the questions made him worried, despite the received advice. What if Elotl was mixed up in something this man was against?

"Now your emperor." This time, the Texcocan shot a quick glance around, then paused, evidently listening. When he resumed, his voice was so soft, Miztli could barely understand his words. "What did he tell you to do this evening in the Palace?"

He didn't hesitate, not this time, his hope splashing in force, against all chances. Oh yes, YaoTecuani was the only person who could help him out. If he wished to do so. "The Emperor, he told me to listen to this delegation, the visiting Tenantzincas. Like I told you before. Back in the Palace, that is, when you saved... saved me from these warriors. I told you back then. I don't know what they wanted, why they attacked..." He forced the welling uneasiness away, determined to talk better than this, with no stuttering. The man believed in him and his abilities to walk this difficult road. He told it in so many words just now. "I was to disguise myself as a servant, a palace's slave. To sneak around and listen to this delegation. Ahuitzotl told the Emperor that I could speak their tongue, so he thought I might hear something of interest, something they wouldn't share while using Nahuatl."

"Yes, I remember that." The Texcocan's eyes lit with appreciation. Even in the thickening darkness, it was easy to see that. "Good thinking. So did they speak that southern tongue? Did they say something of importance?"

Miztli's momentary elation dimmed. "No, they didn't. Well, they did speak in Matlatzinca, two warriors. They looked important and they huddled near the window. But I couldn't listen to them properly, as the others were yelling or demanded that I did things for them. They thought me to be a disobedient slave." The memory of his anger at their nasty way of speaking to him made him wish to hit himself. If only he had stayed despite it all. Stupid, stupid, stupid! His companion was eyeing him with slightly lifted eyebrows, clearly expecting the continuation of the story. "Well, I went out, hoping to listen to them from the outside. But then, well, then Tlemilli came along and then the warriors, and you..."

"What was that you did manage to overhear? Repeat only this, only what these warriors said in the foreign tongue." Again, the crisp command.

"They talked about a threat to their leader, yes. There or on the Plaza, they said." He tried to remember, not sure enough of himself to mention that they did talk about a warning received from none other than a mysterious "Texcocan man." A coincidence? "They gossiped about politics too. Said your *altepetl* was interested in joining the conquests in the south. Said that Cuauhnahuac might be involved, but they weren't sure if this information was true."

His companion's eyes, instead of sparkling again, narrowed into slits. "I think I know who those warriors were. Careless good-for-nothing." Then the piercing gaze was again upon him, cutting the night. "Anything else?"

"No," whispered Miztli, frightened for real. "I... I went out to listen better, but then, well, you know what happened then. And the Emperor, he doesn't want me to retell him some silly gossip. He won't be pleased with me when he sends for me."

The intensity of the piercing gaze lessened. "That remains to be seen, boy. Like I told you before, no need to worry about angered emperors before they are actually yelling at you, bringing in warriors to chop your limbs off." The amused even if brief smile did not make Miztli feel better, not this time. His stomach turned at the very thought; a real possibility, wasn't it? "Now, I want you to do something for me that will help you as well. I didn't count on touring the imperial gardens, enjoying caged animals and getting shot on the way. This wound came at the worst timing possible. So I'll need you to help me out and, on the way, you will be helped in your dreaded confrontation with your emperor." The strong voice again dropped to a mere whisper. "As you know or may easily guess by eavesdropping on those needlessly chattering warriors, I want this delegation to arrive back in their inglorious Tenantzinco safe and sound, to drive our both *altepetl*s to a war in the Tollocan Valley, a good profitable war." A brief pause ensued through which Miztli did not dare to blink or let out a held breath. "So this threat the warriors were talking about but didn't seem to take seriously must reach your emperor's ears. With enough warriors to protect the visiting dignitary, the Palace and the Plaza are relatively safe, but not so the projected tour of the Tlatelolco new marketplace, still full of organized groups of criminals, actually worse than before because there is no one to keep an eye on them. The new Tlatelolcan governor is not strong enough yet, too busy flattering his Tenochtitlan masters to put his attention to the city he is supposed to care for. Do you follow me, boy? Do you understand what I'm saying?"

Not even trying to think it all through, Miztli nodded, eager to please now as well, the possibility of coming to the Emperor with more tangible information too promising, too good to just grab it, in case it wasn't true.

"You want me to go to the Emperor and tell him about the danger of the Tlatelolcan marketplace. To prevent that delegation from going there as planned."

"Yes, I do want you to do that." The generous lips were twisting into a one-sided grin, another familiar sight. An encouraging one. "It'll help you, won't it? How?"

He allowed himself to grin back. "I'll pretend that I overheard it while listening to all sorts of people. And by not mentioning you, not even in passing."

"Oh yes, you mention me and you are dead, quickly and brutally, very much so." That came out offhandedly, a matter-of-fact observation.

Miztli manage to cover his gasp but barely, then tried not to let his apprehension show. "I won't. I know I should never mention you, ever."

"Good." With an obvious effort, the man shifted, then pushed himself off his only means of support, reaching back to steady himself with his good hand, a low groan escaping his tightly pursed lips, his exhaustion suddenly on full display, even in the darkness. It was the rock-hard will that kept him on his feet or even conscious, realized Miztli, rushing closer, ready to catch his companion should he begin falling.

The pursed lips twisted, and the stony hand locked around his shoulder, squeezing the life out of it. "Thank you, mountain lion cub. You are worthy of your spectacular name. The mighty pumas are loyal and not only strong and unwavering, are they?" The formidable head shook, then the smile crept back to dominate the voice once again. "Help me back in, and then go. Make your way back to *calmecac* and wait for your emperor to summon you. Come back here the moment you can. In the afternoon school-free time, I suppose. If I'm not here, I'll leave you word where to find me. Don't fail to do that."

"Leave? Now?" Against his will, Miztli halted, causing them both to sway in a precarious way. "But my brother! I can't leave him here just like that. I need to make sure... to place him somewhere, somewhere to stay. I can't leave him like that!"

His companion's groan had nothing to do with pain this time, of that he was sure. It was too loud, too telling to mistake the professed frustration. "You and your siblings! Will you go on saddling me with brothers and sisters to take care of, threatening to do stupid things if I won't?" Another loud snore. "You and your Tlatelolcan girl!"

Against his mounting worry and a healthy amount of renewed fear, he wanted to chuckle, seeing the parallel too well, unable not to reflect on it. Tlemilli also refused to leave burning Tlatelolco until this very man had promised to take care of her sister with as little enthusiasm as he was displaying now.

"I'm not, not asking to take care of my brother, or anything," he ventured, realizing that he would actually appreciate active help in this matter. "It's just... You see, I can't leave him like that, hurt and alone, or in dubious company. Tenochtitlan is not a place for a foreigner and he has never been to a big city, just like I wasn't, in the beginning. He may end up in an even worse condition, you see. He doesn't know—"

"Yes, I know!" The Texcocan brought his good arm once again, as though imploring Miztli to shut up, or rather, demanding it. "Stop yelling at the top of your voice. The entire neighborhood went silent in order to listen." Even in the darkness, it was easy to guess that the man was rolling his eyes. "If you vouch for his behavior, if you promise that he will do as he is told and cause no trouble until you are back to take him off my hands, I'll make Xochitl allow him to stay here. But only for one day, and only if he behaves. No dubious company or acts like that theft of the stones. And his current companions go the moment they can walk, the wounded and the girl. They are not staying here with him!" Again, it was easy to feel the man shaking his head. Grinning crookedly too, of that Miztli was sure. "You heard Xochitl. The greedy woman is determined to make me pay for these lowlifes' treatment, even though she received the stones back while keeping what she has been paid for it in the first place. The greediness!" This time, the unharmed shoulder lifted in a brief shrug. "She has always been like that, coming from the worst of the slums. Counting every grain of food and every cocoa bean as though they are her last, even though today, she can buy her entire neighborhood or so I suspect. The old fornicating witch." The soft chuckle held none of the professed grudge or the derision. "She is a good woman, a feisty thing that only my brother could handle. But not for too long. She is too much for any man, not that it even bothered the self-assured fowl. On the contrary. She keeps switching them, hungry for new lovers, the younger the better, ashamed of nothing. So be careful if you have to deal with her ever again and I'm not around to make her behave."

"I will," muttered Miztli, embarrassed to no end, remembering the woman's initial remarks and how this man grew angry with her, scaring her off any more teasing, openly threatening even though helpless and bleeding, his wound in the process of being sewed. A hair-raising scene. "Thank you. Thank you for everything. For your kindness and your help, and, well, everything you have done for me. I—"

A bout of soft laughter stopped his words, kind and warm and not condescending. "No need for this, jaguar cub. Everything I did for you, you earned and deserve. And that goes for anyone else, for that matter. Do not mistake that ever. Even your noble friends like Tlilocelotl's boy stuck by you not out of compassion or a wish to help but because of what you are. And the same goes for those *calmecac* cubs who hate you. They sense your strength and they are jealous. Nothing to do with your humble origins or something you might have said or done. Oh well." Leaving Miztli's shoulder in order to squeeze through the doorway, or rather to come in unaided, the man chuckled again. "It's not the time for sinking into reflection on life and its meaning. Anything but. I must be getting old."

Inside, the most painful part of the treatment seemed to be finished, with the healer woman leaning above her half-conscious charge, smearing a sticky-looking ointment collected from a steaming pot. The skinny apprentice was holding it again on her outstretched arms, barely managing, but busy staring at the suffering patient with huge strangely eager eyes nevertheless. No one came to her aid this time.

Miztli rushed toward his brother, now a better sight, with the most of the crusted blood gone, and none trickling out of numerous cuts and bruises, also smeared with something greenish and sticky. "Are you well?"

"Sort of." Elotl's crooked grin made him feel better, bringing the memories of home in force. Oh yes, this was exactly how his brother always was, in trouble and breezing through, flashing a cheeky smile full of admittance and lack of care, not about to behave unless for Father's sake and not always then even, perpetually teasing and needling but in a good way. Well, mostly. Sometimes Elotl would become nasty and brooding, lashing out for real, trying to hurt with words and deeds, many times over the last summers. Mother said it was the age to be like that, but it made the departure for Tenochtitlan easier in a way.

"I can talk to him outside?" he inquired. "Just for a little while..."

The Texcocan nodded absently, leaning against the support of the opposite doorway as though contemplating his next move, his pallor frightening again now that there was no darkness to conceal it, his back dripping something smelly and mixed. Miztli pushed the renewed splash of worry away. Was it wrong to leave now, as the man told him to? And what if something happened to the tough Texcocan in the meanwhile? The healer was not to be trusted. The man had told him so himself.

"Go and lie down in the inner room," said the woman, flicking a worried glance of her own. "The nearest one. There are enough mats there. Little Ayotl will bring you a blanket."

"After I talk to you," said the Texcocan tiredly. "There are things we need to discuss first."

The older woman rolled her eyes while blowing the air through her nose in the most telling of fashions. "I'll come and check on your wound in a little while, you tough man. Smear some of this ointment on it, see if the stitches held from all your running around. While I do this, we'll talk. In the meanwhile, go away. Lie down and do as you are told. The toughest brutes make the worst patients." She shook her head, then rolled her eyes once again. "See this one? Lying there obediently, saying not a word, taking whatever is done to him with not a peep of an argument, no stupid screaming and thrashing about. I wish all of them were like this one."

Poor Tlaquitoc's son said nothing to this spirited praise, too immersed in his agony to respond, was Miztli's private conclusion. He felt his compassion welling, unwelcome and uninvited.

Pushing it away, he motioned his brother with his eyes. "Come outside. We need to talk. You can walk, yes?"

"I can do many things, you tough city man." Elotl's eyes flickered reassuringly, then shifted to Quetzalli, who by now was curled around herself, her head leaning against his brother's thigh cozily, her breath enviably even. "Clear conscience, eh?" Elotl winked, then moved the girl's head with surprising gentleness, making an effort not to wake her up. "Poor fox," he muttered when successful, jumping to his feet with surprising agility. "She's been through a lot this night. None of her fault mostly."

"Whose then?" inquired Miztli, knowing that they had more important things to discuss, much more important questions to ask and to answer. A careful glance at the healer told him that the dangerous woman paid them little attention, busy inspecting her work, critical and proud, like old Tlaquitoc would eye his exclusively thin, intricately decorated copper sheets, a real achievement to boast.

"It's a long story," said Elotl, following an inviting nod with surprising obedience. "A really wild tale. No wonder you got in trouble in this *altepetl*. It's the wildest place I could not even try to imagine. The craziest storyteller of Oaxtepec would not make up the evening I went through. Not even close!"

"What trouble?" Outside once again, Miztli found the darkness to be of a hindrance now, desperate to see his brother, his longing for home welling like a river at the height of the rainy season. It was like that in the melting room's days, but not since *calmecac*, never with such force. "How is home? Father? Mother? Are they good, healthy and all? The mines, there wasn't collapsing, yes? No shifting earth, or fallen down..." He didn't manage to end the question, the terrible suspicion sweeping him, making his chest empty of air. "Father is not... not hurt or something? Not..."

"Actually, there was this mine that decided to fall down on us. The new one. You haven't been there. They stopped working the previous one; remember the one on that dirty-looking hill with two heads?" Elotl's snicker shook the darkness, loud and unconcerned. "It was bringing barely any copper out, let alone something greenish and pretty, valuable enough to pay filthy traders with." The bout of merriment subdued all of a sudden, replaced with a dour frown, of that Miztli was sure. "Father paid that filthy trader two green stones to bring us good news about you. And what do you think the stinking man did? Brought bad news that was not even news. He didn't know a thing about you, only that you had done badly, run off from that workshop of yours, got into bad trouble. But that's no news. Not anything worthy of green stones. Stupid rat of a trader!"

Miztli tried to take it all in, still not over the fright that something happened to Father, even though Elotl would have told him, wouldn't he? And what did he mean by bad trouble? What trader told him that?

"I don't understand," he muttered, straining his eyes in order to see what his brother's face held.

"Nothing to understand, Little Brother. You made us all worried and we are poorer two precious green stones thanks to you, you wild coyote. Had been a good boy for too long, fooled us all, didn't you? All this obedience and nice behavior, doing as you are told, exemplary worker, the best miner, the best hunter, no fights, no trouble. Fooled us thoroughly, eh?" This time, the snicker held the familiar needling, not all of it harmless. "What's with the wild stories and that club, and everyone I run into hating you, telling nasty tales? Then you, running in such a company, oh my! My friends from Oaxtepec that Father is frowning so direfully against are nothing compared to the company I met you with. That man is a scary piece of dung, the toughest. He'll make even Metl and his friends soil their loincloths. What do you do for him?"

"The Texcocan?" His mind refused to deal with this avalanche of information delivered in an overwhelming gush, with no pause for breath and as though full of accusations. But accusations of what? "I don't work for this man. He is... he is a... I don't know who he is. Not exactly. He has his dark side. But he is a great man, a really outstanding person and very kind, well, sometimes. Necalli wants to be his shield-bearer and, well, if he'll ask for me, I'd be honored to serve him in this way. It would be a really outstanding honor, you see? But for now, no, I don't work for him. Just cooperate sometimes. He helped us a lot, all of us, not only me. He is an outstanding man!"

Now it was his brother's turn to gape, his eyes nothing but round holes in the darkness. "What is a shield-bearer?" All traces of amusement were gone from Elotl's voice and it gained that familiar edge that heralded the less pleasant side of his sibling to come on display. Everyone hated when Elotl got into a nasty mood.

"It's a long story," he retorted more curtly than he intended to, beginning to feel the budding wave of anger that kept marking this last day and night, not a comfortable or reassuring feeling. He tried to push his resentment away. His brother was an outsider and he came here looking for him, going through much in order to do that, getting chased and beaten by real criminals but not giving up. No, he had no right to feel angered or lacking in patience, even though it was not the time for silly sibling rivalry, anything but! "A shield-bearer is when they say you are ready to leave school and become a warrior, but you still need to prove yourself, on the real battlefield this time. So if a veteran warrior asks for you or agrees to take you along into a couple of battles until you learn, take your first captive and all, you are in good shape." The silence had a stunned quality to it, so he labored on, trying to be helpful, to ease the atmosphere. "You see, the fiercer the warrior whom you serve as a shield-bearer, the better your chance to become one yourself. To learn from the best. Like learning from Father, you know? We could not learn the mining from a better person, and it's the same in battles. You need a good teacher, someone very experienced, because they can't make you practice for real in that school of theirs. Just teach you the basics, to handle weaponry and such. Others things too, sometimes really boring things. Like rituals in the temples, or what to do with really big numbers." It was turning silly, his lonely tirade, this helpless jumble of irrelevant information. But why should his brother be interested in dividing or multiplying flags of twenty or bars of five? He drew a deep breath, hating the feeling of being lost and ridiculous. "Do you see what I mean?"

"No, I don't," said Elotl slowly, the swollen silhouette of his lips curving in an unpromising manner, openly deriding now, impossible to mistake. "I don't know what you are talking about, Little Brother, but I do know that I liked you better out there in that alley, yelling at people or waving your club like the wildest robber from the road to Cuauhnahuac. Not preaching like a priest at the new calendar ceremony, talking strange, boring everyone into tears. Rituals in temples? Who would let your villager's feet into a temple, any temple? You need sandals to enter those, to begin with. And don't tell me your tough-looking benefactor preaches to you on those things, the rituals and other strange things you mentioned. It didn't look like that in the dirt of the dark alley, when being beaten by thugs that you clearly work with, with your 'great man' masterminding them all, even the nasty witch woman you don't trust unless needing to stitch someone. She'll make your Tecuani-man pay, never fear. She kept ranting about it half the time you were out, even if all you did was discuss rituals and how to divide numbers or behave on the battlefield like warriors do."

To fight the new wave of angered resentment turned harder.

He did it by drawing a deep breath, then another. Elotl was leaning forward, as though about to try and push him back. Initiating a violent confrontation? But he could beat his brother easily, with no sweat at all. A realization that left him breathless in momentary shock. He never thought to challenge any of his older siblings when back home, never attacked but only when pushed into brawling, and even then only pushing back, defending himself. It was only Elotl, of course, who would attack, always with such ferocity and zeal; and it would always leave him scared and on the defensive, not even dreaming of returning measure for measure. And yet, now he knew that he would beat this older brother of his easily, with not much of an effort. And no, it would not be a mere defense, not anymore. He was not a boy of no consequence now, the youngest of sons, on the bottom of the family hierarchy and not caring. He was a warrior, or en route to becoming one and the man of Texcoco just told him that he was worthy of every investment and help.

"You are talking stupid nonsense," he breathed, struggling to keep his voice low, knowing it was not the time and not right, that his brother came here looking for him out of worry, even if he was now trying to put him down and in the nastiest of ways. "I don't have time for this. Not now. If you want to fight it out or do something as stupid, wait for tomorrow, when I come back. Then you can pick fights with me all you like. But until then, you behave like a girl on her first trip to town, all nice smiles and not a word in argument. I promised Honorable YaoTecuani that you will behave. He would not allow you to stay here otherwise."

"You promised my good behavior?" The annoying piece of rotten meat did not even bother to keep his voice low, not caring how loudly it resonated in the tranquility of the pre-dawn darkness. "You are beyond a joke, Little Brother. The stupidest—"

"And you are beyond everything, a joke and serious talk and everything," he yelled back, not caring. "And I don't mind beating your stupid face into an even worse mess. Don't tempt me to do that, because I will, I swear I will! I'm not that silly little boy from the old days and I don't have to tolerate your nastiness. Not anymore!"

The house behind their backs went suspiciously quiet, but the other dwellings beyond the fence didn't even stir. His chest hurt, and deep breaths didn't help. All he wanted was to smash yet another offender, yet another person who was trying to make him feel like dirt.

"Like I told you, I like you better wild and violent, Brother. Suits you more, you drubbed coyote." Through the wild thundering of his heart, his eyes told him that Elotl was shaking his head, radiating amusement once again. Worse than Necalli in that, he reflected, still too stiff with anger to react likewise. "Don't yell at the top of your voice, or the hero you worship so much will get mad and throw us both out of his house for *bad behavior*."

"This is not his house," muttered Miztli through his clenched teeth. "He doesn't live in this *altepetl* at all."

"Where then?"

"Texcoco."

"Where is that?" Elotl's voice rang with marked practicality, pragmatic and matter-of-fact.

Miztli ground his teeth. "Out there. In the east. The eastern shore of the Great Lake and to the north. Huge *altepetl* too, very important. A member in the Triple Alliance. An important one."

"But you've been learning in this stench-filled city, haven't you? Rituals in temples, eh, Brother? Well, good for you." The outlined shoulders lifted with enviable lightness. "Where are you supposed to go now? For how long do I stay here, in whoever this house belongs to, and behave just like you promised?"

"I'll be back tomorrow after midday. Well, sometime after midday, when the sun is halfway down."

"So long?"

"I can't get out before. I'm not allowed. And maybe even then, if the Emperor gets angry. Or the *calmecac* teachers, more likely."

"What?"

"Oh, it doesn't matter. I'll explain it all later." He forced his shoulders into lifting in as indifferent shrug as he could muster. "You just stay here and keep out of their way. The healer woman mostly. It's her house. But the Texcocan man promised to be here or around. He is wounded, as you saw. Likely to stay and keep low as well." The anger was retreating finally, leaving him feeling low, not encouraged in the least. "Everyone back home is good, yes? Not sick or hurt or something?"

"Of course! I would have told you right away, instead of messing with you, you touchy bear. One might think you are a she-bear with cubs. Or a coyote mother, eh? That touchy female ready to yell at you."

"Shut up," he breathed, feeling better by the moment, the tension gone, and not too soon. Elotl's teasing, in a good way, was difficult to resist. Again, he thought about Necalli, missing his friend most acutely, as though he had been gone for two rainy seasons and not just two dawns, because so much happened through the previous evening and night. Would Necalli see the similarities too when introduced to his brother? Would he like Elotl, deem him worthy? Oh, but was he ashamed of his family now? What a dreadful thought.

"Well, just stay here and keep low. I'll be back the moment I can. And..." He swallowed hard. "Whatever that Quetzalli fowl says about me, don't listen to her. She is a nasty piece of work, and so is Tlaquitoc's son. Don't believe what they say about me. They'll lie!"

Elotl's snort could be heard back in the Royal Enclosure. "I told you that I didn't believe what that filthy trader told us, the liar that he was. But Father did." Again, the traces of amusement were gone from his brother's voice. "He took it hard, said that you are young and could be swayed by harmful people or ways. He was not himself through the following day. And well," his sigh was as quiet as the previous snort was loud, "I can't wait to tell Father. He will be relieved." Then the mocking was back, not missed in the least. "When I know what to tell him, that is. So far, I heard about a whole jumble of nonsense, unfamiliar words, places, people, and what I saw with my own eyes, I can't even try to understand. That was a spectacular club you carried, and they did think you would use it, one could see that. And the cloak!" The intrusive hand grabbed the edge of his wear, the loan from the healer, his own so much nicer, not a coarse maguey at all. "I swear that I never thought I'd live to see the day when you appear all dressed like a noble of Oaxtepec, like snotty lowlifes carried in their moving seats. Did you ride one such?"

Miztli fought his smile down. "Tonight, for the first time, and it was no joy. Even though the princess who loaned us her palanquin didn't know that she was doing it. It was stuffed with so many cushions I was afraid to sink there for good, to drown in all this softness. Didn't like it in the least."

Elotl was staring again. "You talk as though you actually mean it, you wild squirrel."

He fought the urge to reply with a rude gesture he learned from Necalli and Ahuitzotl to use to a telling effect, against nasty Acoatl and his friends most of all. The memory that reminded him of school and the disappearing night, and the long way as yet to cover.

"I must go now. I really must. And," he hesitated, overwhelmed once again. "Thank you. Thank you for coming here and going through all this in order to find me. And for not believing their lies. I can't believe Father did!" He swallowed hard, remembering the words of the Texcoco man. No point in agonizing over it now, was there? When able to travel back and see Father and reassure him, he would do it. Or probably through Elotl at first. But now it was not the time. "Please, keep yourself from harm, don't make the Texcoc—Honorable YaoTecuani angry with you. He'll keep you safe until I come back. He is a great man and his word can be trusted."

"And if he feels chatty and starts talking about you, telling me things... Do I discard what he says as lies too?" The twinkle was too obvious, despite the darkness.

"No, he won't tell lies. Not this man."

CHAPTER 17

The sunray was crawling over the floor, hesitating near the open scroll's edge as though unwilling to trespass. Tlemilli stared at it, willing it to move on. It was slender and pretty, and it would break nicely when reaching the brownish paper, the part where it wasn't covered with glyphs. She stared at it her hardest, but it didn't help. The sun was simply refusing to move.

"In the next painting, you can see our Beautiful Serpent Quetzalcoatl blowing at our sun Tonatiuh to set him on his daily journey across the sky." The priestess's voice rose, taking Tlemilli's attention from her battle of wills with the stubborn sliver of light, this same revered deity Tonatiuh not even close to reaching the zenith of this particular journey, let alone begin rolling down the sky in order to symbolize the end of the school day. Oh, but how was she to withstand a whole lot more of this, the monotonous voice relating the story of the previous four worlds' destruction making her eyelids heavy, craving to drop and then stay this way, the wild whirlwind of her thoughts and worries the only one to battle the sleepiness, not letting her mind drift for good.

It had been now half a night and almost half a day since Miztli and the wounded man of Texcoco had left, piling in the litter she had managed to organize for them, so very proud of her own initiative, happy to help them escape. The Palace was certainly not the place for them to remain, with the Texcocan's bleeding back and Miztli's more than ruffled looks. The guards were certain to look for them, hunting after escaping intruders who dared to sneak around forbidden grounds, the impossible, unbelievable place full of caged jaguars and other monsters, of terrible things crawling out of ponds. A real-life *cipactli* crocodile, not something from paintings or stories! And it did devour that guard the Texcocan man managed to wound, didn't it? Oh mighty deities!

Her stomach would spasm every time she thought about it, constricting in a painful manner, remembering the growling jaguars. Real-size, huge, bloodthirsty jaguars and pumas. They said the second cage had a puma in it, didn't they? The Texcocan man was even momentarily frightened, that tough, weathered and scarily fearless warrior. Oh, benevolent Coatlicue, mother of all gods!

"In the painting below, you can see sunset, girls. Just that, a sunset. Someone can explain us how those neatly arranged glyphs are representing the end of the day, young ladies?"

As though someone cared. Tlemilli glanced at the painting everyone was supposed to peer into, a mess of limbs and symbols as expected, its coloring glaring, another merry mix. Tonatiuh's glyph was again easy to see, looking as though it was pulled down or maybe was diving legs first. The sliver of light was flickering next to the very edge of the painting now, about to touch the unfolded page.

She glanced at the wall opening, wondering for how much longer they'd be forced to sit here. Citlalli said not to go to school at all this morning, not after the sleepless night they had faced, and while on any other dawn she would have greeted such a suggestion most eagerly, this time, she wouldn't even hear of it. He might be back in school by now. Where else would he be? Reporting to the Emperor in the Palace, maybe, yes; still, he would end up returning to school. And she would be there, waiting or rather waylaying, as of course he would be trying to find her as well. The goal easier to achieve when in school than back in the Palace, relying on Ahuitzotl and his messages. Wasn't this the reason they made sure to have her joining their local *calmecac* in the first place?

However this time, even Citlalli waited for news only she, Tlemilli, could provide. Her sister did not mince the matters, did not try to conceal her anxiety. She wanted to know what happened to the man of Texcoco, the one who had left so much blood smeared all over their inner room, the stains that they had to scrub off like commoner servants, using the water flask Miztli had brought along with the requested *octli*. The maids could not be asked to do that, could they? There would be plenty of questions to answer, explanations to provide where there were none, no good reason or excuse. And yet, Citlalli wasn't angry, or even reproachful.

As the night wore off, they huddled together, almost like back in the Tlatelolco Palace when the disaster loomed, worried and helpless, forced to wait, unable to do so. And yet it was different now, so much better and promising. They must be fine out there in the city, she knew, repeating it over and over, convincing mostly herself. The man of Texcoco knew what he was doing, always. He surely had a place to stay and a trustworthy healer to send for, someone who would not be running around, spreading unnecessary tales. Nothing of what happened here or in the imperial gardens would come to light. The man of Texcoco could be trusted, and so could Miztli, the best boy of them all. At the last repeated assertion, Citlalli would grimace as though she had bitten into a red tomato only to discover that it was hopelessly green and bitter. Not a pretty grimace.

"This boy is not for you, Tlemilli," she kept repeating as stubbornly. "He will never be allowed to ask for you, had he served Axayacatl for twenty upon twenty of summers. He will never be good enough to have you, so you must put him out of your head. You must, little one! Please! I don't want to see you hurt or heartbroken. You don't deserve it!"

But Tlemilli would tear her hands from her sister's attempted grip, would turn away with as loud a snort as she dared to sound. "Yes, he will be allowed to ask for me. He will. He is good and brave and wonderful. He is good enough to have me! Also," she ventured through their last argument on the subject, having never thought of it before, "Axayacatl will make him a noble. Tenochtitlan emperors did this aplenty, rewarded their bravest of warriors in this way. He put him in noble school! Does it tell you something? He expects him to do nobly enough to receive the honors until he becomes a noble himself. Then we'll see how you'll talk!"

"I'll talk in the same way," insisted Citlalli with matching fire. "Because he will still not be good enough, even if he becomes some minor nobility. This is not the bloodline you carry, Tlemilli. Our mother was our previous ruler Cuauhtlatoa's beloved niece. Think about it! Your bloodline is impeccable on both sides, better than that of our half-sisters who were noble through our father and not their mothers, besides Matlatl and little Yototli."

At this point, Citlalli's eyes would mist, the unknown fate of their half-sisters weighing on her spirit, but not that of Tlemilli. Matlatl deserved to be sold on the slave market of the filthiest of villages, and her parroting barking little dog of a full sister as well. Better yet, the little parrot should be given away for free, or maybe even paid to be taken. However, her thoughts did not dwell on any of these matters, only the fact that no matter how, Miztli was going to receive her and with full honors. He was better than everyone and when he became minor nobility, they would all talk differently, even Citlalli.

"Also think about how long you will have to wait for that lowly boy to become anything of importance. You will both grow old before it happens!"

"We won't! He will achieve great deeds very soon. The Emperor is giving him special missions all the time. Soon he will start rewarding him. You'll see." But the proud talk did not make the twinge of worry disappear, the thought never occurring to her before. She wanted to be given to him soon, preferably tomorrow, or on the day after that; certainly as soon as he finished school, because no schoolboys were allowed to take wives before that. But if they waited even for the end of his schooling, quite a few rainy seasons would pass. At least two, or three, even though his friend was already taken on the spiritual journey only older students were allowed to attend. She tossed her head as high as it felt called for. "He'll be allowed to ask for me soon enough, before anyone else is asking. He'll find a way!"

But Citlalli would only sigh in desperation and shake her head and grow even sadder while surveying both inner and outer rooms for overlooked stains of blood, then curl in her favorite alcove again, tapping her fingers or twisting her prettily done tresses she didn't have time to have maids release upon her return from the imperial feast and before Tlemilli had fallen on her with the most inappropriate troubles and demands.

"This man was wounded badly, wasn't he?" she had inquired only once, staring into nothing as though expecting some help or reassurance to materialize out of the thin air, her frown deeply troubled, concentrated to the point of ridiculousness.

"I don't know. He didn't seem deeply concerned." To recall the sight of the torn, ravaged flesh and the blood seeping from it no matter how they kept wiping it away was disturbing, so she concentrated on the man's matter-of-fact behavior, his lack of politeness, his blunt demands. Those were most reassuring. Dying people did not flare at their rescuers, did they? "I think he will be all right. He is a good man. I hope he feels better soon!"

"He is rude and brutal. And ferocious. He is a ferocious warrior and little else," was Citlalli's surprisingly passionate response. "For a man of as highly civilized *altepetl* as Texcoco, he is behaving with remarkable lack of refinement, civility, and simple good manners."

"He is not!" cried out Tlemilli, offended now on the Texcocan's behalf. "He doesn't spend his time on silly talk, yes. You wouldn't catch him flirting with ladies and wooing after them." Suppressing a sudden bout of mirth, she remembered Miztli's friend telling them that, repeating what his father had said, allegedly. They had plenty of the wildest of laughter discussing such a possibility, imagining the tough Texcocan ogling highborn ladies and talking silly to them. Even Miztli was on the floor, laughing too hard for his usual reserved shyness. "He is very much civilized, Citlalli, and speaking of nobility, he is noble, very much so. Necalli's father said that this man's father was the Chief Warlord of Texcoco and the closest friend and adviser of their old emperor Nezahualcoyotl himself. Also," she added triumphantly, feeling as though she had managed to best her sister on Miztli's behalf as well. "Also he saved you back there in Tlatelolco. He saved you and Matlatl and that little pest Yolotli. Necalli told us all about it! He said he didn't let the warriors come near you and take you away, or do you any other harm. He said that but for this man, you might have been harmed like the rest of those they brought from the Palace. They were all running and screaming and their clothes were torn. Necalli said it looked ghastly."

Citlalli's face fell all of a sudden. "Yes, it was. It was terrible and so... so indecent what they did to us, so undignified. They had no right to treat our nobility like that, our people... Father fought them and tried to protect our honor." Her sigh was heavy and full of misery; however, her head shook resolutely. "This man may have saved me back then, yes, and well, yes, he was not bad or harmful, he behaved with honor and true decency. He is very brave. But..." Her fine teeth were chewing her lower lip, tearing at it unmercifully. "We saved him just now as well. Without us, he might have been killed, or maybe caught and then punished and disgraced or worse. He certainly was in this palace unlawfully, with no permission to be here. So we are even now. I owe him nothing. Life for life, honor for honor."

The surprisingly passionate speech jarred, and now, in the soft sunlight of the class and the monotonous voice of the teaching priestess that kept talking about previous worlds and their spectacular creations and endings, the memory of the night conversation made Tlemilli wonder. It was not like her even-tempered, level-headed sister to hate someone with so much fervor and no viable reason to back the strong feeling up. Citlalli was too rational for that, too cool-headed.

"So who would venture a guess, girls?" The priestess's voice floated in the background, drawing her attention but barely, the sunray still lingering, now touching the page yet refusing to advance any further. Was it nearing midday at least? "How does this writing represent something as simple as sunset? Think about the creations of our world of the Fifth Sun we discussed just now. Remember our previous lesson."

Tlemilli stared at the painting of mixing limbs, catching the outline of a squatting figure with no visible upper body or head.

"Revered Tonatiuh, our sun, is being swallowed by Tlaltecuhtli, our Lord Earth Deity, the way it happens at the end of every day, the time we refer to as sunset." As expected, the commoner girl Chantli was the one to venture a guess, a correct one, as always. Tlemilli shot her a satisfied glance, proud of her. Oh yes, Chantli was better than all noble fowls of this class put together. Of course she was! And yet this morning, the girl didn't look her best, not even near. Had she had as bizarre a night as hers was? Not a chance. And yet, she did come late for the morning lessons, did earn the priestess's wondering admonishment and the other girls' puzzled whispering. Clearly no one expected the best and most hardworking student to be late, not even for one single morning.

"Yes, it is," cried out the priestess, openly delighted. "Good work, girl. The image is indeed representing our Revered Tonatiuh and Tlaltecuhtli, as they meet every evening when it's time for the night to take over. What else is there in the painting?"

The question clearly was not addressed at anyone else but the gifted commoner.

"The moonrise, in which Tecciztecatl, the Moon Deity, rises into the sky, to take over from Tonatiuh until the next dawn. Like he did on the day when both revered deities made their sacrifice, throwing themselves into the sacred fire." The girl's voice rang dully, lacking its usual enthusiastic spark. Her eyes didn't rise from the book they were studying but for a brief look at the teacher, a polite smile to acknowledge the praise.

Tlemilli frowned, wishing that they were seated closer, like on the previous day, when she showed her friend how to solve the riddle of numbers and beans. The way they sat now, she couldn't even try to whisper an inquiry, to find out what happened. Something dreadful maybe. The girl's downcast pose suggested that.

Her thoughts drifted again, the sunray mesmerizing, making her eyelids heavy, craving to close, just for a little while. It was so warm and cozy here, and the priestess again was talking, rustling with another folded paper. Trying to show them its content? Other intricately painted pages? The colors were swirling so nicely, in delicate patterns, no definition to them.

"Tlemilli!"

She straightened abruptly. All eyes were upon her, their faces staring. Blinking in confusion, she tried to focus, the images from the dream intermingling with the reality of the *calmecac* girls' hall, just a large room really.

"Did you sleep badly last night, Tlemilli?" The priestess's nicely round face was wearing the color of a storm cloud – no sunset that – her usually friendly features screwed in a dour frown. "Or are the stories of our previous worlds boring you?"

"No," she said, mostly out of habit to deny anything she had been caught at, a frequent occurrence, especially back in Tlatelolco. "It's nothing like that."

"In the Tlatelolcan *calmecac*, they were sleeping during the day and learning at night." This time, it was Tlazotli, chirping in her lilting, falsely nice voice.

"Unlike Tenochtitlan, where stupid fowls can only giggle stupidly, no matter if at day or at night," retorted Tlemilli, again out of instinct, still dizzy and trying to get her bearings. Had she truly fallen asleep? For how long? The sliver of light was nearing the upper cluster of glyphs, still too close to its previous location at the edge.

"Stop it, Tlemilli!" The teacher was glowing in no promising way. "Go to the pond of the courtyard and wash your face. When you are back, you will be retelling us what we learned of the first creation in our fifth world, everything we had learned about it this morning."

Out of habit, she rolled her eyes and didn't care how angered the teaching priestess grew, even though this one was a nice woman, not like the ugly hag that taught the girls back in Tlatelolco. In the mornings, not at night! Filthy Tlazotli!

Outside, it was delightfully bright as opposed to the semidarkness of the classroom with its partly closed shutters. Elated at being allowed in the courtyard with no supervision, however briefly, she looked around, hoping against hope. What if he was there, heading for the training grounds or sent to one of the temples, on his way to this or that destination? The vast space was empty, save for the servants cleaning the mosaic stones of the pond. The sun was as she expected, reaching its zenith, in no hurry to speed up its progress, not wishing to help. Of Miztli or other boys, there was no sight. Only the drone of monotonous voices, much like that of the priestess's, let her know that the boys' classes were inhabited as well.

Unable to fight the temptation, the slaves on their knees and rubbing the stones of the pond, wholly immersed, she crossed the abandoned yard hurriedly, then crept along one of the buildings, not knowing how to peek in without being detected. Or rather how to let him know that she was out and wishing to talk to him. Just a few hurried questions. She was allowed to ask how the Texcocan man was, or how he, Miztli, was for that matter, wasn't she?

The wall opening was half shuttered like the one in their class. Chewing her lips, she hesitated, then ventured toward the next smaller building, the voices of the lecturing teacher stronger, rolling out in a dull flow. Just as she neared it, it rose, then the footsteps rustling inside made her jump backwards and toward the corner of the building, pressing to the pleasant coolness of its plaster, heart thundering.

The youths who came out did so hurriedly, breaking into a fast walk toward the first building she had skulked around, disappearing into the dimness of its entrance, the bundles they carried looking cumbersome. She hesitated, then crept back toward the opening. There were more voices coming out of it now, boys talking and not only the teacher.

Just as she rounded the corner, it turned quieter again, and to the immensity of her disappointment, the shutters above her head screeched into closing. Jumping back out of instinct, she bumped full length into a youth who was rounding the same corner, carrying another cumbersome-looking parcel. It went down with a bang, but the youth caught her arm first, making sure that she didn't follow suit. Which she might have, she reflected numbly, fighting for balance, disoriented for a moment.

"Fire Girl?" he cried out, astounded, then dropped to his knees, collecting the scattered batons; training swords with no obsidian, a fleeting glance told her. "What are you doing here?"

That other youth from the warring upon the roofs of the

Tlatelolco marketplace? She blinked, trying to remember his name. Something with "water" in it; "a"-something. Axolin? Through the last moon in Tenochtitlan, she had seen this one in Necalli's company from time to time, but not enough to come to know him. Back above the warring marketplace, he was quiet and reticent, barely there, saying little, staring much. There was some tension between him and Miztli, a tension that disappeared after a while. She had been too busy back then to ask questions about it.

"What are you doing here?" he repeated. "The girls aren't allowed..." Then he shrugged and fell silent, but his lips twisted in a knowing grin. "I suppose the rumors about you aren't exaggerated."

"What rumors?"

He shrugged again. "They say you make trouble, do whatever you like." His grin kept spreading. "Not surprising, given the circumstances of our acquaintance with you. And the workshop boy."

She rolled her eyes, not concerned with any of it, yet not about to miss her opportunity. "Where is Miztli? In that class out there with you?"

His grin was gone. "What?"

"ItzMiztli, is he with you in there? I need to send him word. You must have ways to whisper to him or something, let him know that I'm out here."

He blinked somewhat stupidly. "You are asking me to send him out here to meet you? Now, in the middle of the classes?"

"Yes!" Was it really that hard to understand? She made a face at him. "It can't be that difficult. I need to speak to him. For a little while, not for half a day."

"Look," he said, grimacing like a teacher before a particularly slow student. "First of all, no, he isn't there in this class, or any other. Just after dawn, the royal warriors came to take him away. For his usual imperial errands, I suppose." He rolled his eyes tellingly, but there was a slight touch of resentment to his words now. "Necalli would be pissed to learn he had missed out on any of it. Bad timing the Emperor picked."

She stopped listening, the wave of fear sudden and

unwelcome, bringing dreadful suspicion. What if the Emperor learned about their involvement in the place of the animals and the mess they had left behind? What if he was now charging Miztli with something; transgression, resistance, anything? "Royal guards? But... Did they... I mean, did they drag him off or something? Did they..."

He blinked, then remained staring, wide-eyed. "No, why would they? The Emperor likes using him for all sorts of unusual errands. You must know that, of all people."

"Yes, I know." She tried to calm the wild pounding of her heart. "So he was here at night, yes?"

"I suppose so." He shrugged with a new bout of resentment. "I'm not keeping an eye on him or his movements, you know. Necalli would know, but he is not here either. He is on the mainland, fasting and preparing to become a warrior." That came out even more bitterly.

"Yes, I know that too." She shifted her weight from one foot to another, deeply disappointed. "Well, when Miztli is back, tell him to find me. I need to talk to him."

He ran his free hand through his somewhat ruffled lock of hair. "Look, Fire Girl. I'll tell our glorious commoner that you've been looking for him, yes, but..." His nostrils widened as he blew the air through them. "You know, you really shouldn't run around and flaunt your interest in him that openly. What they are saying about you now is nothing compared to what they'll be saying if you've been caught doing inappropriate things with him. And even if you don't, your name can be slandered so easily now. Think about it." His shoulders lifted lightly, as though reluctantly. "Good girls do not sneak into main parts of our *calmecac* in search of boys. Let alone commoners whose right to be here is questionable in the best of cases. Your nobility out there in the Palace would be appalled, and your noble fellow other student girls will have a field day spreading your bad name everywhere. Don't you see it? It's so obvious."

He was looking at her sincerely, not admonishing or even patronizing. Still, his words hurt.

"He'll be allowed to take me to be his woman after he is

through with school."

His laughter shook the air. "Don't be ridiculous."

"I'm not!" Unable not to, she stomped her foot, incensed with them all, this well-meaning youth included. "The Emperor gives him important missions even now when he is so young. When he is a warrior, he will be rewarded. He will become nobility like your friend's father. Necalli told me about his father! He was not always a nobleman, not until he was rewarded for his bravery on the battlefield."

"Yes, I know about Necalli's father. He was never a villager from gods-forsaken fields, a peasant who couldn't even read or write. Necalli's father came from a respectable family of this city before he was rewarded with lands and noble titles."

"So what?" She stomped her foot once again. "Miztli will be rewarded anyway. He is the bravest and the Emperor knows it. You just wait and see!"

To storm away felt childish, but she couldn't help it. How dared they, her sister and this youth, and the others? How dared they berate him and say that he would never be a noble of this city, never would be allowed to claim her for himself. It was simply not true, it wasn't! They didn't understand or appreciate him, but she knew who he was. And the Tenochtitlan Emperor knew it too. And he wouldn't be too snobbish or uptight to give a reward where a reward was due. Even the highest of rewards, yes. There must be plenty of lands to offer to the promising new leaders, plenty of titles to attach to those. But could she wait until it happened? What if it took him many summers and rainy seasons to achieve that imperial favor, the highest of rewards?

The school fence towered ahead, arresting her progress, bringing in sounds of high-noon and the lively activity out there on the Great Plaza. She wondered if the delegation of foreigners were out there again, touring around and gawking like they did on the day before. The thick-branched tree near the curve in the fence rustled with the light breeze, reminding her of the niche where they tucked their notes for each other to find. It was empty, even though on the day before she crammed another note in there, a funny letter that told the story of Smoking Mountain lovers with a different ending of her making. It would not be easy to read, she knew, but he would manage, working harder, yes, but happily. She planned to be around and help in case he needed explanations.

The wave of longing made her stomach hurt. Careful to bypass the girls' hall, in case the priestess sent someone to look for her, angered with her unauthorized absence in addition to the previous crime of falling asleep in the middle of the creation story, she sneaked toward the opening in the fence, her instincts of an experienced eavesdropper guiding her, letting her know that the courtyard was again completely abandoned, save for a few busy slaves, cleaning various parts of the front patio.

A lonely figure was coming through the narrow entrance, waking tiredly, studying the ground, and when she saw him, she broke into a wild run, careless of the need to keep quiet, heedless of possible prying eyes or angered authorities. None of these mattered, as all of a sudden, he was here, coming in and just as she needed to see him most.

He halted abruptly and was staring at her, and as she managed to arrest her own progress but barely before bumping into him, her sandals made a screeching sound upon the cleanly swept ground, like charging warriors back in Tlatelolco. And like back there, he leapt forward, catching her in case she wavered, and the previous bad feelings disappeared and she pressed to him, relishing his touch, and his warmth and his smell, very clean as opposed to their night adventures, delightfully crisp and fresh.

"Where have you been?" she demanded, her smile impossible to conquer, the good feeling prevailing now, all previous misgivings forgotten. "I was looking for you all over!"

"Where were you looking?" he asked, his smile as broad, blossoming out of his pale, bruised face, worse than when she saw him off and into the fancy litter of Lady Jade Doll, his eyes ringed darkly, their exhaustion showing. Then his gaze leapt around, wariness itself. "What are you doing out here?"

"Looking for you, you silly. I just told you." She refused to let her happiness dim. "There. We'll be safe behind our tree. I saw that you found my note from the day before. I just checked and it was missing."

To pull him after her and toward her favorite hideaway turned easy. He followed quite eagerly, without resistance.

"I didn't read it, not yet," he confessed, hastening his own step, clearly as eager to dive into the relative protection of their favorite corner, not adequately secluded, but better than in the middle of the courtyard or the patio of the entrance. The priestess must be livid by now, she thought absently, not caring. As long as they had even if just a few heartbeats for themselves and he was here, with her, looking unharmed.

"How it was with the Emperor?" she asked, enjoying the thickest of the shadow, leaning against the slightly damp poles of the inner fence.

He made a face, something between a frown and a grin. "Not easy. Like always." Then he sobered abruptly. "He is a great man, so very wise and patient. He can see through people easily. I still don't know how I got away without telling it all, about the gardens and the animals and the Texco—and Honorable YaoTecuani. The Emperor, he looks at you with such hard eyes, straight inside you and you just know he sees through you and your lies, and that... well, it's like you disappoint him with this. And I didn't, didn't want to disappoint, not him—"

"You told him about the night?" She cut into his speech, briefly horrified. "About the place with the animals, and that, that man with *cipactli*..."

"No, no, I didn't! He didn't even ask." His hand leapt up hurriedly, defensive. "I was just afraid that he would, but he kept asking about that other thing, the delegation, and well..." His throat moved jerkily as he evidently swallowed hard. "The Texcocan, he told me important things, things that helped me. It pleased the Emperor, that news, so he was busy asking about it. He wants me to be on your side of the Palace again this evening, to listen some more." He shrugged with less enthusiasm than before. "Hope I won't just fall asleep there and get kicked out. Those people, they are so rude. Worse than old Tlaquitoc's sons." His face darkened some more. "It's nasty to be a servant. I never want to do it for real." Another pause. "Or even as a pretense, like this time. But the Emperor wishes me to do that. I wish he didn't."

Sensing his agitation, she caught his arm in hers, wishing to ask about that "old Tlaquitoc" business – it was the workshop man of the wharves, wasn't it, the commoner girl's father – yet somehow knowing that it was not the time.

"You will never be a servant, ever. Of course you won't! And the Emperor should not ask you to pretend to be one. Because you are too good for that. You are a warrior, a brave, fearless warrior and at the age that other boys can barely wave a stick with no obsidian in it." The troubled creases of his forehead were smoothing, the glow of his eyes intensifying as always when looking at her from such close proximity, softening the dark rings, banishing the gloom and the lines of exhaustion. As always, it took her breath away. "You are brave and noble," she went on, enjoying this familiar sensation whenever he looked at her thus brought. It made her stomach shrink as though under an invisible ring and leave her with nothing but this fluttering expectation, the anticipation of what he'd do next scary and wonderful, disturbing, promising, the mere thought making her knees go weak. It was good that he usually held her close at those times, not about to let go. "The Emperor will make you noble for real. You just wait and see."

His lips were dry, cracked at places; still, their touch was the most wonderful, strong and strangely demanding, a perfect opposite to his usual shy demeanor, his hesitation and lack of belief in himself. As though the bottomless pit in her stomach was not enough, it made her head reel.

"I needed to see you," he murmured, not taking is lips away, their faces touching, breaths mixed. "I just needed to see you. I always need this. After all the filthiness, all the bad; it's nothing when you are here. Everything bad goes away."

"I know," she muttered, leaning against him with all her weight now, her legs unable to support her. "I needed to see you as badly. That's why I sneaked away now. Or even went to school this morning." Tossing her head backwards, she laughed into his eyes, liking the way they crinkled now, full of that atypical confidence only his kisses radiated, making him look irresistibly handsome. "I didn't have to come here, so you know. Citlalli told me to stay and sleep. But I wanted to see you, to hear what you and that man of Texcoco were up to." The snicker became difficult to hold in. "Later, I regretted it, of course. When the priestess put me to sleep with her stories of the worlds' creation. I dropped off for real, I swear. She was mad! That's why she sent me out to—"

"You fell asleep in the class?" he exclaimed, looking like a child shown a trick, all eyes and frightened admiration.

"Oh yes, I did. So deeply that I didn't even notice they were talking to me or staring." Leaning backwards in order to see him better, she observed him now from a distance of his arms' length, knowing that he didn't mind holding her, even if in less comfort than before. "The priestess had to yell my name. Only then, I woke up to all their gaping. Then she sent me out to wash my face and come back to recite everything there is to know about Revered Tonatiuh jumping into the sacred fire when Tecciztecatl wouldn't." She snorted happily. "She is still waiting for that to happen, as I went looking for you instead."

All sorts of expressions chased each other across his face, from awe to astonishment, to an open delight. "You didn't!"

"Oh yes, I did. Ask Chantli if you don't believe me. She was there and saw it all."

"Chantli?" His merriment drained off all at once. "Did she come to school today?"

"Yes, of course. Why wouldn't she?"

He kept frowning dourly. "Did she tell you... something, anything?" To her deep disappointment, his eyes slipped away, his face filling again with gloom, losing its magical radiance. "She wouldn't come to school if her brother or someone of her family died, would she? People here don't do this, yes?"

"What?" she asked, irritated but not moving away. "What do you mean? Who died?"

"No one, maybe." He shrugged and didn't try to push her out of his arms either. Which improved her deteriorating mood considerably. Why would they discuss Chantli just now? "But her brother, he got stabbed at night. Stabbed badly, in his side. Deep, scary wound. The healer woman stitched it, but it really looked bad. Even the healer said so."

"Was it when you and the man of Texcoco were in the city?" she asked, frightened against her will.

"Yes. Don't ask me how they all ended up to be where we were, and involved." He shook his head forcibly, as though trying to get rid of all the thoughts. "It was bizarre, all of it. Worse than back in the Palace. It couldn't—"

Outside in the courtyard, probably near the pond and not the girls' hall and their improvised hideaway, conversations burst out, many voices talking at once. He tensed and fell silent, and she pressed closer, knowing that the right thing to do was to separate while heading out each their own way, all innocence and pretense. Still, it felt safer in his arms. Did the priestess send out servants to search for her? Or rather asked other schoolboys, as the voices were young and babbling, pouring from the main part of the school premises.

"Did they finish their lessons?" she whispered, feeling his nod, a tension-filled motion.

"Sometimes after midday, yes," he breathed. "The training grounds, they are going there now. Or out on errands."

"Out on errands" did not spell anything good. Those heading for the opening in the fence would be passing close, liable to peek into this neglected corner if they wished to do so. They never huddled here before. Only placed messages.

"If we stay and don't move..." she whispered.

"Let them get busy training, then we'll slip you out," he finished for her, pressing her tightly.

She giggled. "*I* was going to say that!"

His chest trembled lightly against hers, suggesting a desired reaction. She smiled to herself, proud at making him laugh even in such pressing moment. He was always so serious but never with her, was he?

"Did you read my note?" she whispered, getting bored by the need to keep quiet.

He shook his head, a smile in his whisper. "I told you I didn't. But I will. I had no time."

"No time, huh?" She moved to make herself comfortable while

still facing him. "You just didn't manage. It was a difficult story, admit it. But you'll love the ending. I made it up all for you."

"You made it up? The ending? How so?"

"Easily. That Smoking Mountain, remember I told you about those lovers? Well, they didn't die in my ending. But maybe they had better." She snickered too loudly, unable to hold her excitement in. "Don't try to peek at the bottom of the page. Do it properly, from the beginning. Promise? No peeking!"

His chuckle caressed the air. "I promise. Maybe. Or maybe I'll just—"

More voices poured all around, from closer proximity now, the girls' hall contributing female voices to the general hum. The training grounds further away radiated steady clamor, yet enough boys' shouting burst from their side of the schoolyard as well.

"They are looking for me," she whispered, feeling cornered all of a sudden, even afraid.

Grateful for his arms that pressed her with more force, feeling ridiculously protected, she heard a girl crying out from too close, as though standing on the other side of their tree, eager to confirm all her fears.

"Did she run away from school? I can't believe it!"

"Maybe. She is wild enough to do that. Or maybe..." Tlazotli's lilting chirping was impossible to mistake, dripping smug satisfaction. "Maybe she is still here, hiding. There is that place I saw her sneaking into once..." The shuffling of the nearing footsteps left them with little to doubt, or to hope for.

"Where?" asked another voice eagerly, this one of a boy, familiar somehow, bringing unpleasant memories. She felt Miztli tensing worse than before and his arms steering her backwards and away, just a few paces to the fence, its poles coarse to touch, offering possibilities. His hands lifted her easily, like they always did, and without the need to coordinate their actions, she grabbed the top of the low beam, pulling herself up, wishing to be of help.

Then rustling bushes and footsteps were upon them, and the voices that momentarily died away, replaced by stunned silence. She didn't find enough courage to look back. The silence hung for another heartbeat, then another.

"I can't believe it," someone breathed in the end, a girly voice, its shock genuine.

"Of all things," said another, this one belonging to a boy, this same unpleasantly familiar tone.

Curious against her will, she turned back, then jumped down as though there was nothing more natural in the world to do but to climb fences in the middle of the school day and with the help of a boy. Miztli was frozen beside her, staring back at them and not moving a limb, maybe not even breathing. Tossing her head high, she returned their stares as well, taking in their amount, a few pairs of boys and two girls, Tlazotli's well-defined eyes sparkling, agog with excitement.

"I can't believe it," the girl breathed again. "In my wildest of dreams..." Two red spots glared upon her chiseled cheeks, standing out ridiculously. For some reason, it angered Tlemilli more than anything else.

"Your wildest of dreams interest no one," she retorted. "Go and dream somewhere else, you empty-headed heap of fat!"

As expected, the open attack silenced the venomous snake, but the burly boy she remembered from the Plaza and their last nasty encounter stepped forward, undeterred. His hair was shorter than usual, an open imitation of the warriors' hairdo, and he towered above his surroundings, his muscles bulging everywhere the eye could see.

"So, stinking piece of commoner meat," he said slowly, as though savoring every word. "The smelly peasants straight away from their excrement-filled fields are laying hands on the noble whores these days, against every rule of this noble establishment, eh?" The nastily sweet smile kept spreading and she heard Tlazotli giggling, over her previous setback, enjoying the break in the boring day. "The Tlatelolcan nobility is questionable, yes, and their sanity is even more so. Still, smelly peasants smelling from carrying their buckets of night excrements, pawing highborn whores..."

"Shut your stinking mouth up!" hissed Miztli in a voice she had difficulty recognizing, so low-pitched, like the growl of one of those caged jaguars from the nightmarish night.

"You shut up, you stinking low-born worm fit for collecting refuse on each dawn, and not even this!" cried out the taller boy, taking a step forward, the training sword clutched tightly in both arms, ready to be of use. Tlemilli gasped and moved closer. "You stinking slave from the worst of the slums, you—"

In the corner of her eye, she saw Miztli moving with his entire body, closing the few-paces distance as though it wasn't there, following his shooting out fist, leaping after it. As it slammed against the taller boy's head, it made a dull sound, and so did the gasp of the others who had crammed into their private corner, more and more pushing in, attracted by the commotion, while the foul-mouthed mound of muscles collapsed into the dust as hopelessly as a slab of stone pushed with just enough force.

Not daring to blink, she watched the limp body hitting the dusty ground, shuddering for a moment, then going completely motionless, hopelessly still. The renewed bout of shocked silence prevailed, with only the buzz of the day's insects and the clamor from the rest of the school grounds remaining to reassure her that the Fifth World did not end like the previous ones.

Miztli shifted as though about to kick the inanimate body, then grew as still as his victim, frozen in the same dread as the rest of them were, his face nothing but a chiseled mask, the strong line of his jaw throbbing from the force with which he must have clenched it. His eyes shifted briefly, brushing past their shocked audience, appraising, haunted, challenging, frightened and daring at the same time, a combination that jerked her out of her stupor at once, made her grab his arm firmly, squeezing it with both hands, relaying a message. She was there and with him, not intending to go or move to the enemy's side. Never that! The way his fingers wrapped around hers in an open desperation, hurting, made her heart double its racing, spreading wonderful warmth. He knew, and he appreciated.

Then her eyes caught a glimpse of one of the veterans followed by a pair of priests pushing their way in and the temporary sense of wellbeing evaporated at once.

CHAPTER 18

The dusk was yet to arrive, his eyes told him, glued to the half closed shutters, the wall opening too small to squeeze through, had he dared to play with such ideas. Which he didn't. There was nowhere to run, nowhere to hide in this enormous and crowded city, with so many houses and people, one couldn't count those even if one used twenty *amate*-paper sheets and all the symbols and intricate laws of adding up numbers they taught their *calmecac* pupils, the future leaders and rulers.

Still, he could not get away from paying for what he did, with his life probably, or maybe something even more dreadful. What? What could they do to him for such an outright assault, a possible killing? Had that filthy Acoatl died by now, or had he come back to his senses? Or maybe he had died back when it happened, lying there so motionlessly, so blissfully still.

He shuddered, then took his eyes off the slivers of dimming light, glancing at his surroundings, finding nothing new there. He had plenty of time to eye it all, the discarded old shafts, the half opened crates, the occasional slightly cracked pottery. Since the tightlipped, dangerously silent veteran warrior who was teaching spear-throwing and how to handle *atlatls* and who was usually nice to him, patient and well meaning, but not anymore, had brought him here, half escorted, half dragged, the man's fingers leaving marks on his upper arm where they held on to their prisoner too tightly, he had been here, curled in the corner, relieved to be left alone and away from all eyes. It could have been worse, he reasoned, remembering the brawl of two other boys half a moon ago, upon which both culprits were left out there, tied and on display until the authorities decided how to punish them, for other students to watch and beware. A dreadful punishment. He had been all nerves earlier, afraid that they would change their minds, drag him out after all, to serve as an example and determent for other violent hotheads, but now it had been already well into the afternoon, with no one left to watch his humiliation and learn from it should the authorities decide to go harder on him before determining his final fate. Oh mighty deities!

Hiding his face in the space his folded knees created, he shut his eyes, reliving the terrible moment. Having survived the interview with the Emperor without letting any of the terrible night's details out, so very pleased and elated, he had gone back to *calmecac* mainly in order to see her, or at least to try to do that. She would wish to hear all about it, and about the man of Texcoco and what happened at the strange healer woman's house, and about his brother. Also of course about the Emperor and his appreciation of the information he brought, the information the man of Texcoco had given him for the benefit of them both and their goals and not out of pure kindness, as the man bothered to state with his typical careless straightforwardness. Such an outstanding person, so deep and complex, with so many puzzling intentions and goals, and yet so genuine and sincere, exceptionally kind, with not a drop of pretense to him. Could this man help him out? Would he?

In a short while, the light would be gone, replaced with yet another merciful darkness. Should they leave him here until then, could he try to sneak away before the inhabitants of this school returned? Run into the city, find the Texcocan as he was supposed to do anyway, ask for his help in escaping, never to return. But then Tlemilli would be lost to him forever, and Necalli and others, the Emperor, the school. No, he could not be perceived as a coward, a fleeing commoner with no honor or principles. Necalli would never respect him if he did this. Even Tlemilli with her openly professed affection and loyalty. She would turn away from him like she did from her father, in a matter of heartbeats, and with no regrets. She had admired this man so much, tried to explain his dishonorable behavior, but not after he let her down, did something dishonorable to her taste. Then it was over and with no way back.

His chest was squeezing once again, tightening under an invisible ring. She had insisted on staying with him, facing the others so fearlessly, with fire in her eyes; not even thinking to step away and let him deal with the mess of his own doing. Not her! She was about to argue with the veteran who had taken him away, until he motioned her not to, promising with his eyes alone to solve it all and come back for her. An impossible promise. He had no way of dealing with it, and they were right. She was too good for him, too noble, too highly connected to this same Tenochtitlan royal house and not only her Tlatelolcan one. Like her snobbish sister, she was too high-born to be given to a mere commoner, the stinking peasant from dung-covered fields, fertilized indeed with human waste mostly. How did those snotty nobles of the city who did not see any fields at all know? That dirty Acoatl, but did he keep harboring on it. And yet, it was he who had been unforgivably violent this time, with no cause and no reason, he who had been in the wrong. He could have gone on answering the filthy piece of excrement, fencing with likewise curses that Necalli was so good at inventing, defending his dignity with words and no actions. The schoolyard was no dark alley; the cowardly piece of meat wouldn't attack. And yet he called Tlemilli a whore. Twice he used this word while trying to humiliate him in her eyes.

The sound of his grinding teeth was annoying, tearing the silence. Then hurried footsteps joined it, heading from the direction of the pond, quite a few sandaled feet. His stomach was nothing but a chunk of ice, and when the wooden screen shuddered, then screeched, and he could see a cloaked silhouette coming in, followed by another two, his heart made a wild flip inside his chest, trying to jump out, thundering in his ears. The length of the cloaks and the symbols of the royal house upon them were impossible to mistake.

"Come," said the leading man curtly, neither hostile nor friendly. "Quick, boy. On your feet and out and follow closely."

He did his best to comply, his limbs somewhat watery, not the steadiest of supports. However, the schoolyard was, indeed, blissfully empty, and he thanked all deities for that. The back alleys the warriors chose did not bring them into the usual evening commotion as well, unwilling to push their way through the well-dressed crowds strolling about, enjoying the coolness of the near-dusk, exchanging talks and pleasantries, ladies in their litters unless busy preparing for an evening feast, not an everyday occurrence, according to Tlemilli.

Tlemilli! His heart was again trying to make complicated moves, getting out of tempo, filling with memories of their afternoons, sneaking around these same alleys with her or out there in the city with Necalli and a few others, happy, carefree – well, to a degree, in his case. Never again now? Oh mighty deities!

The back gate of the Palace's wall seemed to be their destination. Briefly, he wondered about it, remembering being let in through the luxurious front entrance even when on his first visit here, barefoot and barely dressed, smeared with the melting room excess and swaying with exhaustion. The warriors even expressed their doubts about it back then. Yet, why was he led through the back gate now?

A maze of corridors and halls, the royal side of the Palace again. He kept his back as straight as he could, remembering the *calmecac* lessons. A captured warrior goes to his fate with dignity and pride, his only way to retrieve his honor is through sacrifice. No other way. No escape. Only two moons ago, he wouldn't even know what it was, honor and sacrifice, their sacred warriors' code, the worshipped hand-to-hand, the strict rules to conducting oneself, better to die with honor than live dishonored. Not even a comparison. Did he feel like they felt now, or was it just a rehearsed role? Elotl would have laughed himself sick now, not understanding a word of it, ridiculing it all.

Elotl! Waiting somewhere out there, under the temporary protection of the ferocious man of Texcoco. Would he help his brother reach home in case of... Oh well! But for the chance to see Tlemilli, to pass through her side of the Palace, to tell her... what?

"Stay here, boy, and don't move a limb."

The room he had been partly conducted and partly pushed into was spacious, with cushioned mats and low tables aplenty. Blissfully empty, it gave him time to collect himself, to pull his thoughts into a semblance of order. Would the Emperor wish to see him in relative privacy like always? But why? What would this formidable man tell him? About his disappointment, his dissatisfaction with the commoner he gave such an unheard-of chance in life? Oh mighty deities, but he would be better off facing impartial courts and the most cruel of their judges. Any punishment was better than this!

The sun was still there, hovering, as though in no hurry to leave, as though curious to see what would happen. He watched the dim slivers playing upon the painted walls with their depiction of this or that deity, a stern squatting figure of many different limbs. She said she had fallen asleep while listening to the story of Tonatiuh being blown across the sky by Quetzalcoatl. Or was it something different concerning the creation of this current Fifth World? They had been studying this same subject under the elderly priest only a few dawns ago, the lessons he actually enjoyed now that it became easier to at least guess some of the books' paintings, the mystery of deciphering glyphs never wearing off, making his insides thrill. One day, he would read them all as easily as Tlemilli or Necalli did, would write her notes the length of entire scroll.

His stomach was again knotted in a hundred painful knots, and it didn't help that at this very moment, the broad silhouette shadowed the doorway, unmistakable in its imposing bearing, the bold confidence of its stride.

"Leave us," said the Emperor curtly, motioning the servants away before they had time to burst in, evidently anxious to take care of appropriate arrangements. "Stay in the shouting range but nowhere near the entrance. Is that clear to you?"

Several nervous voices burst with muttered words of consent. Miztli tried to will his heart into renewed beating, as it had gone alarmingly still, sliding down his stomach as though trying to hide there. The gaze in the Emperor's eyes did this, impartial and aloof, piercing and yet openly measuring, penetrating, gauging.

Was the man reading his inner thoughts again? What did he see there? Nothing promising, surely.

"So, young commoner, you've been brought here again, causing me to interrupt my busy day with no valuable reason this time." The penetrating gaze didn't thaw. "What do you have to say for yourself?"

Miztli drew a deep breath, wishing to have a gulp of water to moisten his throat with. It suddenly became like a hillside with no vegetation during the moons of no rain. The silence, but why was it so deep, so encompassing? Every heartbeat of it spelt disaster, yet he had absolutely nothing to say in the way of response. It was not of his choosing, those Palace's visits, both of them. He didn't mean to waste the Emperor's precious time.

"Tell me what happened in the school and do it truthfully. All of it, boy!" This time, the authoritative voice rang with a measure of compassion, just a flicker of it, but more than enough to make his stomach unknot in order to draw in a breath.

"I... It was bad and I have no excuse for what happened. For what I did." Another deep breath seemed to be desperately needed. "I... I should not have hit... should not have lost my temper in the way I did. I have no excuses for that." Then he remembered and his back broke out in a bout of cold sweat. "Revered Emperor!"

The sternly pursed lips quivered in one corner. "What did that other student do to earn such a spectacular blow? A single one, wasn't it?"

"Yes." His throat was again shriveling into dry nothingness. "He... he was nasty with words, and he talked bad about Tlemilli. Called her terrible names. But... but he did not attack us. Not this time. It is impossible to do when in school. The teachers and other pupils. The *pilli*s, that is. And the priests. Everyone was out, the boys, that is, coming to train outside." He tried to stop the irrelevant flow, dismayed by the silly words that were pouring out of his mouth. "I shouldn't... I have no excuse."

"He didn't attack you this time, but at other times he did?" asked the man quite impartially, as though collecting the needed information. Like they said the judges in courts would. And wasn't the Emperor presiding over the highest Imperial Court?

"Well, yes. We had fought once, yes."

"If you choose to call it a fight." The pursed lips quivered again, this time stretching into a cold grin. "Five youths against one is not what we call honorable fighting. An ambush in a dark alley is not what a good warrior should seek or desire."

Miztli found himself gaping stupidly. "How... how did you know about..." he mumbled, then wished to swallow his tongue for good once again, the raised brows above the aloof gaze questioning his cleverness openly, challenging. "I... I'm sorry. I shouldn't have asked. Revered Emperor!"

The man shook his head and the frostiness left his features all at once. "As a matter of fact, you may be excused at being surprised. The Tenochtitlan Emperor has better things to do than to keep record on the schoolboys and their antics. Until they injure one another too seriously. Then it becomes an imperial matter, especially if the higher of the nobility gets involved. You should have hit one of your fellow gifted commoners into unconsciousness, boy." Then the smile returned, one-sided and decidedly crooked. "Ahuitzotl, my youngest and most spirited of siblings, spent too much of my time orating on your behalf earlier today, making a good defense that would not shame a witness testifying in the Imperial Court. All eloquence and well organized claims backed by names of possible witnesses." The smile was evening out, stretching wider, filling with surprising warmth. "This boy will go far, and when he occupies the reed woven chair of the imperial hall, he will not make this city ashamed. Anything but!" Shaking his head, the man sobered again. "But back to you and your troubles, young commoner. Regardless of my brother's fondness of you, his belief in your possible bright future, I wish you to understand something. What you did was, indeed, deplorable and has no excuse, as you so passionately stated before. Your lack of self-control is appalling, and while I can relate it to your humble background, your total lack of proper upbringing, and only hope that you will acquire enough discipline to become a warrior worthy of this city and its investment in you, I warn you. What happened in school today will not repeat itself, ever. People can and will call you or your loved ones names and you will deal with it properly, in a way worthy of Tenochtitlan future warriors and leaders and not the marketplace brawler waving his fists. If you escape an outright punishment for what you have done this time, it will be mainly due to circumstances; not to any laxity in the laws that govern our schools, *calmecac* and districts' *telpochcalli* alike. Neither will it be a special treatment that you might hope to receive due to the somewhat efficient and useful ways that you serve me from time to time. Your reward for it is the mere possibility to join our noble school and enjoy the extensive learning and education it offers you, something you couldn't have dreamed to achieve otherwise. There will be no leniency, no special treatment. Is that clear to you, boy?"

Bereft of words, Miztli just nodded, his tongue refusing even to think of moving, let alone offering a worthwhile response, his hope soaring. May it be that he would be forgiven, not forced into courts and any other measure to discipline people who waved their fists with no self-control. Was this how the man put it, like a marketplace brawler? There were other ways to deal with verbal insults, he said. But what ways? He had seen Necalli and other *calmecac* boys spoiling for fights every time someone said something even remotely nasty, ready to wave their fists or actually waving them. But yes, not to such a degree. Father would be disappointed in him too for using the punch he had explicitly told never to use but only if his life was being threatened. It wasn't threatened this afternoon, unlike back on Acachinanco road. Only his honor was, his dignity, his self-respect. The wave of anger splashed, then broke under the Emperor's penetrating gaze.

"Do you understand what I'm talking about, commoner boy? Will you follow my advice in all your future dealings?"

"Yes, Revered Emperor. I will. I thank you... thank you for taking your time... to talk about it, to explain..."

The man nodded thoughtfully, pacified in a way. "Good." Then the pursed lips quivered again, this time with pronounced, almost mischievous, amusement. "That punch that you knocked our spectacular ballplayer out with, was it a coincidence, or do you know how to use your fists to such a telling effect?"

"My father, he taught me, yes, all of us."

The amusement fled, replaced with a matter-of-face concentration. "Your father? Is he a warrior?"

"No, no. He just... just works the land. And digs in the hills, to bring out copper and other things to melt. Or sell."

"Obsidian? Precious stones?"

"Well, yes, also. But rarely. It's mostly green copper and granite sometimes."

"I see." The Emperor nodded thoughtfully, almost politely, as though unwilling to terminate a slightly boring conversation. "Well, boy, your unusual fighting skills, those powerful punches included, might come in handy on the mission I'm willing to trust you with. It will be more complicated than your previous errands in Tlatelolco, but the main purpose will remain the same. Your command of the southern tongues could not have come at a better time. Do you speak any other besides the Matlatzinca dialect?"

He shook his head helplessly. "No, only the way the Matlatzinca people speak."

"That'll be enough." His contemplative mood gone, the Tenochtitlan ruler nodded resolutely. "You'll be heading toward your south this very evening, boy. With enough means, cocoa beans, and other ways of paying your keep to last you for a moon or two." The hard eyes were boring at him, forcing his concentration. "You will spend half of this time in Tenantzinco, wandering about, pretending to be whoever you will see fit to pretend, listening to people and what they say. Remembering everything! Everything that can be of use to me, or you suspect that can be of use." The penetrating gaze wouldn't stir. "For the duration of another moon, you will travel to their rivaling town called Tollocan, the one that they came to complain about. Tollocan and Matlatzinco, the one that we call Calixtlahuaca." The man nodded, as though to himself. "Wander around those would-be city-states, listen to what their people on their marketplaces gossip about, what are their thoughts regarding Tenochtitlan and our Great Capital's possible involvement. If it's possible, try to find out what are their war preparations, how many warriors they could, or are willing to, send into battle against Tenantzinco and how many if our Capital gets involved. It should not be hard to acquire some of this information. On the marketplace, people are always gossiping." A smile enlivened the chiseled mask, even if momentarily. "They say you can read and write these days, something you didn't manage to do before. Well, this is an important knowledge and I'm glad you invested in your studies and not only your martial training. It's good to know that you do not treat my advice lightly." The smile flickered again, this time one-sided, holding little mirth. "Write it all down, so you will not forget important parts, the number of their warriors, the lay of their land. I hope you attended enough relevant lessons to be able to draw a map. If not, do it now, study the maps I will give you while journeying toward your current destination. Draw in the same vein, paintings of important places around those towns, places you think I may be interested in seeing in order to use for my warriors to camp or to pitch a battle. I'll expect a few such maps from you, more than one sheet of *amate*-paper that will help you to tell me all that you learned through the next moon or two. Do you think you will manage?"

His head reeling, hard to take it all in, Miztli took a deep breath. "Yes, Revered Emperor. I can try to do all that, yes. It shouldn't be difficult."

His mind rushed ahead, thinking of details, frantic with worry but excited too. All those places to travel, to wander about and with enough means to buy food – actually buy it! – on marketplaces and such, like a great aristocrat. And those prominent towns like Cuauhnahuac that he only would hear about, so influential, prominent, beyond reach, but now just that, towns, not in the league of the Great Capital, not even near. Not frightening or intimidating either, not for him. And there might be an opportunity to detour through home. If he was to spy on Cuauhnahuac as well, certainly. Father would be able to tell him how to reach those other troublemaking cities, wouldn't he?

"Cuauhnahuac. This city, it was mentioned by the delegation. The conversation I told you about. Revered Emperor!" he added hastily, worried. The Emperor's gaze was not steering, narrowing again. "Maybe I should spend a little time there too. Listening to what they say. They might be involved. What happens in the south affects them."

"Of course it does. Cuauhnahuac is an important regional center, involved in everything that is happening in those fertile areas." The man nodded slowly, deep in thought. "It has been under Tenochtitlan's rule for too many summers to suspect it of possible disloyalty. However..." The decorated shoulders lifted in a shrug, making the bracelets surrounding well-muscled upper arms ring. "By all means, spent some time in Cuauhnahuac as well. This town will be well on your way." The stern mask broke with a surprisingly warm smile, suddenly a replica of Ahuitzotl's way of grinning mischievously. "Good thinking, boy; and a right spirit of going about serving me and my capital, with more broad thinking than blind following of orders. You may go far yet, young commoner." The muscled arms rose again, this time in order to clap, clearly summoning the servants back. "If you manage to do this to my satisfaction, you will be allowed to join this war, and in no auxiliary capacity. You have fought in enough clashes and skirmishes to earn an official right to use your newly acquired obsidian sword. The battles out in the countryside are different, more challenging, more rewarding. You'll find it of an interest."

Miztli caught his breath. "Necalli... will be allowed to join too? He was taken to the warriors' quest just now, and..." His words trailed off under the suddenly chilling gaze.

"Your friend has his own fate, his own destiny to follow," said the Emperor coldly. "Do not intercede on other people's behalf, ever. It is not your place to do that." As the broad back shadowed the narrow entrance once again, it hesitated, eyeing the servants who hovered nearby, waiting for instruction. "Leave the Teconal's daughter at peace as well, young commoner. This girl is difficult enough to handle without you to complicate the matters along. Do not try to contact her or pursue her otherwise. When you are older and earned your right to be called a warrior, I may reconsider."

The man was gone, dissipating in the dimness of the paneled

corridor, already lit by torches tucked along its decorated walls. Not daring to blink, or even breathe, for that matter, Miztli listened to the sounds of the drawing away footsteps, his heart fluttering in no semblance of order.

CHAPTER 19

The girl peeked through the woven branches of the fence just as Elotl neared it as well, contemplating his next step. To go back inside the house and try to fall asleep or to venture out and into the clamor of the early afternoon city, chancing more trouble?

The noise of the various alleys came here in force, especially when on the front patio, curiously tempting, making him think wild thoughts. Would he be able to find that alley where that girl lived? Would she be home and willing to see him? He just wanted to find out if she was well after the wild night that almost killed them all, to ask about that other man, the one who was stabbed. There was nothing wrong in his desire to know if they were fine, nothing inappropriate. Or was there?

The wounded warrior – such a formidable man, not to say scary! – had ordered him to keep low and quiet, not to move a limb until his brother came to fetch him. Back then, with Miztli scampering off to an indefinite destination, all mysterious about it, closemouthed and full of urgency, a man with purpose in life – nothing like his little brother back home! – and the others being still around but about to be sent back to their various dwellings as well, the girl and the workshop man, all Elotl wanted was to curl in the far corner and fall asleep. No difficult questions, no nagging wondering, not now. Maybe later, in the morning, when he was less tired and confused. So when the scar-faced warrior, with his bloodied clothes and back, told him to stay in this house and dare to venture not a word, let alone an action, he didn't feel like arguing. Grateful for being left alone, he had collapsed on the mat indicated to him, a nicely plump affair of tightly woven straw and reeds, a surprisingly soft thing to sleep on, completed with a blanket of even softer quality – nothing to complain about, not even remotely. There he had slept like a dead person for the remnants of the night and most of the morning and high noon, not caring about footsteps and voices, people running all over this outer room, talking and arguing sometimes, or crying out in pain. The healer woman was receiving her patients, a quick peek through his half shut eyelids told him, before he dove back into the dreamless slumber.

However, now he was wide awake, and dead hungry, and with no one in sight, neither the surprisingly seductive-looking healer, nor the scary man Miztli trusted so wholeheartedly. Were they asleep somewhere inside the house? Or did they go about their shady business out there in the city?

Imprudent as it was, he fought the temptation to follow the example, wishing to do something with himself, anything. To endure the torture of boredom was always the hardest of feats, since he could remember himself, especially on days of heavy rain, when cooped up inside the house, with nothing better to do than to needle his brothers and try to pick fights. Neither Tletl nor Miztli would ever complain of boredom, busying themselves with various house tasks, carving tools or polishing hammers and knives, annoying pieces of meat that they were. And yet, now Miztli was anything but bored, running somewhere out there, too busy to come back before afternoon as he promised, enjoying himself.

The aroma of something cooking, deliciously spicy and hot, came wafting through the cracks in the fence, making his stomach twist painfully. A skinny little girl came out, carrying a pot that was definitely too big and heavy for her sticklike limbs, emptying its contents into the nearby patch of grass with an open relief, hurrying back inside without giving him more than a curiosity filled glance. What did this one eat in the morning? A moldy tortilla, judging by the state her body was in. Still, he wouldn't refuse even this sort of treat; not even if it had been rolling in the dust, stepped upon. Damn inhospitable people!

The smell was back, stronger than before. Unable to fight the temptation, he neared the creaking opening, not as well kept as the rest of the fence was, then found himself staring at none other than the previous night's girl's prettily dimpled face, pale but fresh in the soft afternoon light, the most pleasant of sights.

"You are a sight for sore eyes," he told her happily, certain that she came here looking for him. Why else would she prowl around? "Happened to be passing by?"

She made a face, something between a frown and a smirk. "Who would have thought you would be still here, skulking around, not gone, or rather, kicked out."

"You. Obviously."

She snorted lightly, with a pronounced challenge. "Where you come from, is that all you do, loiter about and harass girls?"

"Mostly yes," he answered, unabashed, detecting no animosity that made him so mad with her back on the square after escaping the scary priest with too many questions. "Sometimes, when the girls are too busy to pleasure us, we go down the mines, bring out pretty things. All those stones you ladies like so much, green and shiny." There was no harm in such wild exaggeration; they did bring out an occasional pretty piece among all the boringly gray and greenish copper and such.

"Oh, so that's why you were so fond of those stones last night," she drawled, a hint of a smile curving her lips, which were full and tauntingly red, triggering inappropriate thoughts. "A pity the old witch has taken it," she added, dropping her voice considerably, to his immense relief. "Is she in there?"

"I don't know," he said, his frivolous mood evaporating as well. "I didn't see her back in the house when I woke up. And the scary warrior doesn't skulk anywhere around there either. Maybe they went out to hide those stones, or sell them." He eyed her baskets, which were quite a few, weighing her nicely exposed arms down. Her *huipil* was tight around her breasts, having difficulty holding it all in, plenty of treasures there, very well endowed. He forced his eyes away. "Where are you going?"

"Back home." She rolled her eyes, pouting in the fashion familiar from the previous night, yet not annoying now. "First Mother sent me to the marketplace with demands to bring half of their food alley back." She shifted her baskets showily. "First, she yells at me for half a morning for being a bad girl spending nights out there and all, then she doesn't let me, at least, to catch up on some sleep but makes me work like a slave in Father's workshop, cleaning it and bringing in things." Her head tossed challengingly. "You are lucky and have no cause to complain."

"I wasn't complaining," he said, irritated with her again but not enough to prevent him from stepping out and into the dusty alley, reaching for one of her baskets. "I'll help you take it home."

She regarded him with her arching eyebrows, but before he could grow angry again, the disputed basket was tucked into his hand, followed by another. "Come then. It's far enough from here and the old hag will be livid with me for not coming back in a hurry."

He tried to remember how long they had wandered on the previous night, when looking for their dubious destination. It had taken them some time to arrive here, to walk the endless maze of alleys and pathways, and sometimes incredibly wide and well-swept roads, and canals aplenty. But how huge this *altepetl* was, how enormously sprawling. Like walking all the way from Teteltzinco to Oaxtepec just to arrive from one cluster of alleys and houses to another. It made Oaxtepec look like his home village or worse. Probably that snotty Cuauhnahuac as well. Unbelievable. Still, he hoped that she didn't live too far. The short-tempered warrior would be pissed finding him gone, wouldn't he? And when Miztli came back, it could get really ugly if the man accused him of something.

The girl was eyeing him with her eyebrows still high.

"How far is it? Where you live, that is."

"Far enough, but not like to walk all the way to the Royal Enclosure."

"Royal enclosure? What's that?"

She grimaced in a cute sort of way. "You are not asking *that* seriously."

He shrugged, out of his depth again and not liking it. Royal enclosure, mysterious rituals in mysterious temples, tough warriors with bleeding wounds treating his brother like one of them, sending him on obscure missions, him and his club that he held with unshakable confidence. And that monstrously large city out there, making so much noise, full of so many people somewhere beyond this alley and those fenced houses, the clamor reaching, overwhelming even from far away.

"Come, it's truly not that far," the girl was saying, her eyes nicely tilted and large, twinkling with none of her previous tease. "Wherever you came from, you behave and talk like a creature from another world, not a dweller of our world of the Fifth Sun."

"Oh yes, I come from the Underworld. It's different down there."

She giggled, a nicely melodious sound. "I can imagine."

"Oh yes, we walk the valleys between those clashing obsidian mountains when we want to go somewhere," he went on, pleased with the effect, falling into her step easily, his misgivings forgotten. "It's easier than to sneak around your alleys and pathways, expecting robbers and thieves to pounce on you with their knives and clubs." Which brought another thought. "That skinny rat, the little thief, the one who stole the stones at the first place, do you know what happened to him?"

"That filthy little Azcatl?" She snickered again. "I bet he is out there, stealing other things. He has been on the streets since forever, that little rat. No need to worry about him."

"I wasn't worried. Just curious. He bolted away at the right moment, the little rat. As though he could smell trouble. And that fox that took us to the healer woman at the first place. She melted in the darkness like fog."

The girl snorted, hesitating at the small crossroad, then taking the pathway spreading to their left. "She was another street thing. One could see that most clearly. Who would have thought Ome would be messing with cheap marketplace whores. Pah!"

"Ome is the man who got stabbed?" he asked, embarrassed that he didn't remember to inquire about this one before. "How is he now?"

She shrugged with little feeling, if at all. "I obviously haven't been to their house this morning or noon, slaving like I did in my father's workshop. I'm not lucky like my sister, who spends her mornings in *telpochcalli* these days. Or better yet, like Chantli! That little snob I didn't see for days, busy with her noble school and ceremonies in the Royal Enclosure. With no time for her old friends that are now beneath her new status of the future priestess conducting rituals in temples."

He wondered about her sudden bitterness, and who in the name of all great and small deities was that snotty Chantli, busy with rituals and betraying her friends. Speaking of rituals! He snickered. "My brother thinks of nothing else as well these days. Silly things. Rituals and that school-thing. He could talk about little else last night, stupid elk."

Her snort could rival the clamor that burst upon them from yet another alley opening to their right, reminding him of the square where his troubles began on the evening before. It was somewhere nearby, wasn't it? Even now in the daylight, those surroundings looked familiar.

"Your brother is another tale, straight away from a storyteller drunk on *pulque* and crazy from chewing sacred *peyotl*," she exclaimed, hurrying into another alley and away from the clamor. "That one put even Chantli's story to shame. One moment sweating in the melting room, used by everyone and treated like the cheapest of slaves. The next, learning in *calmecac*, wearing a cloak and sandals and sporting a club or even an obsidian sword – I swear I saw him with that thing once, on the night when Tlatelolco fell! – running with *pillis* of noble families, and having that skinny bag of bones from the Tlatelolcan royal house falling all over him. And in front of everyone too, like the cheapest whore of the marketplace that was paid twice her worth."

He found himself staring. "What?"

"Yes, yes, I'm telling you!" She motioned him to keep up, her cheeks glowing crimson now, a pretty sight but for her words. "Chantli told me that this girl is the highest nobility, the daughter of the head adviser or some other pompous lowlife from out there in Tlatelolco. Before it fell, that is." Her shoulders, now free of burdening baskets, lifted testily. "Her sister was their emperor's lusty new wife who took him from our Noble Jade Doll. Imagine! And that other lanky bag of bones now has an eye for your brother, lowly villager that he is."

He halted abruptly once again. "Lowly villager? You better keep your stupid mouth shut when you want to talk about him like that!" It came out in a sort of an ugly bark, too loudly for even his consideration, now clouded with red-hot wave of rage, sudden yet familiar. But how dared she call any of them "lowly villagers"?

She blinked in confusion, one time, then another, staring back at him but with none of her typical spunky challenge. "What... what did I say?"

The wave of remorse was as sudden as the wave of rage before. It angered him even worse. "He is no 'lowly villager'! And neither am I! Your *altepetl* may be huge and ugly, but you are no nobility yourself. So you are no better than us. Especially Miztli, who is now a warrior and whatnot!" All sorts of expressions chased each other across her childishly disappointed face. He exhaled loudly, exasperated but mainly with himself. "Forget it! Let's go. I need to get back to the healer's house."

"You can't yell at me," she protested, refusing to move, her lips pursed but quivering, suggesting a struggle. Oh mighty deities, but a tearful fox was the last thing he needed to deal with! "You are... are nothing but a pushy foreigner involved in bad things, stolen stones and whatnot. You have no right to yell at me like they all do! You just can't—" Her voice broke, choked by the expected bout of tears.

A few passersby, two women with similar-looking baskets, and a man, glanced at them curiously. Another group bore down on them. He caught her with his free arm, pulling her into relative quietness of a smaller pathway. "Stop that, Quetzalli." Her name popped in his memory in the best of timing. "Don't cry. It's not the time, and I didn't mean to yell. Just stop!"

Somehow, she was pressed against him, enveloped by his free arm, enticingly soft and curvy, making his body react in no uncertain ways. Her hiccups alternated with quite pitiful sniffs; still, he enjoyed holding her like this, so well proportioned and trim, delightfully smooth to touch.

His thoughts swirled around in no semblance of order and no

logic or decency as well. He had to struggle against her stupid baskets to make her lift her head without letting them fall for good. She fought against him but only a little, and when his lips found hers, she reacted with such alacrity, he was left momentary breathless, cursing the damn baskets, craving to hold her with both hands in case she changed her mind and tried to break free. He just needed that kiss to continue.

In the end, they stopped due to the simple need to catch their breaths, staring at each other, panting, embarrassed to no end. Her leap aside was so ardent, her back collided with the beam of yet another fence of the narrow alley. Looking away, she began smoothing her blouse and he wished he had something as efficient to busy himself with. As it was, all he could do was shift her accursed baskets and then curse them some, wishing to be rid of this burden.

"We need to hurry," she informed him, not looking at him at all. "*Telpochcalli* boys will be getting out soon and you don't need any more bruises to add to your current collection." She rolled her eyes, then shrugged. "Also, First Mother will be furious with me more than she is right now. She'll complain to Father in the end."

"Who are *telpochcalli* boys?" he asked grimly, not liking her turning patronizing again. "No one will bruise me without going away looking twice as bad and worse!"

She side-glanced him briefly, then returned to watch the dusty stones they trod upon, heading back along the wider alley. "You are tough, one can see that. But they are always going around in groups. Rarely alone. Those who are looking for trouble, that is."

"I can take them even when grouped," he stated breezily, suddenly needing to impress her. She was changing fast, this strange city-girl; and silly that she might be, and in no position to call them "lowly villagers," she was still something of a mystery, not an unsophisticated fox from home, or like Metl's sister, all spice yes, but with no knowledge of real life beyond her family fields and their storage place for the entire neighborhood's crops, the envy of this part of Oaxtepec. In his turn, he side-glanced her as well, taking in the pleasant roundness of her profile, its lines soft and bold at the same time, and the swell of her breasts under the prettily decorated *huipil* of the sort one couldn't spot anywhere around Oaxtepec, even if one wandered that town for days.

"Maybe you can take them, yes," she drawled, again looking him over with measuring appreciation that made him straighten some more. "You are obviously older, and must have seen things in life. How old are you?" Shaking her head, she chortled. "You are nothing like your brother in your looks and behavior. Are you full brothers, or only through your father?"

"Stop talking silly," he demanded, flattered against his will. What she said sounded like a favorable comparison. Or maybe it was the way she said it. "I'll be counting twenty summers not long from now," he declared, exaggerating the truth by quite a few spans of seasons. His real count did not surpass seventeen as yet. Still, those "*telpochcalli* boys" must be much younger, maybe troublemakers of Miztli's age. Didn't this one talk about mysterious "schools" too and didn't this girl tell him that he was attending something inappropriately exclusive and noble but still a school?

"Twenty summers!" she exclaimed, suitably impressed. However now, surrounded by a more lively flow of people, some again with similar-looking baskets, he couldn't enjoy full benefits of her admiration. "How—"

Then her words died as two girls burst upon them, coming from the maze of yet another narrower pathway, running in the direction opposite to theirs, yet halting upon seeing them, staring at his companion, wide-eyed. Or at least one of them did, a very pretty girl, flushed but exquisitely attractive, with a face that would not shame a meticulously carved mask, all definite lines.

"Quetzalli!" she cried out, darting toward them. "I was looking for you all over!"

The other girl, an interesting sight as well, strangely angular and thin but nicely so, curiously attractive, even though offering no competition to her companion in looks, was busy panting, gasping for breath, in bad need to lean against something.

"We've been looking for you, Quetzalli," repeated the first girl, sounding accusing and pleading at the same time, as though about to grab her newfound friend and shake her hard. "You must help us find that healer you've been at all night. You must! Ome said that you would remember. He swore that you should know. He promised!"

"What?" Quetzalli blinked, her eyes turning ridiculously round. "What are you talking about, Chantli? What has come over you?"

"We must find the man of Texcoco, that scar-faced leader Necalli admires so. Ome said he was at the healer's, the woman who took care of his... his wound." At the last words, the girl gulped, then pursed her lips resolutely. "He said Miztli was there with this man. It's true, isn't it?"

"Well, yes, but..." Quetzalli's eyes narrowed with suspicion. "What does it have to do with you? Or her?" she added with marked spite, motioning toward the thinner girl who had managed to catch her breath and now straightened up with matching enmity or worse.

"It has everything to do with us!" this one cried out. "And nothing to do with you, you foul-mouthed marketplace leftover!"

Quetzalli gasped and her eyes sparkled with fire that made Elotl's stomach twist with pleasant expectation, despite the new splash of a nagging worry. It was all about his brother again, wasn't it? But how so? Did Miztli land in new trouble? Last night when he disappeared in the darkness, or this morning when he, Elotl, slept calmly? The wounded warrior, oh yes, his brother did call him "man of Texcoco" when urging him to trust no one else. And now those flushed, upset girls were looking for this same scary individual, talking about Miztli again.

"Keep your mouth shut, you ugly bag of bones!" burst out Quetzalli, finding her tongue after a momentary setback. "You and your lowly villager lover—"

"Stop that!" cried out the first girl, stepping between the two antagonists, both breathing heavily and looking fit to go for each other's hair, even though the thin girl looked too brittle and young to have any real chance in a physical confrontation with voluptuous Quetzalli but for the fire in her eyes. "It's not the time. We must help Miztli and calling each other names won't help him a bit. Tlemilli!"

The younger girl didn't move, still spoiling for a fight, burning her opponent with her gaze, but by that time, Elotl came out of his own momentary stupor.

"What happened to Miztli?" he demanded, stepping forward while readying to insert himself between the enraged girls as well.

The pretty one frowned at him. "Who are you?"

"I'm his brother," he said firmly, not liking the way her eyes widened in open disbelief. "He was supposed to find me here after midday. He promised that last night, and I'm now looking for him as well..." To hear his own voice ringing apologetically, mouthing silly explanations, angered him. "What happened to him? I have the right to know!"

The pretty girl kept frowning, measuring him with a gaze that told him of no favorable impression. Just the opposite. However, by this time, the second girl's eyes were upon him as well, huge and widely spaced, full of matter-of-fact inquiry. "You were with Miztli last night?"

"Of course I was!" he stated with as much dignity as he could muster, incensed with her less than with the other girls, both of them now. Didn't this same Quetzalli just call his brother a lowly villager again? And the other one was eyeing him as though he was a strange insect, something bothersome and unpleasant, beneath her or her time and to be avoided. "And I know where the healer woman lives and where the man of Texcoco might be."

The girl's strange eyes lit. "Oh good!" Her lips were decidedly wide and they curved in a smile as she turned to her pretty companion, giving Quetzalli no more attention, not even a fleeting one. "See? He knows! And he can take us there. So let's go." Her eyes were upon him again. "We must hurry. The Texcocan, he is good now, no? His wound, it doesn't give him trouble, yes?"

He tried to remember, the memories of the night vague, mixing, one impossible happening intermingling with another. "What happened to Miztli?"

Her smile died all at once. "He... he got in trouble. But it was not of his doing, not his fault. Not even close!" The fire that lit his eyes had melting quality to it, a dangerous glow. "That stinking

Acoatl, he had it coming to him. If he dies, he deserves it. I hope he does!"

"If he dies, Miztli will be executed for murder," said her pretty companion firmly, her own eyes flashing as well. "Or at least sold into slavery to that nasty family, to serve them until that dreadful debt is paid. Stop talking nonsense, Tlemilli. You of all people don't want that stinking piece of excrement dead!"

"Yes, I do," insisted the one called Tlemilli. "Miztli will manage to escape. The Texcocan would help him, if the Emperor himself wouldn't. Ahuitzotl promised that his brother would not execute Miztli. He said there is no chance of that."

Her pretty companion rolled her eyes. "And how will he stop his powerful brother if he decides otherwise?" she muttered, then shook her head and looked at him, still frowning with doubt but now curiously earnest as well. "Will you take us to that healer's house? We really must let Honorable YaoTecuani know."

He didn't spend his time thinking who the owner of the spectacular name was. "Come."

Then the woven handles that were still cutting into his palm caught his attention and he looked at Quetzalli, partly hoping that she would decide to accompany them as well, despite her open quarrel with the others.

Her head tossed high, in no promising manner. "I'm not going back there! Certainly not in your current company." Then her eyes narrowed in reproach. "Tell them how to find that healer's house. They can do it all by themselves. It's not far from here."

Amused against his will, he offered her the baskets, understanding her invitation, the clear demand to choose her, pleased by it. "I must go back, help my brother."

Her hands wrenched her belongings quite violently, scratching his arm in the process.

He forced a shrug, then turned to the other girls. "Tell me exactly what happened while I take you to the healer woman."

They fell into his step obediently, the thin one walking in a funny gait, waving her hands as though needing them to help her along, her feet encased in prettily sparkling wear of which he had never seen before. Stones of the like that got him in so much trouble since arriving in this huge *altepetl* glittered from the leather that wrapped around her slender ankles, and her heel flashed in occasional flares that hurt the eye.

"Are you really Miztli's brother?" she asked, when her prettier companion, her feet elegant and narrow, also encased but in simple-looking thongs, kept frowning, glancing at him every now and then, openly suspicious. "You don't look alike at all."

"No, we don't," he said as nonchalantly as he could, not liking this particular comparison, or the glances of the other one. So much doubtfulness!

"I look nothing like my sister either," related the owner of the sparkling sandals, her blouse and skirt glimmering with matching flare, unlike the undecorated wear of her skeptical companion. "No one would believe that we are full sisters. But we are, the fullest sisters ever. With the very same mother. Not like the rest of our father's brood." She gave him a measuring look of her own that, unlike her companion's, did not make him feel an unworthy pretender or anything of the sort. "Are you full brothers too? Or do you have different mothers?"

"What? Why would we have different mothers?"

She made a face. "I don't know? Doesn't your father make love to his other women?"

"What?"

The simpler dressed girl eyed him with her previous lack of enthusiasm. "Miztli has no family here. No brothers or sisters or anyone. Not a single living soul. Trust me to know that." Her nicely slender eyebrows stretched to create a single line, still a very pretty sight but for her filthy accusations. "Why would we believe you now? You can claim being his brother, or cousin, or anyone, but how do we know that you are telling us the truth?"

"Ask him!" Unwilling to face her any further, her gaze making him feel dirtier than mud, he turned toward the talkative fox, a much more pleasant company anyway, with her strange eyes wide open and guileless, accusing him of nothing. "What happened to Miztli today? What trouble did he get himself into?"

"Oh!" A net of creases wrinkled the wideness of her forehead, making her look even more outlandish. "He hit Acoatl. Punched him so hard that the foul-mouthed bag of rotten meat fell dead, or almost dead." Her hands flew in the air, palms up, relaying much wonder. "One punch! Would you believe it? One single punch and this heap of stinking fat went down like a cut turkey!"

"I believe it, yes," muttered Elotl, feeling one corner of his mouth climbing up quite against his will. "Father taught us that punch. Next to the eyes, but on the side of the head, yes?"

She nodded eagerly, all eyes. "It was incredible, yes! He is always incredible, and believe me, I saw him fighting enough times to know what a great warrior he is. Still, that punch was something! That Acoatl brute, he is not the smallest person that walks our world of the Fifth Sun. Still, he went down like a kicked slab of stone."

The other girl's eyes did not veer from him, narrowed to slits, a less pretty sight.

"Father taught us that thing, yes," he went on, unwilling to ask questions, not under such unfriendly scrutiny. To think of his brother as mighty warrior fighting in wars was funny. Miztli couldn't be even moved to get into brawls, let alone something like real fighting, could he? And yet, she said that he just put some impressive brute out with one punch. And that he was in trouble on the account of it. "Our father, he said not to use it, unless in a real need, a real danger. And I never saw Miztli even practicing that thing."

"He practiced it enough times here," murmured the other girl, measuring him with her skeptical glance once again. "You come from his home village?"

He nodded coldly, hating her interrogation, wishing that she would go away and leave him looking for Miztli in the company of the chatty one alone.

"I see." Keeping her pace brisk and closer to the other girl, who was beginning to pant once again, she brought her hands forward, fingers interlaced. "If so, I suppose you really are his brother, even though he had no family visiting him until now. And he wasn't expecting it, was he?" Her gaze shot toward her companion, then came to rest back on him, her brow furrowed as badly as the other one's before. "I apologize for not believing you. But if you are coming from his village and his family, then I must tell you that whatever you heard about his troubles in my father's workshop, it isn't true, not all of it. My father, well, he is angry with Miztli, very much so. But..." She paused, and he watched her licking her lips, frowning as dourly as before but now as though at her inner thoughts. "My brother told me that someone came asking after Miztli. I wasn't around when it happened, or I might have... well, I might have tried to tell the truth. He didn't run away from the workshop, didn't steal or commit any other crimes. He just... well, he left and my father is still angry with him, but only because he can't find half as good worker as Miztli was. Only because of that. So if he said something bad to you, bad about Miztli, well, you shouldn't believe him. But my father is not a bad man either!"

The unexpectedly long and passionate speech had them slowing their step into near lack of progress on yet another crossroad with a gushing flow of people on both sides of it, the chatty girl gaping with as much wide-eyed curiosity, all ears. Elotl blinked, trying to make sense of the disjointed sentences. Those were the answers he came looking for in this huge overwhelmingly crowded *altepetl*, weren't those? But who were these girls? Why did they know Miztli so well?

"Your father is the metalworker? The one from the workshop out there?"

She nodded solemnly, resuming their walk.

"Miztli worked in her father's workshop once," contributed the other girl in her lively way of talking, welcome in her interruption. "But now he is in *calmecac*, about to become a great warrior, and the Tenochtitlan Emperor himself gives him missions worthy of most trusted among his men!"

He blinked again. "All that?"

The first girl grinned with surprising openness. "Tlemilli believes in ItzMiztli more than anyone."

"I'm not exaggerating and not making anything up," insisted the owner of the pretty sandals. "Ask your Necalli. He'll tell you the same!" Her fragile-looking shoulders, outlined through the lavish embroidery of her fancy wear, lifted sharply. "I know more than you do. About the missions the Emperor gives him. Back in

Tlatelolco, it was really important what he did, and your emperor was pleased with him mightily. Necalli said it many times too. And tonight," her huge eyes became too widely open again, "tonight, it was something really wild, something even the Texcocan was involved in. Think about it!"

The reminder of the man they were looking for made them hasten their step with surprising coordination.

"The healer lives at the end of that alley, the broader one," said Elotl, measuring the sun that was already tilting quite sharply, leaving them with not much of the daylight time. "I'm not sure she will let you in. She is not the friendliest person and has nasty men sneaking all over that huge patio of hers. But," he shrugged in his turn, "if the man of Texcoco is there, then we can shout out and let him know. Miztli told me to trust him. They talked about half a night out there before he went off."

"Oh yes, Honorable YaoTecuani is a good man!" exclaimed the simpler-dressed among his companions, while the other one, Miztli's admirer, nodded with her typical vigor. Was that the high nobility fowl Quetzalli-girl was talking about? he wondered suddenly. The one who was reported to fall all over his brother "like the cheapest of whores"? She didn't look cheap or wanton, anything but. And yet, her sparkling clothes and footwear seemed incredibly rich, and she certainly talked about Miztli like the most unsophisticated girl of their village, in love and not clever enough to conceal it. Or rather not bothering, as might be this girl's case. She didn't look simple. Just very sure of herself.

"What do you think this Texcocan man would do?" he asked, striving to channel his thoughts into useful directions, the flood of information regarding his brother too overwhelming and wild, needing too many clarifications, something about which he hoped to question Miztli himself. The dwellers of this gushing *altepetl* made no sense, confusing even worse when asked for explanations.

The noble girl scowled against the dimming sky. "He will release Miztli, make the Emperor let him go, in case the Emperor got angered after all. Which he won't!" she added stubbornly, tossing her head in a ridiculously similar manner to that of the

Quetzalli-girl before. Again, he regretted that the high-spirited fox went away. It was wild to kiss her like that, but so enticing, better than a quick groping with Metl's sister in the rain behind the shed, or rolling around in the fields with Teteltzinco girls.

"It's there, behind the fence. See that tightly woven thing?" he said hurriedly, taking his thoughts off wrong directions. "She makes sure no one gets in easily, that healer. And she has warriors with clubs."

"More likely local riffraff," said the workshop girl quietly, eyeing the fortified poles with her previous skeptical doubt. "Ome said they were criminals, every one of them. Even the healer, he said."

"Because she took the stones?"

"What stones?"

He held his peace by shrugging noncommittally, heading for the opening in the fence. It was obvious why the stabbed workshop man did not wish to relay the details of their nightly adventure. Of course! He didn't wish to dive into any of it himself, certainly not anything connected to the theft. Briefly, he wondered about the fate of the skinny street boy again.

Two of the discussed riffraff loitered on the patio that was abandoned when he had left earlier with the girl. Pretending confidence he didn't feel, he motioned his current companions to follow, stepping in, only to be confronted by a heavyset individual with a badly bruised face that pounced on them from their left, almost pushing Elotl off his feet with the thrust of his massive chest.

"Go away. The Lady Healer is not accepting sick at this time of the day."

Elotl swallowed. "We are not sick. I... I've been here before. The man of Texcoco, he told me to stay here... and the healer woman—"

"Shut up and go away!" His assailant shoved him backwards with no visible effort. Fighting for balance, Elotl dug his heels into the dry smoothness of the stones paving the alley, determined not to yield a pace. Which of course turned out to be a lost battle. The man was infinitely stronger, so much broader and taller, massive beyond comparison. Swaying and still struggling, Elotl resisted for another fraction of a heartbeat, then, sensing his rival's momentary absorption in the battle of powers, gave in by slipping aside, completing his opponent's suddenly unopposed drive forward with a push of his elbow, ready to deliver another in case the first one didn't work. It did. The man went sprawling across the threshold and into the dusty stones. Which made Miztli's girl giggle and left the other one staring with her frown deep and familiar.

Elotl paid them both no attention, concentrating on the men inside, who straightened up curiously but didn't bother to jump to their feet. His knife made its way into his hand readily this time, unlike through the stupid events of the previous night.

"It's that foreigner from last night," one of loiterers called, motioning with his lazily raised hand. "The Mistress did let him in. He was sleeping in there for half a day. Where are your eyes, Ixtli, you stupid basket of waste?"

The fallen man was on his feet, cursing. Elotl held his knife ready.

"Where is that good-for-nothing little rat Ayotl?" went on the man from the patio. "Send her in and ask the Mistress."

"Wait outside," growled the momentarily defeated Ixtli, his eyes burning holes in Elotl's face. "And put your pitiful knife away. If the Honorable Healer doesn't let you in or have any other use for you, you are dead. Dead, rotten, and forgotten!"

The last phrase made the strange noble girl giggle again, however, her companion pushed her way forward with startling determination. "Please," she said urgently, inching herself as close to the angered man as she dared. "The man of Texcoco. Honorable YaoTecuani, if he is here, please, tell him that we must see him. It's a matter of life and death. He will understand. Please tell him!"

Her words caused even the idling men to straighten up once again.

"The man of Texcoco, eh?" repeated their former assailant, shaking his head while drawing back toward the house. "Stay here and don't move a limb. Especially you, filthy foreigner!"

Another murderous glance shot at Elotl, making him wish to retaliate by something viciously matching. A challenging stare back satisfied his pride for the moment, but the workshop girl glanced at him briefly, reproachful and imploring.

"What scum," he muttered, his anger making his limbs tremble, the reaction setting in, annoying him further. "Just who does he think he is?"

"Pushy riffraff, that's who he is," declared Miztli's admirer, stepping forward and placing herself next to him, as though preparing for the attempt to dislodge them both. "What gall!"

Her gesture, while futile and not very efficient if it came to another confrontation, curiously made him feel better; stronger, capable of dealing with what was to come. He clenched his knife tightly, thinking of their possibilities, in case the man of Texcoco wasn't there, or the healer was truly not ready to let him in anymore, or maybe got pissed with the company he had brought along uninvited – too many "ifs."

"The Mistress said to wait outside." This time, it was the scrawny girl he remembered vaguely from the night, staring at his companions, wide-eyed. "All of you."

Their workshop spokeswoman was again the quickest to respond. "We really need to see Honorable YaoTecuani. Will you tell your mistress that?"

The skinny thing just nodded numbly, motioning them with her entire body to move out and away, her eyes pleading. Shrugging, Elotl led the way, only to nearly bump into none other than Miztli himself bearing down the alley, in a dreadful hurry, his cloak sparsely decorated but as fresh and expensive-looking as that of the noble girl, his hair collected in an intricate bun, sandals bright, also undecorated, not looking foreign or uncomfortable, just the opposite. His familiar handsomely broad face wore what looked like a worried frown, and even though it brightened at once the moment their gazes met, his eyes leapt away and toward Elotl's company, widening to enormous proportions.

"Tlemilli," he cried out, leaping toward them, blinking in shock. "What are you doing here?"

The slender girl did not let him close the distance, literally throwing herself at him and into his arms instead, pressing with force, oblivious of basic decency. However, his brother did not seem to be taken aback, enveloping her in his arms with as much enthusiasm, in a gesture of old familiarity, like a man and his woman of many summers. Elotl felt the need to take his eyes away, or maybe his entire presence, feeling an odd person in their obvious intimacy, an intruder. A glance at the other girl let him know that she felt no better or more comfortable.

"What are you doing here, Miztli?" she asked quietly, wearing what by now had become a familiar frown. "We worried about you so! What happened? Did they let you out of school or did you run away?"

Miztli's frown matched hers as he looked up, stroking the back of his girl with one hand absently, again in a surprisingly natural gesture. "No, no, I didn't run away. The Emperor was angry with what I did, yes; he said it won't be forgiven again. Next time, that is. But now, now I won't be punished and I'm to go—"

"You won't? I knew it!" His high-spirited admirer broke from his embrace at once, beaming so strongly it seemed to light the darkening alley. "I said that! Didn't I?" A triumphant glance shot at the other girl. "I told you all that the Emperor won't let them. He appreciates Miztli so! He does, he does!" she added hotly when the subject of this passionate lauding began protesting. "He will make you a warrior, a great warrior. Jaguar warrior, like Necalli's father. You just wait and see."

"Rather a man for dubious missions," muttered Miztli, shaking his head while fighting an obvious smile, this typical shy, reluctant smile that made Elotl miss home and the quiet evenings by the fire, with Father resting or working leisurely, repairing various tools, and Tletl still without his whiny fox and their screamer of a baby, helping, leaving him, Elotl, restless and bored but in a good way, trying to needle Miztli or make him join dubious undertakings.

"We came here looking for YaoTecuani," the other girl was saying, glancing around nervously, clearly wishing to be anywhere but here. "We thought he might be here."

"How did you know about this house?" gasped Miztli, wide-eyed.

"My brother," muttered the girl gloomily. "He was here with you last night."

"Oh." Now it was Miztli's turn to grow sullen, tightlipped and on guard. "How is he?"

The girl sighed. "We hope he won't die. The healer, she gave him medicine to drink and ointments to put on the wound. And our healer from the wharves says he may live if his blood doesn't start boiling."

To that, Miztli nodded reservedly, and Elotl felt bad for the squat man from the workshop, not a bad person, a reasonable man, all things considered; and a brave one.

"Tlemilli told me that about you and my brother, when we were... when all the mess at school happened and we were thinking how to find YaoTecuani and let him know. About the trouble, that is. So that's why we went to my father's house the moment they let us all out."

"Oh." By this time, Miztli was listening, all eyes, his gaze leaping between the girls, his cheeks glowing stronger with every uttered word. "I... I thank you. You are so... so good to me and loyal. And I—"

A sound of shuffling footsteps brought the skinny thing from the healer's house into the opening once again, her eyes round and wide, fixed on Miztli as though he was something scary straight away from the Underworld's second or maybe third level.

"What now?" demanded Elotl, when no one else ventured any kind of response. "Are we to move away twenty more paces, then wait again?"

The girl blinked in confusion, while Miztli's high-spirited fox giggled, as expected. "Make it twice twenty and this time without talking or moving a limb." She snickered again. "They are so very hospitable here."

Miztli's frown deepened. "They didn't let you in?" Then his eyes focused on the frightened servant girl. "Can I come in by myself, pay respects to your mistress? For only a few heartbeats. I can't stay anyway."

"I'll ask," sputtered the girl, then disappeared inside with the speed of a dry leaf blown away by a mighty gust.

Miztli was still frowning. "I'll go in. Try to talk my way in, that is. I'll be away just a few heartbeats. Wait for me here, will you?" His eyes rested on Elotl, imploring. "If the Tex—If Honorable YaoTecuani isn't there, I'll leave him word and then we'll take the girls home. And we can talk then. Plenty of time to do that. I'll be traveling back with you, you know? Part of the way, that is. But later on that. You all just wait. It won't take me long."

EPILOGUE

The rain caught them as they rushed through the narrow pathways, bypassing the marketplace alleys, not willing to chance confrontations. At this time of the deepening dusk, it was a fair chance; they both knew it quite well by now.

"I can't believe it," cried out Tlemilli, slowing her step as another growl of thunder rolled somewhere ahead, stronger than the previous one, present in force now. "The drops, did you feel them? It fell right on my nose, that drop. I swear I didn't imagine it!"

Slowing his step in his turn, Miztli turned his face toward the dark gray of the sky almost out of habit, enjoying the promise it held. It smelled of rain, oh yes, that familiar fresh heavy scent that brought memories of home in force, in a powerful wave. He had come to Tenochtitlan at the end of the previous rainy season, to experience not a drop of the Tlaloc's essence while living here, to associate none of it with the streets of the Great Capital.

"It really is raining," he gasped as a heavy drop splashed against his cheek, then another. "I can't believe it."

"And the thunder! Isn't it wonderful?" exclaimed Tlemilli, pulling him away from the possible cover the warehouses on both sides of the abandoned pathway were offering. "Let's get wet all over!"

"And bring you back to the Palace looking like a puppy fished out of a cooking pot?" he asked, unable to hold his laughter in, happy for no reason, licking the drops off his lips.

She tossed her face toward the sky, opening her mouth wide, trying to catch the falling torrents. "You'll look like a puppy *after* the cooking. They won't let you to the mainland at all."

Against the intensifying downpour, he glanced at her, making sure her smile was still in place and as happily beaming as before, the reminder of his impending journey threatening to make it go again. Earlier, upon hearing the news of his planned departure, she didn't take it well, not at all. Having left word for the Texcocan with the healer – as carefully composed message as he could manage, not trusting the woman but left with no choice – he had come out, to find Tlemilli's face mirroring the thunder rolling somewhere above the lake, screwed in that typical stubborn scowl he remembered too well from their Tlatelolcan days.

"If you are going away, I'm going with you," she had declared before he had had time to step back into the alley where they had waited for him, let alone open his mouth in order to tell something. "I won't stay here. I just won't!"

It had taken him plenty of hushed fragmented explanations with promises to explain it all later, when at a respectable distance from this dubious house, dragging her and the rest of them away from there almost by force, anxious to leave. There was so much to do! A bag with cocoa beans, maps, and other essentials the Emperor must have considered a necessity for his unofficial emissary, or rather a spy, safely tied to his girdle, given to him while being escorted from the Palace by a brisk-looking warrior who kept looking him over with such an obvious doubt it bordered with offensive. Still, before setting off, he knew he would have to find the man of Texcoco and be honest with him, let him know what transpired, not about the school incident – an irrelevant part where the formidable man must have been concerned – but about the Emperor's wish to send a spy to those southern cities, the clearly expressed intention to go and fight there in due time. The Texcocan would appreciate this news, he knew, pleased to have Tenochtitlan warring out there in the south, if the night conversation or what he had overheard while eavesdropping with the serving girl were to judge by. His mission was secret, yes, but the Texcocan was to be trusted. And maybe he would wish to get involved, something Miztli found himself partly hoping for. It would be so good to have this man's guidance and help. But even if not, the formidable warrior would appreciate his information and honesty. He would not forget something like that.

Then of course, there was his brother, to talk at length and take along maybe, if he wished to quit the city, to journey back partway, or maybe even detour through home. Oh, but it would be good to see them all, Father and Mother and Tletl, to reassure them and let them know, to even boast a little. He was becoming a warrior, wasn't he? And who would have hoped or expected something like that?

When running into Tlemilli out there near the healer's house, he had been stunned, even frightened. She couldn't be seen out there in the city and at such time of the day, so near nightfall. The entire Palace might be looking for her now and the Emperor told him explicitly not to contact her until he earned that right. Thinking the last words of the mighty ruler over again and again, he kept catching his breath, unable to believe it just yet. Did the Emperor promise to look favorably at the possibility of her being given to him when he proved himself? Did he say it in so many words, or at least promised to "consider?" Oh mighty deities, but he must find the way of letting her know!

So while hurrying across the canal and along the noble parts of the city, he had kept racking his brain, trying to think up ways of informing her, deciding to detour through Chantli in the end, risk another unwanted encounter with her nasty family for a chance of asking her to talk to Tlemilli, explain and persuade her to wait patiently until he returned. Otherwise, she would do something silly, he knew. Like back in Tlatelolco or worse.

And now here they were, heading back to the Palace after much persuasion and promises and with Elotl volunteering to take Chantli home in the meanwhile, then wait for him, Miztli, around there. Heading back to the Palace, yes, but not hurrying as they should have been, lingering, kissing in quiet corners, needing each other badly. He didn't think about the actual hardships of parting, of actual risks he would be facing while spying on the Tenochtitlan Emperor's behalf, but now it dawned on him. Two moons without her and her lively gushing words and kisses, two moons of no way of communicating, not knowing if she was well and happy, content, not harassed by her snobbish sister or worse yet, by the school's nasty snakes, or even this same filthy Acoatl, may the stinking piece of rotten fish die after all, even if that meant he wouldn't be able to return to *calmecac* because of that!

"What?" Tlemilli was asking, peering at him through the screen of the slanted torrent, a vision of glistening gaze and the wet hair plastered all over her face, eyes sparkling but concerned now, shining with unconcealed care, like they always were. "What happened?"

He pressed her to him with force, needing her so very much all of sudden, the confidence in that vaguely promised future gone. He was going away and leaving her behind, to fend off pressure and hatred, the bullying of certain school elements, the demands of the Palace's dwellers, from her own uptight sister to the strangely playful Jade Doll, toying with them like back in the dark gardens, playing her own dubious games.

"What is it?" she repeated, squirming free but clutching to him as tightly. "You look as though the worst of the Underworld spirits came haunting you."

"Nothing, it's nothing," he muttered, escaping her gaze while pulling her under the relatively dry spot by the nearest wall of a small warehouse, its screen shut but not completely, the edge of the slanting roof providing a sort of a shelter.

"I'm soaked," she said, beaming into his face, so irresistibly happy again. "I love Tlaloc. He is the best deity. When I die, I want to go to Tlalocan, where he and his beautiful Jade Skirt Chalhuiahtlicue goddess rule. It's the best in there, every servant of the gods would tell you that." She made a face. "I'll have to die by drowning or lightning to get there, of course. But there is plenty of time to do that, isn't it?"

"You can't get there unless by drowning?" he asked, lifted from his unhappy musings even if momentarily. A few dawns ago, one of the priests at school was talking about it, wasn't he? About where people went who didn't die as warriors on the battlefield, another thing everyone knew from their cradles, everyone but him.

The rain was intensifying, slanting worse than before. He pulled her closer to himself and the wall, then glimpsed the dark gap of the opening. An exchanged glance and they charged inside together, preparing to dash out and away in case the place was occupied. It wasn't. Not even by crates or tools or other stored goods. Nothing but faintly outlined walls and dirt floor, covered with scattered mats in places, with a pile of what looked like pottery utensils in one corner, flasks and round large plates.

They looked at each other, keeping close to the doorway, just in case. The rain doubled its efforts, beating upon the roof with much spirit.

"Maybe Tlaloc doesn't want you to go and leave me behind," whispered Tlemilli, snug in his arms, her hair dripping.

"I must go, but it won't be for long. The Emperor promised. No more than two moons. He told me to be back in two moons."

"Two moons is a long time. And what if something happens to you?" Her murmuring tickled his throat, her face tucked somewhere there, refusing to look at him. It made him wish to chuckle.

"Nothing will happen to me. I'll make sure of that. I promised you, didn't I?" When walking away from the healer's house, he had told her all this and more, about the two moons and about the Emperor's hint in regard to her. Back then, it made her shine brighter than sun in midday, agreeing to go back to the Palace but only after he promised that it would be no more than two moons and that the Emperor meant what he said. Yet now, he could feel that she was facing new misgivings, just like he did out there in the rain. Two moons *was* a long time and his mission offered enough danger. "The Emperor told me to return in twice twenty of days, and I can't disobey him, can I? And now you also told me to be back in time or else. So? What do you think? Will I dare to disobey both of you?"

He could feel the reluctance of her giggle, her warmth seeping through the barrier of her soaked clothes, making his body react strongly, in ways he didn't wish her to be aware of. Like back at night, under the terrace, when she got scared and tore from his embrace so urgently, leaving him wishing to disappear from the surface of the earth or worse.

"Twice twenty of dawns," she murmured, her face sneaking from its hiding in the knot of his cloak, eyes huge and glittering, piercing the depth of the darkness. "Forty dawns. That's it. If you don't come back by then, I'll run away and into the mainland and will be looking for you until I find you." The wideness of her lips quivered, creating an inverted grin. "So you better tell me names of those towns you are supposed to travel. Or I'll have to go through every settlement of the mainland."

Mesmerized, he stared at her, oblivious of the beating rain and the thunder that rolled now straight above, one after another, raging with impotent fury. Tlaloc or other sky or air or earth deities, they could have very well disappeared or not have existed at all; only the outline of her face remained, the darkness of her eyes, their determination and devotion that he couldn't see but only feel now, hear in her words that meant what they said.

"You... I will always, always come back," he muttered, feeling outside himself, floating, powerful to say what had to be said, knowing it to be truth, however farfetched and impossible to predict anything like that. That perpetual voice of reason, gone now, replaced by unshakable belief. She was to be his, and they would let nothing to stand in their way, nothing. They were together in this, twice as strong, and four times more determined. "I will always come back to you and be with you and do everything for you," he repeated, pressing her with much force, relaying the message. Words were not enough. "I will never leave you alone."

And then their lips were seeking each other, as they always did, but this time, it felt different, the thunderstorms going through his body stronger than those rolling above their heads, more violently thrilling than before, piercing like sturdiest of spears, this multiple-edged spear Necalli was boasting. It made his limbs tremble and out of control, craving to feel her without the soaked *huipil* and the cumbersome dripping skirt.

With the last of his willpower, he pulled away, but unlike back under the terrace, she clung to him as though craving the same closeness, that forbidden thing he didn't even dare to think about.

"Wait," he gasped, bumping his head against the wall they had huddled under. "Wait! I have to... I need... we can't!"

Her arms, wrapped around his torso, pressed harder as he tried to break free. Speechless, he stared into her eyes, two dark outlines, peering at him, unblinking.

"Yes, we can." Was it her voice, usually high and lively, gushing in a childish rush, but now slow and husky, every word distinct, like carving on stone, impossible to un-hear. "We will make love, and then we'll belong to each other for real. This way, they would not be able to give me away when you aren't here or if the Emperor changes his mind. They can't make us separate if we already belong to each other, can they? If I'm your woman for real."

He could feel her body firm against his, not afraid or hesitating, backing her words. His own was getting out of control once again, pressing her to him but differently now, with ownership. A man and his woman, oh yes.

"You... you sure about this?" He heard his voice mumbling weakly, in disagreement with his body that was already lifting her up, as though knowing what to do, walking toward the corner with mats, determined. She was his woman, oh yes. They could not take her away from him, whoever they were, the nobles of this *altepetl*, or anyone else, for that matter. Even the Emperor himself. Even her haughty sister whom she loved and cherished and listened to, but evidently not in this. She belonged to him. It was her decision. And his.

The world outside melted in the thundering mayhem, disappeared into swirling whirlwinds, with lightning and fire bolts aplenty. It rocked the world and twirled it upside down, spinning and swirling, and taking then right up into most wonderful of places. Maybe Tlalocan; maybe that eastern sky paradise the warriors went to after dying bravely on the battlefield. Or maybe it was another place, better than all of the paradises put together and one didn't even have to die in order to reach it.

Breathless, they sprawled on the coarse mats, not even remembering how they got there, their clothes a mess, minds a jumble, floating, raiding clouds of euphoria, refusing to land back. The rain was still beating strongly, but the thunders were receding, rolling every now and then, as though satisfied too, relaxed and not as loaded with destructive powers as before.

He gathered her closer and hugged tighter as she shivered, trying to envelop with his limbs and give her off his warmth. It didn't feel cold to him, but now the thoughts began returning and, with them, the wonder. Did she enjoy it like he did? Did he hurt her when oblivious and under the magic of the spell?

"Are you good?" he muttered, not daring to raise his head and try to see her, the silence pressing, trying to crush. "Did it... Was it... Did I hurt you or something?"

Another moment of silence had his nerves stretching like a string of a bow that was about to shoot really far, but then she let out a breath and a chortle that followed had him relaxing all at once.

"I don't know. I can't even remember. I think I wasn't here. My spirit went to the paradise, some sky world with most amazing things, so if you hurt me, I didn't notice." Then she laughed and broke free from his grip, rolling over and onto her elbow, peering at him from above, more beautiful than he ever remembered seeing her, shining like the Great Pyramid on the night of the ceremony, with impossible light. "You. You are magic. I knew it. No need to die to go to that paradise. So easy to get there and we didn't even know."

"How?" he whispered, awed, unable to take his eyes away, her face silhouetted not nearly enough to see what it held. "Dying and going to all those good places they are talking about, like warriors' paradise or your Tlalocan. And that magic, your magic. How did you know?"

Her smile held it all, the mystery and the wonder, the answer almost there, hiding in the glow of her eyes, of that he was sure. Then she giggled and the spell broke at once.

"Because it's magic, you silly," she chortled, the lively, vital, enthusiastic Tlemilli back, leaving him blinking. "We've been there together, like a real man and woman. So of course I'll remember. Why should I forget?"

He couldn't help snickering as well, actually relieved to have her back, with her ever-changing facets – Tlemilli, the essence of unpredictability. Even in something as sacred as lovemaking.

"You," he whispered, pulling her down and back into his arms. "You are that magic. But you are my woman as well now and no one will take you away from me. Not even the Emperor. So he better doesn't try!"

"He won't," she drawled, making herself more comfortable, her head upon his chest, the wet hair askew, tickling his face. "He'll make you a great warrior and then we'll have a great house to make love in. Nice mats and plenty of cushions. And servants to bring us food and drinks after we came back from those sky worlds. Citlalli will help us to organize it as nicely as her imperial rooms in the old Palace."

The mention of her sister helped to dim some of his euphoria, but he pushed it away, determined not to let it spoil the wonder. The rain was lessening and there was still the need to bring her back to the Palace safely, then find his brother, then the Texcoco man, then the journey.

He held her tightly, hating the voice of reason and his thoughts that dared to rush on, taking him away from those sky worlds of her definition, the doubts and the worries returning, to be pushed away once again. "Promise to behave while I'm away and not get into trouble."

She snuggled yet closer, perfectly at ease, as though already in that great house of her prophecy, with plenty of mats and cushions and leisure to make love as long as they wanted to. "For two moons. I promise you exactly twice twenty of dawns."

And that was as far as she would commit, he knew, his happiness welling again, returning in force. And why not? She was his woman now. They had committed to each other, committed in the only way that made every union real, even if for now, only they knew. But the world would learn too, in due time, and it wouldn't dare to stand between them. The gods had smiled at them, and Tlaloc blessed them especially. Only Tenochtitlan's society remained to be convinced. But like the man of Texcoco said – one problem at a time.

AUTHOR'S AFTERWORD

After Tlatelolco fell and was successfully incorporated and then absorbed in the growing Tenochtitlan's Empire, with an appointed governor and certain reconstructions such as the latter-day famous marketplace hosting tens of thousands of people described by the invading conquistadors in great detail half a century later, Axayacatl reportedly became busy with various renovating projects of his own *altepetl*. A new story was commissioned to be added to the Great Pyramid and the famous Sun Stone was fashioned, the monument that managed to survive the Spanish conquest and is displayed in Mexico City today. These days, the Sun Stone's symbolic significance important to various modern movements of national pride; it also keeps the modern-day historians and anthropologists busy with arguments as to the actual purpose of this imposingly huge monolith. No one knows what the Sun Stone represented for Axayacatl, but as he was busy supervising the engineers working on it, according to Duran, a plea for help came from the south.

In the fertile Toluca Valley to the south-west of Lake Texcoco local cities in power were in disagreement. Tenantzinco, who might have been paying tribute to Tenochtitlan or, at least, recognizing the Aztec Capital's power in this or that way, came asking for help against their neighbors to the northwest, independent cities Tollocan (Toluca of today) and Calixtlahuacan (before the Aztec conquest known as Matlatzinco). Tenochtitlan's reach did not extend to those south and northwestern areas as yet, but to the north of the Toluca Valley and behind the above-mentioned cities, spread the unknown, people and cities that we came to recognize today as Purehpecha/Tarascan Empire. Not as powerful or, at least, not as bent on expansion as the growing Triple Alliance was, this regional power of the Western Mexico was nevertheless strong and well organized, enough to challenge Axayacatl's advance and then to actually stop it in the following years.

However, back in the beginning of 1474, this western empire was not widely known or causing concern in Tenochtitlan. The Toluca Valley, on the other hand, was. So when Tezozomoctli, the ruler of Tenantzinco, came asking for help, Axayacatl did not hesitate.

According to Codex Mendoza, there must have been a rivalry in this same Toluca Valley and in their ruling Matlatzinca society, between more powerful and influential Calixtlhuaca-Tollocan dynasty led by Cachimaltzin (or Chimaltecuhtli, according to Duran) and the lesser center of power in this same referred above Tenantzinco ruled by Tezozomoctli. The need to establish a firm buffer zone between Mexica Valley and the little known Purehpecha/Tarascans is also pointed out by several 16th century historians (Alvarado Tezozomoc among them) as additional motive for Axayacatl to embark on this new series of conquests.

In any case, according to Duran, Axayacatl received the delegation of Tenantzinco favorably, accepted their shields and swords as customary, then presented them with even more lavishly decorated weaponry to cement the agreement. His building projects occupied most of his time, but even this situation he used to his advantage when, upon discovering some allegedly missing building materials, he didn't hesitate to send the request for those to none other than the same troublesome rulers of the Toluca Valley, *altepetl*s of Tollocan and Matlatzinco. As expected, neither city-state reacted favorably to such an audacious demand, their barely polite refusal presenting Axayacatl with another excuse to get involved in the southwestern affairs. The Tenantzinco delegation went home satisfied and in a hopeful mood.

In this fourth book of The Aztec Chronicles, I addressed the possible resentment some of the other influential people of

Tenochtitlan might have felt in the face of this projected campaign into the lands and valleys that weren't the mighty capital's tributaries and were never conquered before. There might have been those who did not think that it was wise to advance so far into the southwest, to expand so widely and so rapidly. The Emperor's brother Tizoc (or Tizoctzin, the customary honorific "*tzin*" used by Chimalpahin without fail, while others like Duran seemed to neglect it, so today we know this seventh Tenochtitlan Emperor by a simple alias "Tizoc") might have been one of those who did not agree with his brother's aggressively military policies. His future reign, even if short and inefficient, certainly pointed at his non-militaristic inclinations.

Still, I admit taking certain liberties while implying that the imperial brother might have been the power behind various political machinations; even the one who might have been involved in the attempt to hurt the Tenantzinco delegation in order to make it leave in anger – a scenario played about in this novel. No source mentions this future emperor's involvement in any of it. Axayacatl's elder brother seemed to remain quiet and unobtrusive through those times and through his following reign as well.

The famous "Moctezuma's zoo" that the later-day conquistadors described in some vivid detail I tried to present as best as I could, having not many sources to draw the information from. The systematic ruination of Tenochtitlan when it finally fell to the Spanish conquerors half a century later left us with nothing but the words of those who managed to glimpse the city before setting to take it apart.

Bernal Diaz, not a satisfactory accurate source to base one's studies on, provides most detailed information on these unheard of aviaries and buildings with caged animals – "*... let me speak now of the infernal noise when the lions and tigers roared and the jackals and the foxes howled and the serpents hissed, it was horrible to listen to and* *it seemed like a hell…"*

"Lions and tigers" must have been rather pumas and jaguars. He goes into a great detail, describing a lavish aviary with enormous amounts of local and imported birds and reptiles, of various ponds of salt and freshwater hosting *"…crocodiles turtles snakes and lizards… kinds of carnivorous beasts of prey, tigers and two kinds of lions, and animals something like wolves which in this country they call jackals and foxes, and other smaller carnivorous animals…"* He also refers to the enormity of the site's size and the amount of servants caring for this unheard of collection of species, the amount of food the animals were consuming, usually fowl (turkeys) and small dogs.

According to fragmented descriptions of other conquistadors, one of Cortes's famous letters among those as well as parts of surviving diary from an unnamed soldier now known to us as "Anonymous Conqueror" who mentioned the famous zoo in passing, there were also monkeys on display, armadillos, a mysterious "Mexican bull" (probably a bison), ocelots and opossums, and so on. One of the conquistadors also claimed that the famous Moctezuma II was fond of strolling through his zoo, feeding jaguars, and even petting them.

For the beginning of 16th century, the concept of caged animals kept for the pleasure of watching them seemed to be largely unknown around the world. The Spaniards were certainly deeply impressed.

However in the late part of the 15th century, they were still safely away, decades from discovering other continents, while Axayacatl seemed to have little time to tour his wondrous zoo, busy with planning his conquests in the southwest.

"Morning Star", the fifth book of **The Aztec Chronicles**, will tell the story of Tenochtitlan's preparations to advance into Toluca Valley and the welcome the Tollocans and their unexpected Chichimec allies arranged for the mighty Mexica Empire.

The story continues with

MORNING STAR

The Aztec Chronicles, Book 5

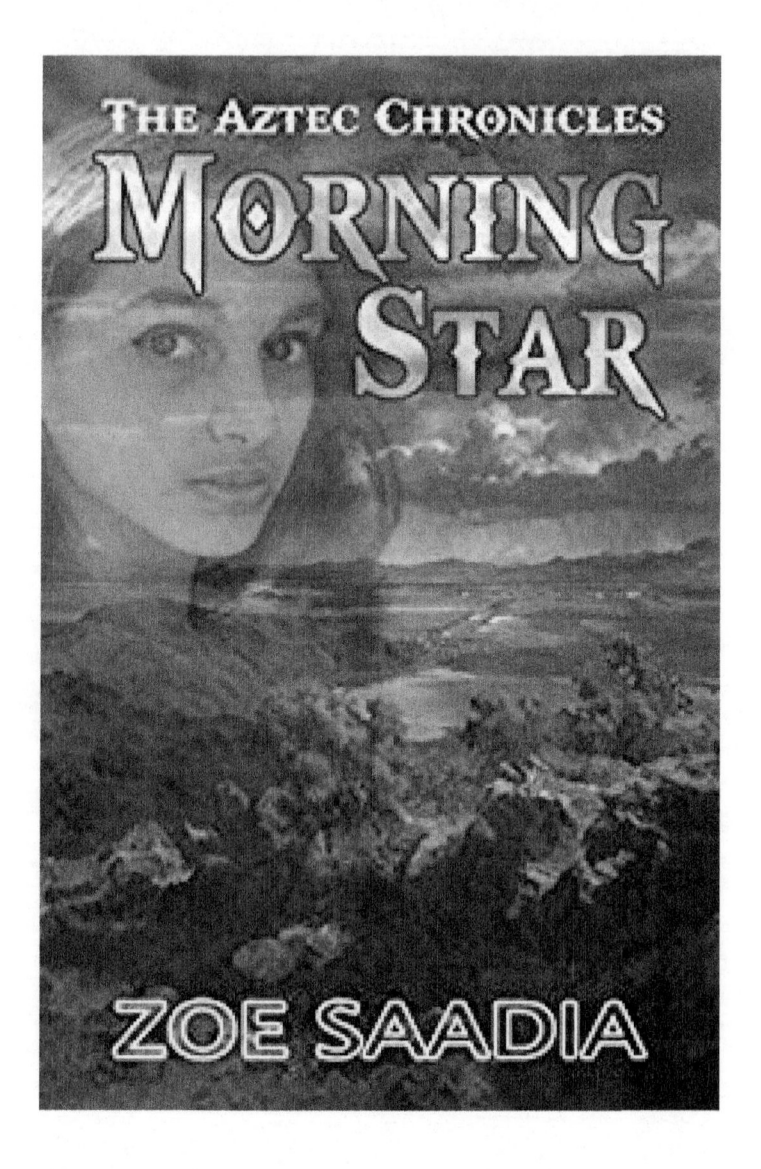

CHAPTER 1

Tollocan,
1474 AD

Tollocan turned out to be huge and sprawling, its slanting alleys and pathways challenging, forcing one to make one's way up or downhill, never in a straight line. It made Miztli miss Tenochtitlan and its flatness more acutely than ever. Even back in Cuauhnahuac and Tenantzinco, it was easier to move around. But the capital of their prospective enemies turned out to be a challenge.

Shielding his eyes against the glow of the early sun, he hastened his step, his ears reporting a nearby square, or rather a plaza, judging by the continued clamor of too many people speaking at once and too many objects moving. Not a marketplace surely, he deduced, forcing his legs up the steep incline. How would they put their mats and stalls on anything so slanting?

"Move away, boy!"

An open palanquin in a form of a richly cushioned seat squeezed its way past him, the litter-bearers having not enough space to spread comfortably even after he flattened himself against the beams of the high fence that flanked the road, letting them pass with enough readiness to satisfy the warriors that led the procession. There was only a pair of those, walking proudly, dressed in an outlandish fashion that made him wonder. Even back in Tenantzinco, which he had left only on the previous morning, local warriors wore regular cloaks, their hair done differently sometimes but not in an unrecognizable manner.

It had taken him many days to grow accustomed to all those various sights, wear, and hair styles, different ways of pronouncing the same words, let alone different tongues. Nearly half a moon spent in Cuauhnahuac alone was full of so much intensive learning, it put his first days in *calmecac* to shame. Back in the noble school, even as a complete outsider and out of his depth on all counts, he had been eased in quite gradually, not forced to learn like the rest of the boys or demanded to keep up with their regular studies. Overwhelmed and frightened and out of his depth, he hadn't noticed that at first, but now, looking back, it was difficult not to appreciate the relative leeway he had been given on this first crazy moon when Tlatelolco was still there, making trouble and threats. Insane, wild, wonderful days!

And yet now, traveling those new faraway places, Tenochtitlan enemies most of them, or at least discontented subjects, he had to learn twice as hard, think and react truly fast, work every moment he was awake, write down everything he could and in the way that made it possible to decipher and understand for any possible future reader, to remember it all and be able to recount, accountable to no one but himself, desperate to succeed. No hope that this or that teacher would not appear for an occasional lesson or a training session, or another would be inclined to dismiss them earlier or go easy on them. No counting one's time to the free afternoons. He had no one to report to now but the Emperor, no one to keep an eye on him but himself.

And it's not that he felt like complaining. Anything but! It was only that the days and the nights kept rushing by, chasing one another, hurrying toward the completion of the two moons, with so much to do yet, so many places to visit, roam around, and listen, and strike up conversations, engage in idle gossiping, pretend to be someone he wasn't and yet be himself, proud and unashamed. An impossible combination, but the only way to go about his mission. The man of Texcoco, as always, knew what he had been talking about. After a day spent with this formidable man around the marketplace of Cuauhnahuac only a moon ago, it had been easier, even enjoyable. Better than school at times. But for the opportunity to run into the stern Texcocan somewhere around here as well! Impossible, of course. The man spoke no Matlatzinca tongues, which here, in the heart of the western valley, were the ones not only to open more doors, but also to put one beyond natural suspicion and doubt. Nahuatl was not a popular tongue in the south these days. Not even in his native Oaxtepec.

Resuming his walk up the slanting cobblestones, now that the palanquin and its escorts had passed, he frowned, remembering Elotl's acquaintances, tough-looking brutes from the rundown side of the town, beside the storage sheds and the fields. Not as ferocious or as nasty as Tenochtitlan or Tlatelolco criminals, and nowhere near as ruthless or quick to do the killing – but did his brother keep carrying on about it, the insanity of Tenochtitlan streets – they still made him use his club against the foul-mouthed leader of theirs named Metl, that Elotl was quick to defy, taking his, Miztli's, side and against his former friends and accomplices. The incident that taught him to keep his thoughts to himself more than ever. He was here to listen and gather information for the Tenochtitlan Emperor to use. Not to defend Tenochtitlan's good name in the places the Great Capital was anything but popular. Oaxtepec's reminder was a good one.

The square opened before his eyes, neither large nor tiny, occupying surprisingly even ground. Not in the league of Tenochtitlan's squares, with their ponds and water constructions and the colorful crowdedness but still well attended, as lively as expected in this part of the morning, full of chattering women and the familiar sight of mats and cooking stones belonging to the vendors who were offering food.

His stomach reacted at once, but the thought of the now-slim bag holding remnants of the cocoa beans the Emperor had given him served to cool his excitement. Food was not the first priority, always available out there in the forest and near the fields. His meager means of payment was better conserved for something more important. Like these *amate* sheets he had to purchase in Tenantzinco, when his original stash of unused papers was stolen. Thanks all mighty deities, the thieves didn't touch the scrolls he had written upon, deeming them probably worthless, of no value with the densely scrambled symbols filling them to the brim, even their edges. Since then, he and Elotl never slept in the cities, bothering to make their way out and into the hills with dusk, no matter how exhausted they were or engaged in interesting findings. There was nothing to rage against but his own carelessness and stupidity. Cities were full of hungry commoners and prowling around thieves. Didn't he learn a thing while running all over Tenochtitlan with Necalli?

"Don't dream with your eyes open, young man." A woman with too many baskets weighing down her massive arms glanced at him briefly, her face round like a plate, crinkling with laughter. "The sun is high enough to wake one up, isn't it?"

Blinking, he stared at her for a moment.

Her smile was wide, openly amused. "Where are you from, boy, to wander around like this and at such a time of day?"

"Oaxtepec," he said, collecting his thoughts hurriedly. "Out there in the east. I… I came to bring things. To traders. My father sent me to do this."

"Oaxtepec?" Her brow creased in an obvious thought process. "Where is that?"

"In the east," he repeated, relaxing gradually. The woman seemed to be anything but unfriendly, and her way of speaking was strange but easy to understand. "Beyond Cuauhnahuac."

"A long way. Could your father find no traders out there in Cuauhnahuac or somewhere around?" Her eyebrows knitting, she studied him with unconcealed curiosity, then moved from the path of yet another palanquin that appeared at the edge of the square, in a hurry to cross it, or so it seemed.

Miztli did likewise.

"Too many important nobles are cruising all around these days, foreigners from the Chichimec north and their cronies." The woman shifted her baskets, then motioned him with her head. "Follow me, young one. The marketplace is not far away from here. You'll find plenty of traders there. Or buyers, for that matter. What did you bring to trade?"

Blessing the man of Texcoco for the thousandth time for his

invaluable advice, Miztli nodded toward his bag that was strapped across his shoulder, not heavy enough to fasten it to his forehead like traders did but containing some necessary commodity to justify his wandering about. YaoTecuani made plenty of faces when meeting them on the marketplace of Cuauhnahuac, discovering that he, Miztli, intended to just wander about with no plausible back story in case of being challenged. Youths of his age and status didn't just roam around the countryside doing nothing productive, claimed the redoubtable man. Not in these rural areas. The first person to challenge him with a question or two would have no difficulty discerning his dubious purpose. And then before he knew it, he would be done for, dragged to the local courts or worse, because spies never fared well when caught, never lasted beyond the time it took to kill them, quickly and brutally if they were lucky.

Oh, but how disgusted the formidable man grew with them both, Miztli and Elotl, who had tagged along, a most welcome addition, but not on this occasion. And the Texcocan was so wise, so farsighted, even if inconsiderate and short-tempered, frightening at times; just witness what happened back in Tenochtitlan and the healer woman's house.

Never lie more than you have to, the man had said back in Cuauhnahuac after leading them away from the lively parts of the city and into the nearby fields, neglected at this time of the season, a perfect place to hold a private conversation. *Have your back story ready but make sure it's as close to the reality as it can be, not too twisted or complicated to have you entangled in your own lies.*

It was two market intervals after leaving Tenochtitlan, half twenty days that this man allowed himself to recover from his nasty wound, visit his home *altepetl*, and then travel southwards after more of his dubious goals that Miztli came actually to understand better, remembering the overheard conversation at the healer's house. The complex man wished to make sure the mighty capital of the world was busy elsewhere, in the south if it desired to expand there, because otherwise, it might come to a confrontation with the powers beyond the eastern highlands where his mysterious brother everyone talked about ruled or at least had been "listened to." Why or by whom? He didn't dwell on these questions, too busy with his own qualms and dilemmas, worried about his own homeland in this same about-to-be-invaded south, not very happy with Tenochtitlan's current interventions and reach as it was. Or so claimed Elotl, himself not enamored with the tribute collectors of the mighty Mexica Capital but willing to listen, for a change.

Elotl! More of a good company. Spiky, yes, impatient at times, turning nasty when triggered. Yet a surprisingly good partner to journey with when away from boredom-induced spitefulness; lighthearted, enterprising, easygoing, finding the right words and worthwhile solutions, never intimidated or scared. Not even by the toughs of Oaxtepec, his former friends and accomplices, now discarded as stupid hotheads after learning about Tenochtitlan and what it meant to him, Miztli. It was surprising and so very encouraging to have Elotl on his side, standing up for him and against this bunch of Oaxtepec thugs. It made him love his brother and respect him more than ever before. And rejoice in the fact that Elotl insisted on staying around, on traveling on, convincing Father to give them both his blessing, somehow.

A good thing for them, but maybe not for the rest of the family. The guilt was nagging again, the realization that they had left Father with so little help, depriving the hardworking man of two additional pair of strong hands instead of just one. The contents of his bag with the cherished Tenochtitlan cocoa beans helped, but only a little. Leaving half of this treasure with Mother made Miztli feel better, even though Father tried to refuse. But on that, Miztli stood firm. The family must have something out of his changed position, until he was able to help more. When he became a warrior, he promised himself, his family would be showered with goods and cocoa beans, not forced to work as hard or live in such poverty. It was difficult not to notice their reduced status after Tenochtitlan and its noble and commoner parts alike. But he would change it, somehow. After becoming a great leader of Tlemilli's prophecy, with that great house that she insisted they should have and plenty of maids to serve them refreshments after they made love all over this wonderful place. *Oh mighty deities, all great and small spirits and everything in between, please keep her safe until he came back.*

The worry would return with renewed force, and with it the longing, the need to be near her and bask in her open adoration, her magic, and her love, lawful and unlawful too, that wonderful thing that they shouldn't have done. And what if they had been discovered, what if someone saw them entering that abandoned warehouse, to love each other in the ways they weren't allowed, the mere memory of which had enough power to squeeze his insides into the inability to breathe and his mind into the impossibility to think. Wonderful, magical, ethereal, and yet real and theirs to enjoy but for a few complications. And yet, what if she was in trouble on an account of it and he didn't even know, wasn't around to protect her and take the blame?

And then, there was his village, not on the path of the impending invasion but still dangerously close, around. If the war broke, it might become entangled, and he would have to make sure it didn't happen. Somehow he would have to keep it safe, protected, not harmed by reprisals Tenochtitlan would be certain to send in order to make places like Oaxtepec behave. His entire village would have to be left out of it. Somehow he would have to ensure that.

All the while they had spent in the village, two dawns of blissful respite, resting and pampered and at home, Elotl was glowing with excitement, happy to escape the boredom the mines and the fields spelled for him, busy planning their journey to Cuauhnahuac but through Oaxtepec first, to sound out all sorts of people he was anxious for Miztli to meet. Not the hotheads he used to associate with before, he had promised, but serious people, those who did not oppose Tenochtitlan and its possible intervention; serious people Miztli must meet and make an impression on. What presumption!

Not that Miztli minded that. It was actually good to let his brother take the lead sometimes, especially after he had proven himself loyal and unafraid back in Oaxtepec. Through their journey, Elotl's leader-like inclinations proved useful, let Miztli free himself from mundane details of taking care of their progress, dedicate some of his time to watching the countryside, trying to memorize and then actually write his observations down at nights, huddling next to the small fire they would dare to make, unwilling to attract the attention of possible robbers or even just passersby.

Father had said that it was actually good to have Elotl busy with something useful, even if not to the family directly; that it was better that they were together to keep an eye on each other. Apprised of Miztli's mission to its fullest – he didn't even dream of keeping anything from Father, the most trustworthy person in the entire world of the Fifth Sun – the older man gave plenty of advice and warning, impressing on Miztli how important it was to have his back story prepared, how dangerous it was to get caught while spying for the enemy nations. Echoes of YaoTecuani's later admonishment, come to think of it. Well, he didn't listen when back at home, not to the fullest.

In large cities like Cuauhnahuac, Father said, spies were abounding. Usually traders, people who knew how to blend and listen and ask questions without appearing suspiciously curious. Those men were also experienced in warring, capable of defending themselves or escaping from difficult situations. They were no youths of little learning and experience, however unique his position with the Great Capital and its ruler was. The Tenochtitlan Emperor could obviously afford to sacrifice his unofficial messenger if necessary. He must have plenty of such foreign elements at his disposal, to send out and spy on whoever needed to be spied upon.

Told in most worried and not dismissive tones at all, the assumption hurt all the same. He was well capable of defending himself, Miztli had protested hotly, offended to no end. The Tenochtitlan Emperor valued him and his bravery and skill, enough to put him in noble school and make him train hard, enough to send him on missions of spying back in Tlatelolco; enough even to forgive him transgressions that saw other students – noble *pilli*s all of them! – severely punished. He wasn't just a messenger or a sniffing around trader. He was to become a warrior and was spying for the Emperor in this capacity. He had his club from Acachinanco road with him now and the obsidian sword stored back in Tenochtitlan, the marvelous elite weapon he had earned in a real battle, real hand-to-hand and with a veteran warrior. He was anything but an expendable youth of no worth. The Tenochtitlan Emperor believed in him!

The heated protest had the entire family staring at him speechless, even Elotl, by now used to the change, or so his brother had claimed later on, but not to such outright boasting. He had never dared to formulate any of these thoughts even to himself before. Yet now he knew that those were true, not just silly boasting. All of it, even the belief of the Emperor in him. Still in no time, the familiar hated hot wave was washing his face in the most embarrassing of fashions, the wish to disappear under the surface of the earth returning in force, harming his ability to defend his position with words if not actions. However by then, Father was shaking his head thoughtfully, nodding a sort of approval, smiling with little amusement, saying that if so, it must be the case, yes, that the account of his last moons in the great city did support his claims. And then Elotl was busy talking about Tenochtitlan and its wild ways again, taking everyone's attention to himself as he always did, most timely now, and he felt his equilibrium returning, gradually but it did, while Father's gaze flickered at him from time to time, thoughtful and somehow sad.

When sending him, Miztli, to the Great Capital, Father confessed later, in the privacy of the outside and just the two of them this time, he had hoped to bring the best out of him, seeing his potential being hindered by natural shyness and lack of presumption. And it was good that he overcame those drawbacks with such marked success. Still he must be careful, less trustful and more observant, never forget his roots, never presume that the nobles of the Capital of the World would eye him as an equal, would stand by him as they might by one of them. Life of an ambitious warrior was a great achievement, beyond the wildest of dreams, but this road was difficult and fraught with dangers. He must never forget that.

However, despite such openly sounded misgivings that hurt even though this time he managed to keep his thoughts to himself

– the Emperor, and Necalli and his father, and above them all, Tlemilli, *his woman*, oh but they could be trusted, they did eye him as one of them, equal, worthy! – Father did not seem to be disappointed. Perturbed yes, worried; but not disappointed. And he did give Elotl his blessing as well, even encouraged that hotheaded second son of his to continue beyond Cuauhnahuac, all the way to the west and the mysterious Tollocan Valley of Matlatzinca people only Father heard about before. Their alleged ancestors whose tongue Father made them all learn when mere children, but about whom he never bothered to talk at length.

However, this lack was rectified later on, when the man of Texcoco had found them on the Cuauhnahuac marketplace a few dawns later and just as they entered this fairly large sprawling city, not in the league of Tenochtitlan but still putting Oaxtepec to shame, momentarily at a loss but trying to pretend that they weren't. Well, Elotl certainly put out an effort, holding his head ridiculously high and his back exaggeratedly straight, making Miztli wish to snarl at his brother or at least to put him back in his place with this or that sneering comment. Both options were out of the question, of course. They were here to sniff around while drawing no attention, a fight or a loud verbal exchange with plenty of swearing thrown in being anything but. After a market interval of traveling, spending days and nights together, needing to coordinate their actions without too much bickering – oh yes, he had learned how to handle his restless sibling or what to expect in most of the cases, how to avoid an outright conflict. All things considered, Elotl was making an effort to behave as well. Even the man of Texcoco seemed to be impressed, eyeing Miztli's brother with slight but pronounced doubt, with one eyebrow arching. Still the formidable man didn't demand explanations or venture a comment. Instead, he got straight to the business at hand, led them away and out into the hills, then got to as detailed questioning as expected, and then some more. Where had they spent their time so far? What did they learn? What was their next destination?

After making a temporary camp, with a confidently large fire they never dared to make before, and edible goods that had their stomachs react almost violently after two dawns of traveling on a very light diet – they could not let Mother pack too much food for them, not with the low supplies of this time of the season, could they? – the man mellowed as well, examining their back story and helping to refine it. Village youths like them could only pretend to be what they were if traveling with goods he had volunteered to help them obtain. A claim that their father sent them on a trading mission now that the fields were temporary out of use could do to a certain point. Simple items and tools, nothing expensive to tempt the city criminal elements with.

Before the darkness set, the man even volunteered to help Miztli rewrite most of his scribbling until it become understandable to people's eyes, reading it carefully, and of course, asking questions. To what end? Only gods knew. Miztli did not spend his time thinking of possible other uses their companion would make out of his scrolls and findings. The Texcocan was a law unto himself, and it was of no use to doubt him or try to outsmart, or even to avoid. If the forceful man decided to use his newly acquired knowledge while helping him along, then that was that, and he could only hope that the redoubtable warrior would see further use for him and his cooperation, go on and help him on the way and teach and give more of his offhanded, often harsh, matter-of-fact kindness.

The cozy night spent out there in the hills, away from various travelers and their possibly prying ears, warmed by the fire, blessed with lack of rain, was another memory he cherished, feeling ridiculously safe after many dawns of watching his step, wishing the darkness would not disperse. It was good to be able to talk freely, to retell the happenings of the last market interval, pore over his growing collection of notes, painfully composed maps, and comments that he didn't manage to decipher himself at times, to explain them all and thus make an order out of it in his own head. Not to mention the learning, the man's way of explaining what he did wrong, how to draw this or that glyph correctly, comments as crisp and as helpful as the man himself. No patronizing, no grownups' condescension or derision of an educated person toward uneducated youth, a villager – nothing of the sort! Just matter-of-fact comments and sometimes longer clarifications, then sinking into interesting stories, then back to perceptive questioning, as always, with no way of avoiding telling the truth. He didn't even try this time. The man was on his side!

"It's not a market day, boy, but there might be still enough traders sniffing about. What did you bring to get rid of?" The woman's voice brought him back from his reverie, the vastness of the plaza opening before his eyes, staggering in its expanse.

He blinked, trying to make his mind work. "Tools. I brought tools. Ladles and scrapers. Things like that."

His guide made a face. "What do you use those for?" Another palanquin swept by, nearly shoving them into the stones of the nearby wall. "I thought you brought foodstuff. From your fields, you know. You should have told me!"

"I didn't know," he said, glancing at the group of warriors that followed the palanquin, their attire strange, bright grayish shirts instead of colorful cloaks, their hair pulled up in an outlandish fashion. "You didn't ask."

The woman grimaced once again, following his gaze. "Xiquipilco visitors. What posers!" Bettering her grip on the largest of her baskets, she gave Miztli a skeptical look. "You are a strange youth. Good luck at finding someone silly enough to be interested in your so-called goods."

He forced as polite a smile as he could muster, in the corner of his eye noticing that the warriors that followed the palanquin split, some disappearing in the mouth of one of the alleys, while others rushed to greet another group of armed men. But this city was crawling with fighters! He thought about Elotl, loitering at the foot of the craggy hill they had spent the night at, keeping an eye on their belongings, Miztli's club, and his precious papers. Usually, they would hide those things as best as they could, preferring to enter towns they encountered together, split somewhere inside if need be, then reunite as soon as they could. However this night, Elotl didn't manage to sleep, coughing and heaving, vomiting twice and running to do his needs in the bushes too many times to count. With the dawn break, it was obvious that he was in no position to accompany Miztli as far as the nearby road, let alone the river and the enemy city towering beyond hill.

Full of misgivings, Miztli had made his brother as comfortable as he could, filled their flask with cool water from the nearby stream that trickled toward the river they had crossed on the day before, then promised to come back as soon as he managed, rolling his eyes at unsuccessful attempts of the stubborn hothead to come along anyway, in some part of his mind sympathizing with his brother. It was a bad timing to become sick just as they reached the legendary capital of the enemy. Having never even heard before about this pair of *altepetls*, Tollocan and Matlatzinco, which ruled the Tollocan Valley, they had listened to plenty of litanies concerning these two capitals since leaving Cuauhnahuac, especially in the smaller and less hilly Tenantzinco full of complaints and unconcealed hatred. Tenantzinco people clearly did not regret making mighty Tenochtitlan involved. They were spoiling for a fight, and judging by the amount of warriors he had seen upon entering this same presumptuous Tollocan, the locals were determined to return the fight, if not to mount the attack themselves, just as the complaining visitors of Tenochtitlan claimed.

"What are you staring at, young one?" called out someone, a woman with a mat full of maguey fruits. "Have you lost your way? You could use something to chew, judging by your looks. What do you have to give me for a fruit or two?"

"Leave the villager alone, sister," shouted another woman, this one surrounded by baskets of colorful flowers and roots. "Can't you see that this one can't pay you but with his youth or vigor, you dirty-minded old bag?"

He moved away hurriedly, not liking the attention he drew. Why were those women determined to sell him things, the marketplace fowl from the previous square and now these two?

More warriors swept past him, leaving him with barely enough time to jump away from their path. Those wore cloaks and looked more like the warriors he had glimpsed back in Tenantzinco aplenty. Upon reaching the previous group that lingered nearby the stall with a delicious aroma of cooking tamales coming from it, they halted their progress, greeting their outlandish peers in a tongue he didn't manage to recognize.

Thoughtfully, Miztli moved closer, fascinated with the man who seemed to be leading the foreigners, a slim, richly decorated individual with the most spectacular pelt covering his shoulders, his upper torso exposed as opposed to his over-clothed peers, chest covered by glittering breastplate, the muscled arms encircled with bracelets, glowing brightly. Plenty of gold in there; evidently more than copper. Miztli narrowed his eyes against an intricate image of a snake that wound its way around the man's upper arm. Such a beautiful design! Would Tlaquitoc manage to create something like that? The thought and the familiar wave of anger it generated served to bring him out of an unseemly staring in time. One didn't gape at warriors or their spectacularly dressed leaders.

Hurriedly, he took his eyes away, then glimpsed a youth of about his own age stepping away from the nearby palanquin, his attire like that of the outlandish warriors even if simpler, his sandals sparkling vividly, the oiled hair collected in an intricate bundle, glistening in the high morning sun. There was something about this one, something strange, contradicting. The youth's head was held high, challenging in the manner of Tenochtitlan noble *pilli*s, unmistakable at that, yet his eyes darted around with alertness worthy of a marketplace thief out to steal something.

This time, Miztli wasn't quick enough to take his gaze away, and as their eyes met, the youth's frown deepened, then filled with scorn. An arrogant toss of his head summoned a simpler-looking boy of about the same age, sending him away, to slip behind the cover of the nearby stone column, looking as furtive and maybe even afraid. Puzzled, Miztli followed this one with his gaze, then put his attention back to the lively gathering, more palanquins arriving to dazzle with their colorfulness and the richness of their ornaments, the market getting as busy as back in the towns and cities he had wandered so far, richer and larger than many, even the main square of Tenantzinco. He regretted not bringing Elotl along. Sick or not, his brother's presence was always of a great support.

"The foreigners are flooding our alleys today!" A woman with baskets full of round tomatoes spread upon a neatly arranged mat waved at a passerby, this one weighed down by a crate full of unbundled cloths, prettily patterned and folded most neatly. "Should have brought twice as much fruit and more."

"Didn't you know, sister?" The man shot a satisfied glance at yet another procession that sprang from a further alley, a broad avenue, clearly paved and maintained. "Xiquipilco warriors came at long last. About time, I say. Took them long to get organized, lazy good-for-nothing northerners that they are. Fierce Chichimecs each and every one of them. Not like our Otomi people from here."

"Did they bring their families to fight together with them? Plenty of noble ladies are cruising all over the city, I'm telling you!"

Grateful that the woman spoke Matlatzinca and not that other outlandish tongue so many seemed to prefer to converse in here, certainly the spectacular-looking warriors, Miztli hesitated, his gaze still following the arrogant youth who by now slipped behind the same column as his simpler-looking companion before, seeming more furtive than ever, undecided. Tempting to follow.

He hesitated again. The woman spoke freely and in the tongue he understood, giving out interesting information. At this point, everything he managed to overhear should benefit him and his mission, the dwellers of this side of the valley still an enigma, they and their outlandish guests. And yet, a richly dressed noble youth sneaking around like a marketplace thief bore watching. What was he up to?

"Of course their ladies would come," exclaimed the tomato woman, rearranging her half empty baskets around the prettily glittering pile of her treasures. "Their gods-forsaken Xiquipilco is nothing compared to our Tollocan."

The youth motioned at his poorer-dressed follower, then disappeared behind the shadow of the nearby set of high poles. Unable not to, Miztli slipped after him, resisting the urge to find out what that was all about no longer. There was enough time to return and eavesdrop all he liked. The sun was not even nearing its zenith yet.

A narrow passageway behind the densely placed beams teemed with more passersby, the patterned cloak of the sneaky *pilli* swaying at its far edge, in an obvious hurry now. Miztli pushed his way through, the lively chatter reaching him everywhere, offering possibilities. So many warriors! Oh, but these people were spoiling for war. There could be little doubt about it. Yet, how ready were they, how well prepared? And would they war against Tenochtitlan with as much zeal as against their southern neighbors? Too many questions, too little time to get answers. It had been more than a moon and a half and she promised to wait for forty dawns only before doing something wild. How could he send her word, let her know that he was well and unharmed, and intending to come back as soon as he could? Back in Cuauhnahuac, he'd had a hard time restraining himself from asking the Texcocan to pass her a message in case the redoubtable warrior was intending to visit Tenochtitlan again. If only he had enough courage to do something like that!

Another square, as spacious as the first one, burst upon him with its animated activity, this time crowded with men, merchants and buyers alike. The goods spread upon the mats explained it: tools and building materials, ropes, rough maguey cloths. Nothing feminine and refined. Against his will, Miztli's gaze lingered, enjoying the rich assortment, craving to be able to pick up some of those better tools for Father, that polished hoe or a hammer decorated with copper ornaments. Such pretty things, so useful! Father would enjoy working with those. He and Tletl. Would he ever manage to buy something like that for his family?

As though eager to reinforce the temptation, his wandering gaze brushed past another mat, less crowded than the others but looked upon by everyone, glittering with glassy obsidian. Arrowheads, blades, neatly carved knives, even a pair of spears, other razor-sharp items he didn't even know their purpose, club-like tools crowned with cutting edges – oh, but here was the paradise, that haven for an aspiring warrior. Necalli would go cross-eyed over such treasures. Would his friend have enough cocoa beans to buy something out of this temptingly spread commodity? Maybe those clubs with their vicious-looking spikes, crowned with flint judging by the brighter hue of their cutting edges.

Oh, but for the opportunity to get something like this, something rare that his friend or his noble father didn't have, to gift them with! Necalli's father would appreciate something different to enrich his collection of weapons with, wouldn't he? Did he have flint-spiked clubs in that wondrous room of his? He tried to remember, watching the arrogant youth and his shady companion devouring the spread-out wonders with their gazes as well, openly wistful. Reminded of his purpose, Miztli moved into the shadows, not taking his own eyes off his prey.

"What do you fancy, young noble?" called out the trader, clearly the owner of the mat, a burly man of uncertain age, not too approachable-looking yet not terribly intimidating either. Or maybe it was the richness of his prospective customer's clothing that made the man mellow in a way.

The young *pilli* drew himself up before strolling toward the mat, exuding importance. Or rather, pretending it. After more than a moon of observing people, Miztli couldn't help but notice the furtiveness, less pronounced than back in the other square but still there. The youth's words were not loud enough to decipher their meaning. Straining his ears, he drifted closer, bypassing two warriors that almost bumped into him, too absorbed to mutter apologies.

"Watch your step!" flared one of them, his eyes flashing at Miztli, his speech accented heavily.

To mutter an apology seemed like the best course of action. He wasn't here to pick fights, certainly not with foreign warriors. The seller of weaponry was talking to the youth, his speech gushing, unintelligible even from closer proximity. Nor were the hesitant answers of the visitor.

Miztli stifled his disappointment. What was the tongue those locals were speaking? Something Chichimec, they said. And who were those Chichimecs anyway? The highlanders from behind Tlemilli's favorite Smoking Mountain? But they weren't anywhere near there now. The Otomi people the gossiping trader mentioned out there on the square? Were those also part of the legendarily fierce Chichimecs everyone knew and remembered for their barbaric ferociousness and rare warring skills? In Tenochtitlan, there was a whole unit of elite warriors called Otomitl. Necalli said so, and the *calmecac* boy would know. Again, he wished he could bring the flint-spiked club for his friend as a present upon his return.

The negotiations progressed lively, the noble boy evidently gaining confidence, speaking louder now and with enough conviction to hold the interest of the owner. The man seemed to be hesitating, offering something, then shaking his head. The sparkling bracelet the boy had taken off and tried to press on him was pushed back into its rightful owner's hand after an offhanded, openly condescending inspection. The simpler-looking youth was shifting his weight from one bare foot to another, shooting worried glances whichever way. Miztli followed suit, looking the crowded square over briefly, reassured by the relative lack of attention they drew. Besides a small group of warriors that was nearing this same mat unhurriedly, busy in conversation between themselves, no one seemed to be interested, certainly not in the potential buyers of such goods. Still, the second boy didn't relax.

The sun was reaching into his shadowed hideaway, pleasing in its strength at this time of the season, the breeze barely entering the walled enclosure, another good thing. In the countryside, he would he chilled to the bone now. Was Elotl well out there, feeling better?

The negotiations advanced into a more agitated stage, the noble *pilli* offering his necklace now, an intricate jewelry of glittering copper and green stones. A very rich thing, even Miztli could tell that. Still the owner of the treasured weaponry did not let himself be easily persuaded. By the time both boys went away, the rich one clutching the spiked club with both hands, with plenty of reverence and excitement, Miztli was all nerves, knowing that he should be lingering among the regular townsfolk, listening to their chatter that he was able to understand. Trailing after foreign warriors or their offspring, fascinating in their outlandish looks and ways that they might be, did not enrich him with knowledge worthy of sharing. Not for immediate use.

Absently, he began drifting away and back toward the narrow alley, noticing that the weapon seller was turning toward the nearing warriors but not before giving him, Miztli, a scrutinizing look. Not good. He hastened his step, only to bump into none other than the youth with his newly acquired weaponry, who apparently dove into the same pathway but somehow had changed his direction and was hurrying back toward the second square. To demand his expensive necklace back?

Bewildered, Miztli stared at them for the length of more than a heartbeat, the second boy, so uncertain before, now glaring at him with anger that matched the scowl of his haughty companion, very much so.

"Why are you following me?" demanded the angered *pilli* after another heartbeat had passed, this one in mutual glaring. His Matlatzinca words sounded clear, surprisingly understandable, with barely any accent at all.

"I'm not!" To insist on something like that felt silly, but he found nothing better to say for the moment, chancing a quick glance around, checking possible routes of escape. This first day in the enemy capital was going in all sorts of wrong directions and he had no one but himself to blame. Why did he follow this youth, indeed? There was no good reason for that, no explanation.

The annoying *pilli*'s grimace said it all, his spiked club balanced easily in his right hand, the other one thrust forward, ready to join the grip around the carved hilt. His follower stepped closer, unarmed but as though ready to join a possible brawl. Miztli felt his own fists bunching hastily, the knife in his girdle forgotten, the thought of his club left out there in the hills with Elotl pushed away. The simply dressed boy looked skinny, not very well developed, an easy target, unlike the other one, with his wide frame and his club-like new weaponry. Still, he could take them, maybe. They were nothing but pampered schoolboys. If there were schools in their hometowns at all.

"You are really asking for it, aren't you?" The richly dressed brat shifted, both hands on his new club by now. "I won't mind testing this axe on the traders' scum. Eh, Kjua?"

The other boy nodded eagerly, his eyes sparkling with excitement. "See if it's any good, yes. The filthy trader asked too much for it."

"No he didn't!" This time, the owner of the new weapon whirled at his companion, his fury spilling. "It wasn't too much and if you ever tell anyone, I'll beat you really hard before telling Mother to sell you for one cocoa bean on the meanest market that ever exists."

The threat had its horrified recipient taking a hasty step back, then another. Fascinated against his will, Miztli watched, understanding too well. The other one was nothing but a servant. Easy to guess. He concentrated on the rich *pilli*, detesting him now, wishing the fight to ensue. Not wise in the least, but the presumptuous piece of work was so sure of himself, so nasty.

"That trader did make you pay too much," he declared, glancing at the passing by group of men, their chatter loud, gazes brushing past them, not curious or demanding. "You were stupid to leave that necklace. The stupid club isn't worth it."

The youth whirled back at him with an admirable readiness. "Shut your stupid commoners' mouth!" he cried out, stepping forward while bringing his overpriced weaponry up. "You understand nothing—"

After Tenochtitlan and Tlatelolco, not to mention the last moon of traveling and facing all sorts of riffraff on the roads, or Elotl's so-called friends in Oaxtepec, he didn't need to think before reacting. His fist, not even bunched before, shot forward, burying itself in his assailant's belly, the rest of his body tilting away from the anticipated path of the returned blow. Which proved unnecessary as the club-like weapon was apparently only threatening, not set on attacking for real, something his punch forestalled even so.

The haughty piece of work was busy doubling over, gasping funnily, in a silly squeak. Before his companion came out of his dumbfounded stupor, Miztli spun around, intending to race up the alley and away, putting as much distance between himself and those unreasonable people. No city authorities would take his side, or even bother to investigate possible causes of his assault. He was not the spoiled noble *pilli*, anything but.

The relatively clear path beckoned, more people hurrying past, not blocking the way. The second boy's sweaty fingers slipped against his arm, unsuccessful in their grabbing attempt, his thinner frame easy to push away, the vacant corner of the square temptingly empty. Two men busy measuring what looked like slabs of dark marble squinted at him as he raced past, slipping upon the polished pavement, changing his direction while glimpsing another blissfully clear alley, this one inclining sharply, a steep uphill. A few passersby paused to glance at him, then at his unmistakable pursuers. The shuffling of two pair of feet, one sandaled and one bare, was impossible not to hear. Tenacious pests! What did they want with him anyway?

At the edge of the alley, there was another square, then another. He rushed past what looked like a walled pond and across the paved space, fenced with vegetation on one side and rows of warehouses spreading from it in the rest of the directions like rays from an imaginary circle of sun. Turning abruptly, he veered from the possible path of the outlandish club in case it reacted to his maneuver with enough alacrity. Both his pursuers panted mildly, the thinner boy's cheeks glaring like round tomatoes. The owner of the expensive weaponry clutched his precious new belonging with both hands, determined to use it this time, warmed by the pursuit. His charge was admirably swift; still, at the sight of Miztli's knife, by now out and ready, thrust forward to relay the message, he halted halfway, then changed his tactic, attempting to reach him from the side, in a swift, arching blow.

Feeling as though he was back in *calmecac*, Miztli swayed away, the strange club shorter than a training sword, easier to avoid. Probably lighter to maneuver as well, he reflected, wishing to try it himself, maybe with Necalli. But for the opportunity to present his friend with such gift upon his return!

His leap aside had him slipping, bumping his back against a stony wall and a few passersby who gasped, then moved away swiftly, clearly pausing to watch. The opportunity to slash at the unprotected ribs that tempted his eye, momentarily exposed under the swaying cloak, presented itself, which he disregarded in favor of another leap aside, having enough presence of mind to know that he could not kill noble *pilli*s and expect to get out of this city alive.

The other boy pushed himself forward clumsily, nearly getting hit by the tip of his companion's club. A thrust of Miztli's elbow had enough drive to send this one sprawling. He topped it by the kick at his other opponent's shin but didn't pursue his success by another as the boy wavered, clutching the same warm stones of the wall for support.

For a long heartbeat, they glared at each other, the foreign *pilli*'s eyes nothing but a pair of slits, brimming with fury yet measuring, displaying a thought process. Keeping the other one in sight, Miztli tried to make his mind work. It was the time to walk away, wasn't it? Or make a run for it.

"Who are you?" the aristocratic brat growled, back to being aggressive with his words alone.

"It's none of your business." The memory of Tenochtitlan and his longing to go back helped. To use Necalli's words made him feel better. The *calmecac* boy would toss it twenty times a day while bickering with the annoying piece of filth Acoatl, and in other, less harmful instances. And Tlemilli too. She said this phrase often enough while facing the haughty school snakes. The longing splashed in force, as fierce as on the evening of his departure. Was she well? Happy? Sad? Missing him? Not harassed or harmed or nagged by her annoyingly haughty sister? Did she do nothing silly or rash?

The boy shifted impatiently. "Yes, it is. I wish to know whom I will kill with my new axe. I have a right to know."

He forced his concentration back, out of his depth at this new demand, not knowing how to proceed. Were people expected to make formal introductions, exchange their names, or maybe ranks, when setting to kill each other, even if in some stupid alley and under no appropriate circumstances? And what alias should he use? Not his real name surely. And not the one he used on occasions, the one the Texcocan told him to have ready, in case of a need. That one was too simple, good for villagers and traders, not the snotty noble spoiling for a fight.

"And you?" he demanded, trying to gain time, the routes of escape beckoning, quite a few of those, temptingly open but for the nagging realization. He couldn't turn around and flee, he just couldn't. Necalli would never contemplate something like that. "What is your name?"

More passersby slowed their steps, their glances full of curiosity, mildly amused.

His adversary's chin shot yet higher. "I'm Xedi Dehe Ma'ye. The son of Honorable B'otzanga, Xiquipilco's war leader. His Chief Wife's son," he added hurriedly, as though afraid it might be assumed otherwise.

As though someone cared. Miztli rolled his eyes tellingly, trying to remember. The name Xiquipilco sounded somewhat familiar, mentioned several times through his last moon's wandering, certainly when skulking around Tenantzinco, which was still glowing over its brilliant move of making Tenochtitlan involved and on their side, but the man of Texcoco said it was a mistake, that Tenantzinco would be absorbed into the growing Triple Alliance's domain as readily as the cities they tried to best by inviting the Mexica into the Tollocan Valley and its internal affairs. In the long run, the results would be similar for this same Tenantzinco as they would be for Tollocan and Matlatzinco they hoped to best by such questionable means, paying as much tribute and doing Tenochtitlan's bidding. Yet he said not a thing about the people who inhabited other settlements, somewhere there to the west or the north. Elotl claimed that those were not even Matlatzinca people anymore, but mysterious Otomi, or wild Chichimecs one only heard hair-raising stories about. Just last night, his brother was talking about a conversation he was having with some trader on the day before. There were plenty of Matlatzinca people in the Tollocan Valley, yes, but plenty of other speakers of strange unintelligible tongues, fierce Otomi or Chichimecs included. Was it this tongue these boys were speaking with the trader?

"Are you Chichimeca?" he asked, unable not to, his opponent's curious chattiness having a calming effect. With so much ceremony around a stupid brawl in the shady alley, one could expect the snotty brat to conduct himself with a measure of decency. Like Necalli and his friends maybe, violent and as dangerous as a snake in the early spring, and yet surprisingly decent and trustworthy, following certain rules of honor as though it was a matter of life and death. Yet were the rules of the nobility out here in the west the same as back in the Capital of the World?

"Of course! Who did you think I was? A lowly Matlatzinca like you? My people are fierce and invincible Otomi, and we are related to our Chichimec past, very much so! Not lowly Matlatzinca peasants."

He came off his musings at once. "I thought you were a barking coyote. The one who barked in strange words."

It came out well, a rebuff worthy of Necalli's or Elotl's quickness of wit. He readied to leap aside from the possible range of the outlandish club.

"Shut up, you filthy piece of smelly—"

The men who came up the narrow pathway looked decidedly out of place, their clothes drab, faces grim, limbs smeared with fresh earth. Two of them wore plain-looking cloaks that bulged, suggesting concealed clubs. The briefest of glances informed him of that, not needing to stare to arrive at this conclusion, his last moon's traveling combined with the first Tlatelolco kidnapping leaving little to speculate. Through the last moon and a half of wandering, he had met such types by twenties, starting from Elotl's former friends in Oaxtepec and ending with coarse unscrupulous types that seemed to inhabit outer neighborhoods of every *altepetl* or town they roamed.

Another quick glance informed him that the small square they had halted on offered possibilities of escape, something a few of those who lingered around seemed to exploit rather hastily.

The men slowed their step and were measuring them through their narrowed eyes, clearly taking in the richness of his unwanted companion's clothing, the sparkling of his jewelry impossible to miss despite the lack of the traded off necklace. The alley leading back toward the market square beckoned.

"We better..." He shot a glance at his unasked-for company, unwilling to just bolt away and forget all about it for some reason.

The thinner boy gave him a disdainful glance, but the Chichimec *pilli* frowned toward their new company with an open suspicion.

"What are you bickering about, boys?" One of the men stepped closer while another moved aside, clearly trying to block the rich brat's way of escape. Miztli shot a glance at the wooden façades of the warehouses, a seemingly solid obstacle but not really. There were always passages between such constructions; evenings of wandering around Tenochtitlan with Necalli and his troublemaking *calmecac* friends taught him that.

"It's none of your business, working commoners," declared the bejeweled boy haughtily. "Be on your way."

"Not so fast, foreign brat," drawled the man with the bulging cloak, a grimy affair with no decorations and bare remnants of the original coloring. "First give us those pretty things you wear. And don't make noise while doing this!"

The last words came out in a hiss, accompanied with a swift movement that had the surprised boy pinned against the wall, with the hand of his assailant digging into his shoulder with no visible effort, the other grabbing his throat, uncompromising at that. The second boy uttered a funny squeak, then tried to come to his companion's aid by throwing himself into the fray with little fighting spirit, achieving no results besides an indifferent kick. Another cloaked man yanked him away contemptuously, using one hand to do that, not bothering to secure his grip even but shoving the skinny thing to the ground instead.

Miztli didn't think it all through. With the little square clearing as though by a gust of wind from the rest passersby, he squirmed away from an attempted grip of someone's grimy hand, then planted a fist at the belly of the man who rushed toward him, doing so carelessly, clearly unimpressed by the previous rescue attempt, expecting no worthwhile fighting. The groan that accompanied his assailant's fall drew the others' attention if momentarily, such a stupidly loud sound. Even the leading robber, the one who was still pinning the rich brat to the wall, glanced away in an open puzzle, a distraction that the aggressive *pilli* did take advantage by kicking viciously, with much spirit. His attempt to push the assaulting hands away did not crown with success, although it did result in a renewed struggle, as the victim's position was actually more solid thanks to the prop the wall behind his back provided. Miztli didn't wait to see the outcome of this. His fist leading the way, he threw himself forward and onto the cloaked man, eyes scanning the wooden planks briefly, seeing an opening between the different-looking beams.

The man wavered at the collision but didn't go crashing down. Himself nearly crying out at the intensity of a sudden pain in his wrist, his bunched palm crashing into something more solid than his target's ribs, Miztli shoved with his elbow, then grabbed the boy's shoulder in his turn, pulling with force.

"Run," he breathed, pushing his unasked-for charge toward the narrow gap. "Over there!"

The thinner boy was heading in the same direction, a quick glimpse informed him as he ducked someone's shooting fist, acting more out of an instinct, not seeing clearly in all the melee. The man he assaulted was still on his feet, in no hurry to throw himself at him, fiddling with his cloak. Getting a club out, or something even more lethal?

Miztli hurried to charge for the narrow opening himself, colliding with the servant boy who evidently had the same target in mind. Steadying himself with the help of the rough wooden surface, the planks coarse and full of splinters but helpful by just being there, providing support, he felt the blow from behind hurling him forward, this time sending him sprawling in a heap of limbs.

Disoriented and on the verge of panic, he pushed himself up, frantic to turn around and face the next assault, to know what it had in store for him. These people were vicious, and they had clubs, not only knives, while he had no space to maneuver, to roll away or escape in any other manner, not in the narrowness of this passageway.

He fought the fingers that grabbed his upper arm, pulling him up in an actually helpful manner, then recognized the familiar by now face, holding no haughtiness this time, only a matter-of-fact frown. The realization dawned, sending him rushing into the dimness of the crammed lane, following the familiar panting. Those other boys were no runners!

In the brightly lit square, they paused for a heartbeat, getting their bearings. The skinny one was huffing too loudly, looking as though about to faint. His companion, or rather the overlord, didn't look better, his cheeks glaring with red of a ripe tomato; still, he was the one to look around and then motion them into a wider pathway, then another. By the time they reached the hum of the marketplace, they were all out of breath, even Miztli, still confused and disoriented, his heart pumping in a mad race. People around them gushed in an animated flow, shooting curious glances but not pausing to ask questions or try to harass them in any other way.

"Who were those people?" demanded the Chichimec *pilli*, wiping his face with the back of his free hand, the other one still clutching his wondrous new weaponry, eyes boring at Miztli, glaring with previously displayed suspicion.

"How should I know?" retorted Miztli, his presence of mind returning as well, even though his heart was still pounding. But it was stupid, this entire incident, stupid and unnecessary.

"You acted as though you knew they were a danger." Another accusing scrutiny. The club was again grasped too tightly in the youth's palms.

"Of course they were. One has to be stupid not to notice. Haven't you seen robbers and criminals before?"

"No, I haven't!" cried out the annoying *pilli*. "Why should I? I'm no Matlatzinca commoner like you." His thinly pursed lips twisted, then relaxed all at once, even if his suspicious expression didn't change. "You helped us back there. Why?"

Incensed even further, Miztli shrugged. "I have to go."

"Where?"

Another shrug seemed to be in order. "Marketplace. I have things to sell."

"What things?"

Growing more uncomfortable with every passing moment, Miztli motioned at his bag, noncommittal.

"He is a commoner, like you said," contributed the servant boy, catching his breath at long last, his face still glistening, glowing in fiercest of hues. "Trader selling on the marketplace."

"Shut up, Kjua! You were useless out there, the filthy piece of slave's meat that you are. You didn't even fight!"

As expected, the thinner boy quailed in already a familiar, pitiful manner. You *weren't that much of a fighter yourself*, thought Miztli, but was wiser than to say it aloud this time. To pick another argument and in a public place again was beyond regular stupidity. Enough that he had managed to get into this mess the moment he stepped upon this *altepetl*'s streets. How stupid. And it was not getting any better, with the sun being already high and with him learning nothing, not even the silliest gossip about prices and crops.

He glanced at the people that squatted beside piles of beams and boards, enjoying their shadow. By now he knew that those must have been traders too, offering building materials. In Tenochtitlan, such hefty goods were also sold on the outskirts of the marketplace, nowhere near edible merchandise.

"Where did you learn to fight?" the foreign *pilli* was asking, peering at him with what seemed to be a genuine interest even if still colored with a frown.

Miztli considered turning around and leaving for good. "Here and there."

"Are you coming from one of the villages?"

"Yes."

Which village? he asked himself uneasily. What to tell? There was that town they passed through on the day before with Elotl. What was this place's name? He was too far away from home to use his real village as a cover, wasn't he? Even though the Texcocan said not to lie more than necessary.

"Will they round up your people for the battle against the Tenantzinco lowlifes?"

That snapped his mind back to attention. "What?"

"That filthy Tenantzinco. Those southern *altepelt*s will fight it, you can be sure of that. And your villagers will be drawn into their forces. My father said that they would. He gathered warriors from our villages too."

"Your father? Who is he?"

The boy grimaced in the way that made Miztli wish to smash the handsomely defined face into a pulp. So much haughtiness!

"You are not really that bright, are you? What do you do in your village besides working fields and fighting?" His short nose wrinkled toward Miztli's bag. "And selling things."

"That's none of your business," he began hotly, but his mind was running amok, interfering with his ability to form an offensive enough response. Did this boy just tell him that the fight against Tenantzinco was a sure thing, with both problematic cities involved and some mysterious, clearly influential father bringing more forces from elsewhere? He took a deep breath. "I'm... yes, our villages, yes, we will be called upon to fight. Of course we will be. They always take warriors from the villages. But why your father..." He tried to collect his thoughts in a hurry, to stop the stupid stammering, to form the right questions. "Where are you coming from?"

The annoying *pilli* was eyeing him with most skeptical expression. Both of them did, even though the serving boy's grimace was a bad imitation of his master's genuine scorn.

Miztli pushed another wave of welling irritation away. He was supposed to be a villager, wasn't he; a simple boy, with not much understanding. The faltering speech was a good thing. And who cared what the stupid foreigner thought of him? He wouldn't see this one ever again probably, unless on a battlefield. A battlefield! His pulse quickened at the memory of the Emperor's promise, *both promises*!

"I told you before, you thickheaded villager," the richly dressed brat was saying, shaking his head with exaggerated forbearance. "My father is the war leader of Xiquipilco and all its provinces. He is the best warrior ever, the fiercest. And I'm his third son, the first son by his chief wife!" The last phrase came out stupidly proud, childish to the extreme.

Miztli tried to suppress all sorts of appropriate expressions, from rolling eyes to a tellingly loud snort. Necalli would be having a field day at this one's expense, such a stupid *pilli*.

"Where is Xiquipilco?" he asked innocently, the thought of his friend giving him strength to cope with unwarranted insults. He wasn't being stupid or humble, not for real. He was doing the important work and this bragging feather-head was a gift sent by benevolent deities that didn't want him to fail or be late to return to Tenochtitlan, to miss war preparations or make her upset. He had less than a market interval to start traveling back.

"You really know nothing, don't you?" This time, he was bestowed with an openly amused and smugness-filled gaze dripping with derision. "Who doesn't know where Xiquipilco is?"

"Only stupid villagers," echoed the Chichimec *pilli*'s worthless shadow, agog with excitement.

"Also stupid foreigners," retorted Miztli, unable to take any more of this. "I bet you don't even know where this same stupid Tenantzinco is. Or Cuauhnahuac. Or Tenochtitlan!" he added, deciding that everyone knew about the Great Capital of the Mexicas without making themselves implicated with it.

"Who cares about those stupid places!" cried out his opponent, as expected taking the bait, knowing not a thing about most of the mentioned names, let alone their actual locations. "Who cares about your pitiful villages and what are they called?"

"No one cares about your stupid Xiquipilco either!"

"Shut up!"

He readied for a renewed attack, noting the boy's hands tightening around the decorated base of his wondrous new weaponry once again and with evidently too much force; however, a sharp cry from the more crowded part of the square drew their attention, made his opponent stir, then glance away in a somewhat dismayed manner. The servant quailed again, more visibly than ever, his eyes fixing on the group of warriors that bore on them, their determination unmistakable.

In another heartbeat, the controversial club was thrust into Miztli's hands. "Tell them it's yours!" breathed the outlandish *pilli* with all his previous bossiness, not asking but giving an order.

"Tell them you brought it with you from your village, that it's your father's axe. Give it back to me later. I'll tell you when."

He wanted to tell the stupid bragger to go and dump his stupid corpse off the nearest cliff, to take himself out of whatever trouble with the warriors he was in all by himself. However, the polished handle felt good in his hands, satisfactorily light and lethal, a promising combination.

"How can I find you later, to give it back to you?" he asked, deciding that it could be actually useful to meet this one again, to pump him for more information. The foreign *pilli* clearly knew plenty about his homeland's possible forces those enemy towns might be reinforced with.

"You come with us," declared the annoying brat without a pause to think or rather consult his prospective guest. "They don't mind who I bring along if my guests are of no importance to anyone. And you are clearly no Matlatzinca noble." His gaze brushed past Miztli, relaying it all before drawing back to the approaching warriors. "My mother is too busy with that marketplace, and her servants wouldn't dare to ask questions. They are afraid of me. Aren't they, Kjua?" A somewhat spiteful glance was shot at the slave boy, making him lower his own in a hurry.

Miztli tried to suppress his fury. "I don't want to come with you," he said, unable not to. "I have things to do."

"They will wait." The boy's eyes measured him with surprising lightheartedness. "You can sell your silly things after the sun begins rolling down. I bet the marketplace scum won't go home in a hurry, not with so many visiting ladies falling on them. My mother will make her litter-bearers' feet sore before she'll leave all those alleys and squares." His grin held plenty of unexpected mischief, still unbearably haughty but somehow less annoying than before. "And you'll get to eat nice before you go back to your stinking village. That'll pay you for covering me about my new axe, and," the grin disappeared, replaced with a frown, "and for fighting that scum out there. You could have run away, but you didn't." The cloaked shoulders lifted briefly, with grudging admittance. "It was nice of you not to scamper away. No commoners' behavior that. My father may wish to take you among his warriors when we'll be fighting the Tenantzinco scum. I'll ask him to test you. How about that?"

"I..."

Miztli's head reeled too badly to form a worthwhile response, his instincts urging him to leave now, while it was still possible. To go with this snotty boy and to some clearly important war leader of the people he was spying on and was supposed to fight against not very long from now was dangerous, an unnecessary risk. And yet, in the vicinity of a lauded foreign leader he could learn much, extract plenty of useful information. These people – fierce Otomi or Chichimecs, no more and no less! – came here from their distant Xiquipilco, a town or *altepetl* he hardly heard about before, bringing warriors and important leaders, talking of war openly enough to have their young progeny blabbering about it, clearly not making a secret of their intentions. This could mean only one thing. A war on Tenantiznco and soon, and what if it happened before the Emperor had time to arrive with his warriors?

He caught his breath, trying to think fast. How to learn it all, then make word reach Tenochtitlan as fast as it could? Oh, but if he managed to hear enough in this afternoon, then maybe, maybe...

"I'll come," he whispered, as the warriors were already upon them, five in all, dressed in blinding regalia, all sparkling metal and jewelry. "I'll keep that axe until you tell me to give it back to you."

His companion nodded in a businesslike manner, relaying little acknowledgment or appreciation. Miztli pushed the renewed wave of resentment away.

ABOUT THE AUTHOR

Zoe Saadia is the author of several novels on pre-Columbian Americas. From the architects of the Aztec Empire to the founders of the Iroquois Great League, from the towering pyramids of Tenochtitlan to the longhouses of the Great Lakes, her novels bring long-forgotten history, cultures and people to life, tracing pivotal events that brought about the greatness of North and Mesoamerica.

To learn more about Zoe Saadia and her work, please visit www.zoesaadia.com

Printed in Great Britain
by Amazon